# BEAUTIFUL PLACE

AMANTHI HARRIS was born in Sri Lanka and grew up in London. She studied Fine Art at Central St Martins and has degrees in Law and Chemistry from Bristol University. Her novella *Lantern Evening* won the Gatehouse Press New Fictions Prize 2016 and is published by Gatehouse Press (2017). Her short stories have been published by Serpent's Tail and broadcast on BBC Radio 4 as Afternoon Readings.

*Also by Amanthi Harris*

NOVELLA

*Lantern Evening* (2017)

# BEAUTIFUL PLACE

## AMANTHI HARRIS

SALT

CROMER

PUBLISHED BY SALT PUBLISHING 2019

2 4 6 8 10 9 7 5 3 1

Copyright © Amanthi Harris 2019

Amanthi Harris has asserted her right under the Copyright, Designs
and Patents Act 1988 to be identified as the author of this work.

First published in Great Britain in 2019 by
Salt Publishing Ltd
12 Norwich Road, Cromer, Norfolk NR27 0AX United Kingdom

www.saltpublishing.com

Salt Publishing Limited Reg. No. 5293401

A CIP catalogue record for this book is available from the British Library

ISBN 978 1 78463 193 2 (Paperback edition)
ISBN 978 1 78463 194 9 (Electronic edition)

Typeset in Neacademia by Salt Publishing

Printed and bound in Great Britain by Clays Ltd, Elcograf S.p.A

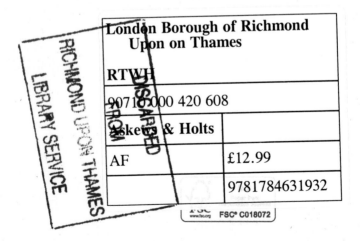

*For J and K*

'And the perfect morning, so fresh and fair, basking in the light, as though laughing at its own beauty, seemed to whisper, "Why not?"'

*from* 'At the Bay' *by* KATHERINE MANSFIELD

# PART I

I

THROUGH THE EARLY-MORNING house Padma went
out to the veranda. A breeze came in from the sea, easing in
past the araliya trees. Ever since returning to the villa she'd had
nightmares. In them she was always a child, alone at night in the
villa's garden, then propelled by an unseen force into a room. And
it was the front room of the brothel down the lane as she had seen
it one time when the black polythene over the windows flew up
with the wind: plastic chairs pushed up against the walls, bottles
of arrack, beer in buckets of ice. And men. There were always
men. In the dream they crowded over her. She had woken up safe
in her room at the villa, but the fear stayed real, fear of the sheer
randomness of her luck - for it was only luck, illogical, slight,
unfathomable, that had lifted her to safety. Luck didn't make you
feel lucky. Being saved didn't make you feel safe.

A grey dawn lingered over the garden. Soon strangers would
sit looking out at the sea, being at home in the villa, her world.
The veranda was where all life at the villa flowed, to that view of
changing waves out beyond the frangipani trees tangled around
the front of the house. Already the room was altered: three new
tables for guests had replaced the long old pine table now stored
in the shed. The room seemed bigger. Past the trees, the sun made

a red-gold rim over the sea. It burnished each ripple of the waves drawing back from the beach, simmering, settling, stilling itself after the wildness of the night. A thin yellow streak spread across the sky, growing to amber, green, turquoise – becoming the blue to come. The birds' shrill waking cries faded and the garden came to life, filling with the quiet new brightness of morning, the new day begun.

The dog, Gustav, came out of the house and nuzzled her, wanting to be stroked. He licked her hand and went out to the porch and into the garden. He ambled contentedly around the lawn, the grass bright with dew.

"What are you doing, Baba?" Soma came up behind her, making her jump.

"You're up early," she said.

He had refused to wake before his usual time when the villa became a guest house – one of his many protests against her new business – but there he was, up bright and early on their first day! She smiled at him and he tried to look as if he didn't care.

"Go and get ready. Your guest will be here and you'll still be in your pyjamas!" he scolded.

"He's not going to be here for ages."

"How do you know? And you have to eat breakfast. There's no time to make milk rice, though."

"Oooh, milk rice! So you do think today's auspicious?"

"I'll make you scrambled eggs and toast, that's all. And hot chocolate."

"Fine!"

She stood on the porch and looked over at the lane.

"I said, get dressed!" Soma called after her.

"Later!"

She ran down the steps to the garden, alone again in the morning. But someone was coming along the lane – one of the village men, dishevelled looking after a night on the beach. He was a waiter at the Kingfisher Bar, the biggest of the beach shacks, where the backpackers lay in hammocks all day getting stoned. The man stopped outside the villa's gate. He could see her there. Even from a distance she could see him glowering at her, see the hatred in him. The villagers all hated her more now because she was the competition. Competition! What a joke! As if any of their low-life clientele could ever afford to stay at the villa. She looked back coldly, unsmilingly at the man – that was the way to show them you couldn't care less what they thought of you, all the lies they made up about you and spread everywhere. Such effort it took to stay hostile, but she stared him down and he went away.

⁂

The taxi stopped at a white picket fence, an impenetrable green grown high above it. The driver didn't help with the bags, but Rohan paid him a tip, for in the new Sri Lanka, as he had discovered, anyone could feel aggrieved at the slightest denial and respond with the true viciousness of the thwarted. He was no longer surprised by the cruelty of ordinary people, the malevolence lying in wait for release. The taxi drove away and he pulled his two suitcases behind him and went into the garden of the guest house. A dappled green shade closed over him, coconut, cashew, plantain and paw paw trees crowding in, bushes of yellow-speckled, magenta and lime-green leaves, reaching out to stroke and scratch and poke at him, examining him as he followed a path to a white-painted house up ahead. With its clay-tiled roofs and bulbous white pillars it looked like an ancient relic magnificently preserved, like his grandmother's house of long ago on a coconut estate, but as he drew closer he saw that the villa had been far more recently built.

An Alsatian rushed onto the porch and barked down at him.

"Easy, easy, boy." He held out his hand, backing away. "Hello! Is anyone there?" he called.

A young woman with long wet hair ran out.

"Gustav! Stop it now!" she cried and knelt beside the dog, hugging it to her with a dramatic sweep of a slender arm. "Hi there! Can I help you?" She smiled down at Rohan.

Her face was a perfect oval; a perfect face.

"I have a room booked. I telephoned last week."

"Ah, then you must be Rohan." She came lightly down the steps, her hand outstretched. "Welcome. I'm Padma. I'm the manager." Very regally she shook his hand.

She was Sinhalese, he noted, the way all Sri Lankans knew about each other, but he couldn't quite place her. There was something too cocky, too theatrical and at the same time awkward about her. She could have been the wife of the owner, a mistress, or even the maid, it was impossible to tell, there was something peculiar about her. She didn't seem like a woman from the village – she was much too bold and outspoken. She spoke English remarkably well, although with a faint Germanic accent. He saw her smile, clearly amused by his confusion.

"Come, I'll show you to your bungalow," she said, still laughing at him.

She had small straight white teeth, disconcertingly even, yet natural-looking and untampered with, an easy spontaneous beauty. She looked like a woman in a Sri Lankan Airlines advertisement; the type of stewardess you never encountered unless you flew First Class or Business. She grabbed the large suitcase.

"Oof, what have you got in here? A ton of bricks?"

"I'll take that," he said, but she wouldn't let him.

"I'm fine, come on!" she said, heaving it up and setting off across the garden, staggering a little.

All he could do was follow her.

"I'm a lot stronger than people think," she said over her shoulder. "I do yoga every day. I'm almost a qualified teacher."

Her orange and red flower-print skirt flared out over slim brown legs and her feet in red rubber slippers. She wore a silver chain with a tiny silver bell around her ankle. Her hair bounced behind her in wet glossy ringlets, swaying against the red t-shirt, her waist supply moving with her stride. The dog trotted, a great wolf, at her side. She looked like a girl in a fairy tale. The whole place in fact was vaguely fantastical, although the exuberant wild garden, on closer inspection, showed itself to be carefully tended. She led him over a trail of circular stepping stones, flat grey bubbles, at the edge of the lawn. Crimson hibiscus flowers hung above, crinkled red lanterns, the papery petals glowing with sun, stamens bowed heavy with thick yellow pollen trembling, about to fall.

The small bungalow was at the back of the garden. Two planters chairs were set out on a veranda with carved old wooden pillars. Padma went up onto the veranda and pushed open the narrow double doors, a bolt dragging over a smooth grey cement floor, waxed and gleaming mutely in the gentle shade of daytime indoors. Something scuttled across the back of the room. The Alsatian pricked up its ears and bounded in barking.

"What was that?" Rohan demanded.

"Oh, it's nothing!" Padma laughed nervously and grabbed a broom and charged in, thumping it under a bed shrouded in mosquito netting.

She ran to the back and crouched by a wardrobe, jabbing the broom under it. The dog howled and jumped around the room, knocking over an antique towel rail.

"Gustav! Stop it!" Padma shouted. "Stop now, you silly dog! Sit!"

Something grey and woolly whirled past Rohan and disappeared into the garden.

"There, it's gone now," Padma declared.

"That was a rat," he said.

"Oh no, no, no! There are no rats in my guest house – that was a little *meeya*."

"Meeya is *mouse*. That thing was a *rat*."

"Don't be silly! A rat is *this* big—" She opened out her hands.

"No, that would be a rabbit."

She giggled. "Anyway, it's gone now, for sure. No need to fret."

"I want another room!"

"The other bungalow is booked – all I have is the room in the house—"

"No thank you."

"You could try one of the other guest houses – although I'd better warn you, they're nowhere near as nice as ours. Maybe you should go to one of the big hotels . . . ?"

"Oh God, not a big hotel!"

"Why not?" She studied him curiously.

He ignored her. There would always be someone he knew at any one of the main hotels; people who thought they knew all about him. More whispering, more stares, more lies made up about him. He sighed.

"I'll take the room," he said.

"Ah, good!" She grabbed the large suitcase before he could take it, and dragged it inside.

"This is crazy heavy! What have you got in here?" she exclaimed. He pretended not to hear.

"Huh? What's in here? Not a dead body I hope?"

"No, not a dead body." He held the door open for her to leave.

"What do you want for dinner?" she asked, not moving. "You

need to tell me now so I can go and buy it from the market, the cook only makes things from fresh."

"Do you have a menu?"

"Yes: fish, chicken or vegetable curry; fried rice, boiled rice or noodles."

"Great menu."

She looked delighted.

"I only want steamed fish with plain boiled rice and steamed vegetables. No spices," he told her. "And what have you got for lunch?"

"The cook doesn't make lunch for guests. He likes to sleep in the afternoons."

"Such great service."

"There are a few cafés up the lane," she said blithely. "You could try the one called Boss's Bar – he's a friend of ours. Dinner's in the main house at seven."

At last she left, running out into the sunlit green, the garden claiming her back. She threw a blue rubber ball for Gustav, who raced after it over the lawn. She stood straight-backed and firm, contentedly watching the dog. She tossed back her hair, the long gleaming mass of it almost dry already. Then she went over to the main house and went inside. It was a relief to not see her anymore.

He went around the room peering into corners; under the bed, behind the wardrobe, searching for signs of rats or other vermin, but everything seemed dusted and well-swept. He gazed up into the roof beams, the roof tiles left exposed with bright slivers of sky showing in the gaps through which anything might crawl in at night and no doubt would. He thought longingly of rooms with minibars and room service and someone to complain to whenever something was not immaculate and perfectly soothing. The still- ness of the bungalow pressed down on him – his first room in Sri

Lanka without his family nearby – no more shocked whisperings on the other side of the door, no more prying glances when they thought he wasn't watching.

He turned on the fan, and with that accepted he was staying at the villa. He unpacked the smaller suitcase, taking out casual clothes but leaving behind the suit and ties and shirts pristinely laundered by the dobi – with one stroke he zipped them all away. The large suitcase he kicked under the wardrobe; he never wanted to see it again. What he needed was a drink. Several. He could drink all day now if he wanted to – that at least was a consolation. Now there would be no maids or the cook keeping count for his mother as he went to the fridge. His mother and her sisters had grown convinced in the past months that he had a tendency to drink – this was how they explained what he was said to have done. They had forgotten of course that it was they who had coaxed and cajoled him on to the worst mistake he had ever made. He was on his own with that.

He looked out at the unknown garden, his new world away from them. It was not love, but the desire to be dutiful, that expectation of all good Asians, which gave others their power over you. Now he was free of them and he could do as he pleased, but he didn't know what that was; which life to choose. What lives were there? How many had he passed by without seeing, without hearing their call? Once he had thought himself fully formed, this half-made man that he was. But how to find a new way, a way to reverse it all? How was time to be undone? He drew the curtains closed and turned back to his cool dark sheltering room.

"He's a bit weird," Padma told Soma in the kitchen. "Nice-looking, though."

She tried to recall him, but she could only remember glimpses: a straight nose, an angled face, dark eyes intense and angry and so scornful as he spoke to her, yet with no hostility.

"They're all weird in Colombo," Soma said, filling his tobacco pouch, his fingers expertly sifting the black snarled leaves.

"He's not from Colombo. He's from England. There were London Heathrow stickers all over his bags."

"As long as he doesn't cause any trouble, I don't mind where he's from," Soma said, putting the tobacco pouch into his shirt pocket with its bulge of lighter and cigarette papers and the little metal tin of marijuana she wasn't supposed to know about.

He patted the pocket lovingly, looking ahead to being alone with its contents.

"Now about this steamed fish nonsense, what exactly am I supposed to be cooking tonight?"

"He said he didn't like spices."

"What sort of a sissy-boy is he? Mummy making white curry every day for him?"

"I told you, he's not from here. He probably isn't used to our spicy food."

"Must be eating fish and chips and mutton stew all the time," Soma mocked. "With pot-ay-toes and carrots. What's the point of having a menu if they can do what they like? Next thing I'll be making waffles and pancakes and chicken biryani with sugar-plums on top."

Padma giggled.

"There's nothing wrong with my fish curry," Soma grumbled. "Who does he think he is, asking for steamed this and boiled that?"

"I think he's used to big hotels."

"He should go to one then."

But the new guest had been horrified by the idea, almost

afraid, like someone hunted. He had run away from somewhere, she sensed. He was at the villa trying to hide - but from whom?

"He's here for a reason of his own," she reflected.

"Oh I'm sure."

"Nothing like that!" She laughed. It was impossible to imagine the moody new guest going into the house with the women.

"You can tell these things, can you?" Soma scoffed.

"I can tell a lot about people. Even Gerhardt says I have a very powerful inner eye."

"Oh yes, your inner eye. Don't worry, I will be keeping both of my outer eyes on him - any sign of trouble and he's out of here."

Soma's efforts would come to nothing. Padma could already tell that the new guest was a different sort of straight-laced compared to the sordid business-men types who gave way to base desires when left to themselves. He was nothing like those lost, heart-dead people she'd seen wandering alone in luxury hotels when she had gone sometimes with Gerhardt on his business trips abroad. The new guest would never resort to such impoverished encounters. He was too proud, too searching. She had seen the way he looked at the garden, his gaze following a passing butterfly and lingering on a mynah bird by the pond and on the new burst of pink in the camellia bushes. He might be a poet or a novelist. The suitcase he'd made such a fuss about could have been filled with books - that would explain its weight. Or he might be a film director looking for somewhere to make a film. The villa would be the perfect place - and what publicity! The neighbours would boil with envy!

"What do you think would make a suitcase extra heavy?" she mused.

"A dead body."

"He hasn't got a dead body in his bag, you silly man!"

"He might do. I read in the papers just the other day about someone who came to stay in a hotel and left a suitcase behind.

The hotel people thought it was a bomb so they called the police, but when they opened it, there were chopped up body parts in plastic bags. The fingers and toes were all smashed so they couldn't check for fingerprints."

"That guy's not carrying a dead body around!"

"How do you know?"

"It didn't smell. A dead body decomposes fast in the heat."

"There are chemicals you can get to stop it stinking – but they won't work for ever – he'll be hoping to get rid of it fairly soon I imagine. All he'd need is to find a quiet beach . . . maybe that's why he's come here."

"No, it's books. Books weigh a ton. And scripts."

"Scripts?"

"For a film. He could be looking for somewhere beautiful to make a film . . ."

"Ah yes, I'm sure, you know best. You're the expert."

He bustled smugly about the kitchen, thinking he'd had the last word. He was gathering ingredients: onions, ginger, green chillies, garlic for the daily masala; peeling, chopping. The stone pestle thumped, skins bursting, juices running, and he drew it all together into a mound and rolled it into a pale green paste on the granite slab. And then came the fizz of oil as he threw in a small wet lump of masala to fry. Soon that familiar beginning-smell, of the day's work getting underway, drifted through the house. Soma wasn't worried at all about the possibility of dead bodies – otherwise he'd have been rushing to ring Gerhardt.

"Now are you going to the market or not?" he asked.

"Yes, of course!"

"It's getting late, there'll be nothing left – do you want me to go?"

"No!"

"I don't mind going."

"I'm going, we agreed."

"Then go! Quickly!"

"Okay!"

Padma put on her trainers and paused on the veranda. There was always the pause, the gathering in and steeling herself before leaving the villa. There was always the chance of a hostile encounter. One needed to be centred and strong to not let it spoil the morning.

She rearranged a spray of leaves in the vase on the dresser. Beside it was her friend Jarryd's new book, such an elegant little volume with its mustard-yellow recycled-paper cover, and the title: *Reflections on a Teardrop* printed in red ink inside a single red line of border. Even the local minister with all his talk of banning the book would have admitted in private that it had style. Padma wrote on a card: 'A guidebook to Sri Lanka by a Local Author' and placed it next to a pile of the books. She would ensure that all of her guests bought one copy at least. They would leave her guest house knowing a little more about the country than the usual tourists, who only cared where the best beaches were for surfing and nude sunbathing and where one could buy ganja. She lifted the cover of the first book on the pile:

## INTRODUCTION

Sri Lanka is a sturdy squat little house with all manner of proud impossible people living inside: Sinhalese, Tamils, Muslims, Burghers, Wanniyala-aetto (or Veddhas, as they are known derogatively by the others), all squeezed in together with nowhere to go to escape from each other, surrounded by soft sand beaches shaded by coconut palms and glistening blue seas with hidden treacherous currents – all the loveliness of Paradise encircling them in their earth-bound entrapment.

Jarryd's book was quite different to other guidebooks. It was the Sri Lanka that Jarryd inhabited and the place he longed for it to be. His book was a cry for peace, a protest against corruption, yet Jarryd's Sri Lanka was a place of beauty and hope, a jewel to prize, to adore and protect with pride. Only Jarryd could make Sri Lankans seem noble and wronged, a people gifted with a Paradise desired by all, besieged by invaders and savagely plundered. For Jarryd, Sri Lankans were ensnared and oppressed by the greed of others. He made even the local yobs seem like promising youths who needed only to be freed from the injustice of poverty and exploitation.

> Everyone is pushed up against each other in the house that is Sri Lanka, their pride, arrogance, envy, hatred – and love – raging. People wanting peace, but fighting each other, people wanting to belong but also to rise up and be apart from all the others, each person secretly longing, reaching beyond their crowded house for something more, somewhere better. Perhaps there has always been a need for Sri Lankans to turn away from each other, to leap across seas to other lands and leave behind their close clinging house of fury and discontent.

Only Jarryd could make Padma feel pity for the lives of the villagers, and to forgive them their bitterness and poisoned tongues. Jarryd was her yoga teacher, but she had learned much more than yoga asanas from him, she had learned more from him than anyone.

"Are you still here?" Soma shouted. "If you don't go now there'll only be frozen fish left and I'm not cooking that muck. You can be the one to poison your guest!"

"I'm going, I'm going!"

She went around the house to the back of the garden. It was

already too hot to be in the sun. Only the sea breeze and the shade of the trees made it bearable. How quickly the day moved forward after its cautious probing at dawn. Crows cawed. A woodpecker tapped high up in the jak tree. She unlocked the shed where she kept her new motor scooter, gleaming in the dark, glinting with possibility.

2

ROHAN STOOD AT his window watching Padma, out in the garden. She looked thoughtful and dreamy, her face tilted to the sun. She went inside a shed and came out wheeling a bright purple motor scooter, big and new and expensive-looking, gleaming obscenely in the sun. She threw her leg over the seat, climbing on with careful fluid grace, sitting bolt upright, strapping on a glittery lilac helmet. She was too much; everything about her was excessive. He had noticed her looking him over earlier, smirking; well, what did he care what she thought of him? The owner and manager – like hell she was! As she rode away, her skirt blew back, revealing a long brown leg, surprisingly muscled. He followed the delicate line of her thigh. There was something defiant and immodest about her. It was dangerous, if nothing else, to dress like that when riding a bike.

He felt himself watched. A stocky Tamil man was staring from the back of the house. The reluctant cook, Rohan presumed. The man looked furious, as if he had read Rohan's thoughts, which of course he couldn't have. In any case, Rohan had only been concerned about road safety. Rohan glared back and the man was the first to look away, going to an outdoor kitchen just behind the house. Soon there was a smell of a wood fire and blue-white curls of smoke wound out from the open brickwork walls.

Rohan left the bungalow and went over the garden. The dog lay slumbering on the porch of the main house, opening one eye as Rohan edged past.

"Good boy, Gustav," Rohan said softly.

The dog thumped its tail and went back to sleep.

A young Western couple strolled past in the lane. He followed them. A breeze shook the coconut trees making them sway high above, branches whispering of long ago – of weekends at his grandmother's coconut plantation, the adults gathered talking on the veranda and his cousins playing cricket on the lawn. He had wandered alone under the trees, safe in that world, no danger to look out for, only mad dogs and falling coconuts. The Western couple left the lane and entered a shack where a group of local men sat arguing at the bar. On the beach beyond the shack, other travellers lounged under palm-thatch umbrellas. Even from the lane he could smell their joints. There were more shacks, more bars along the beach, and on the land-side of the lane, after the villa, was an empty house, then another much larger house where five, maybe six, young local women were sitting outside, all piled onto a chair, their legs entwined. Their breasts were big and rounded, pressing out from thin strappy vests; buttocks curved in tight shorts. The women looked out at him. An arm rose up and waved.

"Hello! How are you? Are you coming to visit us?" they called. "Anè! Where are you going? Come back!" they shrieked as he kept walking.

The lane curved out of sight up ahead. It could have led to a dead end, or another strange house. He turned and went back the way he had come.

"Ah, here he comes! Why don't you come and say hello! Ane!

We're missing you so much already!" the women shouted and burst into wild laughter.

Their jeers followed him. The men in the bars watched him go. He had been warned by his mother and aunts that villages along the coast contained just such places, but he hadn't expected to see one so near to where he was staying. What a place to put a guest house! He paused before it now, innocently reposing in the sun, shielded by its bright jungle garden and high white wall with a burst of red hibiscus falling over it. He had first read of the guest house in a review he had found online: 'elegant, simple, tasteful; a cut above the other guest houses along this unspoilt stretch' a travel journalist had written. It was exactly what Rohan had been craving: somewhere unspoilt and simple, to rest and be alone, to let himself forget.

He headed up the lane, walking the way the taxi had come. The village houses here had rooms to rent, the houses painted in bright uneasy colours: rose-pink, canary-yellow, violet; an unnatural flat green – it was the Asia of his student travels in Goa, Nepal, Thailand – an Asia-without-comfort embraced then as a protest against the hotels with turbaned staff and infinity pools that one couldn't afford and only went to in later years. He came to the top of the lane and a clearing with stalls and tuk-tuks gathered under the shade of a cyambala tree. Buses circled a bus stop. Nearby was a grimy café where a sweating man was making roti over a gas burner. Rohan walked around the clearing, inspecting the stalls. The stallholders reclined under their awnings, smoking, idly talking; a woman tugged a nit comb through a child's matted hair. Rohan bought Jacob's Cream Crackers, mangos, plantains, Bombay mix, beer and bottled water. Other vendors followed him around, offering him marijuana, magic mushrooms; lottery tickets, trips to turtle conservation beaches.

"You want a room? You want to stay in a nice guest house?" a group of excitable young men offered.

"No thanks."

"Where are you staying?"

"The Villa Hibiscus."

"Why stay there – it's much too expensive! There are much better places."

"Thanks. I'm fine."

The men eyed him resentfully. He was glad to leave them behind and return to the lane. He looked past the coconut trees towards the beach. Such an incongruous mass, the sea, with its yearning rising green-blue swell and the deep-blue simmering stillness of horizon – a seemingly impossible whole, its line of division imperceptible. And above it all was the clear pale empty blue of sky – the blue of a shirt that his wife had bought him a long time ago, a shirt he didn't wear anymore, needless to say. The air burned white, drained of all softness; the sun struck out from the sea. It hurt his eyes. He turned away.

There was a man outside the villa, peering over the wall into the garden. He spun round startled and fierce as Rohan approached the gate.

"I'm going in," Rohan explained.

"You're staying here?"

Gustav came down the path. As he came near he growled and started barking.

"Get lost you bloody dog!" the man snarled.

Gustav bared his teeth and hurled himself at the gate, barking wildly.

"Down boy!" Rohan shouted. "Jesus, what's wrong with him?"

The man picked up a large jagged stone from the road.

"Don't hurt him!" Rohan rushed forward, blocking the dog. "Gustav! It's me. Remember me? Calm down, boy!"

"He's just a little excitable, he won't hurt you," Rohan

explained, but when he turned around, there was no one behind him.

Gustav strained to see into the lane with his paws on the gate, then he dropped down and wandered away. Rohan slowly entered the garden. The dog roamed idly under the trees. It barely looked up as he went up the path. The cook was on the porch of the main house, calling to the dog. It trotted up, wagging its tail. The cook frowned, looking over at the gate. There was no sign of Padma. The villa felt too quiet without her, abandoned-seeming. Had she gone to buy food for dinner? Had she met up with friends? He couldn't imagine her friends. She had the careless disdainful confidence of the city girls who went to the fashionable schools and travelled abroad; it was hard to imagine her with villagers as friends.

But she was too unruly and uninhibited to be like the city girls who, for all their worldliness, were highly conventional and conservative – as he had discovered. Padma seemed foreign. She could have come from anywhere.

She had looked to have just run out of a shower when he'd arrived, which meant that she might live at the villa – but no young Sri Lankan woman from a well-to-do family would have been allowed to live alone at a guest house. The cook might have been a relative, but he seemed more like staff. There was something strange at the heart of the villa. He thought of the house down the lane and the hard, brazen laughter of the women. The sullying presence of that house reached into the silence of the villa. Rohan returned to his bungalow. He watched the cook come out of the back of the house and sit on the step and light the fattest joint Rohan had ever seen. The man looked up and scowled across at him. Rohan pulled the curtains closed. He paced about the room. There was nothing peaceful about this new freedom of his. He had strayed too far from the world he knew. A band of sunlight came through between the curtains and fell over the desk and across the floor. He turned on the fan and stood in its cool whorl. Despite everything he suspected, he felt soothed by the shelter of the villa. He chose a book from the pile he had brought and lay down on the bed, returning to a time when he had rested reading, after school. Like then, the fan whirled over him, its drone a rhythm of its own. He laid his face on the cool white cotton pillow smelling faintly of sandalwood, and let his eyes close. Once there would have been the cook scraping coconuts in the yard, the maid squatting at the outside tap washing cooking pots; his mother talking on the phone with her sisters, catching up on the day's family news; and his father at the office, expected back later for lunch. Now there was only this room at the villa, and beyond it a world of aloneness and resentment, where people never wished you as well as you hoped. He dropped down through the silence, the stillness of the villa filling the room.

He slept longer than he had meant to. The sun had already set when he awoke. Someone had left him a bottle of iced water on the veranda, a packet of fried cashew nuts, and, more inexplicably, a hefty volume of all of Shakespeare's plays. He drank the water and ate the nuts, watching the last streak of red in the sky fade to darkness. Dusk descended in one smoky unflinching sweep, the night filling the garden.

Inside, in the bungalow's bathroom, in the buzzing brightness of a neon light, he shaved for the first time in days. He showered, feeling as if he had woken after a terrible illness. He dressed slowly, taking more care than he had in months, even for court appearances. Then he went over to the main house, going up onto the porch where two wooden armchairs posed, two sentry posts, on either side of the doorway. To one side was a low round table with a neat arrangement of everyday objects: ball-point pens, a pencil, a bottle of pills and a newspaper with its crossword half-done. He paused in the doorway with the veranda before him – a low-lit spacious room open onto the garden, wooden roof beams slanting down to white pillars on a parapet. Wicker lampshades cast a warm baskety glow over two round tables, while a third small semi-circular table was pushed up against the parapet where Padma was arranging cutlery around a plate that was round and white like the moon. She was wearing a lunghi with a long-sleeved blouse, clothes he thought of as belonging to a time long ago. Padma's lunghi was printed with red and purple flowers and emerald green leaves, and was wrapped tight around her hips and falling long down to her feet, delicate in silver slippers. Her hair was pulled into a chignon, a red frangipani flower tucked into a fold. She moved a water glass, lighted an oil lamp and placed a fluted glass shade over the flame. There was something artful about her, about her slow smile as she surveyed the table, her face with its small nose and rounded cheeks, the soft curving line of lips and chin. Too much beauty could conceal too much, hiding all that was ugly and ruthlessly self-seeking beneath. Now he knew such things and he knew to be wary. He stepped into the room. She spun round with a gasp.

"What are you *doing*? Standing there like a burglar!" she exclaimed.

She looked terrified.

"You said dinner at seven."

"Ah, yes of course!" She smiled.

"Are you alright? I didn't mean to scare you."

"You didn't! Not at all!"

She looked him over as he went further into the room, then she giggled.

"What's so funny?" he asked.

"You've shaved. You look nice."

It would have been easy to let his defences be prised away, to feel flattered - that's how it began. He said nothing.

"That's your table," she said, indicating the table she had laid. "You can work here anytime you want."

"Work? Here?"

"So many great people have been inspired by the sea," she said mysteriously and gazed up at him expectantly. Her lips were slightly parted and he saw the white gleam of her perfect teeth. He felt her presence; so near, he felt her inside his skin. He stepped back, pulling his chair out between them.

"Shall I bring you a beer?" she asked.

"Yes. Thank you."

She went inside and he sat at the table with its lone plate and glass and fork and spoon, a solitary setting for a single man, for that was what he was now. Had he ever truly been anything else? The oil lamp's flame fluttered inside its glass containment, futile against the darkness.

Padma returned with a bottle of Lion beer.

"Where's everyone else?" he asked.

"Who?"

"The other guests?"

"There's no other guest - just you and me and Soma."

"But you said the place was fully-booked!"

"Others will come, don't worry. There's a couple due in a week, hopefully."

"Hopefully?"

"Who knows with tourists? They see one thing on the news and cancel their holiday - it happens all the time around here. People that nervous should never leave home, that's what I say. Don't worry, Gerhardt will be here soon. You can chat with him."

"Who's Gerhardt?"

"Gerhardt Hundsler," she said importantly.

"Who is he?"

"You haven't heard of him?"

"Should I have?"

She looked astonished. "He's a very famous architect - he's designed many important buildings in Asia. He's the owner here."

"I thought you were?" he reminded her.

She didn't flinch. "We both are. Gerhardt designed the villa and the garden a long time ago, but now it's my guest house."

"And he lives here?"

"No! He has his own house, in another village inland, it's not far from here. He's from Austria originally, but he's lived in Sri Lanka for *fourteen* years - you can ask him all about it."

Rohan hoped very much to avoid such a conversation. Long-term expats were the biggest bores of all, always wanting to tell you in excruciating detail about their discovery of the island you yourself had been born in, and thinking it was theirs to do what they liked with. He would have to be careful not to encourage the man, otherwise there would be no escaping him. And who knew what strange arrangement there was between him and Padma . . .

"Is this Gerhardt your employer?" Rohan asked.

"My employer?"

"Is he in charge?"

"Of me? Hah! That's what he'd like to think!" She chuckled. "*I'm* the one in charge, actually. I don't like working for other people. I have issues, you know, with authority." She grinned infuriatingly.

A motorbike drove past, pausing by the gate, a man in a black helmet waited with the engine on. A woman approached, lit by the headlights, a thin angular body in a dark dress, a plastic lipstick-red belt pulled tight around her tiny waist. She lifted a thin doll-leg over the motorbike and sat behind the man, her hands resting on his waist as the motorbike turned in the lane.

"Interesting goings-on around here," Rohan remarked.

Padma bit her lip.

"I came across a house earlier, further down the lane – there seemed to be a lot of people—"

"It's a wedding. They're having a wedding with lots of family staying."

"Ah, that must be it."

"I'll go and see if your dinner's ready," she said and went inside.

The couple on the motorbike rode away for their encounter of the night, red lights fading behind them. Then all was darkness again.

Padma brought out the food: fried vegetable rice and fish curry – large fleshy chunks in a yellow gravy of coconut milk.

"What's this?" Rohan poked at the fish. "I wanted steamed fish, not curry."

He tasted a spoonful. It was nothing like the crude overdone fare of village restaurants. It was cleverly spiced, rich and subtle, made with care like the curries he had grown up with. But he refused to be seduced; the cook had ignored him on purpose. Rohan had had enough of people not listening to what he said.

"I said no chilli," he protested. "And this is fried rice."

"The cook must have made a mistake. He must have made his usual things. He - er - doesn't like people to change the menu."

"*Menu*? Some menu!"

"But tomorrow he'll get it right. Don't worry. I'll make sure of it."

"I saw him watching me earlier – what's the matter with him?"

"He can be a bit funny." Padma laughed nervously. "He's very suspicious of new people."

"What's he think I'm going to do?"

"It can be a little strange around here sometimes."

"I noticed."

The dog ran out of the house barking. It raced into the garden. Padma darted to the parapet and stood looking out.

"It's Gerhardt," she said with relief.

The barking stopped and some moments later, a tall tanned old Western man came in.

"Hello, there!" He smiled at Padma, then at Rohan.

Gerhardt had blue eyes, very bright and pale against his tan, and white hair parted in the middle. He was dressed in cotton chinos and a pale cotton shirt, elegant and relaxed looking.

"So how's everything? You've settled in okay?" he asked Rohan.

Despite the man's friendliness, Rohan felt himself carefully checked. Gerhardt, he noted, spoke with the same Germanic accent as Padma; a resemblance that persisted in being unsettling.

"I hope the food's alright for you?" Gerhardt said.

"Yes, yes, he loves it!" Padma pushed Gerhardt out to the porch. "You sit down and relax, Gerhardt, I'll bring you a nice cold beer."

Rohan saw him settle in the armchair by the table with the newspapers and pills as Padma returned. Gerhardt sat thoughtful and rested, gazing at the garden. His garden. His house. He seemed very friendly with Padma, and didn't seem to mind showing it. He didn't seem embarrassed, or afraid of being found out. And she wasn't frightened of him, but then who knew what went on behind closed doors? Irregular goings-on among expats and villagers had been going on for decades in Sri Lanka.

"So many foreigners have invaded our villages and are corrupting the poor," his mother and his aunts would often lament.

With their social club, they ran fundraising events to help children rescued from such dangerous influences, housing and educating them in orphanages. Rohan had been made by his mother to donate to many such institutions, and he had seen for himself the solemn scrubbed rows of children watched over by strict unloving staff, protecting them from Western predators. There were many unwholesome households hidden away in remote coastal areas, the natural beauty of the place a mere backdrop for the ugliness going on. The certainty grew in Rohan that he had stumbled upon just such an arrangement.

He watched Padma take out a large tray to the porch with a bottle of beer, a can of Coke, two glasses, two plates of rice and fish curry. She sat eating with the man, the two talking in low voices. To Rohan, straining to hear, their talk sounded like genuine guest-house business. He thought he heard the rat in his bungalow mentioned and Padma suggesting that they cut down a tree, Gerhardt protesting. It was exactly what a manager might talk about with the owner of a guest house, but there was more in their seeming friendliness, a different kind of closeness. Rohan went nearer to hear better, standing at the dresser pretending to read a book.

"That's a fabulous guidebook," Padma said behind him.

He turned and she was there holding the tray with the empty bottles and used dishes.

"You should buy it. Our friend wrote it," she said.

He glanced at the book in his hand: *Reflections on A Teardrop* by Jarryd Gunnerson'.

"It's really good. I'm not just saying it because he's our friend – it's really amazing—"

"Yeah, maybe." He slipped the book back onto the pile.

"No, no – buy it now! You'll love it, trust me."

He searched in his pocket for the money and found some. She took it triumphantly and went off with the tray. He sat down at his table and studied his new purchase, a slim volume, like a book of poetry; it looked slight and home-made. He set it aside. Padma returned and took his plate. She didn't say anything about his having eaten all the fish and rice – it hadn't occurred to her to triumph over him, he realised. She merely looked pleased that he had enjoyed his meal. A knot loosened in him, a sudden easing, a feeling of contentment and safety spreading through him, despite everything. Then Gerhardt came in, asking about the state of the roads on his journey that morning. Rohan told him, alert all the while for sly questions and offers of dubious services.

"How about some fresh coffee?" Gerhardt asked. "We can do real coffee?"

"Okay. Thanks."

Rohan had meant to refuse and get away, but he was suddenly unwilling to leave the gentle glowing veranda with the darkness of the garden and the lonely roar of the sea pushed away, the old man bringing over a chair to Rohan's table.

"Padma - tell Soma to put some coffee on," Gerhardt called into the house.

Gerhardt sat back in his chair, his eyes searched the garden. He seemed to have forgotten that Rohan was there. A scooter sputtered past the gate. Silent shadowy figures passed in the lane; the old man's gaze followed them.

"Have you owned this place long?" Rohan asked.

The pale bright gaze turned back to him.

"Fourteen years. We've only just recently made it into a guest house. We had a good review in the International Guardian Online, did you see it?"

"Yes - a *very* good review—" Rohan tried not to sound accusing.

Gerhardt smiled. "Possibly a little bit over-enthusiastic. What can you do, the fellow came to visit and loved the place!"

"You said 'we' - does Padma also own this guest house?" Rohan watched Gerhardt.

"It's all her business. I have my own architects' practice. I live in the next village now. It's been a year of changes – it still feels strange not living here."

"This was your home?"

"And Padma's."

"She lived here with you?"

"Right from the start! The building work wasn't even finished when she arrived."

"She must have been very young."

"Nine years old, she was. Nine and a half."

Gerhardt didn't look ashamed. There was no hint of remorse or regret at what he had done.

"Oddly enough, this place still feels like home," Gerhardt reflected. "I always believed that work would root me, but it is children who define one's world. Home is a construct based entirely on people, wouldn't you say?"

"Home is where I keep my things."

Gerhardt laughed. "You're still young. Maybe one day you will understand. It's terrifying when a child leaves; you see all too clearly that Time is irreversible. I had a taste of it when Padma went to live in Colombo – it felt so different here. That's when I bought the new house and started working on it. I was going to keep this place for weekends, but she's come back, would you believe!"

The old man had a hold over Padma. Somehow he had made her return after an attempt at escape. Offering her a business to run would have done it. Maybe he gave her money as well. Possibly he paid her family.

"The villagers do anything for money these days," his aunts used to say. "The poor are so easily corrupted."

Padma had been a child when she came – what chance would she have had against a rich controlling foreigner? His control was all she had known. No doubt her family had handed her over for the usual laughable gain – a television or a stereo or money for drink and drugs, perhaps. No wonder the seedy dregs of the West trekked gleefully over to Sri Lanka where ordinary money could be turned into great wads of cash and buy them anything that their poisoned hearts desired.

"Now she has her own income," Gerhardt explained. "She is totally independent. That's the best way."

A guilty conscience if ever there were one. No doubt Gerhardt thought himself superior to all the other dirty old men by being so generous afterwards. Rohan longed to tell him exactly what he thought of people like him, but there was no knowing whom this Gerhardt might know. He could easily turn out to be well connected and dangerous. One had to look out for oneself in Sri Lanka these days; no one cared about the truth or justice; no one listened except to save themselves. Rohan had to stay out of Padma's troubles, he had only just escaped his own.

"I'm going to bed." He pushed back his chair from the table. He couldn't stay near the disgusting old man a moment longer.

"But what about your coffee?"

Rohan faked a yawn that halfway through became real.

"Are you still tired from your journey?" Gerhardt looked genuinely concerned. "Was the traffic very bad?"

"Yes, very bad."

"Oh dear. Never mind, we can have coffee another time, you go and get some sleep."

The face that looked up at him seemed full of kindness.

'He's good, I'll give him that,' Rohan thought glumly as he left.

He walked slowly through the garden, resisting returning to the bungalow faded into shadow at the end of the lawn. At the side of the main house, a window glowed pink through curtains drawn against the night, a secret other life going on inside, private and closed to him. He went to his room, to the bed with its nets billowing with the fan, to lie rootless and empty inside its cool cocoon that felt of nothingness, not even the past.

3

GERHARDT TOOK THE long route to the villa for break-fast, leaving his village and walking down to the sea road and onto the beach – a pale gold smoothness early in the morning. The sea was gentle, just woken, resting across the horizon. The day had opened and a new world was before him; each day a different view, a new configuration of sky and sea and beach achieving its own perfection. An incredible feat, to be so effortlessly, ceaselessly renewed, and so completely, but this was the magic of Asia, this power to regenerate with a new and greater vigour each day. It kept one forever in the first thrill of one's excitement. Mornings in Asia offered such absolution; anything seemed possible in that glorious light, the sun a welcome caressing warmth in the quiet loveliness of the day. It was easy to bask in that hopefulness, in the delusion of endless possibility, even if it only lasted for those first early hours.

But that morning he was uneasy, for he had been thinking about Sunny; Sunny who was really Sugathapala, the most devious, grasping individual one could ever meet. Gerhardt had been expecting Sunny ever since Padma's return to the villa several months earlier, because Sunny's many spies and underlings would have told him she was back – but he hadn't shown up once. And now with Padma starting her own business, it was completely unlike the scoundrel not to turn up to pry and attempt to take something away. Gerhardt reached Nilwatte Beach and walked towards the lane, leaving the sea behind. Stamping his feet on the tarmac to shake off sand, he crossed over to the villa. Gustav ran down to him and he walked with the dog at his side up to the house. Gustav would let them know if Sunny came, the dog somehow knew to resent Sunny's presence. Gerhardt used to sometimes encounter Sunny in the town in the old days, and whenever he'd had Gustav with him, the dog had turned savage. At least with Gustav around, Sunny could never come too close to the house.

Soma brought coffee and toast out to the porch. Gerhardt sat eating and going over his work for the day: two client meetings at his office, back at his house; a site visit and a second viewing of a cottage he hoped to buy and renovate for a holiday rental business of his own. Building the bungalows for Padma's guesthouse had been the inspiration. The young so effortlessly renewed one's enthusiasm. He always had new ideas when Padma was around. What a joy to have her back again. Ruth, his oldest and dearest friend in Colombo, had wanted Padma to travel the world. Even as a young woman, Ruth had believed that a true self was only to be found in foreign lands – but one's true self could be found wherever one felt inspired. Padma had always loved the villa and this was why she had needed to return. Ruth too, in the end had returned from her travels to her homeland. People thought he had followed her to Sri Lanka – possibly he had, but the island had called to him. All of his work, in one way or another, had been fuelled by this single decision to go where he felt called, the island's splendour had inspired him from the start, with its majestic ancient heritage and wild natural abundance. He always returned in his designs to the modesty and elegance of its old buildings. It was hard to imagine what he would have built if he had stayed away. Padma was finally back where she belonged. She had never loved anywhere else as much, so why send her away? The villa was her home, it was a world he had made to hold her safe and Sunny couldn't change that. Gerhardt wasn't afraid of Sunny; Sunny could always be paid to go away.

"Good morning!" Padma came out of the house eating cereal. She bent and kissed him on the cheek.

"What's the matter?" she asked at once.

Like a psychic, she was, so perceptive. And bright as a button; she always had been.

"I'm just enjoying the morning," he said.

"Have you seen that crazy Rohan, yet?"

"No. And by the way, that's not a very nice way to talk about your guests."

"He's strange, don't you think? Why do you suppose he ran off before coffee last night? What a weirdo!" She gazed at the small bungalow.

There was something different about her that morning – so impatient and dishevelled and bright-eyed.

"Soma had a bad feeling about him, right from the start," she mused.

"Soma has bad feelings about everyone."

"Yes, but this time I also have a bad feeling."

"Good God, not both of you."

"I'm telling you, there's something really strange about that new guest. He's hiding something."

"Like what?"

"I'm not sure. He's up to something though, and it's definitely not a screenplay. He's running away . . ."

"It's only his first morning, give him a chance! And by the way, shouldn't you go and get dressed properly?"

She had changed from her nightclothes into her clothes from the day before, unusually for her she was unwashed and crumpled.

"In a minute, I've got something to do first." She crunched on her cornflakes, her eyes still fixed on the small bungalow. "You know, Soma thinks he might have killed someone."

"My goodness!"

"He's got the heaviest suitcase."

"It's called luggage. Guests have it sometimes."

She giggled. "You didn't try carrying it – it was so heavy, not like usual luggage; a dead weight. He could easily have had a body inside."

"He's a bit stressed, that's all." Gerhardt drank down the last of his coffee. "The best thing we can do is leave the poor fellow alone, let him have a good rest."

"Maybe."

Gerhardt thrilled to see her returned to herself, once more full of warmth and laughter. Her years at the University in Colombo had dulled her; each time she returned she had seemed more lost, more lacking in purpose. The university had failed to inspire her, yet the failure had been deemed hers – and it was he who had urged her to go there, to try and try again to succeed where she could not thrive, for he had feared that a lack of a degree might burden her – yet here she was, unshackled from that fruitless pursuit, shining and new again. Ruth had worried that Padma would never meet suitable men away from Colombo, but love could wait. It was work, not love, and certainly not marriage, that gave purpose to life.

"Ah – ha! Speak of the devil," Padma murmured.

Rohan had come out onto his veranda, a tall solemn figure looking out at the day.

"Whatever you do, don't upset your guest, okay? He seems a little fragile," Gerhardt advised.

"Me? Upset Mr Rohan? Look – he's settling down; aha! So he's planning to keep guard."

"He's reading."

"He's got something in that suitcase he doesn't want anyone to see."

"Maybe he just wants to relax."

"Don't worry, I have a plan." Padma darted inside.

Gerhardt watched a fat mynah bird on the mango tree. Two parrots on the top branch calmly surveyed the devastation that their chattering tribe had wrought on the ripe fruit. It was possible that Sunny had lost interest in Padma. No one seemed to know what Sunny was doing these days, but there was talk of him working for someone rich and powerful – possibly one of the many Russian mafia mobsters based on the coast, trading in arms and drugs and women – that would keep Sunny busy. Good riddance to the scoundrel. Even if he did ever come by the villa, Gerhardt had plenty of money set aside, ready to pay him to go away. One thing he knew was how to handle Sunny – he'd had plenty of practice in the past twelve years.

Gerhardt remembered all too well the morning of their first encounter, not long after he had bought the dilapidated little house by the sea that no one else had wanted. It was quite usual at the time for villagers to come and watch the building work: the veranda being erected, the roof raised, windows enlarged; frangipani trees planted. The arrival of the porch pillars alone, reclaimed from an old mansion demolition inland, had raised quite a crowd. Everyday there was someone to watch as the small, mean, inward-looking house grew the languorous features of its tropical heritage. It was the day when he and Soma had been planting choleas along the edge of the path, that Gerhardt first became aware of Sunny beckoning to him over the gate.

"Don't go, sir, he's no good, that one," Soma had warned.

But Sunny was hard to ignore. He had waited and waited. "Hello, sir!" he'd kept shouting. "Sir, I want to tell you something. Can I come in?"

"Don't let him in!" Soma hissed.

Sunny lifted the gate latch.

"Alright, I'm coming." And Gerhardt had gone to meet him.

"Ah, how do you do, sir? You're the new owner here? Very good, very good. Welcome to our beautiful Sri Lanka." Sunny bowed with his hands together, as if praying at temple.

"So you will be living here, sir? You and Soma over there? He'll be doing the cooking, I suppose. Is he cooking Sinhala or Tamil food? A lot of oil they use, I hear."

Race was never a neutral observation in Sri Lanka, race was a judgment, an accusation.

"Soma's an excellent cook. Now – I am very busy here. Is there anything else I can help you with?"

"Oh, goodness me, sir! But it is I who can help you! That is what I am here for!"

"For what, exactly?"

"First of all, let me introduce myself: I'm Sunny. And you are Gerhardt Hundsler, no? World famous architect! Oh yes, we have all heard about you, coming to our small village. You're from Germany, no?"

"Austria."

"Yes, Austria. You love our small island, I hear? That is good, very good. You will build many beautiful houses and hotels in Sri Lanka, I'm sure. Maybe you will build me also a house? I'm only a poor villager, but who knows, maybe one day, you and I can help each other?"

There was an excess of energy in Sunny, pressed back too hard and waiting to burst through. One saw it in the forced eagerness, the hard, bright gaze, the smooth bald head, poised snakelike, as if to strike.

"I really must get back to my gardening now." Gerhardt stepped back from the gate.

"You need someone here, sir – for company?"

"For *company?*"

"Sir doesn't have a wife, no? It can get lonely in these parts. I can find you someone." Sunny smiled meaningfully.

"Thank you for coming. I have to go." Gerhardt walked away.

"Shall I bring you someone – to meet? Just for you to see, that's all? No need to do anything if you don't like them. All completely confidential, sir. You prefer boys? Girls? What age? I'll bring someone for you to take a look. How about tonight? Tomorrow? Anytime you want I can bring them—"

Gerhardt stopped and turned back.

"Let me be very clear: I am *not* interested," he told the man.

He knew not to be angry, or even surprised. Impoverished rural areas were known to attract a particular kind of tourist, and to a local he would be indistinguishable from one of those Westerners arriving on the island with their warped minds concealed by inoffensive middle-aged exteriors.

"I'm only here to build my house and do my work, nothing else," he said.

"But you will need somebody to look after you, no – while you are working? I know a nice young girl you can have. Very well-behaved – she'll do anything you tell her." The man smiled slyly. "Anything at all . . ."

"No. Thank you." This time Gerhardt didn't turn back, he walked away.

"I can bring her here – just for you to look, that's all," the man called after him.

Gerhardt picked up the trowel and dug a hole for a red cholea already turning limp in the sun.

"Just let me bring her, to show you, you can always say no! Sir will like her, I'm sure. Very good girl, she is. Very pretty!"

Soma sprang up and stormed down the path. "Palayang! Dhang palayang!" he shouted, one of the few Sinhalese phrases Gerhardt knew: now piss-off.

Soma rattled the gate, threatening to call the police.

The man smiled past Soma to Gerhardt, then sauntered away up the lane.

"That man is a real devil. He's been in and out of prison for the past twenty years," Soma told Gerhardt. "He's always up to something. Once he was in an armed robbery, another time he killed a man in a fight. Don't get involved with him, sir, he's a bad man. And he has bad friends all around these parts."

"Don't worry, I don't think we'll be seeing him again. I made myself very clear."

Afterwards, Gerhardt had thought about buying a small pistol – for protection only. But where would he have kept it? No room seemed appropriate to house such a thing.

Gerhardt sat on the porch now; it was so many years since that first visit of Sunny's. How much the garden had changed, yet still it would shelter them. Padma could safely be inside it again, surrounded by beauty. She came out of the house, still wearing the same crumpled clothes.

"What are you doing – you need to get dressed!" he exclaimed.

Just then, a great blast of Bollywood music burst over the garden.

"Bloody hell!" Padma ran outside.

It was the neighbours, a fishing family, who had just sold their house to the minister's brother, if the local gossip was to be believed. There was a suspicious lack of information about the new buyer, which was worrying of course, not least as some months earlier the villa's other neighbour had also mysteriously sold their house.

"Padma, just leave it, they'll be gone soon," Gerhardt said, over the din.

Already the new guest was looking over, disturbed by the noise.

"They know we've got guests, that's why they're doing it," Padma fumed.

She picked up a stone and hurled it over the wall, crashing onto the tin roof of the garage next door.

The son or the father shouted a protest and swore at Padma.

"Hey! Don't talk like that!" Gerhardt called.

"We'll call Boss!" Padma threatened and then the music stopped.

"Stupid bloody idiot," Padma muttered, coming back in. "His wife goes to Saudi to work like a dog, so he can buy stereos and annoy everyone."

"Padma, you need to calm down."

"Stupid bastard. Bastards, all of them."

"For goodness sake, Padma. Shouldn't you get ready now? Go and put on some clean clothes. Have you even showered this morning?"

"Later, later! I've got to do something first." And she ran into the garden.

Gerhardt folded his newspaper. It was time to go. He stood looking out at the lane. So much was changing around them, but there was nothing for him to worry about. The minister and his brother knew that Gerhardt loved the villa; it didn't matter what they did on either side, he had already built the wall higher on one side, he could do the same on the other. The only thing he was concerned about was the absence of Sunny. Had Sunny really lost interest in Padma, even now when she had her own business? He breathed out slowly. It would take time to get used to this new freedom, to know if it was real.

# 4

## ACQUIRING SRI LANKA

Many nations have tried to acquire the jewel in the Indian Ocean that is Sri Lanka – once a collection of kingdoms spread over the island, staying proudly apart unless fighting each other.

## THE PORTUGUESE

The Portuguese arrived in 1505 and exported away the valuable spices of the island. They conquered first the Sinhalese Kingdom of the south-west of the country, then the Tamil Kingdom in the north, but the Kandyans in the central hill-country resisted fiercely and held out in their hilltop palaces.

## THE DUTCH

The Kandyan Kingdom also survived the next invasion of the island, by the Dutch, in around 1658. The Kandyan Kings with their pale-skinned beautiful wives imported from India, thrived high up in the green hills. In that distant world of cool misty mornings, the lushness of flowers and ferns, in pleasure gardens and palaces they held out against the invaders, surrounded by Art and beauty. The Kandyans developed apart and distinct from the rest of the country, they had their own style of architecture, fashion, dance and music. Their loud stirring drums and rousing rhythms, the muscled dancers leaping in jewelled costumes of white and red and silver – these are brought back from a long lost past for special occasions still, for weddings and processions, national parades, telling of a time of splendour and pride, the heady power of a true autonomy.

## THE BRITISH

The British arrived in around 1815. More subtle and more sweeping than the previous invaders, they wooed the Kandyan Kings and Queens, guaranteeing their independence if they would only help the British gain control over the others. The vain trusting Kandyans obliged, and through this betrayal of their fellow Sri Lankans, they enabled the British to sweep in and take over the island. Soon, the island was under the control of a single ruler – a Queen far away in a land of grey cold and wetness. For the first time, the country's separate regions, once entire worlds in themselves, were made to form a whole, the different races and cultures sliding uneasily in among each other, compressed into one mass while the country was taken over by the invaders.

The British, a determined organised presence, bore firmly down on island life, smoothing it into a world of rigidity and order: towns of Victorian sophistication, with new administrations, roads, railways, churches, schools, hospitals; soirées in imposing homes. There were new elegant avenues built in cities, where women glided in long pale dresses and parasols and men sweated under suits. A vast native population crowded beneath these new conquerors, made to serve the all-powerful

Empire. Sri Lanka in those Colonial years was a functioning whole, divided only into natives and conquerors.

Rohan tried to read on from the little book he had bought at dinner, but the words slid meaninglessly over the pages. Nothing stayed with him anymore, his thoughts derailed by the continual charge of reminiscence and regret and endless recriminations; a new absorption. He had never been aware of how he was feeling at any moment, but now a heightened awareness of his every mood assaulted him – a new kind of aloneness, it felt like drowning.

He opened out the arms of the planters' chair and lay back against its woven curve, propping his leg up on one of the extended chair arms. His father and uncles had lain lazy and proprietorial on just such chairs at his grandmother's coconut plantation on weekends long ago, the family all gathered on the veranda, sleepily talking after big country lunches of red rice and chicken curry, jak fruit curry, cashew nut curry, gotukolla mallung, while his aunts whined gently on and on about misbehaving servants and disputes with the neighbours over stolen coconuts. The drone of their voices in those days was simply a part of the day's lull, nothing to fear – but he was only a child then, loved and let be. It was when you were older that they gathered around you, needing to instruct and guide and push you into making their mistakes all over again.

There was a twinge in his shoulders, a pain in his back. He adjusted the seat, but he ached in new places. He sat up, rubbing his neck. Padma had been out on the porch of the main house earlier, marching about in front of Gerhardt, even stooping to kiss the man. Their private arrangements were none of his business, but how was he supposed to relax, knowing what he did about them? He tried again to read the guidebook, but Padma went past, then appeared again with a giant machete, swinging it wide as she came towards him.

"Hello there!" she shouted.

He sank down, pretending to read.

"Good morning! I have to cut some branches, they're too close to your bungalow - that's how that meeya got into your room. You want to go for a walk for a little while?"

"No thanks."

"Okay then, I'll do it with you here."

She came onto his veranda unasked and leaned out, hacking at the tree.

"This is where it must have run into the roof." She struck hard with the blade, slicing through a tough grey branch, leaving a gash of raw green, oozing white milk.

"You have to stop them quickly, otherwise they get in and make nests," she said.

Rohan returned to his book. Branches crashed down around him, leaves landed in his lap. He was surprised at the force of her blows; the tree shuddered and rustled against the house. Sweat showed blood-red through her t-shirt, but she didn't try to hide it - she raised her arm up high, unflinching; her small body arched proudly, supple and sure. He kept losing his place on the page trying not to see her.

"Can't you do this some other time?" he asked.

"Only a few more to go!"

Her hair was tousled around her face. Her cheeks glowed a dark rosy pink, the skin a flawless softness. Rohan threw down his book.

"I'm going for a walk!" he declared.

"Yes, a walk will be good for you, bye, bye! Have a nice time!"

He went over the lane to the beach, crossing over and stepping down from crumbling black tarmac onto sandy earth, passing under the coconut trees, his feet sinking into fine white sand, cold from the shade and streaming into his slippers. He took off the slippers and walked with the hard ribs of coconut leaves cracking under his feet. He looked out for litter and dog shit and broken glass or discarded needles. It was years since he had walked on a beach in Sri Lanka. Where his family usually went, it was easier to stay inside the hotel grounds and use the pool. On the beaches in those resorts there was a constant stream of vendors coming to sell drums and crab feasts and ear-cleans, on Nilwatte Beach there was no one, just the sea, wide and calm, rippling blue. He walked into the edge of the water, the waves frothing around his ankles. His feet underwater were pale and long and bony, veins bulging. Like an old man's feet. As he walked along the beach his footprints filled, all traces of him disappearing.

He had lived by the sea in England on school holidays, going with his best friend Tom to his family's farmhouse in East Sussex. From the room that became his, Rohan had seen across fields to a distant pale view of sea. He had cycled to that beach, to sandy dunes and faded flailing grasses, a lonely restless sea. He had learned to find consolation in that wan blustery beauty, but inside he held a different sea, a different beauty of sunshine and heat and a sparkling blue richness. His sea dazzled, even in the city, glimpsed brilliant and blue at the end of the crowded little lanes as you drove along the main Galle Road.

Stray dogs ran now on Nilwatte Beach, a wild panting pack racing on up ahead, stopping to inspect the tide's nocturnal littering: glistening dark mounds of seaweed; plastic bottles scuffed to pearl, rusted diesel cans dropped from fishing boats. Once on a beach in Colombo, he had watched with his ayyah as another band of stray dogs, yapping and frisky and completely unaware, had been rounded up by the dogcatcher and herded into a van.

The doors with their small barred windows slammed closed on the dogs' barking, suddenly turned frantic. Rohan had begged his ayyah to save the dogs, but she had refused to intervene, and the two of them had stood by the railway line, Rohan crying, his ayyah offering him sweets, as the van drove away. He had been crying for the dogs, but also for his helplessness to alter their fate. He had wished himself older, for he had thought then that becoming a man would entail living his same life but with the power to change things. It was nothing short of a betrayal discovering the real world that adults went about in, where ideals were put aside and forgotten, and one's work was fuelled merely by the desire not to have failed. He had wanted so much more of himself, he had longed to be able to help. He had once fully intended to use his expensive schooling and the mind that others praised, to do good, and live boldly.

He watched the stray dogs scampering along the beach now, free to play. Dogcatchers belonged in a different Sri Lanka, he sensed, a world far away from Nilwatte Beach. Here was a different place. Anything one wished for seemed right and possible; there were none of the usual obstacles; no one to convince, no one to talk the longings away. He breathed deeply, feeling better without trying. The morning sun touched his face, his arms, the back of his neck; it felt like the first morning ever. A new quiet filled him, a sleepy emptiness opening inside, wordless.

Padma watched Rohan go. She gathered up the cut branches and took an armful to the bins. She waved to Gerhardt as he left for his meeting. The shower was running in Soma's bathroom. She could hear his tuneless singing – he could stay there for hours, being Elvis Presley. Now was her chance, possibly her only chance. She had the key ready in her pocket. Quickly she unlocked Rohan's door and slipped in.

He had left the room perfectly tidy, even made the bed. There wasn't a single thing out of place, no dirty socks, no worn underpants. It was impressive, his private orderliness. Blue-striped pyjamas were folded on a chair, a grey t-shirt folded on top. Its label said Medium. He was tall for a Medium. She tied back the mosquito net. The big suitcase was under the wardrobe. She heaved out its dead-weight, only to find it locked with a heavy brass padlock. She had hoped to startle Rohan into leaving, but he had taken precautions. At least the padlock didn't need a code, just a key, to open it. She searched in the desk drawer, but there was only his passport and an envelope of cash. She flicked through to his photograph in the passport, suddenly faced with a quite different him: another self from a happier time. His smile brimmed with good fortune and success. She could imagine him in one of those well-to-do families full of attractive, well-dressed people that one came across at expensive restaurants and five-star hotels, filling vast rooms with their noise and bluster. No waiter would ever ask them to be quiet, for they would be trusted customers, friends of the management. The Rohan in the photograph would have been one of those distant, handsome, unattainable men making jokes and being teased by adoring cousins, while a proud mother and aunties would beam on at him and brag of his achievements. It was harder to imagine the Rohan at the villa being in that world. Something had happened to him to take away his veneer of entitlement and confidence; the assurance of acceptance.

She searched for the key all over the room: on shelves, in the wardrobe and the bedside table, around his teetering pile of books. So many books: three Russian novels – the famous ones; a book about the trees of Sri Lanka, another on Sri Lankan wildlife, and Jarryd's guidebook. She stacked them all more neatly. Gustav barked outside and she pushed the suitcase back and quickly started sweeping, but no one came. She went out on the veranda in time to see someone passing by the gate. Whoever it was, Gustav had scared them off. It may have been a possible guest, of course, but they could always telephone to enquire, the villa's number was on the sign. She locked up the bungalow. Rohan must have taken the key to the padlock away with him. Possibly he kept it with him at all times. The big question was why.

⚘

The sun grew strong over the beach and Rohan turned back for the villa. The man from the day before appeared as Rohan was crossing the lane.

"You're staying at the Villa Hibiscus, sir?"

"Yes."

The man came with Rohan and stood blocking his way, although standing well away from the gate.

"Sir, there are much cheaper places than here, you want me to show you?"

"No thanks."

"It's not too expensive here for you, sir?"

Rohan was silent, trying to get past the man.

"Maybe because you're coming from abroad, no? Sir is from America?"

"England."

Rohan reached for the gate, his arm brushing the man's. The man jerked back, startled, his face vicious, one fist already raised ready to strike. It was an instinctual response, an unexpected glimpse of the real lives of the villagers behind their seeming haplessness. The man recovered immediately, smiling and bowing and stepping aside to let Rohan pass.

"Ah, you need to go this way, of course you must. How nice for you, sir, staying in this fine house. Have a nice day, sir."

Rohan opened the gate.

"Just one small thing, sir - the child who works here - you know her?"

"Padma?"

"Ah, you do know her. How is she, sir? Is she keeping well?"

"I think so - why? Are you a relative?"

"Oh I'm family, alright."

"Where are her parents?"

"That's a long story."

"So you are . . . ?"

"Her uncle."

"So go in and see her."

"If only I could, sir. But Mr Gerhardt won't like it." The man sighed. "He doesn't like us poor villagers. We're nothing to him, just dirty scum from the drains - that's what he thinks of us. Just because we're poor and he has his millions. So many are struggling in this country, but Mr Gerhardt only spends his money on himself - only he is allowed to be comfortable in his fancy houses - two he has now. Taking away our precious children - what to do, no? I don't want his money, all I want is to see that my little niece isn't being mistreated."

"Padma seems fine," Rohan said.

"Ah, thank you, sir, it makes me very happy to hear that."

"How did she end up here?"

"She came marching over, sir, all on her own."

"But she was only nine!"

"Ah, so you know the whole story."

"She didn't come here on her own, did she?" Rohan demanded.

"Mr Gerhardt brought her, who else?" The man sighed. "He brainwashed her, bringing her gifts and so on - you know what his type are like, no? They have so much money, they can buy what they want. And now she won't leave. She's a difficult girl, that one. She doesn't want anything to do with her family – but that's only because Mr Gerhardt has put ideas in her head. He and his friends want her for themselves. They have been having their fun with her all this time—"

"They should be in prison!"

"Oh they should, sir."

So many lost years of Padma's childhood, she would never have them back – and still she stayed, caught in the trap.

"Mr Gerhardt is hoping she will forget all about us, but family is the most important thing, no, sir? A child should be with her family, no?"

"Maybe. Sometimes."

"But of course, sir! Every time! Family is always best. Who else will want the best for their children?"

Family wanted what was best for the family, but that wasn't the same thing. Still, Padma had to be better off with her strange uncle than living exploited by Gerhardt.

"Come with me now," Rohan urged the man. "You can talk to Padma. I'll keep the dog away."

"Ah sir, you are too kind, how much I would like that—"

"Well, come then! We can all go to my bungalow. Gerhardt can't stop me inviting people to my room."

"No, sir, I'm afraid of that mad dog of his – it will eat me alive. You saw for yourself. You won't be able to stop him attacking, he's too big. Mr Gerhardt has trained that beast to kill any of us locals who get too close to his house. If only I could see my little Padma outside here – do you know if she leaves this house anytime?"

"She went to the market yesterday – she might go again today. Around ten o'clock."

"So late! Most people go much earlier! That is when the fish is fresh – you'd better be careful what you eat tonight." The man chuckled. "Ten o'clock, you say. Maybe I'll try and see her. All thanks to you, sir!"

The man beamed and bowed again as Rohan returned to the garden.

Up by the main house, Rohan washed the sand from his feet at the garden tap and went in to breakfast. His table had been laid with a yellow and white checked cloth. There was a pink glass vase with a sprig of jasmine flowers at the centre and jam jars of tea bags, Nescafé and condensed milk.

"There was a man outside to see you," Rohan told Padma.

"A man? To see me? What for?"

"He said he was your uncle."

"My uncle!" She laughed. "It must have been someone selling something! The things they try these days!"

"He wasn't selling anything. He just wanted to know how you were."

"Did he now?" She placed a silver thermos flask on the table. "Hot water for your tea and coffee," she said.

She went to the parapet and stared at the lane. She wasn't smiling anymore. She turned abruptly and went inside the house. It was the cook who brought out Rohan's eggs and toast. Rohan ate slowly waiting for Padma to return, but she never came.

He waited in the garden, inspecting flowers and watching birds. He went to take a look at the second bungalow, tucked in behind a cluster of plantain trees. It was wider than his bungalow, with a long veranda with a hammock at one end. From the steps he could see over the gate, scruffy backpackers strolling past, going towards the beach bars. There was no sign of the man. Was he waiting somewhere for Padma? Rohan was uneasy. It felt as if he had said too much, although he and the man had barely spoken.

The dog came over with his rubber ball and dropped it at Rohan's feet. Rohan threw the ball to the edge of the garden and the dog bounded gleefully behind it. How angry it had been the day before, barking so ferociously at Padma's uncle. And how afraid the man seemed of Gerhardt. People were managed by fear in Sri Lanka now, it was how one got what one wanted. Nobody cared if it was right or fair or deserved, having was all that mattered, and the power to have. Possibly Gerhardt was feared by Padma too, not just her uncle. Rohan had noticed how the men trying to sell him rooms in other guest houses had refrained from speaking badly of Gerhardt. Clearly Gerhardt had money and influence, and that usually came with the backing of someone dangerous. Someone able to command the violent forces that circled everywhere in Sri Lanka these days, in the shadows and under the most glossy and respected surfaces. He had learnt this too in the past months.

The dog returned with the ball and Rohan threw it again. Over and over he threw the ball until Padma finally emerged with her scooter.

"Get the same fish as yesterday," the cook shouted to her from the house. "And get potatoes and some ash plantains – go to the woman in the corner stall, but make sure you bargain – don't just pay what she asks."

Padma did up the strap of her glittery helmet.

"You're sure you don't want me to go?" Soma said.

"Very sure! Goodbye!"

The scooter roared away. Rohan casually walked across the garden, following. Padma flung open the gate and rode out. Rohan walked faster. Was the man waiting in the lane? Had he been telling the truth or was his interest something other than familial concern? Did he mean to harm Padma? Rohan started to run.

## 5

T HE LANE WAS busy that morning. Padma beeped her horn at a group of tourists. They ambled along, travel-worn and bulky with backpacks, searching for somewhere on Googlemaps. They turned in at the Kingfisher, a shabby old guest house. Well, good luck to them! Paying good money for a flea-infested room with a dirty mattress on the floor covered up nicely with a batik bedspread. It was amazing what tourists would pay for. The two horrible sons who ran the place were by the fence, painting alternate slats sugary pink and bottle-green – a truly awful combination. The worst! They scowled at her and she smirked behind her helmet at their ugly fence and pressed down on the accelerator. It was good to leave the lane behind. Sometimes it helped to be away from the villa. Her fears seemed less real and the world felt bigger, full of people who didn't know her. It could have been anyone asking Rohan about her – it was probably one of the villagers, they were the ones with nothing better to do than hang around pretending to be other people's uncles.

At the Green Emerald Café, the Bob Marley flag flapped in the wind, a faded rag, hanging from the mango tree. They should have taken it down years ago. Music croaked from the ancient speakers wrapped up in polythene and hung from branches – what a noise! But it didn't stop the tourists. They would think it all very quaint and take photographs. It made her mad. Tourists expected so little of the country. Someone ran out from the trees. Out of nowhere! She screamed and braked. Bloody Hell! The man leapt to one side and stood grinning at her. And there he was, after all these years: Sunny.

Padma straightened the scooter. She knew she should ride away, spin round in the road and go straight back to the villa, but she stood frozen, gripping the handles. Sunny emptied her. No thoughts survived in her. It was easier to wait until he had said what he wanted. She could never have ridden away knowing that he was somewhere behind her.

"So, how?" he said, coming to her.

"What do you want?" It was an effort to stay apart, to seal herself up and not let him in.

He was chewing betle, his mouth was full of spit. He slurped it all back and swirled it around his mouth and shot it out, a red bubbling jet onto the road – splat! The red bubbles burst on the sand, making a wet rounded imprint.

"I hear you have a business these days.

"You're back here to stay?"

Her skin tightened, her body grew hot. Even as a child she had known her body to change near people to fear – like the friend of Sunny's who would smile too long at her and stare strangely, and another one who used to come up behind her sometimes and put his hands on her breasts or grabbed her by the hips and pawed at her buttocks. She would get rashes whenever those men came near her, red weals rising, itching and seeping a clear fluid when she scratched.

"You're back at the villa again, are you?"

She didn't reply. It seemed wrong not speaking when he wanted her to, but it was her power now. He wasn't used to that; he seemed nervous. He kept jigging about fidgeting, like a boy – a boy with a few strands of dyed black hair oiled over a bald pointy head. He clutched the knot of his sarong and fiddled in a pocket of his shirt.

"You have a guest, I hear? Are there many others coming?"

"I don't know."

"Ah, still, one is good. Who needs too many guests?" He sniggered.

Padma started up the engine. Would she dare to ride it into him if he didn't let her pass?

"You're going, are you?" Sunny stepped aside. "I also have to be going. Good to see you anyhow. I only wanted to see how you were. When are you coming to visit us?"

"Visit you?" This was new.

"Leela has been begging to see you. She is the one who sent me to find you today. You know, she isn't very well these days."

Padma turned off the engine.

"What's wrong with her?"

"She keeps asking for you. I don't get a moment's peace, all she says is: 'Padma, Padma, where is my Padma?'"

Padma couldn't imagine Leela saying any of that, especially not 'my Padma'. She hadn't seen Leela since leaving home twelve years ago. They had never even said goodbye. Leela was a silence, an absence whenever Padma looked back at that night. Had Sunny chosen a time when Leela wouldn't be there to shout to the neighbours for help? To scream and fight and pull her daughter back into the darkness of their shack and its fragile shelter? But Leela had never come to the villa looking for Padma, or written. Padma had sometimes wondered why.

"It's been so long since we saw you," Sunny said. "Even on your twenty-first birthday we didn't get to wish you – there were hundreds of people there, I heard."

Ruth had made Gerhardt hire security from Colombo for the party, certain that Sunny would appear like an evil fairy to ruin Padma's passing into adulthood. But there was no trouble, no sighting of him, and Padma and her old school friends from Tangalle Town and their families – friends now scattered around the country or abroad, starting new lives after university – had danced the night away in a marquee on the lawn where the small bungalow now stood.

"What a sad thing for parents not to see their beloved child on such a day, no?" Sunny said. "We were so surprised to hear you were back."

"I've been back for almost a year!"

Any of his many spies in the area would have told him of her return. It had to be the opening of the guesthouse that had brought him now – just as she had expected it would. Her instincts about him were always right.

"You didn't think of getting in touch to let us know you were back?" Sunny accused.

"No."

Sunny smiled.

"I hear you have done very well at the fine university in Colombo, what a great thing that is for our family, no?"

Did he know really that she had failed her exams, year after year for three years running, starting a different course each year and failing every time, never making it to a second year of any subject. Had he heard all about it?

"And having a business at age twenty-two," Sunny went on. "So young to have your own guest house. My goodness! What a lot you have achieved in such a short time. How could we ever have given you such things?"

He would know that it was because of Gerhardt that she could start such a venture, but the idea had come from her, although at the time she had only talked of renting out the spare bedroom on Airbnb. It was Gerhardt who had grown a whole guesthouse from that, and built bungalows in the garden and talked Soma into making dinners. Gerhardt had paid for it all, and he still gave her an allowance each month – a business loan he called it, but there was no interest to pay, and she had forever to repay him.

"In the village they send the boys to monasteries," Sunny said. "That's how we poor people educate our children. Just think if we'd sent you to become a nun – imagine walking around with a bald head, chanting pirith and begging for food in a bowl. All we ever wanted was to give you the chances we never had."

He didn't mean a word of it. She knew not to listen. Nothing he ever said was true.

"Maybe one day Mukul can own a business also," Sunny said. "All he needs is a chance, just like you. Do you think Gerhardt would give him a job?"

"No."

The one true thing about Sunny was his concern for Mukul. Mukul was the son and he mattered. Mukul mattered more than her – this Padma had always known.

"It's so difficult for him," Sunny said.

"Yes, I can imagine, especially now with a prison record."

"He should never have been in there." Sunny's face darkened. "Those bastards left him to take the blame. They're going to regret that."

It was no idle threat, Sunny bore grudges. One or more of Mukul's gang would pay the price for running away and leaving him behind at the raid they had botched at a jeweller's. Nothing was taken, but a security guard had been shot in the shoulder and Mukul had been the only one caught. When the security guard survived, Mukul had got away with a six-month sentence.

"Poor fellow, he's suffering. He's got nothing, not like you. You were always the lucky one," Sunny said.

"Lucky?"

"You always worked hard, that is good. Mukul might be the one with the brains—"

"He isn't."

"Oh, he has brains alright."

"Mukul's an idiot."

Sunny paused and grew dreamy, erasing her words.

"You know Leela wants so much to make you a meal, a small dinner maybe, to celebrate you growing up and becoming a business owner. Will you come? She is crying every day, talking of you."

"Is she, now?"

"She wanted to have a party for you, so you could see all the relatives again, but what to do? You have forgotten all about your family, no?"

"They're the ones who've forgotten me!"

"What nonsense! People are always asking how you are!"

Nothing Sunny said could be trusted, she knew that – but she had once had a large family, a real Sri Lankan family, like everyone else – with uncles and aunts and cousins to meet at weddings and funerals and festive holidays. She remembered women cooking noisily together in smoky kitchens, uncles giving her sweets, and cousins – so many cousins to run with around wild village gardens. Those cousins would all be grown up now. It was hard to imagine any of them still thinking of her.

"It won't be like the grand parties you're used to," Sunny said. "Just a simple meal, nothing fancy . . ."

"Would you ask the whole family?"

"All the relatives? But of course! If you're coming, I'll tell everyone! My goodness, if they knew you were going to be there they will come running to see you. The house will burst! And

Leela will be so happy. She is so weak these days, who knows how long she will last?"

"What exactly is wrong with her?"

"How should I know? The doctor has given her a list of the medicines she needs - so many there are, but these things cost money, and who has that kind of money these days?"

"How much does she need?"

The warning bells were ringing, but money was what he wanted, what he had always wanted, and maybe now Leela really needed it. Money Padma had. She had more in her account than she knew what to do with. She gave Sunny some of the food money.

"Ah, she will be grateful even for this much." Sunny rolled up the notes and tucked them away. "So will you come to eat with us? One small dinner? We'll call all the relatives."

"I'll think about it."

"How about Sunday?"

"And Gerhardt? I'll only come if he does."

"But of course, Gerhardt must come too - he's like family, no! You tell him he's invited!"

"Alright."

"So you'll come?"

"Yes."

"Ah, Leela will be so happy! I must go and tell her. Oh! I just thought of something! Oh dear me!"

"What?"

"There is just one little problem—"

"What's that?"

"Oh, my, what a nuisance . . . it's just the relatives might not come if Gerhardt is there. They're simple villagers, they are not used to foreigners - not like you, getting to travel all over the world: India, Hong Kong, Thailand, Europe - my goodness, what

places you have been to, no! And staying in posh places, I'm sure
- travelling with Gerhardt you must be staying in the best places
. . . how can we poor villagers even imagine the wonders you have
seen? People will be too nervous with a famous foreigner there—"

"Fine, I'll come on my own."

"Yes, yes, that might be better. Good idea. How about Sunday,
seven o'clock?"

"I need to talk to Gerhardt, I'm not promising anything—"

"But we'll be waiting. Ah, Leela will be so happy! I must go
now to catch my bus. See you next Sunday!"

She rode on to the market. After buying fish there was only
enough money left for potatoes. She would tell Soma she had
forgotten about the ash plantains. It didn't matter if he didn't
believe her. The morning had turned unreal. The empty purse and
the numbness in her were the only proof that she had met Sunny
again. After all after the years of silence, of watching out for him
and waiting, he had come back for her.

# 6

ROHAN WALKED THROUGH the garden defeated, think-ing of Padma – Padma revealed – so small and vulnerable as she rode into the lane on her scooter, then almost crashing into the man. What a strange thing to do, to run out in front of her. She could have been hurt. Rohan had almost broken cover and run to help, but she had sat calmly talking with the man and then Rohan had seen her hand over a great pile of cash. The man didn't threaten or try to grab it from her bag; she had offered it, resigned and business-like, and he had taken the money with an accustomed air, a sense of entitlement. So this was how it was done, the niece was loaned by the uncle to the depraved foreigner who paid in cash. Gerhardt didn't even pay the money himself, instead he forced Padma to sully herself. Gerhardt was a vile hyp-ocrite, hiding behind his cultured sophistication and amiable airs, his silent secret depravities hidden. Deep inside its pure elegant simplicity, the villa was rotten to the core.

Rohan went inside his bungalow and locked the door. Someone had been in to clean: a broom had been left leaning on the wall. His books had been shifted, sorted, the order changed around. Despite what he knew about the place, calm surrounded him. But that was their goal – to seduce you with their seeming playfulness and trusting childlike acceptance and warmth. He had seen through it all. He had seen through Padma, right from the start. All the smiles and artless chatter – there was no truth in such a person. No malice either. She was a victim. She was trapped by the men who controlled her. He pitied her. Beauty was a curse; hers no doubt had led to her corruption. There was a knock at the door. He didn't respond. Another knock. He waited. They would have to leave eventually. He could have been sleeping, he could have been in the bathroom. A key entered the lock. Rohan stormed over and flung open the door. A woman stood outside with a bucket and broom.

"Cleaning," she declared.

"It's fine what you did earlier," he said, although in fact she had hardly done anything other than rearrange his books.

"Room must be cleaned every day, that's what Padma Missie said." The woman slid in past him and started to sweep the floor.

"You left your other broom here," he told her.

She looked at him oddly and carried on sweeping. He took a book, his bag of snacks and water and went onto the veranda, reading to forget.

## ACQUIRING SRI LANKA

## AFTER THE BRITISH

Independence from Britain came in February 1948. The British left the island, and in their wake, a shifting social order: the once prominent Burghers, those people of mixed Dutch, Portuguese, Sinhala and Tamil heritage, who had been most closely aligned with the British, sank down into genteel poverty as the fierce Sinhalese surged upwards onto the stage that the British had once claimed.

The Muslims eased away into their world of blue and pink and green painted blank-faced houses, curtains drawn across windows all day, the women of the house out of sight. Inside the walls were gardens and courtyards and private enclosed spaces. Only the call of the muezzin rode free in the blue open sky over the city, calling the men to pray, drawing them into the sanctuary of the mosque's cool tiled rooms, a world within.

The Tamils, who under the British had begun to identify as a whole and to see themselves as a minority, began to push for representation. The Tamils in Sri Lanka date back centuries, and although the dates are disputed to this day, it is a fact that there have been Tamils in Sri Lanka since 2 BCE. The confusion, sometimes wilful on the part of right-wing Sri Lankans, arises from the existence of the Tamils known as Plantation or Indian Tamils, who were brought to Sri Lanka from South India by the British in the 19th and 20th Centuries to work on the tea plantations built by the British to profit Empire. These Plantation Tamils, at Independence, were offered the choice of expatriation to India or Sri Lankan citizenship and those who stayed were drawn into one grouping with the Sri Lankan Tamils. For in the upheaval of change with the British departure, following years of suppression and conflict, the island's people grouped and cohered according to religion, and the Tamils, even those whose origins were rooted in centuries-old kingdoms, became the resented guests.

A restless discontent stirred beneath the surface of the newly liberated Sri Lanka. The Sinhalese and the Tamils jostled for the empty apex, the mean, small space at the top of the pyramid that the British had built and had abruptly vacated. The Sinhalese, by far the largest group, crowded in and pushed down hardest, trampling on everyone else in the struggle to occupy that pinnacle of power – and ruling as they themselves had been ruled, with arrogance and disregard and without kindness. Sinhala was declared the national language, thus excluding and disadvantaging all those who spoke Tamil or English better. And laws were made to advantage the Sinhalese, and so were built the brittle walls dividing a nation once oppressed together.

⁂

Padma ate at the kitchen table, Soma insisting that she eat lunch where the guests couldn't see her and get ideas. She had eaten at that same small table when she was younger, before going to school, Soma making her roti and scrambled eggs and hot chocolate, and watching her swallow a vitamin pill. In those days she always had homework to complete, abandoned the previous evening as the sun began to set, and she walked on the beach with Gerhardt and Soma. In those days there were always visitors in the evenings, with Jarryd living close by and bringing musician friends and dancers for dinner, staying singing on the veranda late into the night. Later, in bed, she would lie listening to their voices, their long stories and soft gentle laughter, as she fell asleep.

"Do you know how to pick a lock?" she asked Soma.

"Yes, thank you."

"Could you show me?"

"Why?"

"There's a padlock I need to open. I've lost the key."

"Oh yes? Bring it to me, I'll do it."

He was on to her. He was delighted, looking smugly at her. She scowled at him.

"No amount of snooping will tell you what he's really like," he said, serving her more potato curry.

66

"But just imagine if he's hiding something bad!"

"Like what?"

"Drugs. Or guns. Or something he's stolen? He didn't like me even touching that suitcase – not one bit . . ."

"Okay, maybe later I'll show you. Now eat, please."

She grinned. Soma was already searching in the tool cupboard and brought out a spool of wire and an old padlock.

"You can only really know what another person is like when you're in trouble," he said.

He meant Boss and his family during the riots in Colombo when crazed Sinhalese ran amok, setting fire to Tamils in the streets and cars with people inside. Soma had seen children clawing at windows, screaming to be let out of burning cars as he ran home from the restaurant where he worked. As the mob stormed Soma's road, torching houses, razing them to the ground, Boss, his father and brother – members of a volatile Sinhala Marxist group, the most unlikely saviours – had come running to take Soma, his parents and two younger sisters into their own home, hiding them in cupboards when the thugs came looking for Tamils to slaughter.

"Boss and his family could have been killed for hiding us," Soma said. "Our families hardly knew each other – Boss and I weren't even in the same class at school – he was in the Sinhala stream, I was in the Tamil stream – we were just friends from playing in the road."

Soma was still in awe of what Boss had done. Soma's love for the man knew no bounds. Even when Soma's parents and sisters fled to South India, Soma moved with Boss and his brother to Nilwatte Beach where Boss and his brother owned land and planned to build a café.

Soma eased a strand of wire into the padlock. Padma leaned close to watch.

Rohan was subdued at dinner that night, barely speaking and

quick to look away when Padma went to take his order. She was busy in any case, watching for Sunny and thinking of ways to tell Gerhardt of the day's events. How she had come to have an arrangement with Sunny without Gerhardt's knowledge or consent. It was a secret she didn't want; a failure, a betrayal – she wanted to reveal it. Luckily Rohan soon left and she went to the porch and sat with Gerhardt, watching Rohan walk over to his bungalow.

"Our poor guest still seems a little agitated," Gerhardt observed.

"He's very strange," Padma agreed.

She offered Gerhardt a praline from the box Jarryd had given her to celebrate the opening of the guest house. Jarryd had asked one of his visiting students to bring them by hand, all the way from Brussels, especially for Padma. She chose a raspberry flavoured dark chocolate, a dainty pink and red spiral swirled on top.

"I saw Sunny today," she said.

"Sunny? Are you sure? Where?" Gerhardt was trying to sound calm, but he looked terrified.

"In the lane."

"What did he want?"

"Don't panic Gerhardt, nothing happened. He didn't want anything."

"He didn't ask for money?"

"No."

It was for Leela that she had given the money. There was no need to worry Gerhardt with that small sum; even if Leela weren't really sick, it wasn't much – nothing that couldn't be absorbed into the weekly accounts, a minor loss, no different to throwing out stale bread or prawns that had gone off.

"What did he have to say for himself?" Gerhardt asked.

"He's invited me to dinner with the relatives."

"Dinner with the relatives? How extraordinary! All of a sudden now he's a family man?"

"It's because of Leela. Apparently she's not well – she's been asking to see me. She wants to get the whole family together so I can see them all."

Hopefully it would be mostly Leela's family, rather than Sunny's who came – his were prone to arguments and fighting. She remembered drunken uncles stumbling around punching each other and throwing furniture and having to be separated. Even the women on that side of the family were forever grumbling and telling stories of violent triumphs over enemies and neighbours and sometimes their own children. Padma remembered Sunny's older sister telling of the time she had caught her oldest son secretly pouring his milk away into the flowerbeds. "I really gave it to him that day!" the aunt recounted with relish. "Chitty-chitty-chitty, I slapped him, and his face swelled up like a balloon!"

"Do you really want to go back?" Gerhardt asked.

"No, but if Leela is sick—"

"Then you must," he said quickly.

He had always wanted to be fair, to let her own her past before him, to never feel guilty or ashamed of those first nine years. That time was never lost, although it was a life she could never see clearly, a time of shadows and unreality, of shifting moods and faces, but her roots began there, thin and sickly and flailing. Her memories of Leela were dim and uneasy. But now she was calling to Padma.

"It's been so long since I saw her," Padma said to Gerhardt.

"Then maybe this is something you must do."

"Just to see how she is – if there is some small thing I can do to help—"

"Yes. Of course."

"And I'm going to see some of my cousins – I wouldn't mind catching up with them. We used to see quite a lot of each other in the old days."

"Yes, you left a whole world behind. You must go back and see it again, I understand. Maybe Sunny isn't up to anything this time."

"Yes!" What a relief to have Gerhardt agree with her.

"When do you think you will go?"

"Sunny suggested Sunday."

"So soon?"

"I might as well get it over with."

"Of course."

So now she could go. How easily she was pulled back to them. Their hold on her was stronger than she had realised. It was because of Leela. Sunny and Mukul and all the relatives, she could have relinquished but Leela was the void that Padma longed to fill, Leela she carried inside, the missing part, the endless empty unknowing; a cold black longing. Did a new sadness await her when they met? Yet what sadness lay in staying away. This time she would see and she could free herself.

The expensive praline was melting all over her fingers. She ate it whole, her mouth filling with melting chocolate cream and raspberry sharpness, a rich sweetness feeling of comfort and being indulged.

"Maybe it's better if Karu drives you. He'd be less conspicuous than me," Gerhardt said. "He can wait nearby until you finish."

"Good idea."

Karu, Gerhardt's driver would be easier company than Gerhardt on the way home. Karu wouldn't worry as much or ask too many questions; he would simply collect her and return her to Gerhardt who would be waiting up, no doubt, like in the days when she went to parties in Tangalle Town with her school friends. In those days he had chosen which homes she could enter without him; which parents to trust. Now she made those decisions alone. She closed up the chocolate box, retying the golden ribbon like new.

# 7

K ARU DROVE PADMA to Sunny's house. On a night long
ago Sunny had driven her to the villa on that very same road,
in a tuk-tuk he had borrowed for the occasion. She remembered
the lonely long curves of road, a blackness fallen over the paddy
fields, cold winds coming in through the sides of the tuk-tuk. She
had imagined jumping out and running away towards the lights
of houses, but they were too far away. No one would have seen
her, no one would have heard her scream as Sunny came whirling
through the darkness after her, gleefully catching her up with
demonic speed, trapping her with his steel strength. She had not
given him the satisfaction, the thrill of triumphing over her. She
had sat unmoving and alert behind him, knowing he was taking
her to people who were waiting for her. Men. She had known
even then that it would be men. Shame was the need for flight
extinguished at the brain; shame was inaction. Sunny had told her
to wear her best dress. He had watched her comb her hair, with
business-like interest, telling her she would wear it loose later,
but to tie it back for the ride so that the wind wouldn't blow it
about. Shame was built of obedience, of the protest in you that
you silenced. Shame was the emptiness inside you.

In Gerhardt's cream-coloured Mercedes Benz, she sat against

pale cold leather and watched the dusk descend. The air-conditioning chilled the car to an icy stillness. Outside in the paddy fields, distant silhouettes of workers passed along the dark earthen grid of passageways over the fields. In the villages, the verandas of houses had been abandoned for the night. A woman pulled a curtain closed. Life turned inward. Karu consulted a page of directions that Gerhardt had written for him. Sunny's new house was in a development at the edge of a village Padma had not been to before, land hacked out from jungle and not to be found using Google.

Karu turned into a lane and they wound past modest concrete houses with television aerials and corrugated tin roofs, gardens bursting over walls - nature in all its unruly untidiness, asserting itself. In the city people fought it, only the wealthy truly succeeding, with gardeners employed to reign in the abundance, trimming and pruning all day. There was a certain peace in that order, yet she had felt constrained by that primness. One was not held by such a garden. Gardens in the city kept their distance, asking only to be admired and passed through without incident.

Karu stopped the car in front of a small wooden gate. Plantain trees clustered close behind a wall topped with a smear of cement studded with broken glass. Through the trees she could see a small white house, a porch light shining out.

"This is the place, Baba. I'll stay here. Just call me if you need me."

"You can't wait here!"

"Sir told me to stay close by."

"But not just outside the gate!"

"Baba, Sir said—"

"There'll be other people coming soon - they'll also need to park."

They would think she didn't trust them, having a guard at the gate. And in a great big shiny Merc. Cars were luxury items once.

Most of her relatives had ridden around on bicycles and scooters, and the few who'd owned tuk-tuks had needed them for work.

"I'll wait in the village then," Karu said.

"Okay—"

"But call me if . . ." Karu stopped. "He's here," Karu muttered.

Sunny stood at the gate.

"Come!" He gestured to Padma. She got out of the car, not knowing what his expression meant, what he was thinking seeing her. She didn't know what she herself felt, what she was entering.

"I'll come back in two hours," Karu said. "But any problem, Baba, call me - okay?" He leaned out of the window. "Baba - you have my number?"

"Yes, yes. Now go!" She stepped away from the car, away from her world.

"You're sure I shouldn't stay, Baba?"

"No, it's fine. Go."

"Don't worry, we'll look after her!" Sunny laughed at Karu.

Karu withdrew and drove away.

Padma went to Sunny. She had not brought any gifts, not even offerings of chocolates or wine. Gifts and chocolates and wine were from her life with Gerhardt. The relatives used to just turn up with maybe some plantains or a pot of curry or nothing at all, in the old days - but now maybe more was expected. She didn't want to seem stingy or ungrateful. Being empty-handed was disempowering. Sunny played the beneficent host, smiling as he opened the gate to her. He looked strange, smiling.

She followed him through his garden. In the house a curtain moved at a downstairs window, a shadowy figure passed behind it.

"Have any of the relatives arrived?" Padma asked.

"Soon people will be here," Sunny said.

There was a porch reached by three steps. Two chairs were placed on either side of the door.

"You like this?" Sunny asked. "Just like at the villa, no?"

Gerhardt had bought antique chairs from a dealer of fine furniture, having the old seats expertly rewoven. Sunny's chairs were cheap replicas of those same chairs; his looked crude and uncomfortable, the likeness laughable, almost mocking. Sunny opened the door and led the way into a room with red cement floors, low ceilings, white walls, blue curtains. The furniture was traditional: sedan chairs, a heavy round dining table, a brass vase that was remarkably similar to a vase that she owned. A man came down the stairs. He was young and wiry with a wild black tangle of hair. It took a moment for Padma to recognise Mukul. He nodded at her, studying her with the same watchful gaze of the villagers in Nilwatte Beach, thinking things about her that they would never say in her presence.

"Padma's here!" Sunny shouted and a long brown curtain with a print of blue parrots moved across a doorway at the back of the room and Leela appeared. An older, wizened Leela, almost someone else. She threw a furtive glance at Padma then lowered her gaze.

"Nice to see you," Padma said. She could find no more words, no gestures that seemed right; kneeling to worship felt too formal, nor could she hug and kiss like a Colombo urbanite. Amma, she had called Leela once – now even that utterance, failed her. There was only a pained wordlessness in her.

Someone else came down the stairs. A thin dark-skinned young woman with a slightly lop-sided face came to stand beside Mukul.

"This is Kumudini," Sunny said. "She is helping with the cooking."

"Come, Auntie, we should finish the poloss before they come." Kumudini drew Leela away behind the parrot curtain. Padma started to follow them but Mukul moved to block her way. She stepped aside to avoid touching him, which seemed to amuse him.

"Better get the table ready, they'll be here soon," Mukul told Sunny.

"Who's coming?" Padma asked.

"You like the table?" Sunny said.

The table was polished dark wood with a thick pedestal at its centre. Gerhardt had bought a similar table for the villa.

"Like the one on your veranda, no?" Sunny said.

The tables on the veranda were not visible from the lane. Mukul no doubt could sense her discomfort. He looked away with a smirk.

"We saw it on your website, of course," Sunny said. "I'm looking for a bed like the ones in your guest rooms – were they expensive? Must have been, no?"

She didn't reply.

"How much does a bed like that cost?" Mukul asked.

"I don't know."

"Gerhardt's spending a lot on your business," Sunny observed. "Nice. I'm very happy for you."

Sunny and Mukul spread out a white tablecloth over the table, anxiously tugging it into place, smoothing out the folds with their big clumsy hands that had squeezed and strangled necks; punched faces, stabbed knives into chests. Sunny placed straw coasters strategically over curry stains on the cloth. Padma didn't offer to help; she stood apart, not entering their world. Kumudini brought out poppadoms fried in strips, curled bobbled ribbons heaped in a plastic basket. Leela brought out a large covered Pyrex dish.

"Cashew curry's hot, put two mats together," she told Sunny.

"Can I help?" Padma asked Leela.

"No, no, it's alright." Leela put down the dish then scurried back to the kitchen.

"Who's coming from the family?" Padma asked Sunny.

"It's just friends tonight. They should be here soon." He went over to the window and looked out, easing back the curtain.

"You told me the relatives would be coming," Padma said to Sunny.

Mukul and Kumudini exchanged glances and followed Leela into the kitchen.

"Hmm?" Sunny turned from the window, trying to look vague.

"Did you even ask the relatives?" she demanded.

"Of course I asked! Why wouldn't I ask them if I said I would? They can't come today, that's all. Everyone is busy. Pity. You wanted to see them, no? Next time we'll get them here."

She should have known. He was never going to give her what she wanted. But she had come to see Leela, most of all, and Leela he couldn't stop from being there. Padma would find a way to talk to Leela and find out what she had wanted to tell her.

"So who is coming then?" Padma asked.

Mukul came in with a clay pot of steaming pollos curry. "The Rajapalas," he said.

The room filled with the rich savoury smell of the pollos. More curries were brought out, Leela and Kumudini coming and going from the kitchen in silent procession: pol sambol, potatoes in oil, plain dhal, mung dhal, green beans fried with coconut, deep fried sprats.

"They're business people," Mukul said. "Mr Rajapala owns two bars in Galle and a hotel in Tangalle town: The Sea Garden—"

"You know it?" Sunny asked.

"No."

"You should! You're also in the same business now."

That was intended to annoy her, for their establishment was most likely to be one of the sleazy holes near the harbour - a drinking den downstairs and rooms above to rent by the hour. So Sunny was socialising with the owners of such places now; he had advanced from hovering around their staff and clientele. Sunny was on the up, Padma had heard. There were even rumours about him working for the local minister's brother, a greedy simpleton who owned three drinking dens in town and the brothel down the lane from the villa, and was buying up houses. He kept asking Gerhardt if he would sell him the villa – as if Gerhardt would.

Sunny arranged bottles of lemonade, arrack, iced water, and a bowl of sliced limes on a coffee table. Mukul placed saucers of fried peanuts mixed with dried anchovies around the room. A car drove down the lane, its headlights shining.

"They're here!" Mukul cried.

Sunny ran to the window. Leela and Kumudini ran in from the kitchen, Leela clutching Kumudini's hand.

"They're early! Come and help me put on the sari!" she cried, dragging Kumudini to the stairs and running up in a panic, while Kumudini slowly climbed up behind, her face through the bannisters expressionless.

But it was someone else's car. Sunny hovered by the window, checking his watch, drinking tumbler after tumbler of arrack, smacking his lips and crunching on peanuts, his eyes shiny and bloodshot. He left the window and paced around the room. Padma felt him encircle her. At last several cars pulled up in a cluster outside the gate and the guests all arrived together. Wild-eyed, rough-looking men crowded into the house, and behind them, two middle-aged women, stately and plump and well-tended, with good skin and fine features. They wore immaculate white Kandyan saris, frilly and traditional, and heavy gold jewellery full of bright gemstones. Their hair was dyed blue-black, puffed into huge buns padded out with fake hair. While the men crowded around the drinks, the women sat on the sofa, looking haughtily about them, talking only to each other, sipping Coca Cola through straws they had brought with them in shiny leather handbags. They stared at

Padma, muttering together. They seemed to be talking about her; they kept staring at her. She couldn't think why they were there.

Sunny came through the crowd, sweaty and drunk, holding his drink up high. With him were a middle-aged fat man with a bristling moustache and a younger man, well-groomed and slick, with a slim brash body in a purple silk shirt. The shirt was unbuttoned too far to show a gold chain with a diamond-studded dagger pendant against a pale smooth-plucked chest.

"Sir, this is Padma," Sunny said, and the older man looked her over with keen eyes.

"This is Mr Rajapala," Sunny told Padma, and he sounded awed. He seemed to want her to do more than just nod. She did nothing, enjoying his frustration.

The younger man was introduced as Nishan, Mr Rajapala's son. He gave her a strange suggestive smile.

"And the foreigner? He isn't here?" the older man asked Padma.

"Which foreigner?" Padma replied, although knowing full well.

Sunny spluttered, glaring at her.

"She means sir, Mr Rajapala, he couldn't come today. Next time, sir, I will make sure he is here next time. I didn't know that sir would like to meet him."

"But of course I want to meet him! Why wouldn't I?"

The room grew loud, the voices of the men rising as they argued about business and politics. More than once, she heard the minister and his brother mentioned. Leela and Kumudini came through the crowd, bringing fish cutlets that were grabbed by the handful by the men as they passed. Padma looked to the clock. One and a half hours more and Karu would be at the gate, and she could go. That wasn't such a long time really.

"Good cutlets," Mr Rajapala said, licking away fried breadcrumbs from thick pink lips, wet like molluscs.

"My wife made all the food," Sunny said.

"You see my wife and her sister over there – they are very great cooks," Mr Rajapala said.

"I am sure they are excellent," Sunny gushed.

"Why else would I marry her?" Mr Rajapala chuckled. "Although now of course we have a chef."

"Of course, sir, these days you must be having several chefs!"

"That we do!" Mr Rajapala turned to Padma. "Now miss, explain to me, what exactly the foreigner is to you? Officially, at least?"

"Officially and otherwise, father." It was only strange that it didn't feel strange to say it in front of Sunny. "Why?" she asked.

"Sir, she is fully adopted," Sunny said quickly. "She is living in his house just like a daughter. He is devoted to her."

Mr Rajapala was one of the new type of businessman risen up behind a government of rough-cut traditionalists. Men from the villages, Ruth called them. Unpolished, uncultured, with no command of the English language – for Ruth that mattered. One could never converse with such people as equals, Ruth said. Jarryd had disagreed. It was only natural and right that these men should be enabled to succeed in their own country, he argued. Wasn't it time to stop looking back to our colonial oppressors to define ourselves?

"*Themselves*," Ruth had corrected him. "You aren't one of them, remember?"

But Jarryd had disagreed with her about that too; he was Sri Lankan, he insisted; he had lived and farmed and prayed among the people for over twenty years, he loved them and they accepted him – surely that gave him the right to feel Sri Lankan? Gerhardt stayed out of these conversations. People, for him, were solitary individuals, each a separate encounter, each of interest in their own way.

"Gerhardt only cares about the world in his head," Ruth would grumble. She didn't like it when he didn't take her side against Jarryd.

"You must go and talk to my wife," Mr Rajapala told Padma.

"What about?" Padma said and Sunny glared at her.

"Anything you like," Mr Rajapala retorted. "Go on! I want to eat some rice now."

"Go and talk to Mrs Rajapala," Sunny hissed, pushing Padma towards the women who had served themselves and were sitting eating with fingers, heaped plates balanced on their laps. Leela stood fanning the dining table with a newspaper to keep away flies. There were a great many flies, darting in to settle on the dishes or waiting poised on the backs of chairs to dive into curries. Padma went to Leela.

"Can we talk here?" she asked in a low voice.

Leela flapped the newspaper harder, refusing to look at Padma, her eyes wide with fear. Was she really so afraid of being heard by Sunny? After all, hadn't he brought Padma to her, just as Leela had asked? Sunny went past carrying a new crate of beer. Leela saw him and dropping the newspaper, she hurried to the kitchen. The flies danced over the dishes and swooped down.

Padma pushed through the crowd towards the front door. She could wait outside by the gate for Karu. The voices of the men grew louder, growing more agitated, their arguments turning fierce. Dark sweating faces leered down at her as she eased her way through. Her buttocks were squeezed and caressed; an arm snaked around her to touch her breasts, she slapped it away.

"You want to go outside?" a voice said beside her.

It was Nishan, the younger Rajapala.

He pushed back the men to make room for her and they reached the front door together and stepped onto the porch.

"It's quieter outside," Nishan said.

He was a different breed to the others. He didn't belong there either. Ruth didn't have a description as yet for his type – the son of thugs sent to the finest schools, preening and cushioned in lives gilded by the profits of crime. She stepped into the garden with him, into the easy warmth of night, no breeze, no sound of waves like at the villa. Inland was still and close, the crickets sounded too loud.

"Do you like parties?" Nishan asked.

"Sometimes."

"You don't drink?" He finished his drink and balanced the glass on the porch railing.

"Sometimes I do."

"You say 'sometimes' a lot, don't you? Or do you only say it sometimes?" Nishan giggled.

He was an idiot, one of those schoolboy-men who never grew up, but became greyer and fatter and more awkward.

"You want to see my car?" he asked.

She turned back to the house. Kumudini, Mukul's girlfriend, was watching them from the window, a moth caught in a fold of net curtain.

"Yeah, why not?" Padma said.

The moth watched them leave; the shriek of drunken voices faded over the garden as they left the house behind.

Nishan's car was parked behind all the other cars in the lane, his was black and sporty, with dark streaked windows and a dent in the side and painted-over rust patches.

"You want to go for a drive?" he asked.

She got in. Gerhardt would never have let her go, and Ruth would have physically dragged her away from both Nishan and his ungainly vehicle. Nishan was quite unlike the sons of judges and surgeons and university professors whom Ruth kept introducing to Padma at parties at Ruth's house. Parties that were thrown, Padma suspected, with the single aim of finding Padma an appropriate husband. Ruth failed to see the fatal flaw in her scheme, that the first man to get serious would run a mile when his family asked about Padma's origins. Ruth went on hoping that love would override all, even the past that Padma was burdened with. But at Sunny's now, for the first time, Padma's past was known to all and she was free of it. Nishan started the car. She sat sealed inside that alien vehicle. She was heading to nowhere, for the first time unburdened of her secret.

"You like it?" Nishan asked.

"What?"

"My car."

In the low seat, his lithe body was an easy muscled arc. The diamond dagger on its gold chain glittered against him in the dark.

"You like the tinted windows? I did them myself."

"Ah, I see!"

"What?"

She laughed.

He glanced across at her.

"You're strange," he said. "I heard you were strange."

He turned the car down a narrow road, driving past a Buddhist temple. The white mound of the dagoba gleamed in the moonlight, a pure pale milkiness piercing the inky windows.

"So what do you think of all this?" Nishan asked.

"All what?"

"The marriage proposal?"

"Whose marriage?"

"Ours, of course!"

"What?"

"Who else's?" He sounded affronted.

They drove under majestic old village trees, tall and thick and venerable.

"Have you've been to the lake before?" he asked.

"No. What marriage proposal?"

He stopped in a clearing. Black water gleamed in the moon-light. He let down the windows and they sat with the sound of crickets, the whine of mosquitoes; the far away splashes of frogs and fish.

"Didn't you know?" he asked.

"Obviously not."

"That's why we came to your house." He started to laugh. "My father and Sunny have been talking about it for ages!"

"Have they now?"

There was no need to feel foolish or to be angry - she hadn't been tricked, not really. Even Gerhardt had failed to see Sunny's plan this time. There was always a plan with Sunny - that was the thing to have known. After all this time she should have known. Why did she never learn?

"Anyway, I have a girlfriend," Nishan said.

"Can't you marry her?"

"She's Muslim. They want a Sinhalese for me."

"But you want to marry her?"

"Yeah, she's hot."

"Can't you talk to your father?"

"It's not a problem, don't worry. I don't care who I marry - I'll marry whoever they want, I'm still going to keep seeing my girlfriend, she doesn't mind."

"Well, that's brilliant. She sounds very sensible."

He laughed. He was enjoying talking with her - men always seemed to. They could tell she wasn't like the other women of the social class she now came from. She wasn't bound by the same conventions as them, taught to be clever and quiet and nicely closed up at all times, only saying what was expected, never what they were really thinking and feeling - these were the women that the men would marry in the end. But in the meantime they liked the freedom of being with her. Nishan was gazing at her now with the look she knew. He leaned across and pressed his lips on hers. She let him. It had been too long since lips had touched hers; too long since a man had been so close. The skin of his cheek was warm and smooth and scented. A tongue probed. She let herself be opened, explored. He pulled back after a while and she wiped her mouth discretely.

"So what's the deal with you?" he asked. "You like old guys? You like foreigners?"

"Yeah." She played along.

"And ladies?"

She smiled and looked mysterious. He was impressed.

"I heard you got up to quite a lot at the architect's house," he said.

"Yeah, I guess I do."

"Cool. He's friends with the minister, no? My father wants to open another hotel closer to yours – that's where all the tourists will be coming soon, but the minister's brother won't let him. He thinks he owns the place. You're only allowed because of your architect. Do you think he could talk to the minister for us? My father will pay him really well, if he helps us and give him more work."

"The architect isn't friends with the minister," Padma said.

"No? That's not what Sunny said."

"What does Sunny know! Gerhardt's just done a few projects for the minister, that's all. Official projects. He used Gerhardt because Gerhardt is a brilliant architect, no other reason."

"So they're not good friends? My father was wondering if Sunny was lying!"

"Oh Sunny lies all the time. I wouldn't believe a word he tells you."

"You're not a very loyal daughter!"

"Sunny's not my father."

Sunny was a liar. He was shameless. She should never have listened to him. Was Leela even sick? Had she ever wanted to speak with Padma - she certainly wasn't showing any sign of it.

"If we married, you can keep seeing anyone you want - even the architect, I'm not the jealous like that."

"No thanks, I don't want to get married."

"Ever?"

"Never. Thanks anyway."

They sat looking at the lake in silence. He checked his phone, reading messages then typed a reply.

"Let's go, I have to meet someone," he said.

The windows rose up, and the streaky blackness surrounded them again. The air conditioning rattled on. He turned the car around. It was late. Karu would be waiting at Sunny's place, worrying, wondering where Padma was. A walk, she would say. Just to get some air. That was what she would tell him, and Gerhardt later, when he asked her about her night.

8

THERE WERE NO cars outside Sunny's house, and no Karu waiting.

"They must have all gone," Nishan said. "You want a lift to town?"

"No, thanks. I'm being met here."

Padma got out and Nishan raced off down the lane. She stood looking up to the road. Soon the blinding white headlights of Gerhardt's car would swing down towards her. A tuk-tuk passed up on the road, then a car turned into the lane and came driving past her, but it wasn't for her. The driver leaned out leering drunkenly. She went into the garden. The white fluorescent light of Sunny's porch shone emptily. It wasn't like Karu to be late. Of course she should never have gone with Nishan, but Karu should have waited. She checked her phone; he hadn't rung, but then she may not have had reception by the lake. She started to ring his number, but the front door opened.

"So? How was it?" Sunny asked. "There's no signal from there. Come in, inside is better. Has Nishan gone? He could have come back for a drink, no? You didn't invite him?"

"Did the driver come?" she asked.

"He'll be here soon. Just wait inside."

In the living room Leela, Kumudini and Mukul were clearing the table, seemingly so absorbed they didn't look up as she entered. They carried stacks of dishes to the kitchen.

"Did you eat anything?" Sunny asked.

"Oh yes," she lied.

"You can still eat some cutlets, no?"

Her stomach churned emptily, but she didn't want to eat, not there. She wanted only food that Soma had made. She longed for the pure simple order of the villa. Sunny wouldn't know what to make of that calm, his mind would leap wildly filling it with plans and tricks; strange surprises one had to be on the lookout for. Always there were tricks to look out for with Sunny.

"Are you sure my driver wasn't here earlier?" she asked.

"Let's ask the others, shall we? Leela? Mukul!" Sunny shouted. "Did Gerhardt's driver come earlier?"

There was silence behind the blue-parrot curtain. Was it whispering Padma could hear? There was the rumble of argument, first Mukul's voice then a woman's voice protesting in a loud whisper. Kumudini stumbled into the room as if pushed.

"Earlier the driver came," she reported.

"So where's he now?" Padma demanded.

"He said he didn't want to wait."

"He wouldn't just go away! What did you tell him?"

"Didn't he say he will come back in the morning?" Sunny added.

Kumudini nodded and darted back behind the curtain.

"But I have to get back tonight!" Padma exclaimed.

"Such a lazy fellow." Sunny tutted. "You should give him a good scolding when you see him."

She brought up Karu's number on her phone, but Leela came out from behind the curtain bringing Padma a plate of cutlets and a mug of tea.

"Why not stay the night?" Leela murmured, coming up close. "Why not tell him to come in the morning for you?" She lowered her voice. "Please stay, finally I have a chance to talk with you?"

"What are you mumbling, stupid woman?" Sunny scolded Leela. "Stop bothering her! No wonder she doesn't want to stay."

"Please?" Leela begged Padma.

In her pleading eyes was a promise to be together, for secrets to be revealed when the others were sleeping perhaps, and the arrack had finally stilled Sunny.

"I'll have a cup of tea first and then go." Padma wavered. She put her phone away and took the tea from Leela.

"Here – cutlets." Leela pushed the plate into Padma's hands.

"Maybe later." Padma put the plate on the table.

"Here, sit, sit!" Sunny came rushing up with a wicker chair.

Padma sat on its edge and took a sip of tea. It was too strong, made the way the villagers liked to drink it. And it was far too sweet. Padma hadn't drunk sugar in her tea for years, but then none of them there would have known that.

"It's okay? You like it?" Sunny asked.

"Mmm."

"Kumudini makes nice tea. Eat some cutlets."

Her phone rang. It was Gerhardt.

"What's going on? Where are you? Are you okay?" he demanded

"I'm fine. Where the hell is Karu?"

"He came, but you weren't there!"

"Well why didn't he wait? I was only gone for a few minutes – twenty minutes, at the most—"

"Gone where?"

"Nowhere, just outside. Why didn't he call?"

"He tried but he didn't have a connection."

"He should have waited."

"They told him someone else was giving you a lift."

"What? Who told him that?"

Gerhardt spoke with Karu; she heard Karu's urgent voice and Gerhardt, concerned-sounding. They were probably on the porch at the villa. Rohan would have gone to his room. The villa seemed distant and unreachable, she felt stranded, too far from them.

"Who told the driver I was getting a lift with someone?" Padma asked Sunny.

"Not me! I never even saw the man! Someone must have thought you were going home with Nishan."

"And why would I do that?"

"Karu says it was Mukul," Gerhardt said.

"It was Mukul," Padma accused Sunny.

"Me? What about me?" Mukul charged out from behind the curtain.

"Never mind now, don't argue with them. Just wait there till we come," Gerhardt said.

"I didn't do anything! I didn't see anyone!" Mukul stormed towards her, but Sunny barked a warning and put his hand out to stop Mukul before he reached her.

Sunny dragged Mukul outside.

"Padma, it doesn't matter now! Don't aggravate them. Karu and I are coming!" Gerhardt insisted.

Kumudini unlocked a cupboard and took out a handbag, opened it and checked inside, then left.

"Padma – don't move from there until we get to you – okay?" Gerhardt said

But Leela was at Padma's side; a thin cold hand gripped Padma's arm.

"I never get to see you," Leela whispered, her eyes filled with tears. "Please stay, just tonight. Maybe it's our last chance."

"Padma? Did you hear me?" Gerhardt called.

"I want to tell you something," Leela whispered, glancing fearfully at the front door.

"Padma? Padma?" Gerhardt cried.

"I'm here," Padma told him.

"I have so much I want to tell you," Leela whispered. "Will I ever see you again?"

Silent desperate tears flowed down her withered face. Somehow Leela had grown elderly, that face that had once been so much like Padma's own was now shrunken with dark blueish circles under the eyes. The body once strong was stooped and weak, the stiff cheap sari falling off her shoulder. The ill-cut blouse gaped open, breasts puckered and sagging inside. Padma glanced at the clock. It was already past one, less than five hours before dawn.

"It's nearly morning now, Gerhardt. Could you send Karu in a few hours?" she said.

"What are you talking about? We're coming now."

"I don't mind staying till the morning."

"What's going on?" he demanded. "Get Sunny on the line! This isn't what we agreed - what's that bastard up to?"

"It's nothing to do with him, Gerhardt, nothing's going on—"

"Put him on the line—"

"Really, Gerhardt - he's not even here—"

"Go and get him for me."

"Gerhardt wants to talk to Sunny," Padma told Leela who went to call him, wiping her eyes with the fall of her sari.

Padma held the phone away from her. Gerhardt was angry - with Sunny, but also with her, although he would never admit that. She didn't know what to say to him. He didn't understand. Sunny came in, he was red-eyed and staggering a little, but he was still excitable and sprightly. He grabbed her phone.

"Hello there Gerhardt, sir! Of course we will look after her!

She is safe in my house - why wouldn't she be? No need to worry, sir. Yes, here she is—"

"Is he making you stay?" Gerhardt asked Padma.

"No, really."

"Okay, fine. You're sure? You really want to stay?"

"Just until the morning, that's all. It's just . . . I don't get to see Leela that much—"

Leela looked alarmed and hurried to the kitchen. Was it Sunny being there that had made her nervous? Hopefully soon Sunny would go to sleep. Sunny was drunk, it wouldn't take long. He stood holding a chair, eager and watching her. Gerhardt was giving instructions: she wasn't to leave the house until he arrived in the morning; and she wasn't to drink any alcohol or sign any papers. She agreed. There was nothing more to say; they ended the call.

"Come, let's go to sleep, you must be tired," Sunny said. "We have a spare bedroom. You never had a spare bedroom at the villa, did you?"

"No."

"You forgot your tea," Leela said and brought Padma the mug.

"Take the cutlets, you might be hungry later." Sunny handed her the plate of cutlets. Padma carried them and followed Sunny upstairs to a small dingy landing with many doors.

"This is the bathroom." Sunny showed her a room with bare cement walls dappled with mildew, a shower and a Western toilet, not the squat toilet of her childhood.

"And here's your room." Sunny opened another door.

There was a bed, a desk, a chair, a cupboard and a standing fan - exactly what they had in the guest rooms, except these were ugly. The bed was made up - was it always kept ready, or had Sunny hoped to make her stay? But what for? Her head ached from thinking. It took effort to stay suspicious; one had to think in new ways to be always alert. But that was how Sunny won.

Nothing was what it seemed with Sunny; all of his statements and suggestions had to be held up to the light, and inspected; dismantled; no dealings with him could be trusted. Sunny stood aside and Padma stepped into the room.

"So you liked that Rajapala boy?" Sunny asked.

"He seemed okay."

"Handsome fellow, no? And rich – his family's very rich – did he tell you?"

"No."

"They're big business people. He liked you, I think. The father seemed to. Did you do anything nice?"

"We looked at a lake."

"Ah, the lake! Very good. Nice and quiet there, no? Very private. You think he liked you?"

"I don't know. Why?"

"It's nice for people to like us – don't you think? Did he say anything to you?"

"What about?"

"Oh . . . anything?"

"No." She knew what he wanted. Well, he and his dumb marriage proposal could go hang.

"Maybe you will see him again," Sunny said. "Enjoy your cutlets. Goodnight."

He left, closing the door behind him. She rushed to grab the handle, flinging the door open, checking that he hadn't locked her in. The landing was pitch black. Sunny had gone. Disappeared, like magic. He couldn't have run down the stairs so fast; he had to be behind one of the doors. Standing in the dark laughing at her, or maybe peering through a keyhole at her, watching her be afraid. She went back inside the room and shut the door. When would Leela come? Would she come at all? The tea still felt warm. The smell of fried fish cutlets made her stomach growl. But there were warnings whispering in her now: hadn't Sunny been a little too insistent about the tea and the cutlets? She picked up one of the cutlets. Its breaded skin cracked open: a ragged little mouth gaped, revealing a grey ball of fish and potato under the crumb. Was there something else mixed in with the black pepper and salt, something to make her sleep, overpowered inside that cell of a room, once more all Sunny's to use as he pleased? She swirled the tea around the mug. It wouldn't have been hard for Kumudini to crush sleeping pills behind the parrot curtain, stirring hard until the bitter white chalk dissolved. Tea could be made strong and sweet to hide the taste. Would Gerhardt have arrived to find her gone, and Sunny acting concerned, saying she had called a taxi herself. Would Padma have woken in a different room with the door locked this time and strangers outside - maybe in a wing of Nishan's parents' house, with doctors perhaps to drug her and keep her silent. Or maybe it would be a maid's room in the Middle East, she smuggled in as cheap labour, unconscious and voiceless? Alone in Sunny's house at night, such ideas did not seem outrageous. Padma sat on the edge of the bed waiting for Leela. What was it that Leela wanted to tell her? Where the hell was she?

Padma went out onto the landing again. A television was on in one of the rooms. There was the sound of gunfire and shots and shouting. It was the kind of film she imagined Sunny or Mukul watching - so where was Leela? Had she fallen asleep? Padma cleared her throat, letting Leela know that she was there, but Leela didn't come out. No one did. There was no sound from downstairs; all the lights had been switched off. Padma used the bathroom. It had no lock. She held the door closed with one hand, trying not to see the rusted pipes and the thick clump of hair in the plughole and waving antennae and glistening brown of a cockroach at the base of the sink. She felt her way back to her room. She took off her jeans and bra and lay on the bed in her knickers and blouse. She wasn't sleepy at all. She would make herself stay awake. She closed her eyes, simply to rest.

She woke with a start. The room was dark and silent – too silent. Something was wrong. She sensed the presence of someone there, in that too-perfect stillness; someone freezing, holding their breath, trying not to be caught. She pretended to go back to sleep, half-closing her eyes but squinting into the shadows – the figure at the foot of the bed – was it moving? Was it real? Yes. It was Mukul. He had been watching her sleep. He had done the same when they were children. In those days he had been creeping in to see if she'd been pricked by the pins he'd placed in her bed. Sometimes it was needles because Leela had told them that even a single needle could kill if it entered the body, riding in blood, straight to the heart. Mukul often put needles in Padma's bed. Padma made herself breathe slowly, deeply. Through eyes half-closed, half-open, she saw Mukul sliding closer, coming around the bed. She saw his stone-washed denim jeans with gold studs and printed-on graffiti in nonsense-English. She would scream if he came any closer. He stood towering over her as she lay exposed in her knickers, her legs bare. She would kick him and bite and scratch and shout out loud, but she knew that no help would come. She knew from before that she would be alone against him: Leela had hovered behind Sunny, blocked from entering; there was no need to shout and make a fuss, Sunny had scolded. It was what brothers did to sisters, he had told her. But she had known even then that he was wrong.

She moved a leg, stretched out an arm and sighed deliberately, pretending to wake. Mukul backed away. He moved fast – he always had – suddenly he was at the door. It opened. She blinked, seeing double. But no – another figure had entered. The two shadows passed each other, a smooth exchange, with no words of explanation, no surprise; Mukul slipped out and the other came in, one replacing the other. The new someone was short, slight – Leela at last? But it was Sunny. There was the whiteness of a vest, the red stripes of a sarong. Padma slid her hand under the pillow to her phone, her thumb blundering over the keys. She would never find Gerhardt's number without taking her phone out to look. And what could he do now, anyway? She lay still, slowing her breathing like someone sleeping, seeing Sunny search the pockets of her trousers draped over the chair. He took out her purse, and all the money inside and counted it, then put it back – all of it, as far as she could see. He flicked on a torch and inspected her bra, holding it up, a specimen. The torch snapped off. In the dark she saw him bend over the plate of fish cutlets. He sniffed them, one by one, then popped one whole into his mouth and left the room.

She sat up, peering into the darkness, sparks, flashes, dots exploding across her eyes. She texted Gerhardt:

'Can you send the car, first thing?'

He texted back at once: "Now?"

So he was awake at three a.m., his phone at his side.

'No, morning is fine,' she texted back.

There was victory in not showing her fear. Sunny gorged on the fear of other people. She would deny him that; that was her power now.

'Are you ok?' Gerhardt texted.

'Yes, fine. Just come early."

'I can come now."

"No. Come at six."

Only two hours and fifty-four minutes to wait.

"Call me if you need me sooner," Gerhardt sent.

"OK."

She held the phone close, feeling his presence. Then she jumped up and wedged the chair under the doorknob. She put on her jeans. The bra that Sunny had handled she pushed down into a pocket – that, she would throw away the first chance she got. Dressed, she was empowered. She sat on the bed, ready to go. Hunger gnawed at her. In her purse she found a cough sweet and chewing gum. She sucked on the sweet. Then she chewed the gum. She sat up watching the door, chewing with the flavour all gone. She waited for the dawn, for release.

Gerhardt arrived at 5:42 a.m., just as it was turning light. She saw the car pull up in the lane and ran downstairs. Sunny stepped out from behind the kitchen curtain.

"So you're up, are you?" he observed, amused. "Didn't sleep well? Wasn't the bed comfortable enough?"

Leela came out from the kitchen behind him. She was hunched over, wrapped in a faded old housecoat. She didn't look at Padma, as she scurried past. Had she been stopped by Sunny in the night? Had she been cowering from him in the kitchen, or had they been drinking tea together, waiting for a marriage proposal to come through at first light?

The doorbell rang. Sunny started and ran to a bureau, pulling out a drawer and reaching his hand in.

"No!" Padma cried.

"Sunny!" Gerhardt shouted and banged on the door. "Sunny – open this door! Now!"

Sunny smiled, closing the drawer.

"Here comes Daddy!" He giggled and danced with silly small steps to the door and drew back the locks.

"Where's Padma?" Gerhardt was bleary eyed and pale, pushing in as Sunny opened the door.

"Easy, easy, sir. Goodness me!" Sunny murmured.

"I'm here," Padma said, trying to get past Sunny.

"My, you two are early birds, aren't you!" Sunny exclaimed, not moving from the doorway.

Gerhardt reached for Padma's hand and Padma edged past Sunny, flinching from the touch of his belly against her. But she was outside finally in the cool early morning with Gerhardt, and Karu at the gate, ready to run over.

"What a pleasure it has been for us to see our precious daughter." Sunny bowed solemnly to Gerhardt. "Thank you, sir, for letting her come to our humble home. Please, come again soon, Duwa."

But Padma and Gerhardt were already walking, Gerhardt holding tightly to Padma's hand.

"See you very soon, Duwa!" Sunny shouted.

"Like hell you will," Gerhardt muttered.

It was strange that a garden belonging to Sunny could hold the same sweet clear air of morning as at the villa; that the birds still sang in trees polished with dew, touched by the same sun. Karu looked exhausted. Had he too stayed awake all night, ready to come to her? She suspected they may have been parked close by, the whole time. Karu opened the door for her and Gerhardt. Parked behind was Boss's van. The dark windows slid down and Boss looked out, checking that Padma was unharmed. Three of Boss's men were sitting behind him in the van, pouring tea from a flask. So much trouble she had caused, just by going to the lake with Nishan - had it been Sunny's idea for Nishan to take her away before Karu came for her? She would never know for certain. It was impossible to ever know the full extent of the trap, all its jagged edges and hidden corners.

From the car, Padma looked back at the house. Mukul was at an upstairs window watching her leave. As a small boy he would push her out of the house and lock the door. Once, it was raining and she had gone soaked to a neighbour's home to wait for Leela, and later Sunny had beaten her for leaving her brother alone in the house. Mukul wasn't grinning at her this time. Now no one would make her return to him. Now she was the one cared for and given to, and she had far more deserving others to care about.

She breathed in the cool scent of leather and sandalwood letting her other life, the real one, take over. She would never know what Leela had wanted to tell her, but she wasn't going back to find out. Leela had to find her own way out of the trap.

"Baba, I'm so sorry I didn't wait," Karu said. "Mukul told me you'd gone with one of the guests. I went inside and looked for you. I even ran up the stairs and shouted for you, but you weren't there, so I came home."

"It wasn't your fault, Karu."

"I should have waited. I should never have believed him."

"Everything they say is a lie," Gerhardt said.

Padma leaned back and closed her eyes. The car purred homeward. Sleep rolled over her, she sank down beneath its weight.

9

PADMA WOKE IN her bed, the fan's cool whirl a cocoon suspended inside the heat of daytime. She had woken late. The sun was bright behind the curtains. She lay in the lost new day, memories of the night unfurling, demanding to be deciphered, but she pushed them away. Soma brought her a glass of king coconut water and she sat up to sip the sweet salt milkiness, the taste of old times of sickness and being healed. It was the cure for all ailments, according to Soma. He used to tell anyone who listened about a doctor he'd read about using a king coconut as a saline drip in a jungle emergency.

"What time is it?" Padma asked.

"Eleven." Soma felt her forehead for her temperature, stroked her hair back. "Another guest is coming," he said. "Tonight she'll be here. She telephoned yesterday evening to book for ten days. She wanted a bungalow—"

"You did all this in English?"

"She spoke Sinhalese - English accent though. You friend is still here in the small bungalow—"

"He's not my friend—"

"We'll have to give the new guest the large bungalow."

"Fine, I'll make up the beds."

"You rest Baba, I can do it after lunch. Gerhardt Mahaththaya is coming back soon – he had to go in for a meeting earlier. We were all so worried, Baba – did Sunny send you somewhere when Karu came?"

"No, I just went for a walk. I got lost."

"I knew you shouldn't have gone back there. What did Leela want?"

"She didn't say."

"Typical! You must never go back, Baba – do you understand? Whatever they say, don't listen."

She went to shower, closing her eyes against the world. Under the warm running water, she glimpsed the landing and closed doors of Sunny's house. Had she been in danger there? Was it luck that had brought her safely home? She would never know. She was helpless, not knowing. She stood bathed and naked before her wardrobe, out of reach of the cold of the fan. She breathed in the scent of polish and lavender and mothballs, choosing from the neat folded stacks of clothes. Her perfumes glowed like nectar against the dark wood. She put on a green wrap-around skirt, her favourite red t-shirt, returning to the skin of her life, returning to her world.

"Hello? Padma? Is anyone there?" Rohan called from the veranda.

She waited for him to go. From her bedroom window she watched him walk over the lawn back to his bungalow. She sat in a corner of her room in Full Lotus and kept her eyes open, for when she closed them all she saw was Sunny's house. Still she could hear their voices. She followed the rise and fall of her breath. The anger would pass. All bad feelings passed, Jarryd had taught her. He had told her to name them as they rose up: shame, shame, hurt, confusion. She noted each one, freeing herself. Breathing in, breathing out. One day she would leave Sunny far behind her, and there would be no more need to watch out for tricks and traps.

She breathed in deeply. The villa's air was pure and clean. Its calm spread in her. She let herself open to receive it.

Gerhardt returned and they ate lunch together on the veranda. Padma talked of Mr Rajapala and Sunny's plans for her.

"And the son, what did he make of it?" Gerhardt asked.

"He had a girlfriend, but she didn't mind him being married to someone else."

"Wonderful. He didn't hurt you?"

"No!"

"That's the last time we listen to Sunny. Don't ever go near him again, okay? And Soma will do the shopping from now on. You can't go around on your own with Sunny hanging around. I see I'm going to have to come to another arrangement with him—"

"No, Gerhardt! Don't start all that again!" Padma pleaded.

"It's okay, I knew I'd have to, if you ever came back. I'm only surprised it's taken him this long before he made a nuisance of himself."

"Please Gerhardt, you mustn't pay him anymore. I won't go out on my own. Promise me you won't go talking to him?"

"Fine." Gerhardt sighed. "But you must tell me if he comes back here—"

"Of course."

She ate some rice. She was safe again at the villa, her world, her island, with Sunny circling outside, a crocodile. He hadn't got what he wanted this time, but he had made her world a little smaller. This was his only triumph.

"It isn't even a nice market," Gerhardt consoled her. "Markets are one of the few things I prefer in Europe."

He had told her about the market in his old home town, with stalls of whole hams and cheeses stacked like towers. And sausages hanging from strings: wild boar, venison, pork with figs, gnarled old saucissons spiced with paprika. He'd had a whole other life before Sri Lanka, before the villa and her. His house in the Austrian forest, inherited from his mother, he rented out for conferences and weddings, but it was always there for him if he wanted to return. For Padma there was only the villa, all her best life had been lived within its confines.

After lunch Gerhardt left to meet a client. Padma drank coffee on the porch. Rohan was out on his veranda, getting up to arrange and rearrange his chair, and glancing over at her. Every time she caught his eye he turned away. He gave up pretending to read and played ball with Gustav instead. Standing on the lawn, throwing the ball further and further, Rohan looked stronger, more energised, maybe even happier. After a while he strolled over.

"So you're back. Did you go anywhere nice?" he said.

"Yes, a lovely party. I met some very interesting people."

Was there anyone who could even imagine the night she had had? Certainly not Rohan. Nothing of his city life and no doubt highly-respectable, civilised relatives would have prepared him for a world like Sunny's. For Rohan it would be normal, not unfathomable good fortune, to sleep in a room like hers at the villa, to lie on a mahogany bed with pure cotton sheets, to have a lock on the door and Soma nearby to come running with the knife he kept under his bed, in case of intruders.

"I meant to ask you, does your family live around here?" Rohan said.

"My family?"

"Do you have other places you can go, away from here?"

"No."

"No relatives nearby?"

"You're very nosy for a guest, you know that?"

"Don't your parents mind you being here?"

"How could they? They're dead."

That stopped him. He looked shocked.

"I'm so sorry, I had no idea. I'm really very sorry," he stammered.

"It's okay, it happened long ago."

"Maybe we could talk somewhere private," he said.

"About what?"

"Would you come out for a drink sometime? We can go somewhere close by?"

"Why not here?"

"It might be easier. I really need to talk with you."

"Easier?" And then she understood. He wanted to talk about the suitcase. Clearly the guilt had got too much for him. She had heard of thieves and murderers confessing to crimes even after they had succeeded in fooling everyone, the burden of their guilt too much to bear. Secrets could be buried as deep as one liked, but it took effort to keep them there. Secrets would always reach towards the light, finding air, finding their way back to life. True forgetfulness was harder than people imagined.

"It wouldn't take long, just one quick beer or a cup of tea?" He was desperate.

She sighed. Why her!

"You must know somewhere we could go?" he begged.

Boss's bar was the only place. Gerhardt would know she was safe there from Sunny, and she had been wanting to go there at sunset time like the tourists – to sit on the clifftop and have a drink with someone not Gerhardt, and watch the sun go down.

"I know a place," she said.

"Great! Shall we meet at five thirty?"

"Okay." She would listen calmly to his revelations and offer advice only if asked and strongly advise him to speak with a lawyer. She would be careful not to dress up and seem interested in him; she was not to be dragged into his crimes. She would wear the most casual clothes: something baggy and shapeless and no bright colours; no fancy jewellery. Oddly, she wasn't dreading the evening. In fact the day was suddenly tinged with a new expectancy.

❦

Rohan went looking for Padma and they went to Boss's bar together. He glanced across at her as they walked, the deepening gold of the early evening sun glowing on her face, shining in her eyes. Sea winds lifted long curls of her hair, making them dance. She wore jeans and a loose olive-green blouse that the winds blew against her body, into its curves and tender hollows. She wore a simple necklace of moonstones and moonstone drop-earrings, pale gleaming droplets. With her long neck and rounded cheeks, the smooth curve of her brow, she looked like an ancient queen, a goddess carved on an Indian temple to astonish and elate the devoted.

"I hope you're not taking us to a dodgy bar," he teased her.

"It's the finest on Nilwatte Beach."

"Yeah, exactly!"

"If you don't like it, we'll go to The Savoy."

He laughed, feeling the new lightness in him when he was with her.

Boss's bar was a low blue-painted building that he had passed before on walks. A jasmine bush was trained around the door and grew up to a tin roof. Inside there was a narrow corridor with a kitchen on one side, with clean empty worktops and shelves neatly stacked with steel cooking pots and pans. Then a small bar with three red stools in a row at the counter, two tables and chairs. Padma went through to a garden on the clifftop, thick young coconut trees growing over plastic tables and chairs, the lush green lawn spreading right up to the edge of the cliff, which hung low over a strip of rocky beach.

Padma chose the table closest to the edge and they sat with the sea gently swirling around the black boulders below and black pitted arms of a laterite reef.

"There's Boss," Padma said, waving to a man who had come out of the bar.

He came over with drinks.

"Rum and Coke, on the house," he announced, placing a glass before Rohan.

It was not a drink he would have ordered. He tasted the sweetness of evenings long ago on a beach in Goa with an old girlfriend.

"There's no rum in mine," Padma said, sipping from her glass.

"I'm not getting in trouble with Gerhardt!" Boss exclaimed. "Ask him if you want rum."

"I drink alcohol!"

"It's not good for you, it kills the brain cells."

"I've got loads of brain cells, thank you!"

"You're here on holiday?" Boss asked Rohan. "Where are you from?"

"England."

"England where?"

"London."

"Ah, London. Good! Nice place I hear."

"Bring me some rum, Boss! I'm not a child anymore!" Padma complained.

"Just drink your Coke and stop fussing! Here's Jarryd, I have to go!" Boss greeted a leathery old Westerner scrambling up from the beach and went back to the bar. The Westerner approached, limping a little.

"That's Jarryd, my yoga guru," Padma said.

The man was tall and tanned, his white hair scraped back into a top-knot. He wore faded pink trousers and a white collarless Nehru shirt. Padma jumped up and hugged him.

"I miss you," Jarryd said, holding her tightly. He seemed rather too comfortable with her, and she didn't dare to protest. "Gerhardt tells me the business is going well. Are you still keeping up your practice?"

"Of course I am! This is Rohan, our first guest. Rohan, this is Jarryd Gunnersson."

"Ah! The guest!" Jarryd let go of Padma and shook Rohan's hand; a tight eager grip, no flinching, no looking away as Rohan took him in. The name was familiar - was it possible that they had met before? Rohan couldn't think where, or why.

"But now I must leave you, I have to get ready," Jarryd said.

At the next table he took off his shirt and trousers and stood in a loincloth, breathing deeply, baring his chest at the sea.

"Is he going to do yoga here?" Rohan muttered.

"Shhh!"

Jarryd climbed back down over the rocks, onto the beach and limped towards the water.

"He comes here every evening to celebrate the sunset," Padma explained. "It's his way of giving thanks to the day."

A sitar twanged over the speakers and a deep full chord thrummed over the garden.

"Boss even keeps Jarryd's CDs in the bar," Padma said.

Breathy flutes blew their lilting notes over the drone of the sitar, a tabla pattered in. Jarryd waded into the sea and bowed in namaste to the red ball of sun. He raised his arms, his head swayed inside their arc; he unfurled a long muscled leg up high.

"He used to be a ballet dancer," Padma said. "Then he went to India and studied Bharata Natyam before coming to live here. He used to teach and perform all over the world, but then he was injured. Now he teaches yoga. But he can still dance in the sea, with the waves to support him."

Padma's uncle had mentioned Gerhardt having acquaintances

with similar unhealthy interests – no doubt this Jarryd was one of them. With their wealth they would buy silence. Hidden away in remote villages, they could corrupt the innocent and trail their destruction unchecked.

"Does Jarryd know Gerhardt?" Rohan asked.

"Of course! They've known each other for years! Jarryd used to live near here, but he refused to pay Boss for protection, so he got robbed. He had a small antiques business at the time – the robbers took all his watches and jewellery. They thought the place was empty, but Jarryd was at the back and when he came to see what the noise was, they panicked and fired a gun and hit Jarryd's leg. The cowards ran off and left him bleeding. Luckily the neighbours heard and brought a doctor, but Jarryd's knee was shattered. The worst thing for him was going into the village, he was worried he might recognise the robbers – it made him so sad. He thought he was friends with them all. As if anyone can be friends with those morons. So then Jarryd moved inland."

"I'd have gone somewhere much further than inland!" Rohan said.

"And let the arseholes win?"

"It's called self-preservation."

Sri Lankan thugs, Rohan now knew, were casual killers. Those hired by Shalini's father, who had come to visit Rohan at his parents' house on the night before the court case, had been eerily business-like with their guns and quiet steady repetition of Shalini's ridiculous demands. Had she ever found out how Rohan's agreement had been extracted? Who exactly had arranged for those cold-eyed burly men to come banging on the door in the dead of night, pointing pistols at Rohan's parents' elderly cook and making Rohan go outside into the garden for a talk? For Shalini's father, the ruthless tycoon, it would have been business as usual, but had Shalini known what he had planned?

Had she tried to make him stop or urged him on? Rohan could not even guess. Even now it surprised him how little he had known her.

"There's nothing noble about being killed," he said to Padma. "Jarryd should get the hell out."

"But he wanted to stay close to us! He and Gerhardt are best friends."

"I'm sure they are." People with unhealthy absorptions were bound to stick together.

"Jarryd's got a beautiful yoga retreat now. It was Gerhardt who designed it. The guests stay in thatch huts around a lake and there's an amphitheatre for dance performances. Dance troupes come from all over the world to perform, and yoga teachers. Jarryd lets the villagers come for free."

The music reached a frenzied peak. The sky turned pink, orange. Jarryd dived into the darkening waves and glided out to the red horizon. Sea winds swirled as dusk fell. Rohan felt Padma's gaze, a warmth on the side of his face. He turned to her.

"What did you want to talk to me about?" she asked.

"I want to help you—"

"With what?"

"It's very wrong what Gerhardt is doing."

"What's he doing?"

"I know what's going on - and it's wrong. None of it is your fault, not at all—"

"What isn't?"

"In England he'd be sent to prison—"

"Prison? What are you talking about?"

"You must go back to your family as soon as you can—"

"Oh, my family - really?" She gave a mirthless laugh. "You think I should go back to them, do you?"

"I can help you to escape from Gerhardt"

"Escape?"

"There are people who can help you—"

She stared at him. "You don't think . . . oh my God! You do, don't you? You think Gerhardt and I . . . oh my God! How could you? And after meeting him!"

His face burned and, not for the first time, he felt foolish before her.

"But Gerhardt pays your uncle, doesn't he?" Rohan insisted.

"What uncle?"

"That man you gave money to—"

"Ah, you saw that, did you?"

"I happened to be passing, and yes, I saw you. That money was from Gerhardt, wasn't it?"

"No! Not at all! It was my money. It's none of Gerhardt's business what I do with it. Anyway, it was for medicine for someone else—"

"But Gerhardt does pay him, doesn't he?"

"He *used* to give him money—"

"I knew it!"

"But only so that I'd be left in peace. Sunny's the one to send to prison! Gerhardt's my father."

"He's what?"

"Legally Gerhardt's my father. My uncle brought me here and Gerhardt adopted me - ask anyone if you don't believe me - ask Soma, ask Boss!"

"Like they're going to tell the truth!"

"That *is* the truth."

In her indignation was truth. He saw it shine bright, ringing out, clear - but did he dare to believe it?

"So Gerhardt adopted you? As a daughter?"

"Yes!"

"And he didn't . . . ?"

"No, he did not! How could you even think it? You have a very weird imagination, if you don't mind me saying."

The red sun slipped down to the sea. The waves turned heavy, rippling like molten metal, spreading to a new wide openness, a new world opening to him. It felt like a reprieve, a magical transformation in the ways of the world.

Jarryd swam to the shore and climbed back up the rocks into the garden. He wrapped himself in a towel and sat looking out over the sea. Boss brought him an oddly shaped teapot and Jarryd drank from its spout.

"That's *maté* he's drinking, it's tea from Mexico," Padma said. "It keeps him young."

Rohan laughed.

"I have to get back – a new guest is arriving today," Padma said.

Boss was pouring drinks for a tourist couple at the bar. He gave them a cheery wave as they left. The lights had come on in the gardens of the cafés, strings of coloured bulbs in the trees and music playing. Tourists were settled at tables or headed to the beach bars for the night.

"And look who it is!" Padma muttered.

She was looking at a young local man leaning against a coconut tree and gazing at her.

"Let you out early, did they?" Padma asked the man.

"No, I did all my time. Time goes fast when you're having fun, that's what they say." A cluster of dog tags hung from a chain around the man's neck. He looked Rohan over with a smile.

"Just ignore him," Padma muttered and walked faster.

Soon they had left the man behind.

"Who was that?" Rohan asked.

"We call him the Spy."

"The *Spy?*"

"He gets paid to see what I do and report back to Sunny – crazy, huh?"

Rohan turned and looked back at the man still coiled against the tree, watching them.

"Is he dangerous?"

"In his dreams! So far his big news has been that I went to university, came back, and that I got myself a scooter!"

"You have to get out of here!"

"But this is my home!"

They reached the villa's gates and the lane was left behind. The house was a fading white gleam through the shadows. The garden's last colours shone out: moist velvet pink and redness; a flash of orange at the heart of petals closing for the night.

"Please, don't say anything to Gerhardt about Sunny," she said.

"Surely he should know what's going on—"

"He'll only want to pay Sunny off, but I don't want to be paid for anymore."

He longed to free her from the darkening entrapping beauty of the villa, the shadows growing deeper around them.

"Don't look so sorry for me!" She went up the steps and paused in the doorway with the glow of inside behind her, and she was the ancient temple princess once more, remote and unknowable.

"Don't be late for dinner," she said and went in.

Rohan returned to his bungalow, the garden becoming its night time self, new life awakening in hidden crevices; creatures stretching, creeping, probing, bright-eyed and hungry, eager for their time in the world to feed and fight and pair with another in the long restless hours of the night. He followed the stepping-stone path to his bungalow, one round grey disc after another, appearing through the dark.

## 10

RIA SAT BACK on the steps of her veranda, resting after morning yoga. She closed her eyes, the sun making her eyelids glow red-orange and womb-like. She heard the sound of waves and crows cawing, a scooter beeping far away, and she was returned to a long-ago Sri Lanka - the very place she had come back to find. You should never return to lost places, people had warned her, but who knew when a world was truly lost? It was how one returned that mattered - it had to be with no expectations, no assumptions made, no memories clung to. To travel stripped bare was important. Ria could think back now without sadness to the moment of realisation at the airport that no one from her family had come to meet her. They had thought she would make her own travel arrangements, they claimed, for hadn't she travelled all over the world by herself? They made it sound as if she only had herself to blame for their non-attendance. But the incident had served a purpose, for it was only in that moment of acute aloneness in the white-marble blandness of the arrivals hall that Ria had understood that never again would her grandparents be there for her, pressed against the barriers, waving and reaching out through the crowd to grasp her back to them. Never again would she be claimed so completely.

After all the years since their passing, she at last understood its finality.

Ria opened her eyes to the sunlit jewel green of the villa, the garden throbbing with life; flowers spreading their petals, leaves reaching for the sun; butterflies flickering through in soft coloured flashes. The villa's calm held her. An eker broom scraped over a garden nearby. She breathed in the scent of jasmine and wood smoke and fish frying and she let herself drift. There was a movement in the shade of the plantain trees, then Padma, the manager, approached with a plate of cut pineapple.

"I thought you might be hungry. Breakfast isn't for a while," Padma said, giving Ria the plate of pineapple.

"This is so kind of you."

"I'm always hungry when I do yoga," Padma said.

It was the strangest guest house, a place one might long for, and wish were possible. Padma passed Ria a pepper pot and Ria knew to sprinkle black pepper over the thick yellow discs of pineapple. It was how her aunt and mother and grandmother had eaten pineapple, the way she liked it herself.

"Please, join me," she invited Padma.

"Oh no, I've already eaten – okay, just one."

Padma sat beside Ria and they ate juice dripping down chins, wiped away with fingers licked clean, relishing the sweetness like children.

"I saw your headstand earlier, you're really good," Padma said.

"Thanks. It took me ages to learn – I was always afraid of falling. I didn't think I'd ever get my teaching certificate!"

"You teach yoga? Last night you said you were a lawyer!"

"I do both."

Padma looked intrigued. Most others were confused when Ria told them of this second life she had created for herself, for the self she became for three months of each year, living in a village in Goa, working at a yoga retreat.

Ria had come to Colombo that year instead of Goa because she had received an invitation to the wedding of a cousin, but once in Colombo she had discovered that the cousin barely remembered her, the wedding invitation having been sent by his parents through extreme thoroughness and family correctness, rather than any real desire to reconnect. Ria's return to her family had stirred up a flurry of marriage proposals, as her relatives, reminded of her existence, were spurred into action. They had been horrified when it dawned on them that she was already aged twenty-nine and still single. She had turned all the proposals down, of course, all educated men with eager watchful mothers. Ria's relatives already knew from the accounts of Ria's own despairing mother that she'd had boyfriends – any old Tom Dick and Harry whom she had encountered at university and work, and fearful of her finding such unsavoury companions in Colombo and causing a scandal, Ria's aunts had kept a close eye on her, not letting her out of their homes. Those beloved elegant houses she had once longed to return to, gave a hollow, lonely shelter and Ria had run from their confinement when a fellow guest at the cousin's wedding had mentioned a new guest house opening in a place called Nilwatte Beach.

"Do you teach in London?" Padma asked.

"No, Goa."

"I love Goa!"

"Me too, it looks like Sri Lanka, and sometimes it feels like it too."

"But without any Sri Lankans," Padma said approvingly. "Do you like London?"

"I love London." It was a response she had made many times in the past weeks; sometimes though she wasn't sure if she really meant it.

"I only like Europe for visits," Padma reflected. "I've been to Paris and Cologne and Barcelona, but I only feel at home in Asia."

"Lucky you."

"Lucky?"

"To know what you want. I wish I did."

Padma was easy to talk with. One didn't have to hold back or be met by the terrible silence of incomprehension of the clever driven people Ria usually met. Mostly one kept back so much of one's past, one's secret immutable otherness and talked in the code that others expected. It was the same, but in a different way, with the yoga teachers in Goa.

"Oh look, there's Rohan!" Padma said sitting up and staring thorough the trees at the guest Ria had seen at dinner. "He's going for his jog," she murmured. "I have to go."

She hurried off, then came running back to Ria. "By the way, in case you were wondering, I'm Gerhardt's adopted daughter. It's all legal and everything," she said.

"Okay."

"I just thought I'd mention it. People get such strange ideas about us sometimes."

And with that, she grabbed the plate with its left-over pineapple centres and ran away. Ria saw her pause behind the trees, staring after Rohan until he had gone; he who had eyes only for Padma, watching her move around the candlelit veranda, gazing with wonder at her. Ria smiled as she watched Padma run to the house. She had expected her to be reserved and traditional, seeing her the night before at dinner wearing a lunghi and blouse, all high neckline and long sleeves, dressed like an old aunt, albeit one with a beautiful well-toned figure. Ria had steeled herself for Padma's disapproval, for being an Asian woman travelling alone, speaking with an English accent, eager to talk and not just murmur niceties. These very qualities had caused many of her relatives great consternation. She had observed how certain aunts kept young impressionable daughters away from her – just in case, Ria supposed, she should influence those well-trained, highly-educated, tightly-leashed young women adversely with tales of her life in London. But the people at the villa had welcomed her in. She basked in the pleasure of loving the villa and its people; of being liked and let be. She watched a line of ants heave a great pearl of rice along a crack in the cement floor, burdened by their treasure yet never letting it go. She had always thought that the incompleteness she felt came from living in England, away from the people she belonged with, but now, at the villa far from everything she knew, she belonged, just as she was. For once she didn't long for anywhere else or for what had been left behind. In the sweet gentle stillness of the villa it wasn't shameful to want to be seen, admired, loved. It was love she wanted most of all. She could see now that she had been searching for the wrong type all along: it was not the family's love but another kind of love altogether that she longed for.

Padma looked back one more time, looking out for Rohan, then entered the small bungalow. Straight to the suitcase with the wire all ready. She twisted it inside the padlock, as Soma had shown her, and heard the faint click inside – but the padlock stayed locked. She tried again, easing the wire in, probing, turning. This time it kinked and gave up. She started again with a new wire, but the padlock resisted. She sat on the floor, defeated. His room was impossibly tidy. He had told her that he had been sent to an English boarding school when he was young. They must have trained the students to keep their possessions in order. Possibly they were beaten if they didn't, or punished with the sadistic penalties meant to make boys strong but secretly broke them. The bed was made perfectly. All his clothes had been put away. Shoes and slippers were lined up neatly. Inside a canvas sneaker was a crumpled-up sock – the one untidy detail in the whole room. She had never seen him wear those shoes. Why hadn't he given that sock to the dobi, or washed it by hand? Two pairs of boxer shorts, two pairs of socks and two t-shirts were hanging to dry on the wooden towel rail. Why keep back that solitary blue and red sock? She went over to take a closer look, lifting it out gingerly. She gave the shoe a shake: there was a clink then a clatter as a small silver key fell out onto the floor. Padma grinned. He must have thought he'd found the perfect hiding place – but she was too smart for him!

The padlock opened with one turn of the key. She opened the suitcase. Inside were – papers. Letters, forms, reports, receipts bound into files and tied up with long pink ribbons – these she undid. 'The Colombo High Court. Family Division', she read on the tops of documents, and his name: Rohan Arjuna Fernando set against a woman's name, not anyone Padma had heard of, and repeatedly the words: filing for divorce. So that was the big mystery. There was no film script. No stolen jewels. Why make such a fuss about some dull old divorce papers? She undid more knots, opened more files, flicked through pages. A line here and there jumped out at her. She stopped and read more closely. There were lawyers' letters full of accusation and defences: carefully worded hostile exchanges. She started at the bottom, working her way up to the most recent pages. Her stomach tensed, her eyes hurt. She couldn't believe what she was reading. Yet it was all too possible. So much that one couldn't imagine happened in reality. She followed the correspondence from file to file. Finally she could take no more. She threw the files back into the suitcase. Some of the papers came loose from the files. The pink cotton ribbons trailed in a tangle, she didn't stop to neaten them; she closed up the suitcase

"Just you wait, Mr Rohan! Just you wait until Soma hears what you've done!"

Soma had to be told. This he would want to know; he wouldn't care how she had found out. As she pushed the suitcase under the wardrobe, the door to the bungalow was unlocked. She sprang to her feet as Rohan came in.

"Hi! What are you up to?" he said.

He was a good actor – so pleasant and friendly, it was hard to believe what he had been hiding all this time.

"Is it the rat again?" he asked.

"You're the rat!" She threw the padlock key at his feet and stormed out, a hateful disappointment like bile in her mouth.

Outside his dark lair with its sordid secrets, she gasped for air. She felt sullied; tricked into liking him. He had to go. They would have to ask him to leave. They couldn't have people like him staying at the villa. Gerhardt would agree – he would be horrified when he found out what Rohan had done.

❧

Rohan stared at the key on the floor, for a moment uncomprehending, then unwilling to understand. But he knew, and he knew that she knew. He ran into the garden after her, but she was already at the house.

"Padma!" he shouted.

She came out to the porch and looked down at him, full of contempt. He ran up the steps to her and saw the fear in her and how she backed away from him now, and he stopped and backed away himself. It was futile to try to change how things were.

"What were you doing in my room?" he demanded.

119

The alarm and defiance, the wariness in her eyes was the proof that she had read the files and believed it all, just like everyone else. So many had believed, he almost believed the lies himself.

"I only looked a little, that's all," she said.

"You went through my personal possessions?"

"Only to check if you'd done something illegal! You were being so strange about your stupid suitcase – you shouldn't have brought it here if you didn't want people looking."

"You had no right! No right whatsoever! How could you?"

He wished he had never met her. The thought of her reading all that ugliness, the madness made official by stamps and seals and signatures – signed by him too, of course – was a new shaming; he was to be tarred forever. Already the lies had resurfaced; they could never be buried; no one would ever forget. Padma too would remember.

"You should be ashamed," she told him. "I want you out of here."

"Don't worry. I'll be leaving tomorrow."

"I know everything!" she called after him as he walked away. "There's no use acting all high and mighty – I know what you did!"

"Like hell you do!" he shouted back.

Inside his room he packed wildly, uncaring where things went. He searched in his travel guide for somewhere to spend the two weeks he had left until his flight home, for the court case had ended remarkably early. Shalini had to have known about the thugs. She hadn't seemed at all surprised when he signed his confession. Everywhere he went now, someone would know and someone would find out. This was his punishment. There was no limit to where the poison of an ex-wife could extend. There was no use staying in Sri Lanka; the only thing to do was book the first flight back to London.

That night he stayed for dinner, more to annoy Padma than to eat. He insisted on sitting at a different table, which she then had to set, bringing over the brass lamp and spilling oil on the tablecloth. She didn't bother to wipe it clean. She stayed away from him, hovering around the other guest, a Sri Lankan woman who sat trying to read in the dim light of the lamps. She kept looking out at the sea, a shining blackness with the blue-white curls of foam riding to the beach. The woman sat with her view. It was hers now, and the villa was hers too for as long as she chose to stay. He wished he had never come.

Padma brought him fried rice and chicken curry that he hadn't ordered, both spicier than anything he had ever eaten. A red-or-ange gravy pooled around the meat, speckled red as if sprinkled with powdered brick. The food was inedible. He pushed the plate away. He saw Soma watching him from the garden, threatening, vengeful. So she had told him. Possibly Soma would deem it necessary to teach Rohan a lesson that night – Rohan almost didn't fear him; it felt right, in a way, to be so unseen, so wrongly configured; there was a certain welcome privacy about it.

"I'm going in the morning, please have my bill ready," he told Padma.

"Of course. It'll be my pleasure."

Gerhardt was drinking a beer on the porch as Rohan left. Rohan said his goodbyes.

"Leaving? Already? But weren't you due to stay for another week?" Gerhardt looked startled. His surprise seemed genuine. So Padma hadn't told him. Not yet.

"I have to get back for work," Rohan said.

"Oh, what a shame!" Gerhardt rose and shook Rohan's hand, clasping his arm, full of friendship and warmth. Soon he would know and regret it. Anyone Rohan was drawn to, who began to like him, would grow to regret it when they found out – this was what Shalini had wanted, more than the money; this banishment from the world of good people was her true revenge.

Rohan walked through the dark to the bungalow. He had forgotten to put on the porch light and stood fumbling with the keys. He felt himself being watched. He turned but there was no one to see. He went in and locked the doors behind him – although anyone could break in easily and Soma would have a key. Rohan lay awake for hours with the fan on full and the mosquito net a billowing torn cage around the bed as he replayed and re-worked the exact wording of what he could and should have said to defend himself. Once he went to the desk and looked out of the window, seeing the light on in the room that was Padma's. She who was free to live, to tell her story and be believed, free of blame. She could live out in the open with nothing to hide, while he was to be silenced and shunned and despised.

He let the curtain fall, blocking away that red-pink glow of promise and contentment. He paced around the room, gathering things, preparing to pack. He opened the large suitcase and there were folders all left undone and the pages loose, the paper limp with humidity. He would have to pay extra again to take the files back to London. But who needed them? He carried the suitcase out, picking up the box of matches from the veranda table. At the back of the bungalow, out of sight of the house, he burned away the records of two wasted years, the flames creeping around the long lines of falsehoods and just enough truths to make the lies believable. The fire burned bright. He kept it small, not wanting to be discovered; in this new furtive life it was better to be cautious. It took an hour to burn it all. He was sweating and sooty and exhausted when he returned to his room, and slept restlessly through the rest of the night.

Early, very early the next morning, he marched through the garden to the main house. For the first time he refused to admire it, or feel its welcome; it was a place soon to be denied him. He went onto the veranda. The tables, stripped of their cloths, were scrubbed and unready for the day. There was no bill left out for him. Gustav barked a warning inside. Rohan banged his fists on the doors, relishing the noise. There were voices in the hall then the doors opened and Padma stood blinking up at him.

"What's the problem?" she asked.

She wore a patterned dressing gown, pulled on over yellow pyjamas, her hair loose around her in heavy waves. She held the dressing gown closed over her breasts. She was barefoot, her feet pale against the smooth polished dark floor. Behind her the cook hovered, bleary-eyed and angry.

"Where's my bill?" Rohan demanded.

"You want it *now?*"

"Yes."

"In a hurry to get away, are we? You don't want breakfast?" she mocked him.

"No thanks, just the bill."

"Fine. I'll bring it to your room."

"Good."

In his bungalow, with his bags packed, he sat at the empty desk, curtains closed, listening for her. At last she came, changed into a t-shirt and short denim skirt. Her bare legs were flexed tense as she stood at the door, not coming in. Gustav flopped on the veranda behind her. She held out the bill to Rohan and he scanned the neat handwritten scroll of daily room charges: breakfasts, beers and even the inedible curry of the night before. He wanted to argue the unfairness of the latter, but he was tired of fighting. He took out his wallet.

"So you beat your wife, did you?" she said.

He held the money out to her, but she didn't take it.

"You did, didn't you?"

"No, actually, I didn't."

"Oh yeah? That's not what it says in her statement."

"I know."

"You admitted all charges. There's no use lying, I've seen all the papers."

"So?"

"So damn good she won!" She looked furious. "I *knew* there was something weird about you - I knew it the first moment I saw you."

"Did you really." He wanted to laugh. How stupid everything was. There was nothing special about her after all. She was as small-minded and ungenerous as the rest of them.

"You're not even sorry, are you?" she accused him.

"No, because I didn't do anything."

"Then why did she say you'd hit her?"

"Because she was angry at me for wanting a divorce."

"Then why didn't you deny it? You've admitted to slapping her and pushing her and subjecting her to extreme verbal abuse—"

"I signed papers, that's all. And I signed them, if you must know, because her father, the big-shot businessman, sent some rather large men to see me on the night before the court case, and they suggested very strongly that I do what was asked."

"So you lied in court?"

"It was that or go to hospital."

"Who's her father?"

"Alec Somasinghe."

"Alec . . . Isn't he in construction? Didn't he build those casinos?"

"Yes."

"Gerhardt refused to work with him."

"I'm not surprised."

"And you went and married his daughter?"

There was no explanation he could offer that would make any sense. He himself didn't understand it. All he could recall was a light-headedness at the time and a fading of all his instincts as he gazed at Shalini, while their families gathered around beaming and glad and full of love and hope, closing in around them.

"So you're saying you never hit her?" Padma said.

"No, I bloody didn't."

"Is she beautiful?"

"She was pretty hideous by the end, I can tell you."

"Hmm. I see."

"What?"

"Now I understand."

"Understand what?"

"She had money and you had good contacts – it would have worked fine, but you went and fell in love."

"That's ridiculous!"

A new hurt throbbed where his anger had been. They had never spoken of love, but he had been happy – he remembered that. How quickly it had gone. He remembered the blankness in her when he spoke, her sullen unresponsiveness. He had resented her distaste, her boredom in him. Those deep brown eyes he had revelled in had turned cold and hating and he had turned away. How he had dreaded returning to her in their home that had been his home alone, where her glowering presence had taken over. It was the loneliness of being with her that he had wanted to end most of all – and for that she had punished him, ensnaring him in a poisoned fog of lies that obscured him from others and smothered any chance of new life.

"So, she said you'd abused her and got all your money?" Padma mused.

"She didn't get *all* of it."

"She's smart."

"Yeah, she's smart alright."

Padma chewed her lip. In the silence he felt something change; he could hardly believe it, but there was a lightening in the air, like something leaving.

"I'm sorry I read your papers," she said.

"It's okay."

"I knew you were alright, really."

"Oh, did you, now?"

There was a new calm in him where there had been throbbing and tightness before and hope, frail and fantastical growing, too incredible yet real.

"Can we start again?" she said.

"Some manager you are. Is this how you treat all your guests?"

"Only the ones I like." She took back the bill and tore it in two. "You don't need to go now, do you?"

"Your food is bloody awful."

"I'll fix that, I promise. Will you stay?"

"I might as well."

"I'll see you later, then!" She smiled and quickly left. Gustav had to run to catch up with her.

Rohan sat on the veranda in a new day. A day stretching out long to an evening with oil lamps and flowers and Padma - Padma who believed him and seemed to still like him, despite all the mess and mistakes. So many mistakes but nothing was irreparable - here was the proof. He extended out the arms of the sedan chair and propped his legs up, resting like his father and uncles on the veranda of the old house on the coconut plantation. He gazed out at the world he had discovered for himself, his own world without them.

Soon after Shalini was introduced, his mother and his aunts had taken him on a long trip out of Colombo to see their astrologer, a skinny bespectacled man sitting cross-legged on the floor of his house, pointing at ancient charts and ola leaf books, predicting the outcome of pairing two strangers. Rohan had indulged the silliness to please his mother, but maybe he too had needed the reassurance of those astral calculations to bolster his first steps into the unknown. Now his future spread empty before him, uncharted, unguided; he floated free into its immensity to drift among unknown stars and constellations. The cook came out of the kitchen and stood smoking in the shade. He nodded over at Rohan. So Padma had told him – and he had believed her. They both believed in Rohan. His truth grew real, grew strong. He could speak it out loud and it was his to have, to prove what he was now, who he had become. He nodded back at Soma.

That night at dinner his fish was perfectly steamed and made with a delicate blend of spices. The rice was the finest basmati, boiled and plain, just the way he liked it.

## II

Padma sat on the parapet, waiting for the guests to finish eating dinner. Ria was reading again. Rohan looked thoughtful. Padma had seen him study Ria the night Ria arrived, but he didn't seem interested in her that evening, although Ria was looking impossibly elegant in a long white cotton dress, a blood-red shawl slipping down around tanned golden shoulders; sleek hair tied back with an amber silk scarf. She looked like a woman in a café in Paris. Padma had been around elegant beautiful women at university and at Ruth's parties and they had never troubled her before – but Ria made Padma feel ungainly and young and needy. She made Padma act strangely, placing Ria's table as far away as possible from Rohan so that they would have to shout across the room to each other if they wanted to talk. Ria didn't seem to mind, only looking up from her book to eat pumpkin curry and fried rice and gaze at the garden.

Padma looked away. A new dissatisfaction simmered in her when Ria was near. Yet there was so much Padma wanted to ask her. How it was that Ria had known to make the life she had, full of everything she loved. And how she had known what desires were true passions and which mere whim. Where did one learn to select the parts to discard and those to preserve and stitch carefully together? Soma came out to clear the tables, stopping at Ria's and hovering near her.

"Would you like a coffee?" he offered.

"No, thank you. I'm just going." Ria rose from the table. "I'll see you in the morning." She smiled and Soma stood beaming after her.

Rohan too, smiled up at her.

"See you," Ria said, turning to Padma, and Padma was surprised by a sense of warmth and friendship that swept through her. How could it be possible to feel so reduced and inspired and encouraged by the same person?

"Would you like a coffee?" Padma asked Rohan once Ria had gone.

She ignored Soma's frowns as he mouthed 'no!' at her.

"Yes, please," Rohan said and Padma went to make it, following Soma into the kitchen.

"Don't keep offering them things," Soma hissed.

"You started it!"

"I only meant the young lady!"

"Well that's not very fair, is it?"

"She seems nice," Soma said.

"She is. So is Rohan."

"I'm sure." He watched her with a grin. "Now no hanky panky while I'm out. Otherwise I'm telling Gerhardt."

"Don't be ridiculous!"

"Just take your time getting to know him first."

"What a foolish man you are! There's nothing going on."

He smirked at her in the mirror over the kitchen sink as he wet his hair and slicked it back with the green plastic comb he kept on the window sill. Every night he went to Boss's Bar to play cards and drink beer and smoke weed with Boss and his brother and their friends, like in their boyhood years. With Boss, Soma returned each night to a time of innocence and trust. Every night Soma found proof that life could go on after bad things happened – proof that there was always someone who cared; that true friends existed. Soma was essentially a happy man. He knew he was loved. He accepted that he was lucky and he didn't question his luck; the Gods had looked after him, as far as he was concerned, and he repaid them with gifts of money and flowers at the kovil. Padma didn't know whom to attribute for her luck. Lord Buddha was not a god, he was an enlightened mortal; her luck had come from nowhere, it could have gone to anyone. She took the coffee to Rohan.

"Would you like some?" he asked.

"Sure. Thanks."

She took a second cup from the dresser and pulled up a chair to his table. He poured the coffee. She stirred milk into hers. He sipped his black. In the office, the telephone started to ring.

"That's the new guest house line," Padma noted.

"Wow, somebody's keen." Rohan glanced at his watch.

"Must be calling from abroad."

"Shouldn't you answer it?"

She didn't move, she didn't want the moment to stop. Gustav barked from her room. What kind of idiot didn't check the local time before calling? The ringing stopped. It was no loss – she didn't want ignorant travellers staying at her guest house.

"Hope it wasn't important," Rohan said. "Could it have been Gerhardt?"

"He'd have called on the other line."

That other phone started to ring in the hall. She sighed and went to answer it.

"May I speak with Mr Rohan Fernando, please?" a woman commanded in a deep haughty voice. So formal she sounded, like a business acquaintance, or a new girlfriend in Colombo, perhaps.

"I have no room number for him, but maybe you could put me through?"

The accent was high-class-Colombo, with a drawl that sounded Indian. Once it would have been a British accent they aimed for, but always anything other than Sri Lankan. Very few Sri Lankans really liked being Sri Lankan, so many well-to-do people aspired to be something more, something other.

As Padma placed the receiver on the table, she was aware of Rohan's real world alive elsewhere, on the end of the line, a place of privilege and affluence where only the entitled could enter. His people would soon smooth over the scandal of his divorce and establish order; already they were calling him back to them.

"It's for you," she told him on the veranda.

"Me?"

She tidied the dresser, listening to him in the hall.

"I'm fine," Rohan informed the woman. "Yes. Really."

Padma peered into the hall. He had his back to her, leaning against the wall, his body tense. His shirt had lifted up at the waist; the skin of his back was smooth and even-toned, there was a single dark mole above the belt.

"There are no direct lines here," he said. "I'm telling the truth, there are no phones in the rooms – because it's a guest house, not a hotel."

What a ridiculous woman! Nobody should have telephones in their rooms where they came to relax. For one thing, it stopped them getting calls from annoying people. The woman may have been the ex-wife, calling to make new demands. Rohan listened to her in silence.

"You did *what?*" he yelled.

Padma ducked, pretending to be sorting napkins.

"What the hell is the matter with you?" Rohan cried. "Which part of 'never again' can't you understand?"

Was it the ex-wife making new demands? She had a nerve.

"Of course I'm angry," Rohan said. "I should never have given you this number. *Emergency*, I said." He sighed. "Oh God, don't cry," he added softly.

The woman was incredible! Trying for the last of his money with crocodile tears! Someone had to say something - Padma marched into the hall.

"There's still time for grandchildren, Ma," Rohan said.

Padma stopped but too late - he spun round and saw her.

"I have to go, Ma, someone wants to use the phone."

"No, no, it's fine!" Padma backed away.

"I haven't changed my mind, it's a *categorical* no. Goodnight." Rohan ended his call and came out to the veranda.

"That was my mother," he said, sitting down. "She and my aunts want me to go back to Colombo for a marriage proposal - can you believe it? They're mad, quite mad. I'm sorry - did you want to use the phone?"

"I wonder who they lined up for you?" Padma teased.

"I couldn't care less."

"Hopefully someone with a great body."

He stared at her.

"And great big tits," she added.

He smiled. "And if not a medical doctor, then at least a PhD," he said.

"Or a medical doctor with a PhD - a doctor-doctor."

He laughed. Just then Gustav came running out and raced onto the porch, barking loudly.

"Probably a cat," Padma said, but she went to check.

There was no cat to be seen, but Gustav barked angrily out at the darkness. Padma looked to the gate, but there was no one there. She hushed Gustav.

"Hello?" Padma called.

Something moved in the plantain trees. Gustav charged as Sunny stepped out.

"Easy," he warned, his eyes fixed on Gustav, one hand reaching behind him.

"Gustav!" Padma cried, running to catch hold of Gustav growling and lurching towards Sunny.

Soma had asked if they could finally keep a gun at the villa, now that strangers would be staying, but Gerhardt had refused. There was more chance of them shooting each other by mistake, he'd insisted. Padma held tightly to Gustav's collar. Sunny wouldn't shoot him, not with her there.

"What do you want?" she asked Sunny.

"Good news! Nishan's asked to see you again! He really likes you it seems!"

"That's great. Thanks for letting me know."

"He wants to marry you – just think! Such a nice family. You will be very comfortable with them."

"Unfortunately I don't want to marry him."

"Ah?" Sunny feigned shock. "But then . . . what you both did at the lake—"

"We didn't do anything at the lake—"

"But he can't be allowed to just have his way with you! You must do it properly, it's for your own protection."

"He didn't have his way with me."

"That's not what I heard."

He smiled and she was sullied, reduced. Never again would she let herself listen to him; never again would she enter his world.

"I'm not interested, sorry." She dragged Gustav back towards the house.

"Really? You're not interested?" Sunny sounded amused, but she sensed the anger in him, the fury that would suddenly flare and grow - she knew how quickly; and she knew its force. She went backwards up the steps with Gustav growling and snarling and straining.

"According to Nishan, you were very keen," Sunny said.

Had that dumb guy talked, or was Sunny just guessing? She saw again the black lake and the ink-smeared windows, the stranger leaning close and her own base urges overtaking her. Nishan may well have talked, perhaps exaggerating that mindless encounter.

"You should be thanking us for helping you to meet someone like him. His family have a lot of money – did I tell you?"

"You did, but I'm not getting married to him."

"Other children obey their parents. Other children care about their family's wishes. Other sisters try to help their brothers – poor Mukul, he might have got a good job with the father—"

"Ah! So that's why!" She laughed out loud, knowing his reasons at last, and with the dismay of betrayal came relief, for there was always a hidden truth with Sunny, a challenge, a trick, a puzzle to solve. There was always a motive she hadn't considered. Now she stood on firm ground again, strong before him.

"So Mukul gets a job if I marry the dumb son with the Muslim girlfriend – I should have known! You never know when to stop, do you?"

"How can I make big business men promise jobs for people? Huh? You tell me that! Talking rubbish! Utter rubbish, you talk."

"Thanks for the visit. I have to go now. And so do you."

She wasn't afraid anymore. He was simply a stupid angry old man, a bully, but he had no hold over her anymore. He would never sell her to anyone, not again.

"Alright then, I'll go, if that's what you want. Lady of the big house now, aren't you? Too good for us. Fine by me . . . if that's how you want it, that's how it will be."

He walked away down the path, and it was all over. All her life she had been afraid of him coming to the house, turning up suddenly in the night when she was alone – but she had survived, she had known what to do. She went slowly up the steps, gathering herself to return to her real life, to Rohan sipping coffee on the veranda. He must think she was talking to a visitor, a neighbour perhaps. She would say it was someone asking for directions. She would not think any more about Sunny. She had dealt with him – for the first time without needing anyone's help. She felt a coolness, a strange lightening behind her, her hair was being lifted up, so gently, as if someone were coming in to kiss her. Hands locked around her neck, a hard band forcing all life out from her. She struggled, a cry died inside her. She was twisted back and Sunny's face loomed over her, his eyes bright in the darkness.

"Don't you ever talk to me like that again," he murmured.

She couldn't breathe, her hands couldn't move his fingers locked tight around her, her lips had gaped open, her throat felt crushed as if broken.

"Next time you'll find yourself flying across the garden. Do you hear me?"

All she could hear was Gustav barking and leaping at Sunny. Sunny kicked out, jerking her back. She couldn't shout, she couldn't call out, no sound could leave her.

"What the hell do you think you're doing? Get your fucking hands off her!" It was Rohan. He must have heard Gustav and come out.

Sunny's hands unclasped and she was released. She stumbled back towards the door.

"Come inside," she told Rohan, her voice sounding compressed, distorted. But Rohan stood watching Sunny descend the porch steps.

"You didn't say you had company," Sunny said to Padma. "I see you are offering quite a lot of services at this hotel of yours."

"I told you to get out!" Rohan shouted and took out his phone.

"Are you going to ring the police?" Sunny sneered. "Or that dopehead Soma?" Sunny laughed. "Go ahead, I'm off to bed." And he sauntered down the path. "I'll be seeing you," he called back to Padma.

He stopped and looked straight at Rohan. "And you too," he said, then he left.

Padma's neck burned. The pain spread under her hair, up into her face. She felt sick.

"Are you alright?" Rohan helped her inside and poured water into a glass for her.

He kept turning to check the porch.

"He won't come back," Padma said.

Her voice still sounded strange. Well, this was a first. Sunny had never come past the gate before, let alone right up onto the porch. She shuddered, thinking of him silently, determinedly coming back to hurt her. How easily he had overpowered her. And Rohan had seen it. Shame twisted inside her.

"You have to report him to the police," Rohan said.

"There's nothing they can do. I'll put the dog out at night from now on. Sunny would never have been able to come into the garden if Gustav had been there. Gustav - you're sleeping on the porch from now on, I'm sorry to say."

"You do know your uncle was going to hurt you?" Rohan said.

"No, he wasn't! He was just trying to frighten me. But I'm not scared of him - stupid bastard! Don't talk to him if you see him again - just ignore him."

"I'm not afraid of that idiot."

"No, really, keep away from him, he's not a nice man."

"Your neck's gone red." Rohan peered worriedly at her.

"I'll be fine."

They stood looking at the lane, searching, checking. He put his arm around her. His body felt familiar and right against her.

"Please don't say anything about this to Soma or Gerhardt," she said.

He seemed anxious, agreeing. But she was warned now, she was ready for Sunny. He would never catch her out again. In the mirror on the dresser she saw herself – she was the same still, nothing had changed. The red band around her neck would fade, maybe in a few hours, maybe a few days. The pain too would end. Never again would she turn her back to Sunny; nothing he said would convince her to give him any money or go anywhere near him. She left Gustav on the veranda with Rohan and went into the house, locking the hall doors from inside. In her room it was quiet and safe. Soon the night would be over, just a few hours and it would pass into a clean sunlit morning and life would begin all over again.

# PART II

## 12

"YOU MUST SEE our little rock temple before you go," Gerhardt told Ria at breakfast.

"Is it far?" she asked.

"Forty minutes by tuk-tuk. Shall we arrange one for you?"

"Is it safe for her to go alone?" Padma interrupted.

"Wilson can take her."

"Of course. Good idea." Padma had been about to offer herself as a guide, but Wilson was a much better choice – he could drive Ria in his new tuk-tuk and stay with her if she wanted. Lucky Ria, not having to stay at the villa all day, avoiding people.

"We can ask Wilson to climb up with you," Gerhardt told Ria.

"Thank you so much! That would be great!"

Ria was free to clamber over the granite boulders to ancient painted shrines, to gaze at views of jungle and plains. Ria could walk at ease among the lotus-flower sellers and the good Sri Lankan families out for the day, out being happy together. Having family was a virtue in Sri Lanka, and the bigger the family, the better. Definitions of relatedness were expanded to embrace even the most tenuous connections. An extensive vocabulary of labels existed to claim as many as possible:

amma/i (mother/mummy)
thaththa/i (father/daddy)
ayya (big brother)
malli (little brother)
akka/i (big sister)
nangi (little sister)
loku amma (maternal aunt older than one's mother)
punchi/podi amma (maternal aunt younger than one's
    mother)
loku mama (maternal uncle older than one's mother),
punchi/podi mama (maternal uncle younger than one's
    mother)
mahappa (paternal uncle older than one's father)
bappa/i (paternal uncle younger than one's father)
loku nanda (paternal aunt older than one's father)
punchi/podi nanda (paternal aunt younger than one's father)
seeya (grandfather/ elderly male relative)
aachchi (grandmother/ elderly female relative)
loku seeya (elder brother of a grandparent)

Even the most distant relatives were given titles of uncle, aunt, brother, sister; a seal of belonging, but how could mere words bind a family that beat you and gave you away, or came into the room at night uninvited. Padma had never found a way to use 'thaththa' with Sunny, yet she had never used it with Gerhardt either, the word was too alien attached to him. She was bound to Gerhardt by an unnamed feeling of affection and rightness, a simple directness between them.

"Padma, will you make the arrangements for Ria?" Gerhardt asked and Padma went to the office to telephone Wilson.

"I'm on my way!" Wilson declared, delighted.

"Not now, she's still eating breakfast. Come in an hour."

"I'll be there! Make sure she waits for me! Don't let her go up the road and go with someone else."

"Don't worry, she'll be here!"

Wilson was still excited by his business several months after he had begun. It had taken him two years working on building sites to save up enough to buy the little blue and orange tuk-tuk he had driven ecstatically around the neighbourhood on his first day. Wilson's pleasure in this small success was brazen, but it was all his own – perhaps that was why no one seemed to mind, for the tuk-tuk hadn't been stolen or damaged in the night. Padma was proud of her guest house, but her pleasure in it was hard to hold onto. Sometimes she found herself wanting something else, but she never could pin it down.

She stayed on in the office and worked on the accounts, making the small adjustment to allow for the money she had given Sunny for Leela's medicine. Maybe he had kept the money for himself; she tried to shrug that thought away. Thinking of him made her throat constrict and start hurting again. Through the window she saw Ria in the garden, changed into long trousers and a modest long-sleeved shirt, covering up for her trip to temple, for Ria knew to respect even an ancient rock temple as a place of worship, rather than a tourist site. Padma wanted to join her outside, but she resisted. She would only end up asking more about Ria's life, and whatever she discovered, Padma suspected, would taunt her further. Ria was bound to live in a chic vibrant neighbourhood in London, in a Bohemian apartment with rooms full of clever books and tasteful art. Ria's life would be arranged just as she wanted it, doing intriguing things with fascinating people, and she would think anyone could have a life like hers. What was it that stopped one having such a life?

Padma left the desk and looked from the window as Ria took photographs of the small green parrots that had gathered in the mango trees. Soma came out to pick curry leaves for lunch, and stopped to talk with Ria. He nodded attentively as Ria pointed out the same parrots that he usually loathed and despised and chased away with a big stick.

"Beautiful, aren't they?" Ria said.

"Oh yes." Soma watched the parrots eat his precious mangos.

Padma giggled.

"Can I get lunch here later?" Ria asked Soma.

"There's no lunch menu, but I can make you something," he offered.

Padma stared.

"But something simple—" he added. "You like roti and seeni sambol?"

"I *love* roti and seeni sambol. I could eat it every day for the rest of my life!"

Ria smiled ecstatically, like an eager beloved child, in love with the world; she opened up fearlessly to everyone, as if wanting them to enjoy the world with her.

"We used to have roti and seeni sambol for breakfast at my grandparents' house in the school holidays," Ria told Soma. "Early morning we went for a walk on the beach and came home to breakfast. I remember the smell of hot coffee and rotis cooking. Sometimes we had coconut sambol."

"I can make you coconut sambol," Soma said.

Ria grinned, grateful for even that slight kindness. Soma looked proud. Padma understood. She had felt the same way about the pineapple. It was hardly any trouble to cut up a pineapple and arrange it on a plate, but Ria made you feel so good and kind and generous for that one small act, and she made eating it together seem so special. It wasn't often that people were so grateful. Ria had known a particular kind of sadness, Padma sensed. And she felt a strange stirring of recognition.

"I will make roti and sambol for you everyday lunchtime," Soma told Ria. "Chicken curry also you like? Okay, I make it as well! And fish? You like seer fish? Prawns?"

Padma hid behind the shutters, stifling her laughter.

Then Wilson arrived and Padma went outside and watched him settle Ria into the red leatherette seat at the back, tucking a great many flowery cushions in around her, and showing her how to pull across the curtains that he'd had his mother sew, to keep out the glare. Ria looked amused by all the fuss. Already she and Wilson were chatting happily, Ria admiring the brand new tuk-tuk. Wilson was delighted by her; like Soma, he would be devoted to her from now on. He jumped into the driver's seat and they sputtered off up the lane. Padma waved from the gate.

She walked back through the empty garden, with the spare keys to the bungalows in her pocket. She made her way to the large bungalow and let herself in. It was much too large for one person, meant for a couple with a child, but Ria had made herself comfortable. The room looked cosy with the extra bed made into a seat. Ria had spread her red shawl over it and made the spare bedside cabinet into a coffee table. There was a pile of books she had brought with her: a yoga manual by a yogi whom Padma admired; free booklets from a Buddhist monastery, several books of poetry, some novels in English and French. Padma stood at the centre of the room, trying to imagine it hers, but it stayed resolutely Ria's. Padma sat down on the red shawl and flicked through the Buddhist pamphlets, but there was nothing to show how Ria had pieced together a unique whole life. How did one ever know which sudden idea to follow? Which to work at, and never regret, and which to ignore? Ria's things revealed little of her reasons and methods. Padma imagined her at the rock temple, climbing up to the top, a speck growing smaller as she went higher and higher.

"Baba?"

"Aargh!" Padma cried. Varuna, the cleaner, was standing in the doorway.

"You made me jump! I was about to start cleaning the room," Padma declared.

"I'll do it now, Baba. I'm sorry I'm late." Varuna looked anxious; she had been late on many occasions recently and Padma had asked her to be on time. "I tried to be early today, Baba, but something happened."

"Again? I told you, we can't keep cleaning the rooms later and later now we have guests. It has to be done early."

"I know, Baba, I'm sorry, Baba."

"Is everything okay?"

"Baba - it's all because of Sunny, he's the one to blame."

"*Sunny?*"

"I know I should have told you, but I didn't want to worry you, just as you were starting a new business. Sunny's such a nuisance – every day he's been waiting for me at the road into the village, asking all sorts of foolish questions."

"Like what?"

"Just how many guests are staying and how much they are paying, you know how he is? I didn't tell him anything, don't worry. But I had to go the long way after that, that's why I was late all the time. Today I tried the village road again, and he wasn't there, but then Hema Amme came running to me—"

"What did *she* want?"

"She kept talking and talking, I couldn't escape. I told her she should talk to you herself, Baba, instead of dragging me into it."

"Into what?"

Varuna paused uncomfortably.

"What did she want?" Padma asked.

"She told me to tell you to go and see Leela Amme."

"Again she wants to see me!" Why on earth had Leela not talked to Padma when she had the chance?

"She wants to meet you somewhere outside of the villa; she doesn't want to cause any trouble for you with Gerhardt Mahaththaya."

"When did they ever worry about causing me trouble! I suppose Sunny also wants to see me, does he?"

"No, Baba, Hema Amme said your mother went to her in secret, about some trouble she is having. Sunny doesn't know anything about it. I don't think she is very well, Baba. She's going to wait near the bus stop at the top of the lane at three o'clock on Friday, if you can go and see her."

"What's wrong with her?"

"Hema Amme didn't say. It doesn't sound good, Baba. Poor woman, how much she has suffered. It's not her fault she's married to Sunny, no? What could she do? She fell for him as a young girl and he made her get pregnant—"

"Yes, with me."

"What to do? Everybody makes mistakes. You mustn't be angry with her, Baba, after all, your mother is your mother, no? You only have one."

Padma retreated to the office. She sat in the revolving desk chair that had belonged to Gerhardt's father, who had kept it in his yacht. She spun slowly round and round in the chair, the seat creaking and tipping at uneven points in its trajectory. Sri Lankans spoke of mothers as if they were special beings, a deity, almost, but a mother was an ordinary woman, sometimes a ghost, sometimes she was nowhere when you looked for her. Some mothers stayed away for years without a word, without sending the smallest note, then they asked you to go to their house and even there they disappeared. What Sri Lankans didn't seem to know was that there were mothers who never touched you except to hit and slap and pinch; and mothers who cringed from you if you tried to go too close, shrinking from the feel of your skin on theirs - this was not what people meant by mother, but it was just as real. Did one have to obey such a mother when they summoned you?

Padma waited until lunch was over and Ria had gone to her room to rest. Rohan hovered on the veranda, wanting to talk, but Padma told him she had to work. She stayed in the office until he was gone. In the stillness of the afternoon all was quiet as Padma tiptoed past Soma's room, hearing his snores, and went out through the back door to the shed and took out her scooter. She wheeled it through the garden, only climbing on in the lane and riding off through the village, going inland to Jarryd's house. Away from the beach, the land was greener, more peaceful, the houses more spread out in large lazy gardens and not clustered together, straining for a view. There were only a few cars out in the heat, the sun blazing down. The tall gates of Jarryd's estate appeared and she turned in and rode along the tree-lined driveway towards his house at the far end, a stately pale yellow, single-storey building with a circular lawn in front.

Padma parked in the shade at the side of the house and went onto the veranda. "Hello, Jarryd? It's Padma!" she called.

She didn't go into the house. One never knew who might be staying at Jarryd's place. He often had friends over from abroad, and romantic companions.

"Jarryd?" Padma called again.

Geetha, who came each day from the village to cook and clean, came to the door.

"Ah! Padma Baba - I only just heard you! Have you been waiting long? Phoo, it's hot today! Come inside."

Geetha showed Padma into the sunny yellow sitting room

with its red chaise longue, pale blue sofas, and a blue and saffron antique bedspread from Jaipur hung on the wall.

"Baba, come and sit here, it's nice and cool." Geetha turned on the ceiling fan. "Jarryd Mahaththaya is sleeping – shall I wake him for you?"

"No need. I can wait."

"I'll make you some tea?"

"Okay, thanks."

Padma perched on the sofa, the fan picking up speed above her. She leaned back and gazed at the room Jarryd had lined with tall bookshelves of old valued books and sepia-print photographs of Sri Lankans in Victorian clothes, awkward and unsmiling before the camera. Jarryd had bought the photographs from the previous owners of the estate who had convinced him that the glum posed subjects were the original owners. Jarryd had paid rather more than he should have for the photographs, but he had been delighted with them. 'A house must have its people,' he had declared.

"Geetha?" Jarryd's voice came out from the bedroom at the far end of a corridor going down through the house. "Is someone there, Geetha?"

"Padma Baba's here to see you."

"I can come back another time, Jarryd," Padma called.

"No, wait! I'm coming!"

Jarryd came in a few moments later, rested looking in a freshly ironed shirt and shorts, his hair smoothed back in a ponytail. He bowed to Padma in namaste then hugged her.

"What a nice surprise! What brings you out here?"

"I was just passing."

He gave her a quizzical smile, for they both knew she didn't pass by his house to go anywhere. He sat down in an armchair, stretching out his bad leg. The white gash of his scar flashed through the leathery creases of his knee, which grew stiff after sleeping or sitting for meditation. He lifted the leg back into place with his hand, an automatic gesture for him, something he accepted about his body without judgment or regret – it was just the way it was now for him.

"Actually, I came to ask your advice," Padma said.

With Jarryd there was no need for preliminary talk or the usual evasions.

"Leela has asked to see me."

"Leela? Your mother?"

The word seemed more potent spoken by Jarryd, but even 'Amma', which she had used in the past, brought no feeling of connection; it was only a murmur on the lips.

"Apparently Leela's ill. She wants to see me this Friday," Padma said.

"Who told you this?"

"Varuna. Hema Amme gave her a message this morning."

"A complicated chain . . ." Jarryd mused. "Well, the way I see it—"

"Not now!" Padma hissed, as Geetha appeared with the tea.

Geetha's face was inscrutable, yet her disinterest was perhaps a little too determined. Had she stood for a moment in the corridor listening? How much had she heard? Possibly she imagined they were discussing the threats that Jarryd was receiving because of his guidebook. Geetha had taken some of the calls and been shaken by their violence. No wonder she was so nervous. Low voices, a note of concern, were all it would take to make her pause outside a door and listen for new developments. Poor Geetha. All day she cooked and swept and dusted Jarryd's house, waiting to go home, while the minister's men stirred up the villagers ahead of the local elections, inciting anger at other religions and the damning words of a pacifist who loved the country more than any politician. But Jarryd's love was too simple, too direct; his words were too easily misconstrued and misrepresented. Even people in surrounding villages had started to grumble and call him a traitor, Soma said. It didn't take much to make trouble among bored and dissatisfied villagers - even those whom Jarryd had helped over the years, finding them work and giving money to their children for school books and university fees and medical treatment. People forgot favours. They had no gratitude for those with money to give. Jarryd stirred honey into his tea, waiting for Geetha to leave.

"Was there any mention of Sunny?" he asked Padma, when Geetha had gone, but he kept his voice low, perhaps knowing that she might be listening at the door.

"No, it seems it's just Leela who wants to see me. Three o'clock at the bus stop on Friday. She wants me to come alone."

"It could be genuine, but you must definitely take Soma with you. Don't go alone."

"I can't tell Soma any of this! He'll go running straight to Gerhardt."

"Hmmm. Yes, Soma can be a little hot-headed. But what if I'm nearby to keep an eye on things? Just to make sure there's no dirty business - would that be of help?"

"Of course. So you think I should see her? You don't think it's another trick?"

"How can this be a trick? And what would Sunny gain?"

"I don't know. But I never know, that's the problem. I never see until it's too late."

"Well, nothing much happened last time, did it? So what if you ended up staying a little too long at their place? Gerhardt had kittens for one night, but ultimately everything turned out alright, didn't it?"

"Yes, but—"

"You see, our minds can conjure up terrible eventualities - an infinite array of ghouls and demons, devils, thieves; the masked murderer coming with his knife to slash our throats while we sleep – but in actual fact, life flows on with mostly very minor disruptions. People behave unskilfully, as the Buddha called it from greed, and desire and the fear of pain – and they are a nuisance, but that is all. You must always remember that it is unskilful thinking that lies beneath what they do."

"Sunny's different. He's mean. He likes to hurt people. I'll tell you something if you promise not to tell Gerhardt—"

"What?"

"First promise."

"Okay, I promise. What?"

"When I was at Sunny's house, I was sure they'd drugged my tea, or my food."

Jarryd looked disbelieving.

"He came into my room at night," Padma added.

"What? Sunny came into your room? At night?"

"And Mukul."

"Both of them?" Jarryd was sitting bolt upright.

"They came in separately, but they didn't do anything. I pretended to be sleeping and I saw Sunny look through my bag. But he didn't take anything. Then he ate the cutlets I hadn't eaten."

Jarryd laughed with relief. "He came for the cutlets! What a tale! You had me scared there for a minute!"

"But there was something odd: he sniffed the cutlets before he ate them—"

Jarryd just chuckled.

"It was as if he was checking them, as if they were drugged."

"But you can't smell a crushed pill, silly! I think you can put his behaviour down to poor table manners."

"I thought maybe he did it unconsciously because he knew they'd put something in the tea – an instinctive need to check, maybe?" Even she had to admit that her fears sounded excessive.

"Sunny makes me crazy," she conceded.

Even in the days when Gerhardt paid Sunny to stay away, there used to be sightings of him – a sudden glimpse from a car window of Sunny darting out of their way as they were driving somewhere. She had spotted him inside a half-built building once, watching her. It took her weeks to forget seeing him, and to become again the Padma who was Gerhardt's own and lived safely at the villa. It was surprising how much effort was required to regain that version of herself.

"It was a bad party, but it's over now," Jarryd said. "And you survived Sunny's tricks – that is what you must take from this."

She could have told him that a few days later Sunny had come to the villa and tried to strangle her, but it was too ugly, too frightening still to say out loud. Jarryd would try to understand and explain why, but she didn't want to be confused this time, for she knew what she had seen when she looked up into Sunny's face. Jarryd would never admit it possible, but she had seen the dark venom in Sunny meant for her, for Sunny had lost control that night and revealed it. Of course, he had frightened her before when she was young, but then he had been relaxed and commanding, the beatings an exercise of skill, a measured release of the violence in him. He was able to judge when to stop and how much pain he was going to give. At the villa his anger had burst its containment and overtaken him. She tried not to imagine what would have happened if Rohan hadn't been there. Jarryd's belief in mankind's inherent goodness was unsafe extended to Sunny. On this one thing she trusted herself.

"You know, maybe this has nothing to do with Sunny, it's Leela who wants to see you," Jarryd observed.

"Why now though? She had plenty of time to talk to me when I was at their house."

"Maybe she couldn't get away from Sunny. Could he have drugged her cutlets? What if she's finally found a time when he won't be around? Maybe this is her one chance? A cry for help, perhaps?"

"Oh God! I wish I could know for sure!"

"Go and see her. You need to. Girls need their mothers," Jarryd urged. "A mother is the central most important figure in a person's becoming-Self. Here in Asia, the Mother Goddess reigns supreme, for the Hindus at least – think of Kali, the Divine Mother, ferocious and angry and full of love, so much love emanates from her. The Hindus are not afraid of love, their mythology embraces it, rejoices in it – pure unfettered brilliant love, they believe in it unfailingly. This could be your time to find it, my little one – maybe your mother is finally holding her arms out to you."

"You think so?"

"I feel it, yes. There is something compelling her to meet you. She's gone to so much trouble to get in touch with you."

"She probably wants money."

"So wait and see, and you can refuse her if she asks – but hear her. What harm can it do to listen? Of course, if you are proven right, your feelings will be hurt; and of course your heart will long for more and ache from being denied—"

"I don't want anything from her."

"A mother's love is something that we all desire. When it doesn't arise, it is life's way of making us grow, and your love may make *her* grow. Your kindness might be what she is reaching for to help her transform, to live a more pure and radiant existence—"

"I suppose I could go and see what she wants. Will you really come with me?"

"I would be honoured to help. I will go to the site a little earlier than your meeting and I will walk around the stalls, keeping a look out for any skulduggery. Then I will sit at the bus stop like

I'm waiting to go somewhere. I'll bring a newspaper – I can hide behind it – how about that?"

"It might work."

There was no chance of him not being recognised, but he often took the bus to visit his friends in the area, preferring to travel like the locals. Even if Leela guessed that he was looking out for Padma, why shouldn't he be there for her?

"I will be at or near the bus-stop from two forty-five p.m. onwards," Jarryd declared. "I will wear a hat – my Panama, and maybe a jacket. I've got an old linen one that I haven't taken out in years, no one will remember it. I'll try and look like some old expat guy – all very British and pukka." His eyes glowed with intrigue.

Padma stood up as if to stretch her legs and glanced into the dining room. There was no one there, but she ran barefoot, silently to the doorway at the back, and there was Geetha sweeping the corridor of the back courtyard, just outside the door.

"Do you need anything, Baba?" she asked innocently.

"I came to say goodbye."

"Okay, see you soon! Go safely. Ah! I just remembered – I made some jaggery cake! Wait a moment, Baba – I'll get you some to take home with you."

Geetha hurried to the kitchen, a large sooty room off the old-fashioned courtyard with its sacks of coconuts and stacked firewood. Inside the kitchen, during the yoga retreats, village women arrived to cook on a long, raised hearth, curries simmering in charred clay pots: pure vegetarian feasts that were carried over to the retreat huts. The students from all over the West sat on the floor and ate with their fingers off plantain leaves cut fresh that same morning.

In the kitchen now the clay cooking pots were stacked in rounded black columns. Geetha was cutting cake on the cement worktop. In the shadowy room, the faded pink of her blouse, the green of her long cloth tied at the waist, glowed, dense bright flashes of colour.

How much had Geetha heard? Would she tell anyone? But there was nothing to tell. Padma calmed the unease inside her as if settling a child.

"Here Baba. There's enough for Gerhardt Mahatththaya and Soma as well – say hello to them from me, won't you?" Geetha pressed the foil-wrapped cake into Padma's hands. "You take care, okay, Baba? You shouldn't be riding around here on your own, it isn't safe at the moment."

"It's fine, I didn't see anyone."

"You can't see them, Baba. But they're there."

Padma hugged Geetha. She had never hugged her before. Geetha looked like she was about to cry as Padma left.

Jarryd watched from the veranda as Padma rode away. He smiled and waved, always at ease in his sweet luxurious home. Soon he would go to Boss's café and dance in the sea. The graceful old cashew trees and jak trees rose high over the driveway as Padma left Jarryd's world and went out into the sun.

## 13

FROM THE GARDEN, Padma watched Ria on her veranda, doing yoga again – a long fluid sequence full of supine poses followed by a headstand which she held for many minutes before coming down with perfect control. It was a well-structured sequence with many difficult poses that Ria performed simply, modestly with no flashiness. Ria's students would feel inspired, not intimidated, seeing her.

Padma went inside to find Soma who had just woken from his afternoon nap.

"Can you make chai? Like in India?" she asked him.

He took out a pan and poured in milk.

"For two people," she added.

"Are you going to charge him?"

"It's for Ria. I thought she might like it after yoga."

"Ah, then it doesn't matter." Soma carefully measured out tea and cloves and cardamoms to boil with the milk and took out two fine china cups and set them on a tray, adding a small bowl of milk toffee chunks.

Padma took the tray to Ria on her veranda.

"What's this?"

"Chai tea, it's on the house."

"Thank you! We drink chai in the evenings at the yoga retreat in Goa."

"I thought you might." Padma sat on the step next to Ria. "I trained as a yoga teacher too," she added.

"You're a teacher as well? Well why didn't you say?"

"I'm not fully qualified. I never took my final exam."

"Oh. That's a shame."

"I was doing badly at university so I gave up the yoga to study, but I failed the university exams anyway! And now I'm back here."

"So you can finish the yoga training," Ria said.

"Oh no! No more exams! I'm no good at exams."

"But the teacher training one isn't like an academic exam."

Ria was clever; she would never understand. Padma had trembled uncontrollably and almost vomited onto the desk as she sat in the silent rows of hunched-over figures in the university's great hall.

"They're mostly practical, the yoga teaching exams," Ria said.

"The institute would never let me go back. My teachers were really disappointed when I left," Padma said.

She had never told them that she was enrolled at the university – at fact of her life that she had left outside in the street as she stepped into the tree-filled courtyard of the institute, becoming a simpler version of herself; unburdened, unfettered.

"You should contact the institute and tell them what happened, I'm sure they'd understand," Ria said.

"No, they won't. I ignored all their emails and phone calls – they'll be furious. Anyway, I don't think I'm good enough to teach."

"Aha!" Ria grinned. "I knew it! A perfectionist! It means you'll make an excellent teacher."

"Yeah right."

But now Padma remembered one of her teachers praising her technique, and Jarryd declaring her a gifted teacher.

"If you get your certificate, maybe we could teach together

in Goa," Ria said. "We could sit by the beach and drink chai together!"

Padma smiled. She sipped her tea and sat looking through the trees at the sea with the sky changing above, the colours deepening.

"At my aunt's house they drink Nescafé with condensed milk after their naps," Ria said. "We used to all sit on her balcony and plan our evening. There used to be so many parties when I was younger."

"Do you have lots of family in Colombo?"

"Yeah."

Like Rohan, Ria would belong to an educated elite, their children sent abroad to study and travel, able to stride easily around the world. The silky folds of family would await their return with aunts and uncles eager to see what they had learned; cousins to share secrets with and family jokes. Padma's own family circle was odd in comparison, made up of Gerhardt and Ruth, Soma and Jarryd and the friends they had made all scattered across continents. She had never needed anyone else, but she had gazed at those sprawling settled families at weddings, and weekends away at expensive hotels, such impenetrable clusters, so solidly formed.

"It must be nice to come back and see them all. Didn't they mind you leaving to come here?"

"They were delighted to see the back of me," Ria said.

Padma laughed.

"I'm not joking. It was a disaster, my big trip back to see them."

"Really?"

"Just because I'd had a few boyfriends my aunt wouldn't let me go out of her house alone – in case I made off with someone in Sri Lanka and caused a scandal. They didn't seem to understand that I'd come back just to be with them."

Ria looked up into the jak tree where a woodpecker rapped boldly, tock-tock-tock.

"Why are people here so afraid of difference?" Ria mused. "What gives them the right to imagine your private thoughts and deem them wrong and think they can change you?"

How could Ria's relatives have been so blind to her? What misery for her, to be so powerless to change how others saw her.

"You're a wonderful, intelligent, beautiful woman - if your relatives can't see that that, they don't deserve you," Padma exclaimed. "They're missing out, not you. I'd be so proud to be related to you."

Ria seemed taken aback, she looked embarrassed. Padma blushed, wishing she had not spoken.

"You're so kind," Ria said. "All of you. Gerhardt and Soma and Wilson too - and I'm just a guest."

"But now you're our friend."

"Who needs family when you can have friends?" Ria said.

"One day, our families may need us more than we need them," Padma reflected.

This was her power now. Leela hadn't come near the villa for twelve years, but now she was old and sick and all she wanted was Padma. Leela wanting her and needing her was what Padma had longed for. It was love, in its way.

Rohan seemed as eager as ever to talk at dinner that evening. Ever since the incident with Sunny, all Rohan had wanted was to hatch plans to help Padma escape. Padma avoided him. In the end Rohan turned to Ria and talked with her across the veranda. They both knew the same places in London. Maybe when they returned they would go to them together. Ria matched Rohan perfectly: educated, good-looking, intelligent, they would be happy together. Padma tried not to listen to their conversation. She rearranged Jarryd's books on the sideboard and waited for the guests to leave. A few times she saw Rohan glance over at her, but he went on talking with Ria. Padma went to the office, closing the door on his voice recounting an incident and Ria's laughter. Padma turned on the computer and typed into Google: 'Yoga. Teacher training. Colombo. Sri Lanka'. And there it was at the top of the list: the longest established yoga institute in the country. It had five stars and long glowing reviews from satisfied students. It was Padma's teacher there who had told her about the teacher training course after Padma had been going regularly for a year. She had signed up in secret, only telling Gerhardt and Ruth many months later and even then, claiming to only be doing it to study more complex postures. She had progressed steadily, until her university tutors had warned her that she was likely to fail again, which was when she stopped going to the institute and went to the library instead, trying to compel her mutinous mind to absorb the very facts that it resisted, and refused to take in. Strangely, true desires never protested when they were abandoned; the most cherished dreams could slip so quietly away, they went unnoticed.

There were new photographs of the institute on their website. Nothing had changed: the rooms were still painted white, with deep shuttered windows and ceiling fans. In the courtyard garden there were still benches under the trees where students sat during tea breaks. She clicked on 'About Us' and familiar faces smiled out: there were more teachers now, photographed standing before the walls of the garden where jasmine and magenta bougainvillea trailed. Padma typed out an email and pressed 'Send'. There! She couldn't undo it now. She didn't want to. She had wanted to return all along. Would they reply and politely refuse her? For behind the smiles and kindness, the institute's directors were demanding and serious. Prospective teachers had to have chosen their path with clear unwavering intention; this was the only way to belong there.

Padma returned to the veranda and found Ria and Rohan gone. Had they left together? They were not in the garden. Possibly they had settled in one of their bungalows, talking, growing close; or maybe kissing on Ria's makeshift sofa, tangled in her red shawl . . . Padma went outside and peered through the trees at Ria's bungalow, but the curtains were drawn tight. At Rohan's too, there was nothing to see, just the dark screened windows.

The next day Padma slipped out of the house just before three o'clock, as the others rested in their rooms. Leela was nowhere to be seen near the bus stop, but Jarryd was already there, browsing the stalls in his disguise, a crumpled linen blazer and pale linen trousers, his hair in a bun under a Panama hat. He glanced once in her direction, his aviator glasses glinting darkly. He pretended not to know her, appearing to be busy buying incense. Buses came and went from the bus stop. The sun blazed down. The minister had promised the villagers improvements to the old dusty roads, and this he had provided, just before the local elections began. The new tarmac was spongy and soft in the heat, glistening black, giving way under her sandals. She stopped by the tree where the tuk-tuk drivers gathered and watched the bus stop. A bus arrived and people descended. Others went on board. As the bus pulled away, a figure wavered into view through the fumes: Leela, ghostly pale in a white cotton sari and white blouse, like someone bereaved or taking sil. Padma waited as Leela approached. Would other daughters have run to embrace a mother? What would they say when they reached her?

"Let's go over there, under that tree," Leela said as she came up to Padma.

She didn't seem surprised that Padma had come. Had Leela known that she would? There was no reason for her to assume that Padma would obey her. Should Padma have refused?

In the shade they were hidden from the stalls. Jarryd could not see her now. But he would have seen where they had gone, she hoped. He was watching from somewhere, she assured herself. She glanced around but she couldn't see him, but she didn't see Sunny or Mukul either; Leela appeared to have come alone.

"So you got the message," Leela said.

"Yes. Are you alright?"

Leela was silent. Then tears sprang from her eyes.

"What is it?" Padma asked.

"I'm not alright." Leela briskly wiped away her tears with the back of her wrist, like when she chopped onions, when she would squat in the yard by a mound of small red onions, peeling and cutting them fine with the knife that Sunny had brandished over her in a fight that Padma had watched from behind a curtain. The knife that Padma had held later, imagining sliding it into Sunny as he slept, slicing it across his neck or sinking it deep into his heart, freeing them all. But she had put the knife back in the drawer. Murderers went to prison and Padma had never wanted to give Sunny that victory over her.

"Are you ill?" Padma said to Leela.

"I have to leave," Leela whispered. "I can't live with that man anymore – not now that I'm sick. All the bad things he's done – I don't want him near me. I want to be on my own somewhere. You'd come and see me if he weren't there, wouldn't you?"

"Of course I would – you know I would – that's why I stayed that night at the party, to talk with you, but you never came."

"When he's there I can't talk – all that night he wouldn't leave me alone. But he's gone out somewhere today, that's how I could come. Mukul is just as bad – hopefully he will marry soon and go and live somewhere else. I've done enough for those men. In these last few months of my life, all I want is to see my own daughter."

"What do you mean, last few months?"

"I haven't got long, Putha." Leela's voice broke. "I have this sickness now."

She fumbled in her bag and brought out a letter. It was from a hospital in Welligama. The Urology Department. Treatment for the part-failure of the kidneys. Leela didn't live anywhere near Welligama, but it was one of the larger hospitals. Had Leela been sent there because of the severity of her condition? She did look frail. Her eyes were red from crying. Fear crept over Padma. Did Leela need a transplant? Padma had read of family giving up a kidney for an ailing loved one – was that what Leela had come to ask for? Padma's head swam with fear. She couldn't. She wouldn't – she'd be left with only one. And if that failed, there would only be those who loved her, to ask for a spare – and they were unlikely to be a match. The people she was related to would never give up anything for her; they would slink off and leave her to die. No, Leela wasn't getting a kidney from Padma; it was too big a sacrifice to ask. Guilt swept through Padma, and the fear grew, for now she would be haunted by her refusal for the rest of her life. She looked down at the small weeping figure before her, wishing she had not met her.

"The doctors say they can make it better if I have the medicine," Leela said.

"Medicine? Is that's all you need? Well why didn't you say?" Padma almost shouted with relief.

"How can I ever afford such things?" Leela said sadly.

"I can help you."

"It's not cheap, how can I ask you to pay for my treatment? Gerhardt will never let you."

"He doesn't have to know. I make my own money now." Even if that money came from Gerhardt, it was still a business loan; it was hers to spend as she needed.

"You're sure?" Leela asked.

"Of course. But where will you go if you leave Sunny?"

Tears ran down Leela's thin cheeks. "All I pray for is to live my last years in peace," she sobbed.

"You will. I will make sure of it." One day maybe Leela would beam with love and admiration for the daughter who had helped her to safety.

"I want to go to Galle," Leela said. "My mother's side are still there; how happy I was with them as a child! They will look after me. I only need a small place, just a couple of rooms - one for me, one for you if you come to visit. I'd keep it so clean and nice, no one would bother us there."

"And I could meet your family?"

"Oh, yes, how they would like to see you, all grown up and doing well. How proud they will be of everything you've done."

"We'll find you a nice house near them, when you're better." Padma promised.

Leela pulled out a handkerchief from between her breasts and wiped her eyes. Padma tried not to stare at the dark withered skin of those empty breasts, their flaccid shivering flesh. Padma's own breasts were plump and rounded - would they ever grow so depleted, so spent? "When is your treatment?" Padma asked.

"At the end of the month. I don't have to pay for all of it at once - just one treatment at a time. But can you find ten thousand rupees?"

Padma had it many times over, yet to Leela it was an impossible amount. Wealth created distance, a secret gradient of ease and hardship; privilege and envy and guilt.

"How will I get the money to you?" Padma asked.

"I opened a bank account." Leela fumbled in her bag and handed Padma a slip of paper. "Here's the number. Don't tell Sunny, will you? I'm trying to save up for when I go. He'll be getting back soon - I'd better go. Don't say anything to anyone, alright?"

She couldn't tell Gerhardt, not this. He would have stopped her. He would have called the lawyer and asked him to investigate

– and somehow Sunny would find out. A daughter could have secrets with her mother. Leela needed her now. Leela wanted to have a house with a room kept ready for her.

"I'll let you know the amount," Leela said. "I won't be able to travel once the treatments have started. I'll send Hema Amme. No need to give her the money, just pay it into the account."

Leela wasn't dumb. She knew how to handle that old rogue Hema Amme. How lonely, having only such friends.

"That's my bus," Leela said as a bus pulled into the bus stop.

Padma reached out to embrace her but Leela started to run. She hauled herself onto the steps of the bus and went in. Padma saw her lurching along, sinking into a seat. Padma waited as the bus drove away. Leela didn't turn back. Padma went around the stalls, searching for Jarryd.

# 14

PADMA'S PHONE RANG. It was Jarryd.

"I'll meet you at Boss's. I've hidden some clothes at the dobi's house – I'll change and be with you in five minutes," he whispered.

Padma kept to the shade of the lane, leaving the village behind. The lane was almost a place of safety, almost her domain. She stepped out of the way of a bicycle, then a scooter racing past. A monitor lizard strode through the long grass, then clambered down to the ditch and disappeared down a drain. Padma went through Boss's Bar into the garden. She ordered a Fanta, for the first time not able to tell Boss of a strange unsettling encounter. Jarryd arrived soon after her, tucking his bag of disguises under the table.

"Well? What happened? You two were talking for ages," he said.

"She's leaving Sunny."

"*Leaving* him? Really? They've been together for a very long time . . ."

"All the more reason, don't you think?"

"But why now?"

"Because she's sick. And Mukul will probably get married and go soon. Leela needs to stay and have medical treatment, but then she wants to move to Galle, to be near family."

"What's wrong with her?"

"Kidney trouble. All she needs is the right medication. Falling ill has made her question how she's been living . . ."

"It's possible," Jarryd considered. "The kidneys are instruments of cleansing – maybe in healing them Leela is being inspired to cleanse her life."

"Maybe, yeah . . ."

Boss approached and they stopped talking. Boss brought Jarryd a mango lassi, made to Jarryd's precise instructions, with crushed cardamoms and pistachios sprinkled on top. Jarryd sipped it appreciatively. He practised mindfulness even while eating and drinking, savouring every instant of his experience.

"Sir – there's something I have to tell you." Boss hovered anxiously behind Jarryd.

"A problem?" Jarryd asked.

"Earlier some people came and told me to stop selling your book."

"But that's ridiculous!" Jarryd laughed. "You only sold six copies here!"

"I don't know what to do, sir. This is my bar and I can do what I like, but I don't want any trouble – not with the minister's people, they're too much for us." Boss looked crushed by having to admit his impotence.

"You have been a good friend," Jarryd assured him. "How very many months you have promoted my small pamphlet – that's plenty. I will take the copies away today. But my goodness, what an absolute fool that minister is, making such a fuss."

"It's getting him support from the locals," Boss said.

"Why are people so easily galvanised by invented enemies?" Jarryd exclaimed.

"You could do a reprint with the politics taken out," Padma suggested.

"Yes! Even if you just took out the part about corrupt politicians," Boss urged.

"But I don't name names!"

"You wrote that the South has always been run by bandits and ruffians," Padma reminded him.

"If our venerable minister wants to think of himself as a bandit and a ruffian, that is his choice!"

"He's too powerful these days," Boss said glumly. "So many have been killed or disappeared by him - some just for refusing to do business; my men can't fight his. His have money from the government for training and arms. You wait and see, he'll be in the cabinet soon."

"Only because of his cousin," Padma said.

"Of course." Boss didn't begrudge him that. Like most Sri Lankans, he had no quibble with nepotism; family were the people who helped you to succeed; they were the only ones to trust. Family wanted the very best for you - that was what everyone said.

"My book is still selling in the bookshops," Jarryd consoled himself.

"And you can sell it online," Padma suggested. "You could sell it abroad - that way it won't attract so much attention over here."

"But that's the very idea!" Jarryd cried. "It's our people who need to read my book most of all! They need to see that they must stand up against these scheming politicians doing deals with corrupt businessmen and manipulating divisions between us all."

Boss left them to serve new customers and Jarryd sat in silence, looking out to sea.

"Aren't you dancing this evening?" Padma asked.

"Maybe later."

"It's still a great book," Padma consoled.

Jarryd smiled. To him, insults, betrayals, even crimes rose from the frailty of people; they were to be forgiven and understood. An idealist, Ruth called him – Sri Lankans had always fought each other, she argued; peace was not in the Sri Lankan's nature and the social inclusion he strove for was a Western liberal fantasy. Gerhardt blamed Jarryd's innate perfectionism; dancers controlled their bodies and pushed them to new extremes in search of ideals, and Jarryd, Gerhardt maintained, had been trained from an early age to strive for the impossible; he was driven by the unattainable. But Padma knew that it was love that drove Jarryd. Jarryd loved Sri Lanka and its people – he didn't see their faults, all their hatred and spite and cruelty, or the ugly nationalist pride, or the envy. Jarryd never saw ugliness, he looked past it straight to the source – to the pain of prejudice, and disadvantage; the injustice of race and wealth and class. He longed to heal those rifts, to nourish lives and restore them to a time of respectful ancient ways. His book was a call to everyone who loved the country as he did, to rise up to protect and preserve it. But Jarryd loved too easily. Sri Lanka was not the precious secret isle he longed it to be, for however much its people smiled and gave you gifts, Sri Lanka was a country riven at the heart; a fissure made of years of division, gouged too deeply to make whole and new. Love alone could not fuse those fractured shards; love could only reach longingly across the divide.

"Isn't it fascinating that our dear minister is so troubled by my book?" Jarryd mused. "It's as if he has seen himself for the first time and recognised his reflection."

"I don't think he likes what he's seeing."

"Of course not, and rightly so! He has much to be ashamed of. This could be the start of his rehabilitation."

"He's not going to change, Jarryd."

"Then he must learn that he cannot stamp out the voices of change! I will be that voice! I will write of this latest infringement;

it will make a fantastic article!" Jarryd's grey eyes blazed blindly. He was angry about the ban, just as he had been angry when he wrote his book - of course he would never have admitted as much, but he had written it in the year when he was recuperating after the robbery and the senseless destruction of the life he had built.

But even then, his anger had spared his attackers, seeing them as the dispossessed and disadvantaged of a system they couldn't change, thus needing to be forgiven and understood. His anger was at those who exploited the country, denying its people their share of its natural abundance and beauty. Jarryd believed that beauty and freedom could be enjoyed by all - this was where he differed most from Gerhardt. Jarryd refused to accept the need for high walls and guard dogs to preserve what one prized most. Padma longed to believe like Jarryd in the power of truth and openness - this mattered more to him than inspiring vistas and surroundings. Like Jarryd, she longed to throw open the gates and be free to speak out.

Back at the villa all was quiet. On the veranda of the main house Ria sat reading alone, a pot of tea and a plate of Soma's pink wafer biscuits on the table before her. She smiled looking up as Padma entered, but Padma went on. There was no time to talk. In the office she turned on the computer, opened up her bank accounts. Her own had grown, fattened by the salary she paid herself, for while living at the villa she had nothing to spend it on. She transferred the money for treatment to Leela and the balance shrank abruptly. But it was Padma's money to do with as she liked. So why did it feel like stealing?

※

Ria paused reading and watched the last blaze of the afternoon over the sea. A breeze passed, bringing in the evening, the trees shaking themselves out from the day. A tourist with a backpack stopped at the gate looking in. He came into the garden and started to walk up towards the house. His light sun-bleached hair gleamed pale. He was tall and slim and tanned. The dog started barking inside the house and ran out.

"Padma!" Ria called into the house.

The man had stopped on the path. He didn't seem afraid, even when the dog scudded down to him.

"Padma! There's someone here!" Ria shouted.

Padma came running out, looking frightened.

"Oh! A guest!" She laughed and went out to meet the man.

"Do you have any rooms free?" the man asked Padma.

"There's one left, but it's not a bungalow."

"Can I take a look?"

"Of course. This way."

The dog leaped around the man as they came inside.

"Gustav! Sit down over there!" Padma ordered.

The man looked to Ria and smiled. Then he followed Padma into the hall. Ria opened her book, seeing only the smile and the blue eyes looking across the room to her, meeting her gaze.

Padma unlocked the door of the guest room and Ria saw the man go inside, knowing to feel for the fan switch by the door, and she knew that he had been in Asia before.

"Great, I'll take it," she heard him say.

The man chatted easily with Padma, at ease with himself like someone who had travelled alone before. They talked at the door of the room.

"My friends decided to go to Thailand, but I'm so glad I stayed," he told Padma. "At last I can see this amazing country in my own time, do things my way, you know what I mean? I hate rushing around being part of a big tour group, being told how to see a place."

Even someone strikingly handsome like him would be left in peace in Asia. He wouldn't be judged strange or loose for being alone. He would be able to sit at a bar, or on the beach and there would be no men to avoid, no one to fear; that was what made men bold, the freedom to be themselves, to go where they chose.

"So dinner is at seven, on the veranda," Padma told the man and leaving him in the room, she came out to the veranda.

"Not bad, huh?" she whispered to Ria.

"Not bad at all."

With a quick glance over her shoulder, Padma opened the man's passport: a British passport. Padma flicked through the stamped pages.

"He's travelled a lot," she said and turned to the photograph. "Wow." She held up the page for Ria to admire. "Even without the tan."

Ria smiled.

"He was born in Paris," Padma read. "He's called Louis. Louis Forrester. Do you think his mother's French? The surname sounds English."

No facts that they gleaned about him would undo his otherness. He would stay a stranger unless he decided to let them in.

Ria didn't take her book to dinner that night. She faced the stillness of the evening, its blackness blocking out the world. The day was folding into itself, the sadness of night swirling in, and the fear of having been left behind, of drifting. The waves gleamed with moonlight. Ria watched the sea rocking, soothing itself.

"Hi? Excuse me? Would you mind if I joined you?"

She looked up and the new guest was standing beside her table.

"Yeah. Sure."

He had changed for dinner, into cotton trousers and an

indigo-blue linen shirt, expensive yet careless looking. The sleeves were loosely rolled up, his arms tanned dark gold. He sat facing her.

"You don't mind?" he asked.

"No."

"You're sure? I have my own table – that one in the middle of the room is mine, apparently. Please don't feel obliged—"

"I don't." She smiled.

His eyes were green, not blue.

"Really. I mean it. I can move if you want to be alone."

She laughed. It felt good not to be alone anymore.

"I'm Louis."

His hair was bleached white at the temples by sun and salt. He had swum in the sea. Every day perhaps, striking out far into the blue, unafraid. Unafraid perhaps of currents even – and maybe if you weren't they never got you.

Padma came up, and with a sly smile at Ria, moved the white plate, fork and spoon from his table to hers. Soma brought out blue and white china bowls of fried rice and chicken curry for him and fried rice and pumpkin curry for her.

"You're vegetarian?" Louis asked.

"Only when I feel like it."

"That's the best way, then you don't feel deprived."

"Exactly!" It felt right that he understood.

"Choice is good," Louis said, serving himself rice.

"Cheers to choice!" She raised her glass.

He raised his.

"Are you're travelling alone?" he asked.

"Yes."

"And you're not afraid?"

"Not really. Why?"

"It doesn't seem safe, a woman on her own in a place like this."

"It's safe here at the villa. Anyway, I wanted to get out of Colombo."

"Couldn't you have come with family?"

How little he knew. They hadn't exactly been queueing up to join her when she announced her trip. Some had seemed a little affronted. "Aren't we interesting enough for you?" an uncle had asked unsmilingly. Only her aunt and the two maids had stayed to say goodbye when she left.

"It might have been safer to come in a group," Louis said.

"I don't like groups."

"Me neither."

She laughed. She had known it about him the first moment she saw him, strolling up the path with his backpack.

She loved that he only had one bag for his travels and could still be immaculately dressed for dinner. Louis, she sensed, could pack up his life with ease into that expensive backpack. Sometimes she craved such efficiency, to be pared down to essentials: a few clothes, a yoga mat, a cushion and a blanket – to know what to choose was a skill; it meant knowing yourself and what you really needed. When she packed, she kept all options open, imagining so many eventualities, anxious to be able to make herself at home. Everywhere she went she searched for a home, for the feeling of being at home that eluded her everywhere.

"Do you know any good places for a drink after dinner?" Louis asked.

"No."

"Would you like to walk on the beach?"

"I'd love to."

Padma took away their plates and brought out fruit salad.

"Could I order two more beers?" Louis said. "And could you leave them unopened? We'll take them to the beach."

"Ooh that sounds nice!" Padma grinned.

Ria laughed and Louis smiled with her. There were golden flecks in the green of his eyes, layer upon layer of glassy depths. Gerhardt came in to say goodnight and left for his house in the village. Ria left with Louis soon after. Ria felt the house solid and peaceful waiting for her to return, as she entered the night.

From the veranda, Padma watched Ria and Louis leave, their voices distant and private.

"Ah, the mating rituals of the single traveller," Rohan observed.

"Sour grapes!"

"Sour grapes? Why?"

At school she had hated the way the flirty girls played silly prying games with the boys they liked.

"I was just joking," she said quickly.

"But what did you mean?"

"I just meant that you might have missed your chance with Ria – I'm sure you haven't though, but you should make a move soon—"

"What are you talking about?"

"You need to be quick to get someone like Ria."

"But I don't want her. So to speak."

"You have to start re-bounding sometime, you know."

"Oh, do I?"

"Yes! It's important to enjoy yourself. Otherwise you become old and bitter."

"If I went for Ria, you could go after that dude Louis," Rohan observed.

"Hmmm, not a bad idea." Padma blew out the oil lamp on Ria's table.

"Would you like some beer?" Rohan asked.

"Okay."

They shared his bottle of Lion beer.

"To think that you nearly threw me out a few days ago. Who'd have thought we'd be doing this?" Rohan said.

"You should get your aunts to check out our horoscopes."

He laughed. He didn't know that he knew nothing about her. Sunny would remain a distant uncle. That was the closest he would get to her truth. Without her past she was free; she was just like anyone else.

Ria walked at the water's edge, the foaming black water slyly reaching out to catch her and pull her in. The sea seemed apart from those teasing cold waves, a place dark and heavy and far away.

'All kinds of unsavoury types hang around those remote beaches,' Ria's uncle had warned her. "It would be madness to go to such places, especially at night."

And here she was, with a man she didn't know, no one else around for miles. The wind blew gently, lifting her hair; how glad she was to not have listened.

"This is great!" she said.

"Shall we go in?"

"Into the sea? *Now?*"

"Come on! I dare you!"

"What about the currents?"

"What about them?" He pulled off his shirt and undid the zip of his trousers. "We won't go in far."

She glanced around at the long empty beach, the dense shield of coconut trees. The lane was a long way behind.

"There's no one to see us, they're all at the bars. No one's coming this way."

Louis gently pulled her to him, undoing the buttons of her shirt. She let him, and untied the belt of her trousers. He gazed admiringly as she undid her bra. They held hands as they ran to the water and waded in, the water rising up around her. Before her the horizon spread wide, a vast emptiness. She screamed as the first wave hit. The sea pulled her in and tossed her back. She twisted and was carried away. She grasped Louis as he swam beside her, trying to stay close until the wave passed and she could tread water, her eyes fixed on the heaving blackness ahead, an endless vastness, offering no edge, no limit. One could be lost in that sea forever.

It was how she had imagined Nirvana, this infinite blackness, this smallness and nothingness. As a child she would ache with fear and a desperate sadness, imagining that nothingness. Yet Nirvana was what the Buddhists asked for in their prayers – the very prayers that her father made her repeat after him at night. When she began to leave out the relevant line, her father had insisted she say it and she had fought back harder than he expected and won. But he had stayed disappointed, for he disliked omissions and alterations to tradition. But who in their right mind would aspire to a deathless state, with nothing to hope for, no future, nothing else possible – for *ever*. When she was dead, she wanted to return to the world of people, to be back among the sinners, even as a beetle or an ant or a butterfly with just days of life ahead, but each day rich with possibility. Even her father had gone searching for love in the end, leaving Ria and her mother for a woman in Australia, which was when the tussle of night time prayers had finally ended.

Another wave hurled at Ria, lifting her and rolling her over. She was alone. Louis had let go. She kicked and struggled and fought the water, crying out. Louis swam over to her. She laughed with relief and clung to his cold muscled body.

"I'm going back to the beach," she said, but a new wave came, rising over her and taking her away in its great watery curl, her body small and powerless. She was turned by the wave, inside its black whorl; she was flotsam, weightless, shrill with terror. As the water crashed down, she struck out for the shore.

She stumbled onto the beach, as if from another life. Louis came running behind her.

"Wow! That's the way to end an evening!" he cried, his eyes wild and gleeful.

They dried themselves with their shirts and put on their clothes.

"Wasn't that great?" Louis said.

"I feel like I've been through ritual waters."

"Next time we'll go in further."

"No bloody way."

He laughed. He thought she was joking.

"Would you like a beer?" he asked.

"Let's take it back to my bungalow. We can sit on the veranda."

As they walked towards the lane, two figures stepped out from the dark of the coconut trees; two men, Sri Lankans, one young and slim with a tangled mop of hair, the other older, short and wiry.

"Hello there!" the older man said.

The younger man stared at Ria. He smiled strangely and she wondered if he had been watching her on the beach.

"You want some ganja?" the younger man asked Louis.

"Maybe." Louis turned enquiringly to Ria.

"Not for me, thanks. I want to get back." She couldn't get past the men, who had blocked the way back to the lane. There was no other way through the trees. She stayed close to Louis.

"Maybe not tonight, guys," he told the men. "How much is it, just so I know?"

The younger man told him and they haggled over the price.

"I'll think about it," Louis said.

"Don't take too long. It's the cheapest you're going to get. I'm not even supposed to be selling it here - if any of the local guys find out, I'm in big trouble. If you want some, buy it now."

"Sorry. Maybe another time."

Louis edged past the men and Ria went with him. The men came behind them.

"I have nothing to sell, but maybe I can be of help to sir and madam," the older man said. "How about taking a trip soon? Have you been to a spice garden? I know a lovely place, just a few hours from here, I can get you a car and a driver?"

"No thanks," Ria said.

"Madam, you are from here, no, but what about sir? He might like to see the beautiful spice bushes growing – what do you say, sir?"

"No thanks," Louis said.

"How about an elephant orphanage? Or a safari park? You want to see leopards? Birds?"

"We don't need anything, thank you." Ria crossed over the lane, Louis trying politely to tell the men to go. The villa gates were a few steps away. The lights of the house beckoning.

"You're staying here?" the younger man demanded.

"Yes." Louis said.

"Both of you? Together?"

"No, we've only just met," Louis said.

"Ah, so the place must be full," the older man mused. "All three rooms taken. How nice, very nice, the owner must be happy. You know him? Gerhardt Hundsler's his name; a good friend of mine. We go back a long way. You've met the girl? She's pretty, no?"

The younger man snorted and walked away.

"She'll look after you well – just ask her for anything," the older man gave Louis a suggestive smile.

"Let's go," Ria said, but the man still had Louis' attention.

"She's a funny one, the girl who works there – be careful, sir. All kinds of things are being said about her," the man said.

"Like what?" Louis asked.

"I'm going," Ria said and started walking.

"Hang on a minute, Ria." Louis caught her hand, but she twisted out from his grip.

She noted the little flare of interest in the man watching that single jarring moment. She moved closer to Louis and he put his arm around her. She let him. The man's gaze was fixed on Louis' hand on her shoulder.

"Don't be upset, madam, I also don't like to talk ill of others, what is it to anyone if she is being with an old man?"

"Which old man?" Louis sounded shocked.

"He means Gerhardt, the owner, you haven't met him yet," Ria said impatiently. "But he's her father, for God's sake!"

"*Father?* Is that what she's telling people these days?" the man sniggered. "She's a right one, that Padma."

Ria pulled away from Louis and went into the garden. He followed, shutting the gate. The strange man was still standing in the lane.

"How about temples, then?" he called. "You want to see temples?"

"No, thanks," they said together and went up the path.

"Or turtles? You want to see giant rare turtles?"

Louis turned back.

"The Turtle Watch beach is just up that way – very nice place, sir. You can watch the turtles coming and laying their eggs. I know the boys who work there, nice young fellows, they'll look after you. Just tell them Sunny sent you. You want me to organise a taxi to take you there?"

"No!" Ria protested.

"We'll get our own taxi," Louis said.

"Don't forget to mention me to the boys there."

"We might not go," Ria said.

"I'll know if you do, don't worry."

They walked on up the path.

"What a creep," Ria muttered.

"Do you think it's true what he said about Padma?" Louis whispered.

"No!"

The dog barked and came running down to inspect them, then returned to the porch, and they were alone again. Ria nestled her sandy body against Louis. His arm went around her. The beer bottles clinked in his hand. Only the dog could see them wind through the plantain trees to her bungalow, once more the last two people out in the world.

## 15

GERHARDT STOPPED IN the path, hearing Padma's voice at Ria's bungalow. A male voice joined in her laughter. Gerhardt had been leaving after breakfast with a deadline to meet, but he went closer into the shade of the plantain trees, the cool green flaps of leaves concealing him from Padma, Ria and Louis on the veranda. Louis was bare-chested, wearing only shorts, and upside-down with his legs in the air, and Padma holding them. What was she doing being so familiar with guests? Especially this one. Gerhardt wanted to call her back to the house, but she would never have forgiven him. She had been acting strangely recently. He'd noticed a certain guilty evasiveness about her. She barely spoke when they were together; she seemed preoccupied and jumpy. Soma had already informed him that Padma had sneaked out one afternoon, while he was sleeping. Soma had run to Boss's Bar and spotted her there with Jarryd. Jarryd was vague when Gerhardt asked about their meeting, claiming that he and Padma had merely been catching up. It was possible that Padma was still troubled by her trip back to visit Sunny and had needed to talk. But why hadn't she wanted to talk with Gerhardt? Jarryd had said maybe Padma was missing her mother. Seeing Leela could have unsettled her. A daughter loved her mother however little that mother gave her, Jarryd had suggested. Leela was a mystery to Gerhardt. How many times he and Ruth had sent secret envoys to talk with her, offering to arrange a reunion with her daughter – and always she had refused. Surely a mother would use any means to see a daughter taken from her? Padma knew nothing of his efforts or of Leela's refusal – Leela could remain a phantom of the past; unknown, unsullied. Did Padma really need Leela now, after all these years?

Gerhardt saw Padma smile up at the new guest, the tousled golden young man stretching in an awkward arc before her, as Ria demonstrated a yoga pose. Padma pressed her hand against Louis' bare back. Gerhardt had never seen her so at ease with the body of a man, a stranger. When she was younger, her friends had been girls from her school, and teenage boys were merely danced with at parties, with hawk-eyed relatives watching. Or they had telephoned and talked with her for hours, teasing and telling stupid jokes. Padma laughed loudly now with Louis and Ria. There was none of the new secretive silence he had observed. Was it the new guest, rather than Leela, who was responsible for Padma's change of mood?

Padma had never talked of dating in all the time she had lived in Colombo. Ruth had reported a few close men friends, all of whom had been discretely looked into by Ruth and approved of, but she had never invited them to Ruth's house in Colombo, where Padma had lived during term-time, or brought anyone back to the villa at weekends. Gerhardt was aware that they made an unconventional family, he, Ruth and Padma, and he knew that Padma was wary of revealing this about herself. Most Sri Lankans were confused by her relationship to Gerhardt and Ruth; not to mention Gerhardt and Ruth's relationship itself. Well-to-do Colombo families tended to be a conservative crowd. Even those who thought themselves Westernised, always in the end held to what they knew. Well Padma didn't need any of those dull young men! Whoever truly loved her would embrace her past. She was the same loving, spirited, intelligent child who had lived in the shadows of Sunny's hovel. Padma was special; she had shone through the gloom. People were drawn to her – not only for her beauty. She shone with life, with love.

Louis swayed, losing his balance and toppled with a great yell into Padma's arms. Loud laughter ensued. Padma helped Louis stand, his arm around her. In her yoga clothes, a simple t-shirt and shorts, she looked so young. Louis was all smiles, but there was the sheen of entitlement in his good humour and polite-ness. Those perfect manners would vanish, Gerhardt suspect-ed, if Louis were ever challenged or denied. Was Louis trying to get closer to Padma? Was he making demands of her when Gerhardt wasn't there? Was this what she had talked to Jarryd about, Jarryd who loved to love, and encouraged it in everyone? It would solve all the troubles of the world, according to Jarryd, if people made more love. Gerhardt edged back from the plantain trees, already telephoning Ruth as he left the garden and leaving an urgent message on her voicemail that she was needed at the villa at once.

&#x2766;

Ria wore jeans for the first time since leaving London. It was late, dinner just over, but she and Louis were due to leave on a trip, to the beach where the turtles came to lay eggs. Louis had arranged a taxi with a man in the village –a different man to the one they'd met by the beach, he'd assured her. She sat on the bed waiting for him, alone in her room for the first time since he had arrived at the villa. It seemed a long time ago that she herself had arrived there, being shown to the bungalow at the side of the garden, surrounded by flowers and trees. She had rearranged the furniture as she always did in hotels and even motorway stopovers, hiding unwanted ornaments, ash trays, laminated notices, books that didn't appeal. Even staying for one night she unpacked all her clothes, arranging them in the empty cupboards and drawers, determinedly inhabiting these impossible homes. She inhabited them more fully than her flat in London, lived in for six years but which she was always ready to move on from when she found her rightful home.

Something scuttled past outside. The night pressed in through the window bars like smoke. She closed the shutters and locked them tight. There were geckos splayed on the wall, their dark bead-eyes shining; the shrieks in the night were their mating calls, Padma had informed her; it wasn't the noise of rats at all. Crickets throbbed, expectant sounding. Something thudded along the roof and crashed into the bushes, then came footsteps on the veranda, a knock at the door.

"Come in!" she called.

It was Louis. He was wearing jeans, a navy sweater, tied around his waist. He felt of Europe and abroad, a far away London.

"Ready?" he asked.

"I need to find my jumper."

It was at the bottom of her suitcase. She tugged at soft woolly apple-green sleeves. Louis lay on the bed and watched her. So many days and nights he had spent there, but the room still felt more hers than theirs. The jumper came free and she smelled the perfume she'd worn just two weeks before on the plane coming over, a lifetime ago. An owl hooted outside. A harsh high cry replied. In the dim uneven electric lights of her childhood home there had been these same lives crowded in close: sly squeaks and scratches behind the walls, a scudding up in the ceiling. She remembered the dark under the pantry sink as she washed her hands after dinner, the paw-paw seeds in the waste-bin gleaming wet black malevolent eyes.

"I always hated the night times here," she said. "I used to dread being sent up to bed, going past the kitchen where the maids would be eating dinner at last, from plates too chipped for the family to use, and the cook would be rolling out her straw mat on the floor, arranging her faded old cotton bedding. I'd feel so sad for them, but they didn't seem to mind, they'd just laugh at me and praise me for being concerned. Then in my bedroom I'd lie feeling lost and so utterly alone, even though everyone was just downstairs."

"You have to sleep through the dark like the locals," Louis said. "They sleep early and wake with the sun and everything is beautiful again."

"Yes! In the morning it did seem ludicrous to have been so sad."

A horn beeped outside.

"I want to stay here." Louis complained

"We can't cancel now! Anyway, didn't you want to see turtles?"

"Let's tell him to go away."

"And who would do the telling?"

"You, of course! You're the local."

"I'm not a local. Come on!" She pulled him up from the bed and they went outside. "Where on earth are you two going? You look like you're heading to the North Pole!" Padma called from the veranda.

"We're going to see turtles," Ria said.

"Turtles? Tonight?"

The taxi horn blared louder, longer.

"We have to go!" Louis said, and they went on to a van waiting in the lane for them.

The van followed the bay, passing through villages of houses with dark empty porches. Light shone deep inside in rooms where families had gathered to gossip and tease and worry and scold away the last hours of the night. Soon the van left the villages behind and the sea came nearer, blackly glistening past coconut groves of slanting trees silvery in moonlight. The van stopped at the edge of a grove and they stepped out to the roar of sea and cold rushing winds. Ria put on her jumper. High above her, the coconut trees swayed and bowed against a blue-black sky, the stars a dusty spray of sparkling white.

"I'll come back in two hours," the driver said and gave Louis his card. "Hope you see some turtles."

"But where are you going?"

"I'll just be nearby – call me if you want to stay longer."

"You never said you'd be leaving us," Louis protested, but the driver was already in the van.

"Hey!" Louis cried, but it was too late, the van drove away.

"How come there's no one else here?" Ria said.

"Maybe we're too early."

"Or too late," she replied.

There was a glow through the trees from a thatch hut. They walked towards it. Over the door was a sign: 'The Turtle Watch Museum'. An electric bulb swung from the rafters in the wind, dancing its glowering light over framed photographs of turtles lumbering onto night time beaches, digging in sand, or straining, legs splayed, squeezing out eggs. Louis read every sign, every caption, excited again.

"This place is great – they're a charity employing ex-convicts. They teach them about conservation."

"Ex-convicts?"

"Good evening, sir-madam!" A short stocky man bounded into the hut and grinned at them. His eyes lingered on Ria. The man's face was pockmarked and puffy, the skin yellowed and tough, the nose broken; eyebrows interrupted by the scars of old stitches. His smile though was joyful, unconnected seeming to the damaged features.

"In our turtle watch we don't steal turtles' eggs – we're not like the people down the road," he told them. "Those people steal the eggs and grow turtles in tanks. Sometimes they *eat* the eggs. They're very bad people, don't ever go to their turtle watch, sir and madam."

"Where can we buy tickets?" Louis asked.

"No need of tickets, sir – it's all free at our turtle watch. You only pay if you see the turtles."

"Wow! That's great!" Louis approved.

"So let's go and see if they come! This way, sir-madam!"

The ex-convict came up beside Ria as they left the hut.

"Sinhalese?" he murmured, his voice turned low and adult, a secret voice, brought out for the real conversation. She pretended not to hear. He pretended not to have spoken.

"This way sir, follow me!" He darted away, become the happy child again.

The ex-convict shone a torch ahead and they followed him, winding past coconut trees, their great hooves of trunks stamped in the ground. Ria took off her shoes and the sand was silky-cold and dry, slinking around her feet with every step. A half-moon cast its pale gleam over a wide empty beach.

"No turtles yet, sir-madam," the ex-convict declared, scanning the sea with binoculars.

"When do the turtles come?" Louis asked.

"It can be anytime, sir – soon, hopefully, soon! Dear God, please let there be turtles for sir and madam! Just keep watching the ocean. I will go closer and look for you."

He ran down to the water's edge and strolled through the

waves swirling idly in. He walked around a rocky outcrop and disappeared.

Ria sat down on the beach, a sandy bank firm at her back. Louis sighed and sat down beside her.

"Do you know anything about this place?" he asked.

"No."

"Does your family ever come here?"

"I'm not sure."

"You don't know where your family goes?"

"I know very little about them, it turns out."

There was no way on earth her family would have come to such a place – in the middle of the night, to look at *turtles*.

"You should have asked Padma about this place," he accused.

"You arranged it!" she retorted.

The ex-convict appeared on top of the rocks, walking a little unsteadily. He stood looking out to sea. The pale beam of his torch reached over the waves.

"Something's weird about this," Louis said.

Across the water, at the other end of the bay, lights shone in the town where life went on unknowing of them. It was the first time Ria had been anywhere so deserted in Sri Lanka, so far away from the places she knew, and everyone. The trees leaned over velvet rocks and the pale soft sand of a primal Sri Lanka, a pre-world of hushed dark beaches and a muted rocking sea sweeping the shore all through the night – long still nights, full of unknowable secrets. These were the beaches where war bodies would wash up, maimed and distorted after night-time abductions – even now, in peace-time, the abductions went on for different, more secret reasons. It seemed impossible to end the savagery; it seemed a part of the unreal beauty of the island, so spoiled and churning under the surface.

But here was its raw splendour, its secret night-time source, potent and untainted before it was lost in the world of people.

"Why aren't there any other tourists here?" Louis demanded.

"Maybe they didn't want to see turtles."

He made an exasperated noise and glanced at her impatiently.

"It's better like this, don't you think?" Ria said.

"It feels like a scam."

"I don't see how. We haven't given the guy any money."

"Everything in this country is a scam – that's why my friends left, they'd had enough. It was always the same: hire cars, safaris, Buddhist temples – you name it, there was always a way they could con you."

"But we don't have to pay unless we see turtles."

Louis jumped up, full of a new restlessness, a fierceness in him. "Hey!" he shouted to the ex-convict.

The ex-convict spun round.

"Where are your turtles?" Louis yelled. "Are they coming any time soon? I'm getting tired, I want to go home!"

The ex-convict tensed, his round belly turned solid, thin legs locked. Like a fat sparrow, Ria thought. But dangerous.

"I think I might just call the driver!" Louis taunted, waving his phone.

The ex-convict scrambled down from the rocks and came running.

"The turtles will come, sir! Just wait and see – just a few more hours. Madam – you tell sir, to wait a little!" he panted.

"What's it to you if we leave?"

Louis stood taller than the ex-convict. He looked down with a cold angry smile at the ex-convict's pitted fleshy face. Louis' hair shone in the moonlight, swept back from his fine-boned face, the perfect lines of jaw and chin and lips. Ria looked away from that perfection, winning so easily above the beaten face below. Louis was so much stronger, so much luckier than the fat-sparrow ex-convict. Louis started to type a number on his phone.

"No sir! Please sir, stay!" the ex-convict cried. "The turtles will come! You just have to wait – how can I know what time they will want to lay eggs?"

Louis went on typing then put the phone to his ear. The ex-convict grew still, watching in silence – no more pleading, no more explaining about the turtles. The torchlight made his cheeks seem waxy and hard. 'Tourists missing from Turtle Watch Beach' – Ria could already see the headline. A small square of text with their names, ages and occupations and an inaccurate account of what had happened.

"The driver will be back in an hour, let's just wait till then," Ria insisted.

"Yes, wait!" the ex-convict agreed.

"Maybe the turtles will come later," Ria added.

"Yes, later! The turtles will come later!"

"Yeah, right." Louis ended the call and sat down again, looking away.

The ex-convict jogged away to a distant spot at the water's edge. Ria sat down beside Louis. He didn't look at her. She watched the sea alone, feeling his silence for the first time and him closed to her. He checked his watch. His arm touched hers and she felt the muscle hardness of him under the softness of cashmere, and he felt apart and other. He would always be other, separate from her; she would never truly know what he was thinking – why he had smiled at her that first afternoon on the veranda, why he had asked to join her for dinner. How did you ever know when you knew someone, when it was safe to allow that last private door inside you to open? She understood now why people had horoscopes read before marriages – even the arrangements of stars in their constellations were a comfort faced with the unknown of another's mind. She watched the night-time sea surging in surly bursts onto the beach.

"The sea looks so different at night," she said.

The waves slicked back in an oily sweep, receding into themselves – another sea altogether from its joyful, spraying, sparkling, sunlit self, dazzling all day.

"It looks so pure in the mornings," she reflected.

"You shouldn't have undermined me in front of that guy," Louis said.

"What are you talking about?"

"You should be on *my* side, not his."

"I didn't want to antagonise him."

"It was up to us when we left. What could he have done about it anyway?"

"I don't know . . . He might have friends nearby. Or he might have a knife or a gun – who knows? I didn't want to risk it."

"That's crazy! You're always so afraid of everything!" His eyes were a scornful pale glare in the tan of his face.

She glared back at him. He turned away.

Ria walked alone at the water's edge. The night spread vast and new around her. The ex-convict came running up behind her.

"You're Sinhalese?" he asked, trying again.

"Yes."

"You live here, in Sri Lanka?"

"Of course."

"You're from which town?"

"Colombo."

She hadn't expected him to believe her. Her relatives had found it strange that she had memories of the city, that she could point to where old buildings had been and remember moments of a life they had shared, but her presence then had been forgotten.

"So you remember our little Colombo?" they said, amazed and amused as if she had performed a magic trick.

They thought of Colombo as their place, not hers; and refused to acknowledge her claim to be there as one of them. But it was her city of birth and the place of her early life with her grandparents, a time from where all love stemmed for her. She would always be from Colombo, always bound to it.

"You speak Sinhalese?" the ex-convict asked.

She nodded, wary of revealing her accented Sinhalese that everyone had teased her about. The ex-convict switched to Sinhalese:

"Listen, madam, I'll tell you how it is – I don't get paid for being here, but whether turtles come or not, one of us has to be here, no? Otherwise people will come and steal the eggs. We only do it for the conservation – tell that to your friend. Tell him I'm not asking for the whole amount, just half – something small, for being here all night. Otherwise there would be no eggs, and no Turtle Watch – please, madam, you'll explain it to sir?"

"Maybe."

The ex-convict edged a little closer, confiding.

"You come back in a few months madam, then there'll be turtles."

"I see. It's not the season now, is it?" At last she understood.

"Just a few more months, that's all. Not too long to wait, Madam."

So Louis had been right; there was a scam. There was always a scam. It was how you made something out of nothing.

"Will you tell your friend, madam?"

"I might do."

She turned away and the ex-convict resumed his patrol.

Ria walked slowly, scuffing the wet sand with her toes, polishing her nails the way her grandmother had shown her, on their early-morning walks on the beach, a long time ago. Grampa jogging far up ahead, while the two of them walked and drew in the sand with sticks, together in the new bright day. Their nails had shone like sea shells, pearly pink and pale.

Louis was reading his phone as she went to him.

"It isn't the season for turtles," she said.

"I knew it! I told you this was a con – didn't I?"

"Still, you shouldn't underestimate that guy."

"And still you defend him! I can't believe it!"

"Life is cheap over here; people are so angry, so denied—"

"So they have to be pitied all the time? Given money and indulged whenever they demand it? Maybe if they didn't try to trick every Westerner they met, I'd feel like giving something. What's really annoying is you taking his side—"

"I'm not!"

"You think he'd take yours? He'd rob you just as easily as any foreigner."

"But it wouldn't be personal – I get it now. They don't see us as individuals – we're just people with more. They don't see anyone as individuals, not even themselves – it's all about the group here. *That's* what makes me afraid."

"Afraid – of him? That twit?"

"Alone feels so lonely here."

"What are you talking about?"

Headlights swept over from the road, the van returning.

"Thank God!" Louis cried, jumping up. "I'm out of here!"

He started back at once. Ria followed him. The ex-convict raced towards them over the beach, his bowed legs pounding the sand. He was fast. He leaped in front of them, blocking their way.

"Just pay half!" he cried. "Half is nothing, no?"

"You've *got* to be kidding!" Louis tried to push past but the ex-convict didn't let him.

"Madam, I told you, no, I'm only asking for half!" He switched again to Sinhalese: "It's nothing for foreigners, there's no need for you to pay, but your friend should pay – I was looking for turtles for him, no? Otherwise I could have been at home with my family, nicely sleeping."

He was greedy and grasping, wanting something, anything before they left him behind forever, a wild man on an empty beach.

"Let's just give him half," Ria said to Louis. "It's only a few quid."

"No way. No bloody way! We only had to pay if there were turtles."

Ria counted out the money while Louis went to the van.

"Thank you, thank you, madam!" The ex-convict beamed.

He lowered his voice, speaking in Sinhalese.

"You come back in two months madam, bring your Colombo friends, I'll show you the turtles. I'll take you to the best places. I won't forget your face."

He stood outside the hut waving goodbye, grinning like a child given gifts.

"You shouldn't have paid, he ripped us off," Louis said in the van.

"You haven't been ripped off at all," she retorted.

They sat in silence as they drove back along the bay, two new people on a different journey. The village houses watched them go through the thick black foliage of gardens.

"Did you really mean it when you said that guy might be dangerous?" Louis asked.

"Maybe, but he's gone now."

"He'll be looking out for me though, won't he? You did say he'd have friends in the area." Louis glanced at the driver and dropped his voice. "I bet he's in on the scam as well – and he knows where I'm staying."

"Nothing's going to happen to you."

"I think I might move on though. My friends are still in Thailand, they're having a great time. They keep asking me to join them – I think I'm going to. You can come too, if you want . . . Would you like to?"

"Go to Thailand?"

"I know where they are, I've got an address."

"No. But thanks."

Had he known that she would refuse? There was a new coldness in his gaze, in the green glazed eyes, so beautiful but unknowable. She looked up into them and was not dazzled anymore.

They returned to the villa in silence. The dog bounded down to investigate as they walked up the path.

"I think I will sleep alone tonight," Ria said.

"I thought you didn't like being alone – you kept moaning about being afraid . . ." There was the same taunting note in his voice as when he had spoken with the ex-convict.

"I'm not afraid anymore," she replied.

Far behind her now was the beach and the silent village houses where the families would be sleeping in shadowy rooms with mosquitoes whining, fans humming, bodies bound together, staying safe and close. But all the while, a moonlit world lay altered and new, waiting for those who wandered outside. While others huddled asleep, she was free to see a magical secret life, and free to return alone to her room at the villa with its sagging mosquito net and rusty lamp on the bedside table, the sea shells lined up on the windowsill, treasures of her morning walks. Here she could be safe until the new day came, and she was dazzled anew.

# 16

PADMA HEARD THE banging on the veranda doors through deep dream-less sleep, in the empty silent depths where she had curled, a fossil, pressed down under the sea, into darkness.

She sat up. Someone had called her name. It was just past midnight. There was no sound from Gustav. She reached for her dressing gown, wrapping it around her as she crept into the hall. There was no snoring from Soma's room. He was probably still at Boss's. She reached for her phone. Whoever it was had come through the porch, onto the veranda. Where was Gustav? The person was still there, pacing outside the doors.

"Who is it?" she asked.

"Louis."

"Oh! Just a minute!"

"I'm sorry, I wasn't expecting you," she said, unbolting the door.

He brushed past her a little roughly as he came inside, and stood searching his pockets by the doors to his room.

"Are you okay?" she asked.

"I'm fine."

"How was the turtle watch?"

"Bloody awful. It turns out it wasn't the season."

"Ah! I thought so! I wondered why you were going. What a shame! Next time check with me before you arrange anything."

"Maybe you could have mentioned it when you saw us leaving?" he snapped.

It was strange that a man so handsome could become unattractive so quickly. Beauty was elusive, an unfixable fact, choosing where it alighted and how long it would stay.

"You ran off before I could say anything," she replied.

"You should have come after us."

"I wasn't sure about the season – I'm no turtle expert."

"I should never have trusted those weird guys in the lane, I just assumed the locals would know about the wildlife here—"

"They are the wildlife here! Which weird guys?"

"Just some people we met one night – I suppose they get a commission from the ex-convicts. How was I to know there'd be a scam at a conservation project?"

Louis found his key and opened the door.

"Was one of the men quite old? Short, bald?" she asked.

"Yeah, maybe. Why? Do you know him?"

"And the other one, was he young? Tall? With crazy hair, sticking up everywhere?"

"Yeah, I think so."

She shrugged. It could have been anyone. Louis went inside. She heard him lock the door.

"Goodnight," she called, but he didn't reply.


When she went out to the porch, Gustav looked up hopefully.

"Sorry, no, you're sleeping out here, now," she told him, sitting on the floor beside him, stroking his silky head.

There was no one in the lane – no Sunny or Mukul giggling at all the trouble they'd caused. Could it really have been them, sending Louis and Ria to see non-existent turtles? There couldn't be much money in that, surely? They may have been hoping to sell drugs to them away from Nilwatte Beach, and maybe they had. Sunny and Mukul wouldn't be dumb enough to try doing that on the minister's brother's territory. It might also have been a simple prank to annoy Padma's guests. How well it had worked. Sunny would have enjoyed seeing Ria and Louis fall out. Sunny loved to upset people.

The light was on in Ria's room. Had she and Louis broken up? He had seemed so angry. Was Ria sitting sobbing on her bed? Padma didn't dare go over to see. The loneliness of a break-up was a different type of aloneness. She herself would feel secretly released in those intense sad hours, returned to completeness. It was freeing to drop all the little lies and evasions needed to shield the secrets of the past.

The gate latch clicked. Gustav sat up alert – but it was only Soma returning.

"What are you doing out here?" he said

"I had to let Louis in, he's sleeping in the house tonight."

"Ah, lover's tiff was it?"

"Probably. Do you think Ria's okay?"

"Why wouldn't she be? Now go to bed, please."

"In a minute."

"Make sure you lock up. Goodnight!"

In the old days he would have insisted that she go in with him, and she would have complained while quietly enjoying being safe inside his concern, held by rules.

She walked down to the gate and hid behind the hibiscus bushes, peering out. A man walked in the direction of the beach bars and the brothel. Another man guided a group of tourists the same way. The men looked a little like Sunny and Mukul. Maybe it was them. She felt them near, circling the villa, keeping her in their sights, their terrible endless interest in her making them stay close. How easily Sunny had come into the villa's garden; how silently he had appeared behind her. She tried not to remember the room in his house and waking with Mukul watching from the corner, his solemn crazed eyes so oddly attentive. She would never let them get so close to her again. She called Gustav and walked with him around the garden, checking it all over, right to the edge. Both neighbouring houses were empty now, but no one had moved in. The gardens on either side were overgrown, silent and untouched. Ruth had worried that the minister's brother would extend his brothel into his new houses, but he hadn't so far. There was talk of him making a hotel for foreigners in one, and running a casino in the other – but no work had begun. The minister may have made him wait until after the local elections. In any case, Gerhardt had already built one wall higher and he had plans to build an even higher stronger wall all around the villa if needed.

"This way, boy!" She searched inside the outdoor kitchen, then behind the log pile.

She lifted the lids of the rusted bins with a stick. Something squealed and scuffled in the stinking mass inside. She dropped the lid with a crash. A light snapped on in the small bungalow, the curtain was pulled back. She froze in the shadows. Rohan came to the window and looked out. Had she frightened him? She ought to reassure him. She knocked on his door.

"Rohan?" she said softly.

He opened the door at once.

"Are you alright? Did anything happen?" he asked.

"No! I'm fine! I just saw your light come on – are you okay?"

"I heard a bang."

"Oh I'm sure it was nothing."

He was wearing blue-striped pyjamas with a grey t-shirt, his hair tousled.

"It was loud – didn't you hear it," he insisted.

"Must have been bats. I wouldn't worry, I've been over the whole garden – it's all fine."

Rohan stroked Gustav's head and Gustav looked lovingly up at him.

"I only came to check you were okay," Padma said.

"What great service."

"That's not what you used to say."

He smiled.

"Do you want a cup of tea? I could make you chai?" Padma said.

"Wouldn't we wake Soma? I've got mango juice here if you like?"

Mango juice was too sweet, too thick; she hated mango juice.

"Lovely, yes please," she said.

He went inside and opened his wardrobe. She stood at the door.

"Come in," he offered, but she stayed where she was.

He slept very neatly, she observed, the sheets rucked up only where he'd left the bed. His trousers were folded over the chair, his leather chaporas lined up neatly below. He rummaged inside the wardrobe. He had used one of the shelves for groceries: beer and bottled water and cartons of mango juice. A big bag of potato crisps. Gustav settled on the veranda and went to sleep.

Rohan brought out two of the cartons of juice and they sat on the veranda steps with the candle lit between them. Moths flew at the jar, thudding softly against the hot glass.

"This is nice," she said.

"Yes, it is."

His body felt peaceful beside her, making her body grow tense. His face was so close. He looked gentle and content. He reminded her of a boy from long ago who had stopped once outside her old village, at a roadside stall where she had been helping Leela and the other village women sell fruit and vegetables. The boy was part of a large family group travelling in jeeps and vans, going south from Colombo for the weekend, taking a break to buy king coconuts. They drank them there, the children running around noisily and the parents taking photographs. But the boy had stood alone, looking out to sea. Padma had watched him from the back of the stall, and he had turned and seen her. He hadn't looked away. It was the first time she hadn't minded being looked at - it was a new feeling, the sense of having been seen. She had smiled at the boy, and he had smiled back. She was about to walk over when one of the village women saw her and alerted Leela who dragged Padma back into the stall. Hot with shame Padma saw the boy get into a jeep. Then the families tossed away their empty king coconuts and drove away, the younger children looking back, pulling faces at the villagers.

"Look at her mooning after the rich boy!" the villagers jeered at Padma.

"You think people like them will ever go for people like us?" Leela had scoffed, standing with the faded bitter women.

But the boy's still quiet gaze had stayed with Padma, even after he was gone. His approval was a new awareness in her; a gleam of possibility in the world outside.

"That's Orion," Padma said, pointing at the sky. "Those three bright stars are his belt. And the stars in a line are his shield."

His eyes looked to the flickering white spray of brightness, then at her, and she felt the same warmth of recognition of long ago. He could have been the boy in the convoy. He had been living in Colombo then, and his family often drove down to the south coast, he'd said. Did he remember the skinny village girl in her shabby mended dress? Had fate drawn him back? Two souls longing for each other across time. Perhaps a magical current had brought them both to the villa, a smooth, white shell, formed to hold them like pearls? How strange if it were true, and how right.

The next morning, Padma was woken again by someone banging on the door. It was just past dawn. She threw open the door, thinking it would be Ria coming to make up with Louis - but there was Ruth standing before her.

"What are you doing here? Are you alright?" Padma exclaimed.

"Whatever do you mean?" Ruth beamed, fresh and poised despite the long drive from Colombo, wrapped in her green pashmina shawl.

"You didn't say you were coming!" Padma hugged the small warm figure tightly.

"I just woke up this morning and thought I'd take a drive into the wilds and see how you were."

They walked arm in arm to the kitchen and Padma made coffee for them and tea for Ruth's driver, Lalith.

"Where's that Soma?" Ruth demanded.

"Sleeping, of course."

"So late? What a lazy lump!"

"It's only six o'clock!"

"In my house the servants wake at 5am, no later."

They went to the porch, Ruth settling in Gerhardt's chair, sipping coffee while the morning sun crept over the garden.

"You look tired," Ruth said.

"Yes, you've woken me up!"

"Six o'clock is hardly early, my dear, especially for one supposedly running a guest house."

"I didn't get much sleep last night," Padma said, a smile rising to her face at the thought of candles and stars and Orion's belt; the sweetness of mango.

She had never talked so much with anyone. They had used up

three power-cut candles. She had told him things she had never spoken of – stories of her first life among people he would only have seen from a distance, glimpsed while driving somewhere. It hadn't seemed shameful to confess to being one of those ragged malnourished urchins running around shacks and playing in rubble. She had never been so close to her past while talking with someone new. She only had to remember to say Uncle and Aunt for Sunny and Leela. There hadn't been any need to mention Mukul.

"Why didn't you get any sleep?" Ruth asked.

"Ria had a bust-up with her boyfriend and he came and woke me up."

"Why you?"

"Because I'd locked up the house and his room is in here." Padma lowered her voice. "But he's hardly ever slept in it."

"Because he's been with Ria?"

"Yes! Like I said, he was her boyfriend."

"Ah, Ria's boyfriend. I see." Ruth seemed oddly approving. Just then Louis came out of the house.

"Morning," he mumbled going into the garden.

"That's him," Padma whispered, as he went towards Ria's bungalow.

"So this is the Louis." Ruth stared after him.

"How did you know his name?"

"You just mentioned it."

"No I didn't."

"Yes you did."

Padma frowned. Ruth was acting very strangely that morning.

"He's like a movie star," Ruth murmured. "Beautiful. But looks aren't everything, and I'm not all that keen on this one. But I wouldn't blame you for having a little crush on this fellow. Do you, by any chance?"

"No!"

"Are you sure?"

"Of course I'm sure! What's wrong with you today? You're not sick or anything, are you?"

"Of course not! My goodness, can't an old woman visit her favourite god-daughter once in a while?"

"Only god-daughter. And why didn't you call to say you were coming?"

"I thought I'd be spontaneous. Is Gerhardt still planning to start his holiday rentals business?"

"Of course. I inspired him, apparently, with my guesthouse."

"Good God! I suppose he's still doing up those hideous cottages, then?"

"One's finished already, it looks amazing. And the other two are almost done."

"Who on earth is going to stay in them when there are so many other lovely places to stay? So many beautiful boutique hotels to choose from."

"Some people don't want to stay in hotels, boutique or otherwise."

"But the majority do."

"But we don't want the majority here!" They would be the people tromping around looking for sights to see and demanding attention, and making dull conversation at dinner.

"At your age you should be seeing the world," Ruth said. "My offer still stands . . . ?"

"But I don't want to go to Europe. Not now. Maybe one day for a holiday."

Ruth was about to argue, but Louis started banging on Ria's door, calling to her.

"Oh dear, that doesn't look promising," Ruth observed.

Ria came out, wearing shorts and a vest, her hair tousled.

"They can see us watching!" Ruth said.

"We can't get up now, it'll be too obvious."

"Look the other way, pretend we're just talking!"

"I bet he was in the wrong," Padma said softly.

"Maybe no one did anything wrong."

Ruth was quiet and thoughtful. She was older than Leela, and Leela's body was already frail and failing. Ruth seemed so preoccupied.

"You are okay, aren't you Ruth?" Padma checked.

"Of course I am!"

Padma went to sit at her feet, hugging her legs.

"You silly goose!" Ruth held Padma's face in both of her hands. "You are a lovely girl, you really are," Ruth kissed Padma's forehead and stroked her hair.

Over at the bungalow the door slammed as Ria went in, leaving Louis outside.

"Uh-oh, here he comes! He's been dumped," Ruth muttered. "Look at that face! Like a furious Greek god striding out to seek revenge."

"It's going to be awkward at breakfast."

They talked about the garden as Louis went past into the house. In the office, the telephone started to ring. Padma stood up but Ruth stopped her.

"Let Soma answer it – that's his job. Honestly, whoever heard of staff sleeping in so late? You and Gerhardt spoil him."

"Soma can't speak English properly."

"He can manage. He's such a lazy man! He's the laziest man I've ever met!"

"He does loads! He even makes lunches for guests now."

"Praise be!"

"Certain guests, anyway."

"Who?"

"Ria."

"I see, only the pretty guests get to eat. What a mad guest house this is."

It was Ruth who had told Ria about the villa when they met at a wedding in Colombo. Poor Ria, what a day she was having. She would cheer up perhaps, if Ruth went to see her later. The phone stopped ringing; someone had picked it up.

"There!" Padma declared.

"About time."

"Hello?" Soma said gruffly, answering the phone.

"Growl, growl - what a lovely greeting for guests! People will think it's the house of the three bears!" Ruth whispered.

"Shh!" Padma giggled.

Soma came out yawning.

"Some people just rang and said they'd be late," he announced. "Oh hello, Hamu! I didn't know you were coming?"

"Which people?" Padma asked.

"I don't know - two guests. They said they've been delayed."

"What are you talking about?"

"They said they won't get here until after lunch."

"Obviously they had the wrong number."

"They said 'Villa Hibiscus'."

"Then they must have been trying to book a room."

"No, no, they definitely said they'd booked already."

"But why would they say that?"

"For goodness sake, are you expecting new guests or not?" Ruth exclaimed. "Surely you keep a record of bookings?"

"Of course I do! And there are no new guests coming today!"

"Good, because if anyone came, you'd have nowhere to put them."

"It was a woman - she's called Anjali-something," Soma

recalled. "The other one is Fan or Man or—"

"Oh my God! Oh my God!" Padma raced into the study.

She flicked through the diary – and there they were: Anjali Panditharatne and Daniel Gomes, scheduled to arrive that very day! They'd booked three months in advance – such a long time ago, no wonder she'd forgotten about them by the time Louis turned up.

"What am I going to do?" she wailed to Ruth and Soma standing in the doorway.

"Good grief, Padma, is this how you run a guest house?" Ruth was agog, relishing the disaster.

"I'll have to give them my room," Padma said.

"And where, may I ask, will you sleep then?"

"I'll put a mattress in the study."

"And your things? I'm sure the guests won't want to be sleeping among all your books and incense and yoga mats."

"The lady said she wanted a bungalow," Soma added.

"Well there's no chance of that!" Padma retorted.

"This is just brilliant! The pair of you running a guest house – it's worse than Faulty Towers! I predicted this, didn't I? But Gerhardt was sure it was a brilliant idea – now look!"

"What about asking Louis Mahaththaya to go back to Ria Hamu's room?" Soma suggested.

"What is this, a matchmaking hotel?" Ruth cried.

"Maybe it will bring them together!" Padma said. "I could ask, couldn't I? What harm could it do?"

"You can't force guests to sleep together – that's a very different type of hotel!" Ruth declared. "You're going to have to own up and apologise to these new people, and tell them they have to go elsewhere. There are plenty of other guest houses along the lane."

"There's no way I'm sending those arseholes my business!"

Padma marched across the hall and knocked on Louis' door.

Ruth and Soma darted into the office and hid behind the door.

"Yes?" Louis was cold and sombre. In the room behind him, clothes were strewn all over the bed.

"I was just wondering," Padma began. "Your room—"

"—yeah about that, I wanted to tell you—"

"Would you be willing to give it up and share with Ria?"

"God, no - but you can have the room, I'm leaving."

"Leaving?"

"Yes, I need to go today."

"Oh, then that's fine!"

"But I'm not paying beyond today," he added fiercely.

"No problem at all! Would you be able to leave now?"

"Now?"

"I need to get it ready for new guests, but you can stay as long as you like on the veranda."

She couldn't believe her luck! She ran to get Soma to help Louis move out before he changed his mind.

Louis refused to stay for breakfast. He paid and left at once. He seemed surprised by the cheese sandwich Padma pressed into his hands. Ruth had been astonished when she saw Padma make it, but Padma didn't want Louis to remember his time at the villa too sadly. She dusted and swept his room while Soma cleaned the bathroom and changed the sheets. A room that hadn't been lived in was the perfect empty vessel, easy to order, hungry to be filled. Soon it was ready. Ruth was eating paw paw on the porch, speaking on her phone with Gerhardt. She ended the call as Padma joined her.

"There's no need to go moaning to Gerhardt, even big hotels make mistakes," Padma said. "And it's all sorted anyway. There's a lovely room waiting for them now."

"Didn't Soma say they wanted a bungalow?"

"They can't have everything! They're lucky to have a room at all."

The door of the small bungalow opened. Padma supressed the smile that rose to her face as Rohan came out.

"Who's that?" Ruth sat up and stared at Rohan coming over.

"Another guest."

"You never mentioned him." Ruth leaned forward to get a better look.

"He's just a guest."

"Nice looking chap."

"He's alright."

He had talked in the night about his life in England, his teenage years at a boarding school with turrets, holidays mostly spent with a friend in a farmhouse near a beach with sand dunes. He had described a bleak landscape of cold seas and unsettling winds, billowing white sand, but it had been a time of warmth for him. He had sounded wistful describing the family that had let him into their midst. He had lost touch with them, he said, including the friend.

"Tom and Shalini didn't get on," he had admitted.

"Well, she's gone now. You should write and tell him what happened."

"Maybe I will."

"Do it. He'll be delighted that she's gone."

He had laughed, not minding her directness. Other people she talked with often seemed startled by what she said, as if they had been expecting something else, something agreed on by the rest of the world as acceptable.

"What's his name?" Ruth asked.

"Whose?"

"That fellow over there."

"Rohan."

He had walked her back to the house in the pre-dawn garden, two voyagers arriving after an intrepid journey through the night.

"Rohan who?" Ruth demanded.

"Fernando."

"Hmm – sounds familiar. Is he known for something?"

"I don't think so."

"I've heard that name though, I'm sure I have—"

"It'll only be gossip. I hate how people gossip."

"La-di-da! Hark at her! Since when didn't you like gossip?"

"Since always. Now hush, he'll hear you!"

"Good morning," he said, from the bottom of the steps. He looked bright and clean and new, smiling up at her.

Padma felt her face grow warm.

"This is Ruth, a friend from Colombo," she said.

"How do you do?" Ruth elegantly reached her hand out to him and Rohan came up the steps to shake it.

"Rohan," he said.

"How are you finding Padma's guest house?"

"It's wonderful."

"Really? I'm so glad you like it." Ruth's eyes were fixed on him.

"Do you still want to go for that walk on the beach? Rohan asked Padma.

"Walk on the beach?" Padma tried to look surprised.

"You said last night that you'd like to—"

"Really? Did I?" Padma felt her cheeks burn as Ruth turned to stare at her "I can't now, I'm afraid. We're expecting new guests and it's breakfast soon—"

"But a nice stroll on the beach will do you good, Padma darling." Ruth jumped up and tugged at Padma's chair, almost tipping her out.

"Off you go! Soma and I can take care of breakfast!" Ruth
pushed Padma towards the steps and Padma went to Rohan.

A new shyness swept over her as they walked together down
the path.

"Enjoy yourselves!" Ruth called out.

Padma turned and Ruth was on the veranda, squinting at them.
Padma walked faster away from that intent searching gaze.

# 17

GERHARDT REACHED THE villa, eager to see Ruth. He had been delighted to hear from her a moment earlier that Louis had gone and that there were new guests due to distract Padma, if she missed Louis. Ruth had decided to stay for a few more days, for the first time staying at his house in the village. He would take a break from work while she was staying, he had decided, maybe take her on a drive inland for a day or two, staying in one of the luxurious new places she admired, not doing much, just swimming and lunch and dinner. They would share a room if she wanted to, twin beds of course, or maybe even the same bed – now that would be strange, but not strange enough to seem unlikely.

He found her in the office, talking on the phone.

"Tell Hamu to call me the minute she gets back, do you hear?" she instructed someone in the authoritarian tone she used with staff and locals of lower social standing – a matter-of-fact snootiness typical of her class of Sri Lankan.

He still found these aspects of her a little disquieting, although mercifully the people at the receiving end seemed not to mind, at least not outwardly. Possibly they could sense her innate kindness and good humour, never far from the surface.

"You're sure you've got my telephone number? You've written it down correctly? Read it to me again!" Ruth ordered.

Gerhardt waited on the porch until she came to him. He kissed her on the cheek. She put her arms around him.

"What was all that about on the phone?" he asked.

"Nothing important."

"I heard you say it was urgent."

"It's the only way to get through to her crazy houseboy."

"Whose?"

"Maisie Pieris's. Do you know her? She was a great all-rounder, played cricket, netball and gave piano recitals – I used to be at school with her. She married one of the Matara Wijesinghes – he was the head of the National Union Bank for many years."

He hadn't heard of the man, or Maisie Pieris, for that matter, but he wasn't deterred by Ruth's artful chatter.

"What does this Maisie Peiris need to call you about?" he asked.

"Oh nothing much."

He let it drop. She would tell him eventually.

"Thanks for coming out so quickly, he said. "Sorry it was a false alarm. Do you know why he left so abruptly?"

"I have an idea."

"Was it to do with Padma?"

"No. Definitely not."

"You're sure? She wasn't too upset?"

"Quite sure."

"She's tougher than I give her credit for. I have a feeling Ria also was falling for the fellow's charms. Too much of a charmer, that one! Where's Padma now?"

"On the beach."

"On her own? I told her not to go out by herself! I'd better go and find her."

"Why can't she go out by herself?" Ruth was looking stern. "Don't tell me, Sunny's back?"

"No, not since his ridiculous party."

Still, Gerhardt ran into the garden.

"By the way, she's not on her own," Ruth called down.

"What? Who's she gone with?"

"Someone called Rohan."

"Ah, he's alright."

Gerhardt returned relieved and sat down in his chair.

"You never mentioned him," Ruth said.

"Rohan? There's nothing to mention – he's a quiet fellow, keeps to himself. Padma must have offered to show him around. I'll have a word with her about doing too much; she's so kind and helpful."

"It must be lonely for her after Colombo," Ruth said.

"She's not missing Colombo."

Ruth was silent. The only life she acknowledged was city life. She needed people around, even if she had never quite fitted in her rigid upper-class world, but she liked to think that she had. For Ruth, the countryside was a place to revive in before returning to her real life. Ruth glanced at her phone.

"Maisie always takes so long to call back," she grumbled. "So, when do you suppose Sunny will pop up again?"

"Maybe he won't. If he does, I'll set up a new arrangement."

"Oh no, Gerhardt, not again! How much money you've wasted on that scoundrel already."

"It's worth it, if it keeps him away from her."

"He'll never go away now that she has her own business, he'll want some part of it. He will pull at her heartstrings – that's how he'll get to her. She still cares about those rotters despite everything, and Sunny knows it."

"She's such a kind, loving soul, so tender-hearted." Now

Gerhardt felt troubled too. "That's the weakness they'll go for. Just imagine, a beautiful trusting nature being a weakness!"

"It is a weakness. How else could Sunny have convinced her to go back to his place? After everything he's done, to still go back with him – it's incredible."

"I should never have let her go; I should have known better."

How could he have let himself believe that it was familial affection prompting the invitation? "Such a miserable pair, that Sunny and Leela," he declared. "How can they not see what a glorious precious child they were given?"

"But they do, she's their most valuable asset." Ruth saw straight through to the core of people; she didn't look away from their ugliness. "Send her to me, Gerhardt, help her to free herself," she begged.

"Padma doesn't like Colombo. She loves being here."

"But what sort of a life is this for a vibrant, intelligent young woman?"

"May I remind you that this was what she wanted?"

"You could have said no."

"But it was a good idea!"

"Really? To set up a guest house with the minister's brother's whore-house coming next door?"

"We don't know he's going to use it for that."

"For God's sake, Gerhardt, you're in the middle of his expanding empire! What do you think is going to happen here? And don't tell me again about that wall of yours – the truth is, you wanted her with you in this God-forsaken backwater – that's why you didn't say no. In fact, you expanded her plans – at first she was only talking about renting out one room in the house!"

His stomach was tight with resentment. Ruth understood nothing. He wished he had never asked her to come.

"And in the meantime, Sunny could be hatching up a brand

217

new plan of attack," Ruth went on. "I wake up every night from nightmares about terrible things happening here."

"You want me to send Padma away because you've had bad dreams?"

"Those were no ordinary dreams – my unconscious is trying to tell me something."

"And it's chosen to forget that nothing's ever happened in all the years of us living here?"

"But you're not paying Sunny anymore!"

"I will if I have to – I just told you."

"Oh you're infuriating! You're so selfish! You're stopping her from doing something wonderful. Other young people her age are going all over the world, studying in top universities, setting up incredible businesses, but Padma is cooped up here all day – you've locked her up in this prison you've built—"

"Oh, a prison, is it?"

"Yes, that's what you've made with your great architect's vision."

He wouldn't get angry, he wouldn't let her spoil the morning. She had got herself all worked up, talking nonsense. He should never have asked her to come; she had never liked the world he had made without her. It was his and Padma's; it only existed for them. Ruth's phone started to ring.

"At last! Maisie? Maisie – is that you?"

She went down the porch steps.

"The reception's fine here," Gerhardt called after her, but Ruth had already gone out of earshot.

The sudden quiet felt uneasy. Ruth had destroyed the calm, all the promise of the day. She had always been an overly dramatic person, easily agitated and demanding – was that why he had stood aside to let Ronny step forward, desiring and eager? It had been the end of their happy young trio, so bound to each other once, and so restless for new experiences when they had all met in London. Ronny had been studying for the Bar, Gerhardt for a Masters in architecture, Ruth travelling. But they hadn't always been three – Gerhardt had met Ruth first, when he sat beside her on a bench outside the British Museum and looked up from his sketchbook to find her watching him. They had talked and he had agreed to go to lunch with her. Both she and Ronny asked easily for what they wanted, and always got it.

After that idyllic summer, Gerhardt had been awarded a scholarship to study in Florence and Ronny had returned to Sri Lanka to begin his law career – and Ruth, her visa expired, had gone with him. She hadn't returned to Europe as she had said she might. It was Gerhardt who had moved to Sri Lanka. He had found work with an architect whom he admired, but it was for Ruth that he had gone – too late, as it turned out, for Ronny and Ruth were engaged soon after. They had probably all made the right choices. Ruth had been happy with Ronny, the two at the centre of a vibrant, educated, liberal elite, a tight web of overlapping friends and relatives reinforcing their togetherness. And they were well-suited, Gerhardt had had to concede – so alike: so full of drama, fiercely repelling the usual dullness of life, always demanding more, refusing to be denied or humbled. They had lived extravagantly and neither, even in old age, grew quiet and worn out like other people – there was no gentle rounding-off of ambition, no bounding of horizons, they were defiant. Ronny, to the very end.

Ruth came running around the side of the house.

"I have to get back, call the driver!" she gasped.

"What's the matter?"

"Is Padma here?"

"No – why?"

"They should have returned by now – shouldn't they? He

wouldn't do anything to her in broad daylight, would he? Shall we send Soma to look for her?"

"What's the matter? Have you seen Sunny?"

"No! It's that Rohan—"

"Rohan?"

"There are certain things we didn't know about him. Now Gerhardt, I don't want you to panic, but apparently he's been going through a messy divorce in the Colombo courts—"

"Yes, I know. So?"

"He told you?" She was thrown, but only for a split-second. "Of course, he may have been trying to manage the rumours."

"What rumours?"

"They say he was violent towards his wife. Like I say, it's only a rumour, but we can't risk Padma getting involved with someone like that. Send Soma to look for her, will you! Please! If that fellow so much as touches my girl . . . Soma! Soma!"

"Padma isn't involved with Rohan! Don't be ridiculous!" Gerhardt laughed out loud.

Soma came running.

"Soma, it's fine, it's nothing," Gerhardt said.

Soma looked from him to Ruth.

"It's fine," Gerhardt assured him and he retreated.

"Maybe she's alright . . ." Ruth strained to see the beach. "We'll know everything soon enough. I'm going straight over to his lawyer's house when I reach Colombo."

"His lawyer's house, why?"

"Luckily his divorce attorney was one of Ronny's pupils. I'm sure I can get him to divulge the salient facts."

"I take it this man hasn't heard of client confidentiality?"

"He'll tell me when he knows what a special case this is."

"You do know Padma isn't actually seeing that fellow?"

Ruth really was impossible. Anyone could see that Rohan

wasn't violent just by spending five minutes with him. And nothing whatsoever was going on between him and Padma.

"Haven't you seen the two of them together?" Ruth demanded.

"Of course I have."

She sighed. "You're a clever man, Gerhardt, but you're hopeless sometimes. Just don't mention any of this to Padma - that's all I ask. The last thing we want is to spoil her happiness unduly."

"Don't worry, I'm not saying anything! I want nothing to do with this madness."

Ruth was too much, she was exhausting. Marriage to her would have been a disaster. Here was the proof, if ever he needed it.

"You have a part of your brain missing, that's your trouble," Ruth scolded. "How is she to have a life of her own and meet the right people if you keep her here? You have to let her go, you have to deal with your feelings of aloneness. It's not natural to never be alone, to never be hurt."

Anger flared in him, black and vast.

"You don't think I've ever been hurt? You went with my best-friend. I know how to be alone, believe me."

There, he had said it, the one unspoken fact between them, a gleaming nugget of pain polished from years of handling.

She stared at him, shocked.

"You bring this up now? After how many decades?" she said.

"Better late than never, don't you think?"

"If you say so."

At last he could look at her and see her clearly, without the murky mist of their perfect denial. Her eyes were full of hurt and fear and shame - those black bright eyes, the same eyes still, after all these years, the same girl in her.

"What was I to do? How long did you think I would wait for you to want me?" she said.

"But you chose Ronny."

"You never said what you wanted. You didn't even seem to mind me being with him."

"I waited, but you never ended it. It was him you wanted—"

"I wanted you more," she said.

"We might have had children together."

"You think you're the only one who's thought of that?"

He had never asked, and never been told, why she and Ronny hadn't had children. They had never seemed to need them, the way some couples did; they were so close, so content together, no space between them.

"I'm going to call the driver. I'll wait in the office," she said.

He helped her gather her things from around the veranda. Even in the short time she had been there, she had managed to spread possessions all over the house. She was silent, more silent than he had ever seen her, lost to him. She went to the office and he heard her telephone her driver to take her home. Gerhardt didn't stop her. There was nothing more to say. How could anything change after all these years? He went outside, pacing around a far corner of the garden.

# 18

PADMA WALKED WITH Rohan on the beach. Far down at the other end, a tourist couple walked hand-in-hand. An old hippy from the village was sitting under the coconut trees, a Burgher man with grey dreadlocks, who had lived in New York and Colombo, but now spent his days on Nilwatte Beach selling cigarettes and biscuits and ganja at the beach bars in the mornings, and hard drugs at certain parties at night. He was thought to be friends with influential Russians, which was why the minister's men left him alone. The tourists joined him now and sat laughing and talking and being familiar, the way they became with locals, even after just one night. Padma had never understood why tourists thought they could become friends with the people selling them stuff – but tourists paid to be that gullible, to believe they'd found a place where everyone loved them just for turning up. Maybe that was all anyone really wanted.

"I feel sorry for Louis," Padma said.

"I'm sure he'll be fine."

"It's such a shame, now he'll have bad memories of staying with us."

"The guy was a jerk."

"Don't you believe in holiday romances?"

"As opposed to sex with strangers?"

"Not all sex with strangers is bad,"

How many times she had felt that she didn't know the guy she was with, even though they had been friends and seeing each other every day for months.

"Why should life be so different to holidays?" he mused.

"Because you don't do any work on holiday!" She laughed.

"But love? Why should love be different when you get back home?"

They had walked to a rocky ledge that ran across the beach. Rohan climbed up and walked along the top. He picked something up and came back down.

"For you," he said, bowing as he presented her with a conical shell, green and grey striped, glossy salmon-pink inside.

"Thanks. I'll treasure it my whole life."

"I should hope so."

He looked down at a pool at the base of the rock.

"What are you looking for now?" she asked.

"More treasure."

"All for me?"

"All for you." His smile was all for her.

Her fingers curled into the shell's hollow, glassy-smooth and cool.

"So, how long have you gone without . . . ?" she asked softly.

"I beg your pardon?"

"It's been over a year for me. That's a long time, I think."

"Tell me about it." He sighed. "I'm glad I'm not the only one."

"Oh I can live like a nun if I have to."

"A nun . . . yes, I can see you as a nun."

She grinned. "I'd be like Maria in *The Sound of Music*, singing at the top of my voice in desperation. Just imagine, up on those mountains there'd be no one around – just to know that would be nice, wouldn't it? Is it possible to really be alone?"

"Of course it is."

"But there would always be the chance of a madman hiding and watching you."

"Not necessarily."

"You can never know for sure, though, can you?"

"It depends where you went."

He climbed back up onto the rocks.

"The thing to do is develop your sixth sense," she said. "Like a third eye. Jarryd says it's possible for anyone to develop one, through meditation. We're all born with an instinct for others. He says human beings have lost vital powers of connection by being able to talk."

"What does he suggest? Telepathy?"

"Yes, but also physical communion, like tantra."

"Tantra? As in orgies?"

"Tantra is a philosophy. And anyway, tantric sex isn't only about orgies – you can do it as a couple."

"I thought he was teaching you yoga!"

"Jarryd's my guru! He's not allowed to get involved with his students."

Rohan climbed down from the rocks.

"Let's get back," he said.

"Now? Why?"

"I'm burning in the sun. Come on."

She had to walk fast to keep up with him.

"Are you okay?" she asked.

"Yes, I'm fine."

Clearly she had made him uncomfortable.

"I'm not a tantric freak," she said, but he didn't slow down.

They passed the hippy and the tourist couple.

"Nobody heard anything, we were too far away," she assured him, but he didn't seem to hear. He ushered her over the lane, and into the garden.

It was strange. Who would have thought he would turn out to be such a prude? It was a good thing she hadn't told him about the tantric sex and yoga manual that she had ordered from America, the best on the subject, according to Jarryd, and he would know. She only hoped it wouldn't be stolen in the post. There was so much to learn, now that she was free of university. She had discovered she could study as well as anyone if there was something she wanted to know.

⚘

Gerhardt was tending to the jasmine creepers at the side of the porch when Padma and Rohan returned. They were quiet, coming up the path. He watched them closely. They were barely speaking, certainly no hand-holding or any sign of romance – no sign whatsoever of Ruth's wild claims.

"Morning, Gerhardt!" Padma came over, rosy with sun, stretching to kiss his cheek.

"I'll see you later," Rohan said and walked away.

That handsome well-groomed exterior revealed nothing, but how could there have been anything going on? The two seemed completely lack-lustre, no interest at all in each other.

"Where's Ruth?" Padma asked.

"She's getting ready to go."

"With you?"

"No, she's going back to her place."

"But she's only just got here! What happened? Did you two have a fight?"

"Not really."

226

"She was acting very strangely earlier – she's not sick, is she?"

"No, she's simply suffering from an excess of imagination."

"Imagining what?"

"Whatever Ruth imagines."

Padma gave him a strange look and went inside. Ruth's driver pulled up in the lane in her dark blue BMW.

"Lalith is here!" Gerhardt called into the house and hurried back into the garden as Ruth and Padma came out.

Gerhardt dead-headed the marigold bushes as Ruth, her face ashen, eyes swollen, lent on Padma's arm going down the path. Padma anxiously watched over her. Gerhard followed their sombre procession to the car. Always he followed her. Despite himself, he had gone to her when she returned from months of honeymooning in Europe. He had attended her dinners and parties at the dilapidated colonial mansion that Ronny had bought and had an architect – not Gerhardt – restore to its original splendour for their life together. The same house she would go to now, away from the world that Gerhardt had built, without her and far from her. Lalith opened the car door for Ruth who hugged Padma tightly.

"Won't you stay? Just for one night? Whatever it is, we can sort it out," Padma pleaded with her.

Ruth caressed Padma's cheek. "Thank God for you, you're the one miracle that happened to us," Ruth said softly.

Padma held her, murmuring reassurances, tenderly stroking her back, smoothing her hair. How time passed! How could it have been Padma, the gentle motherly figure now, caring for the elderly woman that was Ruth? Padma turned beseechingly to Gerhardt, but he stayed back. This time they had gone too far, he and Ruth. Too much had been said. There was a reason they had taken such care not to talk too much all these years. Now the wounds of the past had been opened too wide; how could they ever be closed up?

Lalith took Ruth's bag and helped her to settle in the back of the car, placing cushions behind her neck and back. Then he went round to the driver's seat and started the engine. Gerhardt stood with Padma watching Ruth leave.

"I don't suppose I'm going to find out what that was all about, am I?" Padma said.

"Probably not."

Another car came haltingly down the lane, stopping at every gate.

"Oh no! I bet that's the new guests!" Padma cried and ran back to the house.

The car lurched to a halt and a young Asian couple looked out from the back, both somewhat harassed-looking.

"Excuse me, is this the Villa Hibiscus," the man asked.

"That's us."

"Cool! We thought we were totally lost!" The man leapt out of the car, a tall, striking looking Sri Lankan with an American accent and flashes of bleached blond in his short black hair. "Hi, I'm Dan," he said and shook Gerhardt's hand.

"We rang earlier, we have a bungalow booked," the woman said from inside the car.

Her voice was clear and confident, with a slightly Americanised Sri Lankan accent, upmarket-sounding. She was very pretty.

"This is Anjali," Dan said.

She got out of the car and came to stand, slim and lovely, beside Dan, gazing about her with disdain.

"Could you bring the bags up," she said to the taxi driver in the same tone that Ruth had employed with Maisie Pieris's houseboy.

Gerhardt and Dan helped the driver take their many bags up to the house. Anjali paid the man who looked relieved to be getting away. Anjali hardly saw him leave; she stood at the bottom of the porch steps, staring at the house, looking distinctly unimpressed.

"Padma! Your guests are here!" Gerhardt shouted. "I have to

do some work, I'm afraid," he told the couple. "Padma will be out soon and show you to your room."

"Room?" The woman frowned. "But we booked a bungalow, not a room."

Gerhardt edged up the steps, towards the sanctuary of the office, then Rohan appeared – like a Jack-in-the-Box, the fellow was.

"It's much too early for breakfast," Gerhardt told him.

The last thing Padma needed was Rohan hanging around while she settled in new guests.

"I came to help Padma," Rohan said.

"She's going to be busy for a while. Maybe you could come back later?"

Gerhardt noted Rohan's disappointment, guiltily pleased at this petty triumph.

"Okay, fine. I've got a letter to post anyway." Rohan headed for the path. "And maybe I'll buy a paper and read the president's latest fiction about the state of the country."

Gerhardt couldn't help smiling. The fellow was amusing, he'd give him that. Still, he was glad to see him go.

"Is he staying here?" the young woman asked.

"Yes. Why?"

"No reason." Yet she seemed concerned.

So she had recognised him, although Rohan hadn't seemed to know her. Was he known in Colombo for the marital troubles Ruth had talked about? Had Padma's first instincts about him been right after all? Had they been harbouring a violent madman at the villa all this time?

"Do you know him?" Gerhardt asked Anjali.

"Not at all!"

"It's just – you seemed to know something about him . . . ?"

"I know nothing at all about him!" she retorted.

"Padma! Come, will you!" Gerhardt called.

Padma emerged at last, grandly descending the steps to her guests.

"Hello, there! Welcome! I'm Padma, I'm the manager here!" She beamed.

Gerhardt hurried into the office and closed the door. Such welcome solitude! The scent of Padma's joss sticks lingered in the room. Her yoga mat was rolled up by the bookcase. She had cleared a large space for her yoga: her cotton strap and wooden blocks, a fat red bolster cushion were all neatly lined up along the wall. He turned on the fan and sank into the chair. Good God, what a morning. Through the window came voices:

"I specifically requested a bungalow when I booked," Anjali complained.

"But it's no big deal," Dan added.

"Yes, it is! It's a very big deal! I would never have come here if we weren't going to have a bungalow!"

"A guest is leaving in a few days, you can have her bungalow," Padma offered.

"That would be great," Dan said.

"No, Dan, it's not great at all – I don't want to wait!" Anjali protested. "Can I speak to your boss?"

"I am the boss," Padma replied.

Gerhardt grinned.

"And you're refusing to give us the bungalow that we actually booked?"

"What's she supposed to do, Anjali?" Dan said.

"Maybe I could ask the other guest to swap with you?" Padma suggested.

"You mean that man we saw?" Anjali demanded.

"I don't know, did you see him? He's called Rohan. Otherwise you could wait until the other bungalow is free?"

"No, I don't want to wait! Ask him."

"In the meantime, why don't you use your room to rest?" Padma offered. "You can take showers and change and freshen up – I won't charge you for it."

"Thank you so much," Dan said gratefully.

There was no sound from Anjali. It was hard to imagine anyone not appeased by Padma's kindness. She was a wonderful host, and she seemed to be enjoying the work, despite Ruth's disdain for it. Gerhardt glanced at his watch. It was too soon to call Ruth, she would still be on her way home. He might call her later – or maybe he should let her call him. She might not want to talk just yet. Would they ever move on from what he had unleashed?

The guests were installed in their room, and he took his chance to leave the house. He had a meeting with a client at his studio back at the house. He walked fast through the village, leaving the morning behind. He tried not to think of Ruth's small hunched figure hobbling down the path, the sad shocked eyes looking back at him. He had never seen Ruth so defeated; so forlorn. Even as Ronny lay dying, she had been composed, her grief contained. It was Gerhardt who had drifted then, mourning a part of his life lost to them and left unavenged. Was that why he didn't regret what he had said to Ruth that morning? There was a clean new spaciousness inside him now, as if a sullen slothful presence had been forced out forever.

A large, black, armoured Mercedes was parked outside his house. It was a car he knew all too well. He approached it calmly, without resistance; the encounter was inevitable. The window at the back rolled down.

"Ah, there you are, Gerhardt." The round pampered face of the minister looked up at him. Three Special Security Force soldiers sat with him in the car, uninvolved yet alert.

"Hello, sir. Were you waiting for me? Would you like to come in?"

"No, I'm very busy, I have to be going."

Encounters with the minister had turned distinctly frosty ever since Gerhardt had turned down his offer to design a vast hotel in the north of the country in former Tamil-owned land that had been seized by the army. Gerhardt had said he was too busy, but the minister knew his reasons were moral and had taken it personally. The minister had once deemed Gerhardt a friend, enjoying the critical approval of projects he had assigned Gerhardt to work on. When the commendations became international there was no stopping the minister's affection and Gerhardt had been extended the comfort of official protection. His association with the minister had eased his passage through many an official obstacle and no doubt the local hoodlums kept their distance more because of this connection than Boss's protection. But until the minister's latest offer, Gerhardt had not had to compromise his principles for he would never take on any project that could taint his body of work.

"Gerhardt, you never came back to me on that matter I spoke to you about," the minister said.

"Which matter, sir?"

Surely he didn't still want Gerhardt for the hotels? Architects had already been assigned, he'd heard.

"The sale of your villa, of course. Surely you haven't forgotten? I made you a very generous offer when you moved to your new place."

Gerhardt hadn't thought the minister was being serious.

"I can't part with the villa, sir, as you know, it is my daughter's home and her new business is there as well."

"She only has a couple of huts and a room, I heard – surely that's not profitable?"

"She's getting there, slowly, slowly."

"Considering the very generous offer I made you, Gerhardt, you could buy Padma a much bigger house and make her a proper hotel. She could charge top rates - now that would be a real business for her."

"She loves our little villa, sir, and for now it is just the right size for her."

The minister pouted. He didn't like to be refused. The Special Security Force men sat looking straight ahead, acting as if they weren't listening. What those men must have seen and heard. And done. Would they ever be turned on him? Ruth's warnings returned to him; for once Gerhardt felt unsure of his standing with the minister. But the man wasn't stupid; he wouldn't hurt someone with important contacts abroad; he was fully aware of Gerhardt's profile in India and Singapore and China.

"Okay, alright, but the offer still stands," the minister said with a sigh.

"Thank you, sir."

"You know, Gerhardt, these children of ours will always be changing their minds about what it is they want. Mine are constantly finding new things they say they want to do. The other day Nilesh tells me he wants to be a lawyer, then he says: 'Actually, Thaththa, I want to be an architect!' Can you imagine! Maybe I can send him to you for training?"

The thing to do was smile and nod and act as if teaching that buffoon of a boy, who should be in prison for fraud and more than one sexual assault, would be perfectly acceptable.

"So, you're still saying no, are you Gerhardt, about selling the villa?"

"Yes, sir, I'm afraid so. I'll let you know if anything changes."

"Oh, everything changes, Gerhardt. All the time, things are changing. And they can be made to change, of course."

"I'm not sure I understand."

The minister exhaled impatiently.

"You're a stubborn fellow, Gerhardt. But you'll let me know if your daughter changes her mind, won't you?"

"Of course I will, sir."

"It can't be easy for her having her other family nearby."

"Actually, they live quite far away."

"That's not my impression. Sunny is often around these parts, I hear. And the son, also."

"I haven't seen them."

"Must be hard for her, seeing them around everywhere she goes – I hear the man can be violent."

"Fortunately Padma is too busy with her business for family dramas."

"Ah very good, very good. You wouldn't want him being violent with her, would you?"

"No, I certainly wouldn't."

"Isso, isso, isssoooooo!" An old woman hawking prawns came around the bend in the road, her basket balanced on her head.

She stopped, seeing the minister's car and turned and went back the way she had come.

"So bear in mind what I've said," the minister said.

"Yes, sir."

The dark window slid up to show Gerhardt's own reflection looking anxiously back at him. The car pulled away.

Obviously, the minister was making trouble, trying to scare Gerhardt – but there was no doubt anymore in his mind: Sunny had to be dealt with. Whatever money he wanted, Gerhardt must give it and view it as a necessary tax.

"Isso!" The old woman returned with her prawns. "Mahaththaya, isso?" she enquired.

"Not today."

He went inside, through the cool shadowy hall of his house,

into the courtyard beyond. His garden was contained in this house, the rooms in a square around it, looking in. In his study the plans for the client were unfinished on the drawing board. He sat on the stool, allowing himself to be taken over by the clean pliant problems of design, escaping from the weight of something big pushing in from all sides.

## 19

THE NEW GUESTS were awful, the worst ever. Padma wished they would storm out and go somewhere else, but they showed no sign of leaving. Anjali had finally stopped demanding a bungalow, but now she wanted Gustav to be tied up all day. Poor Gustav, he'd never been tied up in his whole life! Padma had refused as politely as she could. Then Anjali had wanted real coffee for breakfast, which she hadn't liked when it arrived. And she had insisted that the toast was burnt, so more had to be made, just for her. Padma retreated to the kitchen to wait for breakfast to end.

"Where on earth have they come from, that pair?" Soma asked.

"Dan told me they've been working at an orphanage in Galle."

"That woman was helping orphans?"

"She must have told all the children to get lost and leave her alone!" Padma sneered, dropping her voice.

"She's mad, throw her out while you can," Soma advised. "You wait and see - she'll do something crazy soon. That's how they get, little by little. I had an aunt once, she was always moaning and groaning and getting angry - she ended up in the asylum. She took an axe one day and ran after her husband."

"Anjali's not crazy, she's just a brat. She'll be on the phone to her mummy and daddy any minute now, asking them to sue us or close us down or something."

"Maybe she's the daughter of someone famous," Soma said. "What if she's a politician's daughter? That's all we need."

"Then she'd have security. No, she's probably just rich."

"Still, what if her father is some big-shot tough-guy? Just give her the bungalow, we don't want the Special Security Force turning up."

"I've already said I'll ask Rohan to swap with them. People like her always get what they want." Padma glumly got up to go and find Rohan.

"Hello?" Anjali called from the hall.

"You go," Padma whispered to Soma.

"They're your guests!"

"Please?"

He went, but he was back in an instant.

"She wants towels - the towels in the room aren't soft enough, apparently. And they're too musty, she says. Freshly laundered, she wants. Please, you deal with her."

He reached for a cleaver and split a coconut with one swipe.

"That woman is trouble, I'm telling you." He held the two halves of the coconut over the sink to drain, then sat down astride the old-fashioned coconut scraper and furiously grated a half coconut against the spiked metal head. "You turn a perfectly pleasant house into a guest house, and this is what you get. They won't all be like Ria Missy and Mr Rohan - most of the time they'll be like that crazy lady, you'll see."

Padma had been thinking the same thing. Possibly one day she would be able to afford to pay someone else to be the manager. But what would she do then? She often thought of going away, to a place where no one knew her. She picked out the fluffiest, most scented towels from the linen cupboard and went to the guest room. She took a deep breath and knocked on the door.

"Come in," Anjali called, imperiously, like a queen.

She was all alone, standing in the middle of the room with all the bags thrown open on the floor. The shower was running in the bathroom where Daniel must have locked himself in to get away from her.

"You can put the towels over there," Anjali said, with a wave of a pale delicate hand. She had showered and was dressed in tight jeans that showed off her small curvy figure. She wore a sleeveless green silk top that made her skin seem polished and golden. Padma had been around women like Anjali before, at university, pampered protected girls untested by life who took their good fortune for granted.

Anjali swept back her damp hair impatiently and moved aside to let Padma place the towels on the bed. Anjali's body looked tense; her eyes followed Padma. Women like Anjali were wary of people they couldn't place, people like Padma, and they concealed their uncertainty with disdain. Padma had never been allowed into their circles. The women in her tutorial groups only ever spoke to her to ask to borrow notes – and that soon stopped when they found out that she had a tendency to fail exams – from then on they had ignored her.

"Wow, that's some fabric conditioner, I can smell it from here!" Anjali sneered at the new towels perched hopefully at the end of the bed. "Have you asked your other guest about the bungalow?"

"No, but I will—"

"How long's he staying, anyway?"

"One more week. Why?"

"Just curious."

"Are you from Colombo?"

"Yes . . ."

"He is too. Maybe you've met already somewhere?"

"I definitely haven't met him anywhere!" Anjali was emphatic.

"Oh, okay. Well, he's called Rohan Fernando."

But Anjali knew that already; she knew exactly who Rohan was – she was too interested in him, and not in the usual way. Anjali had propped a magazine like a shield around her, at breakfast, trying not to be seen by him. Did Rohan know her? Was he pretending not to for a reason they shared? Some secret silent agreement?

"How long will it take to get our room?" Anjali grumbled.

"I'm going now to find Rohan. Would you like a drink while you wait? Some tea? A soft drink? You can have it out on the veranda."

"You have Diet Coke?"

"No. Ginger beer, lemonade, Fanta."

"You have red Fanta?"

"No."

"Just get me ordinary Fanta then."

Anjali followed Padma into the hall. Gustav padded over to inspect her.

"Shoo! Shoo! Go away!" Anjali cried shrilly.

She was terrified, her face contorted with fear as she pressed up against the wall, almost knocking over the telephone table, as Gustav stood wagging his tail before her.

"He's only trying to make friends," Padma explained, dragging him away.

"I've got plenty of friends," Anjali retorted shakily. She adjusted her top and tossed back her hair.

"And you definitely won't tie him up?"

"No."

"I'm not used to dogs. Ours at home are guard dogs – they're not allowed to run around the house."

"Gustav's allowed to run around our house, so maybe you

should introduce yourself. Here, pat him, then he won't bother you again."

Anjali gingerly stroked Gustav with one finger. He gave her a big loving grin that she didn't deserve, then trotted off.

"You see, he's a big softy," Padma said, but Anjali didn't look convinced.

She hovered nervously by the veranda doors as Padma went to the fridge for the Fanta.

"I'll go and find Rohan," Padma said, going out. "Hopefully he'll agree to swap rooms with you."

"Technically it's *ours*," Anjali said. "And it's not like he needs the extra space, is it? He's staying here alone, right?"

"How on earth did you know that?"

"Just guessing," Anjali mumbled.

"But you sounded so sure."

Anjali said nothing, sitting down at the table that had briefly been Louis'. She watched a group of laughing happy tourists go past in the lane, her expression murderous. She inspected her glass then poured in the Fanta, the bubbles fizzing frantically.

"Do you know Rohan?" Padma demanded.

"Of course not! And I'm sure he has no idea who I am either!" Anjali gave a nervous little laugh. "It's a small country, I know, but really!" She got up from her seat, taking the bottle and glass. "I'll drink this in my room. Let me know when we can have the bungalow," she said. She turned at her door. "Oh, and there's just one other thing – we need twin beds, not a double."

"*Twin beds?*"

"Yes. You offer 'twin or double' on your website and we would like twin."

"They're in the shed. Normally you should ask in advance."

"Yes, sorry, I forgot."

But she hadn't forgotten at all. She'd only just thought of it, straight after Rohan was mentioned.

"Well then, I'd better go and find *Rohan*!" Padma watched as she said his name, and yes, Anjali definitely winced. She fumbled with the guest-room door, trying to go in.

"Oh, and thanks for the Fanta," said Anjali, remembering to smile.

"No problem. I'll put it on your bill."

Padma went to Rohan's bungalow and knocked on his door. He opened it and she stepped inside. He offered her grapes from a paper bag.

"I wrote that letter," he said.

"Letter?"

"To my friend Tom, from school – remember, you told me I should write to him?"

"Ah, very good." She plucked herself a grape, looking into his shopping bag.

"So this is your lunch – let's see now: seeni sambol roll, chilli cashew nuts, banana, Kit Kat, how very nutritious!"

"You're welcome to share it."

"Maybe you could eat lunch with us? Soma's already been cooking for Ria, I don't see why he can't for you. And if you're staying in the house, it would be even easier—"

"Staying in the house?"

"Oh yes, Anjali wants your bungalow. Will you swap?"

"What do you mean?"

"The thing is, she did book a bungalow, and you have extended your stay—"

"I see. Okay."

"You will? You don't mind?" She had expected more of a fight.

"When do you want me to move?" he asked.

"As soon as possible. You really don't mind?"

"It could be fun, living in the big house with you."

"And Soma."

"Of course, him especially."

They smiled at each other. She loved being amused by the same things together.

"By the way, the new guests – do you know either of them?" she asked.

"No. Why?"

"The woman's called Anjali . . ."

"So?"

"Are you sure you don't know her?"

"Of course I'm sure!"

"She seems to know you."

"Big deal. I have a reputation now, remember?" He tried to look as if he didn't care.

"Nice people will always believe you. Anyone with half a brain will know the truth the moment they meet you."

"You reckon? You didn't."

"I did really."

He laughed. They stood on the veranda, looking out at the garden; like when they had looked up at the stars, just quiet together.

"I can have my things packed in a couple of hours," he said.

"I'll tell Soma to change the beds – Anjali wants twin beds in here."

"Interesting. She sounds very virtuous."

"She's completely mad. I'll go and tell her the news – maybe it'll cheer her up!"

Ria sat at her desk before the villa's guestbook, trying to write her farewell note. She had been composing it all morning, but every time she began, she started to cry. She had thought at first that she was crying for Louis, but she had watched him leave and felt relieved to have the villa to herself again. It was when Padma gave her the guestbook that she had thought of her departure the next day, which was when the sudden debilitating sadness had swooped down on her, an ambush. She was reduced to a new, inconsolable crying in her room, like a child begging not to be taken away from people it loved and the only place it knew. She flicked through the guestbook to earlier pages, from before the villa was a guest house. Family and friends had been often to stay in those days, writing in German, French, Dutch, English and leaving grateful joyous messages of thanks, with always the words: 'beautiful place' and 'thank you'. She picked up the pen. 'Dear Padma, Gerhardt, Soma – thank you,' she wrote. "Thank you for your welcome and your incredible kindness . . ." Her tears splashed onto the words and made the ink run, the black splitting to yellow and purple, a bruise on the page.

She had not known until then how much she disliked her life in London. Her aloneness there, even among colleagues and friends, was a cold lonely cell she was making herself return to. Of course, the moment she was back, breathing its foul vapours, London would claim her as always, and soon she would be one of the seduced, charmed again by the promise of pleasure and new experiences, a part again of London's hungry eager unquestioning mass. She dabbed at the stain on the page. A sob escaped her. She longed to stay at the villa forever, and never to have to go away.

There was a knock at the door. "Hi Ria? Are you busy?" It was Padma.

"Just coming!" Ria wiped her eyes and put on sunglasses before opening the door.

"Please can I join you? I need somewhere to hide," Padma pleaded.

"Hide?"

"Yeah, from the new guests. The woman's a nightmare. She keeps asking for things. She's got her bungalow now, and twin beds, but I'm staying away in case she thinks of something else."

They sat on the floor of the veranda, right back against the wall, out of sight of the main house.

"She seems unhappy," Ria said.

"She's a total pain! It's been weird, this morning. Ruth turned up, then she left—"

"Ruth was here? Oh, what a shame I missed her. It's thanks to her that I heard about this amazing place—" Ria heard her voice falter and stopped. She didn't want the awful weeping to start again.

Possibly Ruth wouldn't have remembered Ria, just another bored guest at Ria's cousin's lavish wedding in a 5-star Colombo hotel - where Ria had found herself seated at a table at the edge, with the visiting foreigners - university friends of the bride and groom who had flown from abroad for a tropical experience, and talked excitedly amongst themselves, ignoring her. She had slipped out to the bar, which was where she had met Ruth, a chic, self-composed, elderly woman in an unusually bright green sari, worn with a clashing crimson blouse. Ria had admitted to Ruth over a gin and tonic that she longed to escape her entrapment in the city, and Ruth had told her about the villa.

"Ruth would have liked to see you," Padma said. "She came all ready to stay for a few days, but then she and Gerhardt had a fight."

"Not them as well!"

"Yes! Incidentally, you're better off without him, I hope you don't mind me saying."

"My sentiments exactly. Poor Gerhardt and Ruth, though."

"Oh they'll make up, one of these days."

"I didn't realise they were together."

"They say they're not, but they've been in love for years – neither one will admit it, though. They can't decide anything for themselves – even where to live: Ruth says she has to be in the city, but she secretly loves Gerhardt's new house in the village. And Gerhardt says he hates Colombo, but he goes all the time because that's where most of his friends and clients live. They could spend time in both houses, but they're too scared to try."

"Maybe it's easier that way. Love is exposing. It hurts to admit when something matters. I've loved being here so much, more than anywhere else I've been, and now I know that nowhere will feel like this, and I'm so sad to be leaving."

There, she had said it. She let the tears well up behind her sunglasses.

"You still have today," Padma said.

"Yes."

"And you'll be back."

"No, I won't."

"Yes, you will! Silly!" Padma nudged her playfully.

"I'm serious. I'm not coming back to Sri Lanka."

"Ever?"

"I only came because of the family wedding, and that was a farce. Next year I'm going straight to Goa."

"You really love it there, don't you?"

"It's so beautiful it could be here – the same architecture, the same trees and flowers, even the colour of the soil is the same. There's an old mango tree in the garden, all gnarled and bent over, like a tree in my grandparents' garden where I used to have my swing – it's like going back to that life again . . ."

"But you need people, not mango trees!"

"Well, I don't have that."

"You've got us. But the yoga retreat does sound nice. I wish I could go with you."

"Why don't you?"

"I don't want to be in a class with a load of tourists. And I'm hardly a yoga teacher."

"Finish your training, then you will be."

"How can I leave here though?" Padma sighed.

"You'll find a way if you really want to."

"You really think I should become a teacher?"

"Only you know that. Everyone knows deep down what they really want. You just have to get past all the lies we tell ourselves. But don't listen to me – I never know what I really want."

"You seem to know very well. And you're free, you're not stuck running a guesthouse – you can go anywhere you like."

"But all I want is to stay at your guesthouse forever."

"You can stay as long as you like." Padma put her arm around Ria, and Ria was suddenly held in the sweet, easy kindness of the villa's people that surprised her even now – did such open, giving acceptance exist in other places? Was it something one had to actively seek? A world where people cared, and which one could care about without it being wasted?

20

ANJALI SAT ON the bed in their borrowed room, waiting for Dan to finish dressing. He took his time, humming to himself as he searched through the clothes; he was already at home there, even in that room they hadn't wanted. She almost liked it herself, and was suddenly not sure if she had given up something good – but she had booked the bungalow especially. Why shouldn't they have what was rightfully theirs? Through the window she saw the cook go past, grappling with a mattress that kept catching in the bushes.

"What's he doing?" Dan looked up and watched the scowling sweating man.

"I asked for twin beds."

"Aren't you taking this a bit far?"

He was unimpressed. But he wasn't the one being talked about all over Colombo. If Anjali's mother were to be believed, all the relatives and even friends of the family were muttering about Anjali having gone wild. Wild! That was the joke! Not one of them seemed able to see what a shrivelled-up prude she'd become from years of being miserable and saintly. She had thought herself disciplined in those days, but she saw now that she had only let them curtail her, denying her vital precious pleasures. She was damaged for ever perhaps, because an angry wilful self had risen up in her now; ugly and vengeful; suppressed for too long it was a monstrous presence, possessing her and assailing her all day with desires. She had never wanted much before, but everywhere she went now she saw how she was denied – she who had always thought herself lucky! She trembled with fear and fury at what she had colluded in, mourning the years of her youth given up to being good for others – years lost forever.

The cook came past again, going the other way. He looked in through the window bars, his dark face inscrutable. He was probably angry at her, for the extra work she had made for him. Or he could have been laughing at her – old-fashioned virtue would have no place in that strange quiet house with its air of nonchalance. No wonder Rohan had turned up there. Hopefully she had done enough to save the last shreds of her reputation if he did ever remember her. He would certainly have become aware of the rearrangement of the bungalow's beds, and he would hopefully remember this if he ever gave her away to her cousin, with whom he was friends. Rohan, her cousin and their gang of mates had all gone to school in Colombo together. In their teens, Rohan was sent abroad to finish his education, but he had often been at Anjali's cousin's house when he returned for the long summer holidays. It was strange that he didn't recognise her; her cousin's friends had regularly teased and flirted with her in those days. Was this proof that her mother was right, that she had changed completely since those days, changed beyond recognition?

"You want to go out for a walk?" Dan asked.

"It didn't look like a great neighbourhood."

"They only do breakfast and dinner here, we have to go out to get some lunch."

"Fine, let's go then."

As they went along the lane, a group of local men stared at her.

"Missy, are you from here?"

"Hey! Where are you from?"

"Do you come from India?"

"I'm from the moon," she said and kept walking.

It was hard to imagine what Rohan did all day in Nilwatte Beach. It was a far cry from the places he must have been used to, but he had looked quite at home at the peculiar guest house. He was a lot better looking than the last time she'd seen him, some weeks earlier, at a party she'd been dragged to, at the mansion home of one of her cousin's friends. Rohan had sat gaunt and quiet and drinking whisky all evening in the midst of his, and Anjali's cousin's raucous gang who had parted from wives and girlfriends the moment they'd set foot inside the party. Anjali had ended up sipping cocktails with the wives and girlfriends, who had filled Anjali in on Rohan's marital woes while their men stood guffawing by the bar, ogling young thin posing model-type women tottering past on their way to the pool.

On the drive home with her cousin, the subject of Rohan had come up again.

"He wasn't like the rest of us, he was sent to one of the best schools in the world, with royal princes and Arab sheikhs, then Oxford and Cambridge – not just one, but both – and he made a fortune working in an investment bank, and then he went and lost it all in a divorce!"

"You don't sound too sorry for your friend," Anjali observed.

"Everyone who goes abroad gets screwed up."

"I went abroad."

"Yeah."

Her cousin had only asked Anjali to the party because her mother had begged him to, hoping one of his single friends might distract her from Dan. As if she would ever fall in love with one of those stockbrokers or accountants with their rugby tales and ridiculous talk of women. Rohan hadn't joined in with any of it, she'd noticed. Her cousin, like the rest of her family, disapproved of her being with Dan. Only the men in the family were allowed to date openly before marriage. Her female cousins had snuck around, even with their future husbands, stories of their escapades sometimes coming out at the wedding in a best-man's speech, sniggered at by their friends and quickly forgotten by the family. Anjali too had snuck around, but she had been caught – and with a man of the wrong sort: wrong religion, wrong race, and probably not the right class either, although that was confused by his family being in the States and having as much money as anyone in her family, or possibly more.

"You've changed," her cousin said. "You used to be a lot nicer."

"So did you."

It had become easy to say what she was thinking. Now other people had to deserve any effort she made to think her angry thoughts in silence. Her cousin didn't seem too bothered though. He turned on the stereo and a CD started to play, a song she didn't know, but instantly liked.

"Who's this?" she asked.

"A group from the seventies. I suppose you think it's old-fashioned?"

"No, it's nice."

He didn't seem to like her any better for liking his music. The yearning voice singing of love and the mellow strumming of a guitar filled the silence around them in the icy-cool of air-conditioning. They drove along deserted night-time roads, the flash of sleek gleaming cars passing them with a glimpse of an expensive watch, a firm-toned arm, a sweep of glossy hair.

"Are you okay?" Dan said as they paused to look into a café.

At the party, whenever Anjali had looked over at Rohan from

her corner of wives and girlfriends, he'd looked as bored as she'd felt. Even if he recognised her, he might never mention her to her cousin, for why would he draw attention to his own stay in an odd guest house on a seedy stretch of coast? After all, he had far more to be ashamed of than her.

You're very quiet," Dan said.

"I know the guest we're swapping with."

"You do? Why didn't you say?"

"He's just been through this big divorce. He's called Rohan Fernando. The word is he beat up his wife."

"That guy at breakfast?" Dan was shocked.

"Can't say I blame him, she's ghastly. Shalini, she's called – I was at school with her. I'd have liked to give her a good slap, myself."

"So much for the sisterhood."

"Her parents were dodgy as hell. You should see the house they live in – it's got a swimming pool and a mini golf course, and all in the middle of Colombo."

"I'm not sure that justifies wife-beating."

"Maybe he didn't. Maybe she just made it up – that's the kind of thing she'd do, especially if he tried to leave her, which apparently he'd wanted to. She's really spiteful. Even when she was young she was horrible – she blinded an ayyah in one eye."

"Wow."

"She threw a knife at her, then said it slipped out of her hand. Her family covered it up, of course, bribed the police and paid the poor woman to go away."

"They sound great."

"Maybe Rohan's hiding from them."

But he couldn't have looked less like a fugitive. He hadn't even seemed like someone after a bad divorce and facing financial ruin. He looked much too happy. It made no sense.

They went into a café with a large quiet garden. Tourists sat roasting in the sun, their skin a hideous red, their hair bleached white and flossy, unnatural looking.

"Let's sit in the shade," Dan said and they chose a table under a large tree.

The moment they sat down, a speaker tied up in the branches crackled to life and tuneless rave music boomed down. Two young local men came and stood by a wall nearby and gaped at Anjali, one picking his nose, the other smoking a cigarette. She pretended not to see them while she studied the menu. The waiter came over and she ordered a toasted sandwich. Two tourists went past; blond dreadlocks piled on their heads in matted nests. They walked hand in hand, languid and grand, waving proprietorially to the waiter, then going into one of the rooms at the back of the garden. The room was yellow inside with a mattress on the floor and a giant purple mandala painted on the wall as a bedhead. The two men grinned as the couple closed the door, and Anjali knew what her mother had meant when she ranted at Anjali after finding out about Dan. It was true, people knew what you did behind closed doors; people could always tell.

"You're from around here, Missy?" the smoking man called to her. "Where are you from?"

She fixed her gaze beyond the garden, out to the lane.

"You speak Sinhalese?" The man came to their table.

He would never have dared, if she'd been with family. Locals would never have approached her directly then, they would have shuffled up ingratiating and obsequious, addressing the elders, and even then, only to beg for favours or sell things. She was exposed now, she was on her own.

"Could you please not smoke next to me?" she said to the man.

He stamped his cigarette into the sand but stayed where he was. The nose-picking man joined him.

"Missy, we're only being friendly, no?" the new man said.

"Listen guys, we've had a really long journey," Dan tried.

"Where are you staying?" the first man asked.

"The Villa Hibiscus," Dan said.

"Ah, with Gerhardt Hundsler? Ayyo! Expensive there, no? I know somewhere nice and clean and much cheaper."

"You want to see it?" the second man asked.

"No thanks," Dan said.

"You've met the manager at the villa? How's she managing? I hear she's already managed one of the guests." The men chuckled.

"I think I'll head back to the guest house," Anjali said, starting to get up, but the waiter arrived with their food.

He was a solemn, middle-aged man, unimpressed by the two men. He shooed them away and stood nearby, forcing them to leave. Anjali bit into her sandwich. Dan inspected his.

"Miss, you're from Sri Lanka?" the waiter asked.

"Why?"

"You're Sinhalese?"

She sighed impatiently.

"Buddhist?"

Dan started to look uneasy. The waiter glanced at him disapprovingly.

"Do your parents know what you're up to?" he asked Anjali.

Anjali slammed money down on the table and walked away. Dan grabbed the sandwiches and ran after her.

"Don't let them get to you. They're just curious about you," he said. "A beautiful woman near a tropical beach, I'd be curious too."

"They're arseholes. Everyone in Sri Lanka is these days."

He didn't contradict her, but it didn't mean that he agreed – Dan loved everyone. But it was easy for him; they let him be.

They could tell he was a Kalu-Sudda through and through – a Black-Whitie. She'd even had to translate the term for him – and then he'd just laughed. It was hateful that the term existed at all – the idea of being black and pretending to be white, the whiteness something assumed, something aspired to. She loathed the sneering implication of it. Why couldn't you just be what you were, and like what you liked ? All the way back to the villa, there were men staring.

"Hey, Maam! You want a boat ride? How about a crab feast? Is this your boyfriend?"

She ran into the garden of the guest house and marched up the path. A sudden movement on the porch made her stop.

"Oh no," she breathed and froze with the familiar terror, the terrible helplessness gripping her as the dog came loping down.

"Don't worry, he won't do anything," Dan said, stepping in front. "Here, boy!" He coaxed the dog aside, putting out his hand which was instantly licked, the dog's large fangs revealed.

"Go away!" Anjali hissed as the dog looked hopefully up at her.

Dan gave Gustav a gentle shove and he moved off reluctantly. They hung back, letting it go then followed slowly behind.

In the main house they found Padma and Rohan on the veranda, drinking ginger beer. The great hound of a dog lay at their feet, the three a picture of perfect country contentment.

"You're back early!" Padma said, without even a trace of irritation. "Your bungalow's almost ready, the cleaner's just finishing." She gave them a huge smile.

How could anyone be so cheerful all the time? Once Anjali would have pitied her, a woman with no profession, forced to do menial tasks and look after other people – but now she understood that while she had been straining for brilliant pinnacles, furiously striving, terrified of falling, people like Padma had been boldly

living, allowed to move into seemingly lesser pastures that nour-
ished those who knew to love and dream and to envision a world
of their own. Padma, with her little guest house, had far more
than Anjali with all her academic prizes and qualifications. Such
accolades felt irrelevant around Padma. Anjali felt brittle and un-
formed; Padma was all softness, with a bright clever flamboyance
that made her happiness seem effortless, unassailable.

"We'll help you move your bags to the bungalow," Padma
offered now.

"There's no need, you've already done so much," Dan insisted,
although technically it was her job.

"It's nothing, honestly." Padma smiled, all perfect teeth and
cheekbones, playful and womanly. Surely she was aware that both
men in the room were in her thrall, helplessly admiring her? No
wonder she didn't mind the extra work – anyone so adored was
bound to feel generous all the time.

"And thank you for swapping," Dan said awkwardly to Rohan,
not able to look him in the eye after what Anjali had told him.

"No problem."

Rohan didn't look like someone with ugly truths to hide. And
if he remembered Anjali from the night of the party, he didn't
let on.

"Are you staying here long?" Rohan asked Dan.

"Two weeks," Dan said.

"I ended up extending, it's so nice here," Rohan said.

"It is a great house," Dan agreed in a more friendly tone.

So he had decided to give Rohan a chance after all; men would
more easily excuse another man's faults – it was women who
remorselessly punished their own kind.

"I'll go and get our things ready," Anjali said, leaving
them.

Two expensive suitcases – Rohan's no doubt, were in the hall, waiting outside their room. One of them fell over as she moved it aside. It felt empty. Why would anyone bring an empty suitcase to Nilwatte Beach – there was nothing there to buy! Unless it was dope he wanted, but it would take an awful lot to fill a suitcase that size.

In the room she started to pack. Dan joined her.

"At last – you've finally stopped thanking the wife-beater," she hissed.

"Didn't you say his ex-wife set him up?" he whispered back.

"I said maybe."

"Well, he did give up a bungalow for us, we can still thank him for that."

"It was ours in the first place! In any case, I don't think it was all that altruistic."

"Huh?"

"Didn't you think they seemed a little cosy just now?"

"I suppose—"

"I bet you anything he's moved into the house to be closer to her."

"Good for them! They both seem really nice."

"You mean she seems really nice?"

"No, I meant both of them. Just like I said." He folded his clothes and packed his bags.

Anjali was afraid. He was finding her tiresome. He was beginning to like her less and less, seeing her as she really was. She packed the rest of her things in silence, the sadness in her so vast she thought it might swallow her whole.

Later they drank beer on the veranda where Padma and Rohan had sat and watched the sunset. But it didn't feel as it had looked when Padma and Rohan were sitting together.

"Was it a mistake coming here?" Dan asked, breaking the silence.

"Why?"

"We can always move on."

"And go where?"

"Somewhere."

But there was nowhere else to go anymore. Dan looked away, to the view; she felt him drifting from her. The single female guest came into the garden from the lane and stood looking up at the house. She reached into her bag – for a camera or a phone, Anjali assumed, but the woman took out a tissue and lifted her sunglasses to dab at her eyes. Then she blew her nose.

"She's crying," Anjali said, but Dan didn't hear.

He was reading one of his academic journals. He was writing a paper for a conference, but it wasn't for ages. Why bring work with you when you went to watch a sunset? He must have known they would run out of things to say. Padma came out of the house and started to lay the tables for dinner. She arranged flowers in clay bowls filled with water. It was the cheap container that buffalo curd came in, and which most people threw away after the curd was eaten, but Padma had kept the bowls and now she added float-ing candles to the flowers and placed a bowl at the centre of each table, even theirs, then left saying she would be back soon after she changed for dinner. Soon the sun was almost gone. Rohan arrived, then the other female guest, each sitting alone at their table, gazing at the sea. There was no music, not even a television to break the terrible silence. Everyone sat lost and dreaming.

Padma reappeared, dressed to the nines, in a long denim skirt and white peasant blouse with puffed sleeves; a necklace of large, brightly coloured glass beads. She had left her hair down, long and curling, and had worn large hoop earrings; gypsy-like. She drifted among the tables, lighting the floating candles and the oil lamps, and taking orders for drinks. The old German man arrived and she went to him and kissed him on the cheek. The man kissed the top of her hair, which was an odd way for a boss to behave, and so brazen, doing it in front of guests – but then it was that kind of area.

"Would you like a beer?" Padma offered the old man.

"No, I have to drive in a minute."

"Where to?"

"Jarryd's. I'm having dinner there tonight."

"Ah, to moan about Ruth?"

"No – to catch up with my friend! Will you be okay here?"

"Of course I will." Padma grinned up at the man and he tweaked her nose. It was astonishing that she didn't protest. He even put his arm around her.

"I've had to move Rohan into the house," Padma told him, as the two went out to the porch.

"Why on earth did you that? You should have discussed it with me, first!" he exclaimed.

She stood back, looking surprised by his outburst.

The old man seemed furious, towering over her.

"What's the big fuss?" Padma shot back. "Anyway, I had no choice, they wanted a bungalow." She glanced back at the veranda and Anjali looked down, pretending not to be listening.

"And that wasn't all." She lowered her voice. "They wanted twin beds." Padma's voice was full of laughter.

"*Twin beds?*"

"Shhhh!" Padma giggled and the two moved out of earshot, and out of sight. No doubt they were smirking at her. What a guest house. Well Anjali didn't care what that dodgy pair thought of her.

"The owner didn't like Padma letting us change rooms," she whispered to Dan.

He glanced up from his reading.

"What do you mean?" he asked.

"He was annoyed that she hadn't asked his permission. He's

obviously a control freak, but even employees need to be allowed to make decisions."

"She's not his employee, she's his daughter."

"No way!"

"She is. He adopted her when she was young. Her parents died years ago in a train crash."

"Who told you?"

"She did."

"*She* did? When?"

"While you were having your shower."

Anjali leaned back so she could see the two on the porch. Padma stood with her back against the railing, talking with the old man who was sitting in his chair. There was an obvious closeness between them - and an easy apartness. Anjali had seen it before between certain friends and their fathers - a simplicity between them, with no obvious gradient of power - no special obedience required of the daughter, no submission of will. It was a bewildering sight, and tormenting to lesser fathers and daughters. No wonder Padma was happy all the time; being liked for doing nothing would make anyone feel fine. Anjali hated the villa; she wished they had never come.

"By the way, Padma's offered us yoga classes," Dan said. "She wants to finish her training to be a yoga instructor, so she needs to practise."

"Good for her."

"You don't want to?"

"You go and do yoga with her! Hang out all day with her if you want, I don't care!"

"You're being crazy."

He was getting tired of her. He would give up on her soon and turn to someone more likeable, someone like Padma. He looked out into the garden, peering up at the tops of the trees. Every night, after dinner at the orphanage where they had been working, he would go outside with the other volunteers to spot bats and owls and once a grass snake. Even insects fascinated him, all the creatures that the maids sprayed to death at her house, he liked.

"Why don't you tell me about the bats anymore?" she demanded.

"I didn't think you were interested."

"I'm very interested."

"You're always obsessing about weird shit like bungalows and twin beds—"

"Very funny."

But he wasn't joking.

Dinner was served and they ate in the awful silence. If only they would play music, any music at all. At least at the orphanage there had been the other volunteers to talk to. She sat with the din of owls and crickets and motorbikes rupturing; the clatter of cutlery. No one else seemed to mind. God, how she hated the villa! The meal dragged on. Padma seemed to have forgotten the dessert, sitting talking with Rohan at his table. Rohan looked besotted. Padma's eyes were smoky with kohl, her lips deep red. She was slightly darker-skinned than Anjali, but she was definitely beautiful. Soon Dan would watch her too, and be beguiled. Anjali couldn't stand it a moment longer; she stood up to go.

"What's the matter?" Dan asked.

"I'm going to bed."

"But we haven't had dessert yet."

"You have it."

She walked away, but he came with her. They passed through the empty porch. The old man had left. A bottle of ginger beer and a glass stood on a round brass table, the sort you saw in old houses and Government-run tourist shops.

"I wonder where he lives," Anjali said.

"In the next village; he has his own house there with his office. He's an architect, quite famous apparently. He's called Gerhardt Hundsler. He designed this whole place, even the garden. It was just an ordinary fisherman's hut before."

"My, what a long chat you had with that Padma."

"She's nice, you'll like her when you get to know her."

But would Padma like Anjali? Anjali wasn't sure. Padma probably couldn't understand why anyone as clever and kind and nice-looking as Dan would be with someone like Anjali. Anjali was puzzled by it herself. She felt herself shrinking beside him as they walked over the lawn, feeling herself disappearing in the darkness.

⚜

Gerhardt drank his second beer with the black pork curry and rice at Jarryd's. It was a luxurious traditional dish, prepared for his guests over at the retreat. The guests, of course, would be eating it from plantain leaves instead of plates, and using their fingers, playing at being 'local' – that's what they came to Jarryd's for, to live the simple village life, sleeping in huts and swimming in a lake full of leeches, paying thousands of dollars for the experience. Unlike at the villa, Jarryd's guests were well out of sight, surrounded by jungle and a moat that Gerhardt himself had designed to create the illusion of remoteness, but with the safety and convenience of staff nearby. It meant also that one could sit on Jarryd's veranda in peace.

"You don't see a soul here, not even on the road," Gerhardt reflected.

"You're changing the subject, Gerhardt! Go and call Ruth now – I command you!"

"Maybe later."

"Why don't you head over to Colombo tomorrow and spend some time with her?"

"No, it's better to let things settle."

This was how they had navigated each tortuous turn of their friendship, letting time pass between each difficult milestone, recovering alone in a dignified silence, then finding the resolve to pass through each transition, meeting somehow on the other side.

"There's no Ronny now, you can fight like ordinary couples," Jarryd said.

"We're not a couple."

"Yes you are, and I love you both for it. Now please, ring her and get it over with." Gerhardt carried on eating. His phone started to ring.

"Oh God! It's her!"

"Talk to her!" Jarryd cried.

"Hello?" Gerhardt answered.

"I went to see the lawyer," she said.

"Oh yes, what did he say?"

"He refused to tell me anything – can you believe it? All of a sudden he's worried about his duty to his client. He told me nothing."

"Now that is a surprise."

It was also surprising that it was still so easy to talk with her – even after all the things they had said. Still it was prudent to stay cautious, to engage only on subjects outside of themselves.

"Never mind," Ruth said. "I have my contacts. I talked to a lot of people and they all told me the same story: he wanted to end the marriage but she didn't, so she made up some accusations which her people made him confess to by sending thugs round to intimidate him before the court case. Would you believe, some people with guns went to his parents' house in the middle of the night. The poor old cook nearly had a heart attack, apparently."

"How on earth do you know this?"

"Rohan's mother told her best friend, Ranjini Ramachandra, who also happens to be the best friend of Ruwani Sadiq, the parliamentarian's wife – you know her?"

"No."

"Ruwani and I go back many years, I trust her implicitly – she confirmed the story."

"So the boy isn't violent?"

"No, Padma can flirt with him to her heart's content!"

"She's not flirting! She's just being her usual friendly self – just as she is with everyone."

"Of course she is. Just don't go meddling in anything."

"Why should I meddle? There's nothing's going on."

"Yes, yes, I'm sure you're right. Now I'm off to bed."

Gerhardt glanced at Jarryd, checking if he was listening, but he had turned his chair away and was dreamily gazing at the sky.

"Did you get back alright?" Gerhardt asked Ruth.

"Of course."

"You're okay?"

"I'm fine."

"Good." He searched for something to say. "I'm with Jarryd. I'm having dinner at his place."

"Then could you please tell him to stop his nonsense and withdraw that damn book from the shops? And while you're at it, please ask him to also stop writing articles attacking the minister's reaction to the book – it's starting to get a little too much attention in certain circles."

"Ruth says you're getting too much attention in Colombo," Gerhardt told Jarryd.

"Surely any attention is good?" Jarryd said, turning back to the table.

"Put me on speaker – I want a word with him!" Ruth ordered.

"Jarryd? Are you listening?" Her voice carried over the garden. "Jarryd, it's too dangerous - you're playing with fire! These people are not rational beings, they're foolish, jumped-up country bumpkins, they cannot be reasoned with. Don't make them angry."

"Anyone can see that my little pamphlet is a mere personal essay, it can hardly be viewed as political commentary!" Jarryd laughed.

"That is exactly how it is being seen - people are starting to talk. That latest article practically calls your minister a tyrant! He's someone you don't want to annoy."

"Actually, I used 'despot'."

"You have to stop, Jarryd."

"I have no intention of annoying anyone, the man is trying to censor me and I want to let people know about it. I am merely adding my voice to the discussion."

"What discussion?"

"Precisely!"

"Gerhardt, tell him, will you? He doesn't understand the dangers—"

"The danger is to freedom, not me!" Jarryd declared. "These foolish egotistical individuals need to see the folly of their reaction to a simple pamphlet. It's just one man's opinion! Why should it bother them so much?"

"Gerhardt, talk to him, will you?"

Gerhardt was helpless. Jarryd was stubborn, he held fast to ideals - but wasn't that how it should be?

"Gerhardt? Are you still there?" Ruth demanded.

"I'm here." He sighed. "It's Jarryd's decision, Ruth."

"Fine. Just try and be careful, Jarryd," Ruth said wearily. "I'm off to bed. It's been a very long day. Goodnight, both."

"Bon nuit!" Jarryd called.

"Goodnight," Gerhardt added, and then it was just he and Jarryd sitting together in the dark. The one comfort was that once again, he and Ruth had steered past the collision of earlier and appeared to have arrived at more peaceable waters.

"I'd better go and check if Padma's alright," he said.

"Ah, checking on her and this new guest!"

"Of course not! Nothing's going on there! It's Sunny I'm worried about. Do you suppose he's been hanging around like the minister seemed to think?"

"That fool knows nothing! I would take anything he said with a great bushel of salt."

"I can't take the risk. There's a rumour going round that Sunny's started working for him - God knows what he'll be able to do with the minister's backing. I'm instructing my lawyer in the morning to make him an offer."

"Are you sure that's a good idea?"

"It's the only way I know to get rid of the bastard."

One day Padma would leave the villa, and they could all leave Sunny behind - but it was still too soon. For now, Padma wanted to stay and Gerhardt would make that possible for her, for them both.

❧

Inside the bungalow, Anjali unpacked her clothes in the new quiet she had won, the place of their own with the door locked and no one outside to interfere or disapprove. Dan sat working at the desk, reading his journal, returned to his world of graphs and numbers. He never seemed to mind having to work, even on this first holiday since attaining his doctorate. He was eager to know more, and to show what he knew, that was what drove him. When she was studying, she had been hounded by the terror of being surpassed by others. Top grades and the highest scores were her one place of safety. But such a drive was ensnaring, it trapped one; she had freed herself only by walking away. Now the family had nothing to admire or respect; there was only her, this searching uncertain gaze in the mirror.

Dan slouched in his chair, his legs stretched long under the table. He looked so contented. Everything was in balance in him; no opposite desires pulled at him. Anjali hung up her dresses in the wardrobe, folded t-shirts and jeans, but her eyes were drawn back to Dan. His hair, chopped short at a village barber's near the orphanage, was newly dark, only a few traces left of his once startlingly bleached mane. She had wished sometimes, as on the night when he had met her parents, that his hair hadn't been quite such an unnatural colour, but now that it was gone, she missed its strangeness. The last blonde spikes ruffled by the fan were soft like fur. She went to him. He looked up at her. A finger, she noted, kept his place in the journal.

"What's up?" he asked.

She had nothing to say. He reached for her, but she pulled away.

"You're mad at me, don't think I can't tell," she said.

"I'm not mad at anyone – you are, remember?"

"I know you're angry – but I don't blame you. I know I'm repressed compared with all the women you've been with."

"What are you talking about?"

"You knew what I was like from the first day we met." She wore her strait-laced ugliness with pride.

"I seem to remember things being quite different then," he said and smiled.

'So that *is* the problem – you admit it!'

But now he just looked hurt.

"There is no problem – I told you I'd wait until you felt like it again." He held her hand, but she snatched it back.

"This is the real me, this is who I really am," she said and stood glowering before him, feeling shrivelled and empty inside.

"No it isn't," he said gently.

"Yes it is."

"Whatever."

He turned back to his reading. She gathered up her dirty washing for the dobi. Of course it had been different before, when they had met at a dusty old guest house in Colombo where she'd been visiting a friend. Dan had invited her to lunch the next day and she had gone to meet him during a break at work. They had met again the next day, and a few days later she had phoned in sick on her way into Chambers and gone to Dan instead – to his high-ceilinged room with a view of sea and trains chugging past from time to time, along the sea-side edge of Colombo. With Dan she had gladly, eagerly, stepped free of her work clothes to lie naked in his vast creaking bed, become someone new, a secret golden self, wild and free with the fan whirling over them and the midday sun flaring through the red curtains.

She had gone to him every day from then on, to a world all their own. She had imagined they would take it with them wherever they went – but it had dissolved to nothing when they left the city. This was their real life now, this life in the bungalow and the two narrow beds with the parting in-between, like the bedroom of two elderly sisters.

"You've ruined us! You've ruined your life!" her father had yelled when the truth was revealed, when Anjali's Pupil Master, an old friend of her father's telephoned concerned, about Anjali's mysterious illness that had gone on for so long.

"How much you have lied!" her father accused her.

"You have lied to your own parents! What a disgrace!" her mother had scolded. The rest of what Anjali had done, her mother could barely speak of. "Once you have lost you virtue, you can never get it back," she whispered bitterly.

"I don't want it back."

"So you did! Oh my goodness!"

"I'm twenty-two! What did you think? All the cousins - you think they haven't—"

"Don't slander you poor cousins, please - not one of them has behaved like you. None of their families have been shamed like Daddy and I!"

"Only because none of them got caught!"

Anjali had never defied her parents before. She and her mother had never argued, for Anjali had always given in when they disagreed, and been rewarded by being forgiven.

"Now no one will ever respect you," her mother said. "People can see what you're like, just by looking at you. They can tell what you've done."

"Bull shit."

And her mother had slapped her. It wasn't the first time, and this time it mattered least of all. It felt right, a part of a necessary severing, throwing her free of the rules that had burdened her for years. Even thousands of miles away in America, her obedience to those rules had stifled her desires and blocked off instinctual pleasures. But not anymore. Now everyone in the family knew what she had failed to suppress, not only them, important colleagues of her father too now knew of her wantonness. And then, just as she was free of them all, she had started to care. She had discovered, as she fled from Colombo with Dan, that really she minded what people thought of her. She was tormented by shame, her mother's words like talons clinging to her, piercing right through to her heart and poisoning the pleasure of her bold adventure.

At the orphanage where they had gone to volunteer, Anjali had avoided being alone with Dan. At night she slept in a dormitory with six other women, and she and Dan had never sneaked away to a room in a hotel like the other volunteers with partners.

"It's okay, it'll be easier when we have somewhere of our own, just the two of us," Dan had said, but still nothing had changed.

Now she undressed in the bathroom, changing into her night-clothes only emerging fully dressed. She crept into her solitary bed and Dan put away his papers. She watched him stand up and stretch. At the bookshelf he studied the books Padma had put there, moving a twist of driftwood and a conch shell. He chose a paperback, turned up the fan to Max, and sat back reading on his bed. The fan rocked on its slender stem. The curtains rippled and shook, rattling their iron rings.

Anjali looked through a guidebook that Padma had forced Dan to buy: *Confessions of a Teardrop*. There were several oddly named chapters. She paused at one:

## MIXED-UP SRI LANKA

Sri Lanka is a hybrid place, with a composite aesthetic of its many invasions, and peoples of many races and religions with varied ancestors.

Its architecture is a merging of an elegant vernacular style with many Colonial influences: verandas from the Dutch, Gothic grandeur from the British, and bungalows, gables, plant-filled courtyards.

The religions of Sri Lanka are the cause of a rich cacophony in its cities and villages, filling each day with calls to prayer and the rituals of asking Gods for favours. The song of the muezzin, solemn and sonorous and often movingly melodic, call the faithful to prayer at mosques, and from kovils and temples, the jangling of bells and chanting; Buddhist priests reciting pirith in chorus, broadcast on loudspeakers on Poya days. And in cool bare churches with weathered pews, sunlight glancing in through high clear windows, voices soar, tunelessly singing hymns.

There are many colours and sensations of worship. At the kovil there is the wetness of smashed coconuts, spilt milk, oil poured over a black phallic lingum in an inner chamber painted red and orange: a wet glistening scented womb where bodies gather to revere the sacred.

At the temple, the bodies are clothed in white, the voices hushed. There is the smell of incense and newly-washed flowers. There is the white of the dagoba, its smooth chalk mound encircled barefoot on pale sandy ground. In the shrine rooms, there are vivid painted scenes of instructional Jataka tales, bright detailed murals where people sit on cool tiled floors whispering prayers.

Sri Lanka is a mixed-up garden, a hive of buzzing anxiety and passion where dangerous venom lurks, always about to spill over. Boundaries are of immense importance to Sri Lankans who continually strive to assert their otherness, trying to define their belonging more securely. It is a national characteristic to check each other over, and place a fellow Sri Lankan according to religion, class and caste. Questions will invariably be asked to ascertain family, home, origins to precisely place another. However, like children of a family growing up in the same house together, Sri Lankans of all groups often like the same things.

At the edges of the Buddhist temple grounds are where the Hindu gods have been brought in, housed in small shrine rooms painted white outside like temple buildings, but a blaze of colour within – walls painted bright red for wild fierce Goddess Kali; a deep blue for the homes of Lord Vishnu and Lord Shiva alone or with his consort Goddess Parvati and their sons: elephant-headed Ganesha and the war god Kartikeya. Standing in silent garlanded splendour, these great figures of a rival religion lend their powers to the Buddhists with their austere God-less faith when they come to pray for divine attention.

At the holy city of Katharagama, Hindus, Buddhists, Muslims and indigenous peoples all claim the site to be of religious significance to them. On the mountain of Adam's Peak, a giant footprint in the rock is said to have been made by the Buddha, according to the Sinhalese; by Lord Shiva according to the Tamils, while the Christians and Muslims claim it is Adam's, from when he was thrown from Heaven.

Differences continue in dance and music and each language has its own body of great literature. There is divergence of course in the cuisine of each culture, but there are many similarities and everyone likes everyone else's food.

Difference and variety are key aspects of Sri Lanka, and this is its downfall as well as its appeal. The rich heritage of the country is still to be fully embraced; its varied groupings live bounded, defined. Now after warring for decades, after the spilled blood of lives needlessly wasted has been washed away, Sri Lanka strives to grow and be mighty, trying to follow India, China, Russia, the new great economies of the world. But there is a new brand of Sri Lankan politician asserting itself, fiercely divisive, and unheeding of its colonial heritage. They are dismissive of an elite trained at the prestigious institutions of their colonial rulers – the new firebrand leaders have risen from villages and provincial towns, and they have been urged on by the masses, burdened for years and suppressed. These ambitious new political men (and they mostly are all men) will flout the rule of law and abandon the old ways, even physically fighting in Parliament during a particularly heated debate; this is the new face of politics, this open embrace of nationalism, driving division.

Despite the end of war, fear and resentment persist in Sri Lanka. Journalists are imprisoned for reporting injustice, business rivals disappear in midnight raids. Sri Lanka is a clamorous place of many voices, many hands grasping, too many bodies pressed too close and striving for freedom. But a way to peace must be found, for living in fear on this jewelled riven island, with at its heart a torn conflicted soul, is to be in the loneliest place in the world.

For Anjali, the loneliest place in the world right now was their bungalow. Dan had fallen asleep sitting up, the paperback fallen open, pages flickering with the fan. How long ago it seemed, that time in his guest house in Colombo. She remembered the sweet spent warmth of afterwards, as they lay heavy-limbed and wound in each other, the approach of evening her one sadness, when she had to return to her parents' house and pretend. She hadn't minded lying; it hadn't felt immoral at all, she had known to guard her precious golden self. It was only later that she hadn't kept it safe. And somehow she had lost that glorious loving, feeling self that she had been. She longed to be it again. How much she had felt then, and how fully, even crying with happiness afterwards. Now there was nothing. All she was now was this withered angry watchfulness.

Dan's breathing grew heavier. She went over to his bed and set his book aside on the bedside table. She switched off his light and went out and sat on the veranda, just another shadow in the blue-darkness. In the distance, a pale figure went up the path to the house. It was the old man, Gerhardt. The dog barked at him.

## 21

GERHARDT STOPPED AT the threshold of the veranda surprised to find the guests still there, still eating dinner. Padma was only now bringing out dessert.

"Hello! Shouldn't you be going home to bed?" she greeted Gerhardt.

"The guests are eating late tonight," he said.

"Oh, we were chatting! The other two went early. Do you want something to eat?"

"No, I ate at Jarryd's. I'll just sit out here for a while."

"Are you okay?" Padma asked. "Shall I call Wilson to drive you home?"

She bent, concerned, to look at him. She seemed about to feel his forehead for a temperature! So caring she was, and always had been. Lord knew where she got it from, certainly not her people! But there it was, shining out of her, a clear uncomplicated kindness. No wonder everyone loved her. He reached for her hand and squeezed its cool smallness.

"Have you spoken to Ruth?" she asked.

"Yes, and everything is fine."

"Really?"

"Yes."

"Good, I'm glad! Now you really need to be going home, Gerhardt. It's getting late and you need the rest"

Was he imagining her eagerness to send him away? What was she up to? Surely not what Ruth had imagined with Rohan?

"You know, I think I will have some dessert after all," he said. "What's Soma made?"

"Fruit salad."

"Ah good."

"You hate fruit salad."

"I'd like some today."

She looked at him suspiciously but went inside. He stifled a yawn. The important thing was not to fall asleep. If only Rohan would hurry up and go to bed. Gerhardt crept to the door and peered into the veranda. Rohan and Ria sat talking, Padma had gone inside. Gerhardt settled in his chair to wait. Motorbikes prowled the lane as usual. There was the beep of a tuk-tuk further away; voices by the gate of people going to the beach. In the old days there was no one around at night other than the fishermen. Now there were people who came from other villages – not only to the minister's brother's establishments, but also to the cafes that had sprung up along the beach, all reporting to the minister and his brother. Gerhardt was hardly surprised that the minister and his brother should want to own other holiday properties as well, but why did it have to be next door? If they hoped to buy the villa to join up the two houses on either side, they certainly had a long wait The villa would always be Gerhardt's first significant project, built of everything he had loved and learned as he travelled around the country, studying old buildings. He had moved to the south coast to get away from Ruth and Ronny, then newly-married and at every party he went to in Colombo. In Nilwatte Beach he had planned to heal himself. He had not known, of course, what was to come – that had caught him entirely by surprise. But the rightness of his decision then was something he knew with all his heart, with the whole of his being.

On that night, moments before his whole world changed, he had been sitting on the steps of the porch with Soma, the two of them drinking arrack with lime after a day's hard gardening. A whole life could change in a single second. No future should be relied on, no past held onto, that was what the Buddha had taught; a moment's possibilities were minute and endless. He had barely heard the squeal of the gate.

"What was that?" Soma whispered.

Gerhardt, in those days, hadn't known to be afraid, only curious. He took his time setting down his glass where it wouldn't be overturned, trying to remember where he had left the torch. Soma jumped up, but Sunny was already standing before them. This time he wasn't alone – he had a small girl with him.

"What the bloody hell do you think you're doing! Get out!" Soma yelled.

"You keep out of this," Sunny said softly, a darkness in his tone that silenced Soma.

"Here, sir, this is the girl I told you about," Sunny smiled at Gerhardt. "Just take a look, that's all I ask."

The child stood with her face turned away to the bamboo scaffold around the unbuilt veranda.

"Take a good look, sir. See what you think," Sunny urged, then muttered a command to the girl who turned her head reluctantly in Gerhardt's direction, still looking fiercely down at the ground. Sunny pushed her forward. She shrugged sharply away from his touch. He flashed her a look of warning, his arm rising as if to strike her. Her body flinched, but she held his gaze; she was small and thin and fearless.

"Didn't I tell you, no, this morning?" Gerhardt said to Sunny. "Which part of no didn't you understand?"

"Don't be angry, sir. Just say if you want her or not. So many people have asked to have her already - but a father only wants the best, no?"

"You're not frightened for your child? What these people might do?"

"But I'm not giving her to just any passing person!" Sunny was indignant. "It is only for you that I make this big sacrifice. You are a world-famous architect, making a beautiful home in this village - this is why I am making you an offering of my only daughter. It is a privilege for me to help you. Who else would I make such a precious offering to?"

"All you good Buddhists . . . so this is how you behave?"

"Anything you want, sir, she can do," Sunny said brightly. "Cleaning, sweeping, making beds - and any other things sir wants. Sir doesn't have children, no? It is nice to have a child, after all, what is a home without children?"

It was useless to rail against the logic. A morality of survival ruled the poor, it ruled the whole country, its once endless war destroying all faith and hope and making normal the abject suffering of people.

"So many are adopting from here, these days," Sunny said. "Dutch, German, France - all are coming here. Our children are very good. You ask anyone."

If not Gerhardt, then another foreigner would no doubt be approached. Sunny would keep on trying. It was only a matter of time before he found someone to purchase the child. How often had he taken the child to places where such people lingered? Gerhardt anxiously studied the girl, standing so pure and young, defiantly apart from the father. Her gaze was bright with anger and fear. He suspected that this was her first time before the reality of a customer. Gerhardt tried to look away from that small proud face, so clear-eyed and unsullied. How could he stand by and allow what would happen to her? Her feet moved and he saw her toes, under the straps of faded red rubber slippers, clench and unclench without stopping. Such pale small childish feet. Her toes flexed frantically.

"How old is she?" Gerhardt asked.

"Nine and a half, sir. Born in October. Very good horoscope she has."

Gerhardt felt his heart start to pound, and his mind soar high above reason. He was dizzy knowing what he was about to do. Soma stared at him with sudden suspicion. What a place this country was turning out to be, everyone rotted through with distrust, the possibility of corruption ever-present. It was not quite the involvement with locals he had envisioned, such as sitting drinking on mellow moonlit beaches with friendly fishermen.

"If I take her, I want all her papers," he said, noting Sunny's surprise. So he hadn't expected Gerhardt to agree to his offer, which was some consolation.

"And I'll need to see a lawyer and have contracts written," Gerhardt added.

"Lawyer, sir? There's no need for lawyers – they're all crooks. They only take your money."

"No lawyer, no deal. I want all rights to her."

"Any rights you want, you can have, sir. All I ask for is a small sum, simply as a token – once a month, say? That's okay, no?"

"I'm not giving you anything until I have signed papers. My lawyer can come here tomorrow afternoon, otherwise nothing doing."

Sunny hesitated. Gerhardt moved as if to go inside.

"Okay, what time shall I come?" Sunny said sullenly.

"Two o'clock."

Sunny waggled his head reluctantly agreeing, then he left, leaving the child. She stood staring after him. Gerhardt willed the bastard to look back, just once – God knows, maybe even change his mind – but Sunny kept walking. The child stood looking at the lane, small and forlorn in her shabby pink dress. She was a ghost; an inheritance of the damaged island; she had attached herself to his house. Soma glowered at him.

"Well, what was I supposed to do?" Gerhardt protested. "Let him take her to someone else? What if they harmed her?"

Soma looked confused. "What are you going to do with her?" he asked.

"How should I know? Take her inside. Give her something to eat."

Gerhardt retreated to his study and telephoned Ronny in Colombo.

"You've done what? You've taken on a *child*? Are you serious, Men? Have you been drinking?"

Ruth took the phone from Ronny.

"Have you gone mad, Gerhardt?" she scolded. "The last thing you want is to be mixed up in something like this. Didn't I say you'd do something crazy if you left Colombo? These wild places aren't good for anyone. You must call the authorities, first thing in the morning. Do you hear me? Then take her to the nearest orphanage, they'll know what to do with her."

He went to find the child. She was in the kitchen, still mute, shaking her head at pink wafers, milk, even water. Gerhardt and Soma made up a bed for her on a Dutch couch that had just been restored, that he was keeping in the hall until the veranda was completed. The child curled up and pulled the sheet over her head. Gerhardt lay awake in his room listening to the sea rocking itself, the house slumbering as if nothing had happened. Soon he too would forget. He waited, longing for sleep.

The next morning he was already dressed for his walk on the beach when he remembered what he had done. He sat dazed on the edge of the bed, seeing himself in the wardrobe mirror, not knowing himself. It had been a moment of madness. He would call the Municipal offices the moment they opened and by the afternoon, at the very latest, the child would be in appropriate hands. He would deal with the father later – maybe even give him some money to go away. But first, she needed breakfast. She would be hungry. And they had to find her some clothes – the fool of a father hadn't brought her anything to wear. Gerhardt opened the door to the hall, half-hoping to find her gone, but there she was, wrapped in the bed sheet, sitting on the couch, and he was surprised that he was relieved to see her.

She jumped to her feet as he approached her. She stood red-eyed and dishevelled, the cocoon of her sheet unravelling around her, not speaking as he asked what she wanted to eat. He left her to Soma, who gave her toast with butter and jam and a glass of hot milk, which she took into the garden, only eating after she had hidden behind the plantain trees. From what he could see from the study window, she devoured the bread and gulped down the milk. He was gripped by a furious sadness watching her.

"Sir?" Soma stood at the door. "You're not thinking of keeping her here, are you? Because that father is a very bad person – Sugathapala, he's called, not Sunny. Any child of his will be trouble."

"It's not her fault what her father is."

"She'll turn out the same."

"Don't worry, I'm sending her away today."

"Ah, good. Very good! That is the best thing to do, sir"

Gerhardt watched the girl sitting hunched on the grass, gripping the sheet tighter around her against the morning chill. Her interest was caught by something under the trees. She peered closer, her face grown alive as she seemed momentarily to forget herself. But when she sat back, the lostness returned to her.

Gerhardt reached for the phone. The authorities needed to be called – immediately; the sooner she was taken into care the better. But he couldn't finish dialling the number. He had been involved with too many charities to believe in the orphanages of Sri Lanka – those barren houses full of hollow-eyed children and staff grimacing with the effort of smiling to look kind before visitors. What a place to send the beautiful child nestled in his garden. He redialled a different number – the number of his lawyer.

The child stayed outside the whole day, hiding in bushes when her father and the lawyer came. Soma took her food and drinks and hovered close to her, while inside the house, papers were signed transferring ownership of her. That night after Soma had dragged her indoors and made her stand under the shower, she put on a different set of clothes from a ragged pile that her father had brought in an old rice sack, and went to sleep on her temporary bed in the hall. But this time she was a part of the house, a part of his life. Gerhardt sat on the porch reading the documents that were proof that the day really had happened, for there was his signature beside Sunny's scrawl, and the lawyer's neat flourish beneath making it official. Gerhardt read through her identity papers: she was called Padma and she really was nine and a half years old, born in October. It should have felt different, surely, to have adopted a child? *Adopted a child!* It didn't sound like anything he could have been involved in. Soma brought him a beer and sat on the steps rolling a joint.

"What are we going to do with her, sir?" Soma asked.

"How should I know?"

Gerhardt's one certainty until then had been his work; his one aim in life: to stay inspired. Each day the imagination had to be indulged, coaxed, allowed to wander alone and soar to where the magic lay. Already the tropical night seemed less mysterious; the island's lure had weakened with the new constraints of a household. The garden flaunted its wild unencumbered life back at him. He felt Soma watch him - how gullible he must think Gerhardt, so easily manipulated by a man like Sunny. But when Gerhardt looked, there was only an admiring new pride in Soma's gaze, and Gerhardt knew that he wasn't alone anymore.

Someone came onto the porch behind him and Gerhardt turned, almost expecting the young Padma of all those years ago, the silent, delicate, unsmiling child, so fearful of him. But it was Ria.

"You're still here," Ria said.

"Yes, still here."

"I don't blame you. It's so beautiful here - everything you've done, everything is . . . amazing." Her voice trembled. She rubbed her eyes.

"I don't know what's wrong with me today," she added. "It's because I'm leaving. I don't want to leave, I want to stay here forever in your beautiful place."

"Then you must come back."

"No. It's too hard to return. Everything changes."

"We'll all still be here."

"You don't know that."

"Why? Has Padma said anything?"

"No! Not at all. I just meant people move on. In so many ways."

"Is Padma planning to go away?"

"She hasn't said anything to me. She'll never go far away from you - she'd be crazy to," Ria said

He smiled, yet he was wary of her all of a sudden - the solitary young woman with her searching eyes that saw everything.

"Well, goodnight," she said.

"Goodnight."

Gerhardt felt the house solid and gentle behind him, but a new emptiness lurked there. It was waiting for him, hiding in the silence, in the darkness at the edges of the garden. The right time to leave would come, and Padma would go on alone into the light; then he must stand firm in the shadows and let her.

"Here you are - delicious fruit salad! It's got every fruit you absolutely hate!" Padma presented him with a bowl full of fruit floating in syrup.

"Thank you very much. This looks lovely." He stirred the chunks of fruit around.

"Is Rohan still eating?" Gerhardt asked.

"No, he's gone to bed."

Thank the Lord! At last he could go home to bed himself - but he had to warn Padma first. A father's duty was to look out for his child.

"You know Rohan's had some troubles recently . . ."

"Yes."

"So this would be the worst time for him to start a relationship - don't you think?"

He saw her closing up, withdrawing from him, perhaps even a flicker of irritation. He had the power to hurt her, and they both knew it. He faltered. Why take away her small pleasures?

"You think he only wants a holiday romance?" Padma said.

"Well, yes . . . I suppose . . . something like that."

Perhaps Ruth would have known to handle this better.

"Don't worry, I can take care of myself," Padma declared.

"Of course you can."

"Anyway, I'm really tired. I'm off to bed." She hugged him tightly, without recrimination. "Please drive carefully," she added.

In the garden he paused, unable to leave. He called his lawyer's private line.

"I'm sorry to bother you this late at night," Gerhardt began.

"Not at all, Mr Hundsler – is everything alright?"

"I wanted to discuss a somewhat sensitive matter – you re-member the arrangement we set up for my daughter? With her biological father?"

"Sunny, you mean?"

"Yes, because now that she has returned home I would like to set up something similar."

There was a pause, of reluctance perhaps, or disapproval.

"I realise this is irregular," Gerhardt went on, "so I would be happy to offer a higher rate for your time."

"There's no need, Mr Hundsler. Would you like me to ap-proach him on your behalf? On the same terms?"

"I expect he will want a higher sum this time."

"I'm sure he will. Are you quite sure about renewing dealings with this individual, Mr Hundsler? Because, as your lawyer, I feel I should advise you against it."

"I have no choice, Mr Aluvihare, I have to protect my daughter."

"Well then, I will contact Sunny in the morning."

"Thank you. I'll wait to hear from you."

It felt like a hurdle cleared, a new bright way forward. Gerhardt walked back to the house. There was nothing left to do, but he checked that the candles and oil lamps had been blown out on the veranda. In the hall, the doors of both Padma's and Rohan's rooms were closed. The Tiffany lamp on a table by the dresser cast its jewelled light on the white wall; a ruby-red dragonfly surrounded by lilac, cobalt blue, emerald and pale green petals in a flowery glass garden. Padma would stand transfixed before the lamp as a child, tracing its leaded outlines. He stepped into the hall. There was no sound from the guest room. It had been Gerhardt's own bedroom when he lived at the villa, where he would wake at night during Padma's first weeks, hearing her cries and terrified wordless protests during nightmares. Was Rohan asleep? Or was he lying in the dark waiting? For what?

The fridge hummed. Padma insisted on leaving the dog outside at night these days, but then Gustav wouldn't have barked at Rohan, even if he entered Padma's room while she was sleeping. Rohan had made friends with the dog early on – had it all been part of a plan? Gerhardt thought about telephoning Soma to ask him to come back early and guard Padma's door, but she would never have forgiven either of them. He stepped closer to her room; a streak of light glowed between the double doors. Uncertain, he looked about him then knocked.

"Yes?" She was smiling, sitting up in bed when he opened the door.

"Oh! It's you!" she exclaimed.

There was no mistaking her exasperation this time.

"Who did you think it was?" he retorted.

"Soma, of course. What are you still doing here?"

She had been reading – something that she had pushed under the sheets. He could see the glossy red corner of a book.

"I really am leaving now, I just wanted to say goodnight," he said.

"Okay, goodnight!"

Was the book a gift? Intended for him, or maybe for someone else. Perhaps it was a gift given to her – but from whom? And why hide it? In some ways she was a secretive child. She flicked the bed sheet over the exposed red corner.

"I'll see you in the morning, then," he said.

"Soon it will be morning if you don't get going!"

But then she grinned, reaching out her arms to him and he went to her and held her, his big grown child who needed him less and less each day.

He stood outside her room again, in the house that no longer felt his. The fridge wheezed and rattled and shuddered to a stop, followed by the sound of trickling fluid. The light snapped off inside her room.

They had cleared the room for her, on the same day that the papers were signed. Before, it was where they had stored furniture until the house was ready: cane chairs for the veranda, a wardrobe, tables of all sizes and the pine dresser that had belonged to his mother. For weeks he continued to be surprised to see Padma emerge from that room, and slip inside at night. At first she had spent most of her time there, the door closed, with a chair pushed up against it. She barely ate - only chocolate, dhal and rice. And beetroot curry, Soma had discovered. She never spoke. Silently she accepted dolls, books, clothes that Gerhardt asked Ruth to buy in Colombo and send by express post, but the toys and clothes stayed in their packaging. Soma discovered them stacked under the bed as if ready to be returned or sold on.

At night she had cried, helpless wordless wails of despair coming from behind the door shut tight against him. Gerhardt had listened to those lonely unearthly cries unfurling across the hall. On the third night he had gone to her.

"Padma? Padma? Let me in. I want to help you."

The crying stopped. Through the silence came a sob, and a snotty breath drawn shakily in.

"Padma? It's Gerhardt. Can I come in?"

A single un-stifled hiccup replied. He opened the door, the chair falling over with a crash. He turned on the light. It glared too bright, the bulb unshaded still. He switched it off and drew the curtain aside to let the moonlight in. Padma, fully dressed, was curled on the bed, small and frightened on top of the sheets.

"Shall I make you some hot chocolate?" Gerhardt asked.

It was what his grandmother had made for him when the wolves threatened to come out of the cupboard to rip him open with their fangs.

"You know what hot chocolate is?"

Her face stayed pressed to the pillow, but he saw her shake her head.

"Come then, I'll make you some. You'll like it, I think."

They went into the kitchen and Gerhardt searched for a pan. Soma came stumbling out from his room next to the kitchen and stared at Gerhardt stooped over the hob, striking matches, the girl standing silently beside him.

"Here, let me light it," Soma said.

Gerhardt poured milk into the pan, broke in chunks of milk chocolate and stirred, the spoon swirling tinnily. He whisked with a fork.

"It's ready. Now where are the cups?"

Soma placed one before him and Gerhardt poured out the silken brown frothing milk.

"Let's go and sit on the porch."

They walked in single file through the house, Gerhardt leading the way, then Padma, then Soma, through the dark bare bricks of the incomplete veranda, its bamboo scaffold creaking and cracking with the night's cold. They sat on the porch steps and Padma sipped the hot chocolate. Soma went down into the garden and began to roll himself a joint, but with the child there, Gerhardt told him to smoke only tobacco. In the moonlight the trees gleamed, barely moving, except for the coconut trees ruffled by sea winds, swaying a little while the sea whispered to itself.

"It's nice, this garden, don't you think?" Gerhardt said to Padma. "You can play in it, anywhere you like."

She looked slowly around her, as if for the first time.

"We're going to have a fishpond down there – really deep so the fish can get away from us when they need to – what do you think? You like goldfish?"

She shrugged.

"You can feed them, if you want."

She sipped the hot chocolate, more hungrily this time. She drained the cup, wiped her mouth with her hand and carefully licked the last sweetness from her lips.

"We have to enrol you at a good school," Gerhardt told her. "You like to study?"

She nodded.

"What's your favourite subject?"

"Singing," she murmured. The first word she had spoken to him.

He had shown her the stars that night, pointing to Orion and the Milky Way and Scorpio, her birth sign. She had yawned and rubbed her eyes. Then he had taken her into his arms and she had stayed, soft and trusting, gazing up at the sky, her eyes wide, listening as he talked. He had held her while being astonished and disbelieving of her presence – so alive, so real, this small stranger who had intruded into the perfect world he had been building for himself. Yet that well-planned life had given way so easily to the new world that had fallen open before him: strange and unknown and startlingly big.

He walked in the garden now, pausing to look at the stars. He was alone, back at the beginning. How barren it seemed now, that freedom he had planned for himself, the life he might have had. He thought of Padma safe in the house he had built – this he had given her, and this he could give her still. On that night long ago, he had made the most momentous decision of his life – what folly if he had refused to let her in. The time for solitude would come. It lay in wait for everyone, no matter which life one chose.

Inside the car he rang Ruth.

"Is everything okay?" she asked breathlessly. She was always alarmed when he rang her at night.

"Everything's fine. Were you sleeping?"

"No."

"You were right, you know. Padma is the one miracle. We got her very right."

"Yes we did, didn't we?" She was smiling, he could tell from her voice.

Was she sitting in the dark, in bed? In her white bedroom by the sea with its view of an eroded beach and an old tanker that had run aground and was rusting away slowly?

"I might head up to Colombo soon," he said. "I cleared some work before you came in case we got to spend some time together."

"Did you?"

"I may as well make the most it."

"You should. When are you coming?"

It would take several days for the lawyer to find Sunny and to get a reply, but Gerhardt knew he must be ready to respond the moment Sunny took the bait.

"Maybe in a few days' time," he told Ruth.

"I'll look forward to it."

The lightness he loved was back in her voice, a hopeful glittering ripple passing from her to him.

He drove back along the coast road to his new house, waiting only for him, returning to another beginning. There were always new beginnings, but nothing need ever end. Over and over they reached for the life they had glimpsed, the right life; over and over they tried to clasp it, compelled to go on like the waves.

## 22

A T THE SMALL bungalow, Anjali sat on the veranda, a candle lit in a jam jar, the flame misting the glass with soot. Her body felt dead. She felt a thin pulse flicker at her wrist, fainter than the distant throb of music from a party on the beach. She imagined fires and firelit faces, drugged swaying bodies, glowing tanned limbs; she thought of couples on lonely beaches, gleaming bodies in black waters, kissing with cold salt mouths. She followed them into darkened rooms, to beds with mosquito nets, the softness of thighs, breasts gleaming in moonlight, hair tangled, warm wet tongues. She shuddered, her hunger grown cavernous. She had become one of the perverts her mother used to warn her about – the people who hid behind rocks on lonely beaches and spied on loose-moraled couples. The night winds drove through the coconut trees, sweeping the branches down with a rush. The garden crept closer, its hidden life jeering, scornful of her sitting yearning and alone.

She stepped down onto the lawn and walked with the thick-bladed grass springing up strong underfoot. She stamped down on it, on the villa's arrogance and carefree smugness. She heard a rustle in the bushes, the sound of breathing, then the leaves parted and there was the great wolf-dog staring straight at her. It came towards her, its mouth open. She mustn't run, she mustn't run - she knew that from another time. Dogs ran astonishingly fast, they could never be outrun.

"Shoo! Go away!" she told it, but the dog didn't listen.

She mustn't run - not even to the bungalow. It would come bounding after her like the dogs in nightmares, effortlessly gaining ground.

"Good dog, good dog. Go away now. Shoo. Shoo!"

The dog watched her reach for a stick and growled. She took a step back. It came forward.

"Help!" she called out.

But there was no one to hear her. There was no one, just her and the big growling dog. Fear, vast and wordless grew to a taut black emptiness around her. The dog tensed, ready to pounce. She screamed into the blackness.

"Help!" she shouted into that hateful darkness. "Help me!" Nobody had heard. She screamed louder.

Someone came running.

"What happened? What did he do?" It was Padma. "Did he hurt you? Where did he go?" Padma looked wildly around her, as if the dog weren't right there in front of her.

She grabbed the dog's collar, still twisting, looking around, then she stopped.

"Are you just shouting about Gustav?" she demanded.

Other people arrived: Rohan and the cook and the other guest, called Ria, who held Anjali's hand, saying gently: "It's okay, it's okay, you're alright now. You're safe, you're going to be fine."

"He won't bite you, there's no need to shout," the cook grumbled.

"What were you doing out here so late?" Padma asked crossly, but Anjali couldn't speak. Her teeth were chattering yet locked; they scraped against each other as she tried to open her mouth.

"She's in shock," Rohan said.

"Someone take Gustav away until she calms down," Ria ordered, wrapping her arm around Anjali.

Padma passed the dog to the cook who dragged it away. Then Padma picked up a ball from the grass.

"See, he was only trying to play," she said, as if that proved anything.

Then Dan came running, pushing through them to her.

"What happened? What is it?" He held her close.

"Gustav surprised her," Ria said.

"I thought I was dreaming. I kept hearing you scream." Dan's arms were tight around her. Anjali leaned against him. His chest was hard and warm. She remembered his smell, the soft cotton of the t-shirts he wore at night.

The others walked away. Dan guided her back to their bungalow.

"So what happened?" he asked.

"I went for a walk. Then – that bloody dog. Why don't they ever tie it up?"

"It was like a bad dream," he said. "I woke up thinking it was a dream, but I could still hear you shouting, and it was real. Horrible." He pulled her tighter against him and kissed her hair.

Inside the bungalow she lay on her bed and he drew up the sheet, its clean white coolness encasing her, seeping into her like medicine. She trembled with relief beneath it, her terror returning in bursts and she kept seeing the solitary wolf-dog appear in the darkness. Such complete helplessness she had felt, standing before it. Now she lay reduced and unresisting as Dan lay down beside her.

"I love you," he said and kissed her on the cheek. "You're fine now. You're going to be okay."

She kissed him back on the lips. She was safe with him, safe inside the hard arc of his body, his arm curved against her spine. In that tight small space of their togetherness, it felt right to need him, to want him; to want to show him that she loved him and needed him. Gratefully he loved her back. But no golden glowing laughing self arose in her – now only her smallness was revealed.

⚜

"Wow, that's what you call highly-strung!" Padma said, watching Anjali and Dan return to their bungalow.

"She does seem pretty stressed," Rohan agreed.

He was still shaken himself from hearing the screams – which he had thought were Padma's. He had run, not knowing who he would find, for there were so many eyes on her now, not only her uncle's. Just that morning on the beach he had seen two men hiding behind a boulder watching her – the spy from up the road and another man with curly hair, a menacing intentness in his eyes fixed on Padma that had made Rohan want to rush Padma away. The men couldn't have known that Padma would be out on the beach that morning – she hardly ever went to the beach – yet they had taken great care to conceal themselves. It was he who went jogging on most mornings, had they been there then? He hadn't told Padma about the men; not wanting to frighten her, or spoil a perfect morning – but she was right, someone was always watching on Nilwatte Beach.

"What are you looking around for?" Padma asked now, as they walked back to the house.

"Just checking."

"If you're looking for Sunny, he's definitely not here – Gustav always goes straight for him."

He stood with her on the porch, gazing over the garden turned wild and secretive. From the fishpond came a faint pop; there was a red-gold flash in its depths; a feathery flicker of tails and fins. Furtive ripples passed over the green dark water. A motorbike drove slowly along the lane.

"Ah, someone's giving their girlfriend a lift back to the whore house," Padma said.

"You told me they were there for a wedding."

"It's almost as romantic, don't you think? Maybe when they go inside they'll have a beer together. Would you like a beer?"

"Now?"

"Yes! Why not?"

"Indeed, why not! I keep forgetting I can do what I like here."

"Weren't you allowed to drink at your parents' house?"

"Not after my aunts convinced them I was an alcoholic."

She giggled.

"They had the cook and the maids watch me all day – you think you're the only one with a spy! Every time I went to the fridge someone was watching me and taking notes. In the end all I ever drank was milk and water."

She chuckled delightedly.

"I'm glad I've amused you," he said.

"Tonight we will celebrate your freedom!" She threw open the fridge. "They sound nice, your family – annoying, but nice. They obviously care about you."

She was right, of course. And he wasn't angry with them anymore, he realised, for without their meddling he would never have found his way to the villa. Without them he might never have found Padma. He couldn't imagine his life without her or the villa. He stood beside her in the light of the fridge, choosing from the rows of coloured bottles. She shivered in her cotton dressing gown, pulling it over the roundness of her breasts.

"I'm suddenly not sleepy at all – are you?" she asked, looking up at him.

"Not in the slightest."

She handed him a bottle of imported lager and took another for herself.

"Shall we drink these in my room?" she asked.

"Sure."

Slowly she opened the doors into the mysterious rosy softness of her world: a bed with tousled white sheets, a lamp with a pink and red shade, handloom drapes at the windows in bright sugary colours. The room smelled of incense. The walls were bare except for a chart of yoga poses and framed photographs of views and sunsets.

"I took those," she said, seeing him look at the photographs.

"They're good."

"They're okay, nothing special. I like them though."

She didn't fish for compliments the way most women did, laying traps and searching for proof of your approval. She was direct and open and trusting. He loved that about her. She sat on the bed and made room for him. Side by side they drank beer straight from the bottle. There was something under the sheets, jabbing into his leg.

"What's this?" He pulled out a book.

She took it away at once, but he had already seen the cover: *Tantric Bliss for Couples*. A stone-carved couple of Ancient India were on the front, amorously enjoined while impressively contorted.

"It's just research for yoga," Padma said, throwing the book under the bed.

"Any good?"

"Yes, very. It's very philosophical. Tantric Sex is a very learned practice, you know."

"I'm sure. What's it say to do?"

"You really want to know?"

"Yes, please."

"You're not going to get upset?"

"Upset? Why on earth would I get upset!"

"I don't want you feeling awkward or anxious."

"Why would I?"

She left the bed and unfurled a straw mat on the floor, placed cushions around it.

"We have to meditate first," she said, lighting a candle, placing it inside a lantern to shield the flame from the fan.

"Now you must sit facing me," she ordered and he sat on the cushions and crossed his legs.

"We need to focus and open our hearts."

He tried not to laugh, tingling with the heady silliness of it.

"Really we should do it naked." She was serious. She loosened the sash of her dressing gown, and it fell away. Underneath she was golden brown and slender, wearing a thin vest. "Let's take off our tops too," she murmured, slipping off the vest.

He gazed astonished at her beauty.

He pulled off his t-shirt and took her into his arms, feeling the rightness of her skin against him.

"Maybe we could go straight to partner yoga," she said breathlessly and she pressed her lips to his. He felt her fingers in his hair.

It was what he had wished for, maybe from the very first moment that he had seen her run out of the house, so beautiful and other-worldly, standing above him on the porch, ruling over her world of beauty; all powerful, unassailable. He had reached her at last. He was with her now, the one place he belonged.

❧

Padma woke in the fading dark of dawn, a luxurious heaviness in her limbs. Beside her, Rohan lay sleeping. His eyes moved beneath the lids, the eyelashes flickering; his breathing deep and contented. She lay with a new tender stillness spread through her, the last traces of dreams easing away, to be forgotten. For the first time in months she hadn't had nightmares. She watched the first golden light of morning sharpen at the edge of the curtains. She left the bed and tidied the cushions, rolled up the mat, threw away the burnt-out stump of candle. Rohan stirred and opened his eyes.

"Good morning," she said.

"Morning!" He smiled. "So it was real. I thought maybe I'd been dreaming."

She leaped back into the bed with him and they lay close together.

"Let's go for a walk on the beach," she said.

"No, let's just stay here."

"But you always go to the beach in the mornings."

"Not today."

There was something wrong, something had made him change the pattern of the past weeks.

"What happened?" she asked.

"Nothing's happened."

"Don't you want to go jogging?"

"Maybe some other time."

"But not today?"

"No, not today."

"Why? Just tell me!"

He sighed, sitting up.

"Okay, don't get upset, but yesterday there were some guys watching us."

"Sunny? The spy?"

"Not your uncle, but the spy, yes, and—"

"The little shit! Where was he hiding?"

"Behind some rocks."

"What an idiot!"

"There was someone else with him," Rohan added.

He had said it wasn't Sunny, so it was most probably Mukul. Sunny took care not to be seen with the people who worked for him - like he was some hot-shot mafia man.

"Was he young? Thin, with big stupid hair?"

"Yes. You know the guy?"

"He's just some friend of the spy's. Don't worry about them - they're idiots! In any case, people stare in Sri Lanka, they're curious about everyone."

"Yes, but—"

"You're too used to British indifference."

At last he laughed. In London he must walk down the road with everyone looking straight ahead, pretending no one else was there. No wonder Ria wasn't happy returning. It would have driven Padma crazy to be so invisible among so many; surely the worst kind of loneliness.

"Let's have coffee on the veranda before anyone else gets up," she said.

He pulled on his trousers and shirt and went back across the hall to his room while Padma remained in hers, her sealed private world that, for the first time, she had let someone enter. She did her morning stretches and showered and dressed as on any other morning, but something new had begun, she felt the order of the old days unravelling.

They met on the veranda as if by chance, she bringing out the coffee pot, he searching for cups in the old dresser. He smiled across the table at her.

"What?" She laughed at him.

"I could stay looking at you forever," he said.

Other men too had said that, but they never did stay forever.

Mostly it was she who ended it, when they started talking of taking her back to meet family, some even planning a life together. That was when she knew that her past would be looked for and asked about, and she knew to push away. With Rohan this moment felt further off – she had revealed more to him than anyone else – but one day Rohan too might probe the story of the evil uncle and then she would have to back away. But he was only visiting Sri Lanka, he would soon be leaving the villa. Gerhardt's warning was a strange consolation that morning.

"What are you thinking about?" Rohan asked.

"That you'll be going back to England soon."

"I can't even imagine it right now."

She smiled, pushing away that time, thinking only of their time safe in her room.

"I love your smile," he said, and she knew that he too was blocking out what lay ahead; it seemed so far away just then. "I've loved your smile from the very first moment I saw you – on the porch over there – do you remember?"

"You looked so fed up that day! But I knew you liked it here when you stayed even after that rat ran out of your room!"

"So you admit it! You kept saying: 'It's just a little *meeya*'!"

She burst into giggles.

Ria came in looking tired and pale and wearing dark glasses.

"Morning," she murmured and sat at her table, writing in her diary.

Padma and Rohan set the tables for breakfast. Anjali and Dan arrived, Anjali mumbling an apology for the disruption of the night, Dan thanking them all. The two sat glumly at their table in the middle of the veranda and looked out at the garden, not saying a word. Padma placed the jars of instant coffee and tea bags, the sugar and condensed milk and a thermos flask of hot water on each table, and brought out glasses of juice. Rohan took his usual seat at the small table by the parapet, returned to being a guest.

"Could I have more orange juice?" Anjali asked.

"Only one glass is included in breakfast."

"You couldn't make me some fresh coffee, I suppose?"

"No."

"I really hate Nescafé," Anjali grumbled to Dan and looked accusingly at the coffee pot on Rohan's table.

"There's a little left, would you like some?" Rohan offered, but Anjali looked horrified and shook her head, refusing to look at him.

"Just order another orange juice and put it on the bill," Dan told her.

"Why should we? What's one more glass to them?" Anjali whispered crossly. "Considering what we're paying for a room with no air-conditioning and no hot water," she added, still whispering, but Padma heard her. She pretended not to. She went inside to see if Soma had started making the toast and eggs, but as she passed her room, the door was open and Soma was inside, making her bed, the sheets of the night before in a heap on the floor.

"What are you doing? Varuna will clean later!" Padma exclaimed.

"Might as well get these rooms done." Soma gathered up the sheets and with them, Rohan's leather chaporas from under the bed.

"He must have been looking for these, good thing we found them," was all he said as he placed the chaporas neatly outside Rohan's door.

He carried on down the hall. Padma ran after him.

"Have you said anything to Gerhardt?" she demanded.

"About what?" Soma looked innocently back over the bundle of sheets.

She glared at him, refusing to be shamed.

"I don't care what you do with that one, he's alright," Soma said gently.

"What?"

"He's a good one." And Soma went off to the utility room.

Padma wandered back through the house to the veranda and leaned on the parapet near Rohan. She watched the garden allowing the morning to grow, opening itself to the sun and brightness. She turned and saw Anjali staring at her, a defiant unhappy hunger in her eyes. Anjali glanced away and Padma thought of her sleeping all alone in her single bed while she, Padma, had had the night that was still warm in her, still real. Poor Anjali, so lonely, even with Dan devoted to her. Padma ran to the kitchen and brought back two large glasses of orange juice which she placed before Anjali and Dan.

"On the house," she said.

"Oh no! Please put it on the bill!" Dan protested.

Anjali drank her juice in silence. Padma willed her to feel cared for; she wanted everyone to feel loved and happy that morning.

Gerhardt arrived. He seemed subdued and thoughtful. He hugged her tightly.

"Any plans for later?" he asked Anjali and Dan.

"None whatsoever," Anjali said.

"There's a turtle watch in the next village, I'm not sure when the season is—"

"Definitely not now," Padma interrupted, glancing guiltily at Ria, but Ria hadn't heard.

"We can find out when the turtles come," Gerhardt offered.

"That would be great!" Dan looked keen.

"I'm not really into turtles," Anjali said.

"Whatever you do, you mustn't miss our little rock temple," Gerhardt added.

Anjali almost jumped out of her seat.

"A rock temple, you say?" Dan cast a sly glance at Anjali. "We've heard about a rock temple, haven't we, Anjali?"

Anjali glared at him, and he smiled, taunting her. Padma watched intrigued.

"It's wonderful around there! I've recently completed a project of my own near the temple – a lovely little rental cottage!" Gerhardt enthused. "Let me know if you or your family are interested."

"Yes, of course," Anjali said tightly.

"Make sure you visit the temple, and go right up to the top of the rock; the view from there is really something."

"Sounds great," Dan said.

"Padma can arrange a tuk-tuk for you."

"We can't go today!" Anjali protested.

"Why not? We're not doing anything," Dan said.

"We know a very good driver – he'll climb up with you if you want him to," Gerhardt went on, oblivious to the battle before him.

"I'll book the tuk-tuk for two o'clock," Padma said.

"Fantastic!" Dan said, triumphant.

"That's a very good time to go," Gerhardt agreed.

Anjali was silent, resigned in defeat. Padma almost felt sorry for her, but the thought of Anjali at the villa all day demanding things was too awful. Padma went inside to ring Wilson before anyone changed their minds.

৵৻

Padma and the cook cleared the tables. Anjali watched a wave begin along the horizon, heaving up blue-green and gelatinous, rolling over, spraying into the sun as it lunged to the shore, crashing with abandon, a gleeful falling. She too was falling, but fearfully, helplessly. Ever since leaving Colombo she had been falling.

"I'll write down the name of that temple for you," Gerhardt said. "Let me just find something to write on."

He pulled out drawer after drawer of an old pine sideboard, a relic from Europe, dry as driftwood, its pale wood pitted finely with the trails of long-ago woodworm.

"Ah, here's some paper. Now all I need is a pen. My goodness, where on earth do you keep these things, Padma? Padma?"

He opened another drawer, rattled a tin.

"Actually Gerhardt, there's no need, we know the name of the temple," Dan said.

He sounded apologetic; he made it seem like a confession.

"Well, why didn't you say?" Gerhardt looked puzzled.

"Anjali's family know the new priest at the temple."

"*Knew. Knew* the priest," Anjali corrected. She glowered at Dan. He was angry at her, finally he was showing it.

"Well then, you have to visit," Gerhardt said. "Does he know you're in the area, Anjali?"

"No, and it was my grandfather who knew him. It was a very long time ago."

"But the priest's known you since you were a baby, hasn't he?" Dan persisted. "You and you mother used to visit him all the time, didn't you? Wasn't that what you said?"

He was merciless, a cruel streak in him risen to the surface.

"Didn't you live really close to his old temple?"

Anjali looked coolly back at him. So this was how it ended, how one became like all those other miserable couples, feuding in public but secretly, right under everyone else's noses. Couples like her parents. She and Dan must never become like them. Would it have been better if they had never met?

"All arranged! He'll be here at two," Padma announced. They turned expectantly to Anjali – what did they all want of her?

"Great!" She smiled brightly.

Defeat looked less like defeat, if one simply gave in.

"Now you can go to the beautiful cave shrines," Gerhardt said, very pleased with himself.

"Thank you for arranging everything!" Dan gushed.

Anjali left them and headed back to the bungalow. Dan came running up beside her.

"I'm sure it'll be okay," he said.

"How do you know? You have no idea what's going on."

"Neither do you."

"So?"

"I don't want us missing out," he said defiantly.

Inside their bungalow he took her in his arms. She didn't resist, letting herself be held. She leaned wearily against him.

"You always have to be going somewhere," she murmured. "You *knew* I didn't want to go to that temple. All I wanted was to rest a little."

"We've been resting for ages! How much more rest do you need?"

"I told you what my mother said about the priest."

"Nothing intelligible, as far as I remember."

"She said specifically not to visit him. He's done something bad."

"How bad?"

"Very bad, to have got himself banished from Colombo - he would never have chosen to go. He loved that old temple - one minute he's the head priest there, the next he's disappeared up a rock - a little strange, don't you think?"

"If what he did was really so terrible, wouldn't he have been de-frocked?"

"Disrobed—"

"Yes, that - wouldn't he?"

"He has friends in high places, that's what my mother said.

They hushed things up and sent him somewhere remote."

"And that's her whole basis for condemning him? How very Buddhist of her."

"My mother knew more than she was saying – she always does. She was trying to protect me from the sordid details." Anjali frowned. "I hate it when she does that."

"You should see for yourself and make up your own mind."

"What if he's done something disgusting? I really don't want to know."

"Maybe you're afraid he'll tell you off for quitting a good job and hanging around with a good-for-nothing Burgher boy?"

"Don't be ridiculous!"

"You can tell him I'm a lapsed Catholic, if you like."

"What do I care what the silly bloody priest thinks of me? He probably won't even be there."

She silently prayed for the priest to have gone somewhere else – the very prayers he had taught her once.

## 23

THE TUK-TUK CAME in the afternoon, the driver usher-
ing Anjali and Dan into the back of his garish little vehicle,
offering them frilly cushions to lean on and soft drinks from a cool
box. The cushions were too plump and hard, Anjali pushed them
aside and leaned back against the seat, sun-baked and burning
through her blouse, as they drove through the village with the
driver needlessly beeping his horn and grinning madly. She got
him to stop at a grocery stall on the main road where she bought
extra-large jars of Marmite and Horlicks for the priest, just as her
mother used to on the way to temple in the old days. Then the
tuk-tuk resumed its journey inland.

Paddy fields spread, a young wet green. A breeze came in,
cool and restful, the afternoon's heat relenting, loosening its
grip on the day. They passed small houses in sprawling gardens,
a stately bungalow in a coconut grove. At a grey cement well
by the road, women draped in cotton cloths bathed, pouring
buckets of well-water over themselves and tiny bare-bodied
children clustered around them. The sweet floral scent of their
shampoo drifted into the tuk-tuk. The women pulled up water
in pails, passed each other soap. Anjali and Dan sat gazing out
from their separate windows. The driver looked determinedly

ahead, his eyes wide and listening, alert to the silence between them.

They passed a red-earth cricket field, where young men in dusty whites had gathered to play. A bowler ran, one arm raised, about to bowl, but the fielders turned to stare into the tuk-tuk with Anjali inside. Someone wolf-whistled. The young men started to hoot and call to her. The bowler stopped and joined in with the others.

"You've stopped a cricket match!" Dan laughed.

She shrank back in her seat, turning the other way. The awful whistle came again.

"They don't mean any harm," Dan said and touched her hand, but she pulled away.

The sun glinted on a lake with purple Nelum lilies risen above the dark shining water. A pure white egret stood at the edge. The tuk-tuk turned a corner and the giant blue-black rock of Sudhugala Temple rose above them. The driver entered a sandy clearing at the base of the rock and parked in the shade of a large rope-trunked tree.

"You want me to come up with you?" he offered.

"No need," she said quickly.

"Okay then, I'll wait here for you," the driver said cheerily and joined the other drivers resting in the roots of the tree.

Anjali and Dan walked in among the family groups strolling around the base of the rock, out on the kind of daytrip that felt of long ago. On family excursions now Anjali's family went to beautiful, numbing hotels – a new Asia made in the West, with fusion food and meditation groups and hamams. It was what the country needed, her cousins insisted: stylish hotels to attract a better class of tourist, not those ghastly package-types; it was time for Sri Lanka to make something of itself, they said. At Sudhugale Rock there were no tourists, no city folk with designer clothes and expensive gadgets – the place was timeless and eerie. Even the flower sellers carrying around buckets of Nelum lilies cut from the lake didn't hassle or ask for too much. Dan bought two lilies without having to haggle. The hard green stalks dripped onto the sand making wet dark discs with raised rounded edges, like platelets.

Dan started up the steps, but Anjali held back, resisting the rock and the secrets it was hiding. Once she knew, there would be no going back; knowledge couldn't be undone.

"Come on!" Dan called down to her.

He stood waiting. The stone banister was hot under her palm as she went up to join him. As they climbed, people glanced curiously at her, then at Dan; they could tell that she was with him. They reached a hut built into a rocky overhang; a thin man was seated inside, behind a greasy pane of glass with a price list of tickets for tourists.

"Ah, tickets, I should have guessed!" Anjali muttered as Dan took out his wallet.

"You're from here?" the man asked, squinting at Anjali.

"Yes," she said sullenly.

Dan pushed money through a gap in the glass.

"He's with you?" the man asked Anjali.

"As a matter of fact, he is – so?"

"In that case, no need to pay."

"What?"

The man smiled at her surprise. He waggled his head in that gesture of yes-no-whatever-everything's-fine that no one from abroad could ever understand, and pushed the money back to Dan. Anjali found herself giving him a small waggle of the head in return, thanking him.

"What a nice man," Dan said as they left.

"They shouldn't charge anyone for going to a temple.".

"Still, it was nice of him to let me off."

"Yeah, it was."

The chatter of the day-trippers surrounded them, a languid bustling contentment all around. There was none of the hardness and mean profiteering that seemed to have taken over the whole country in the years she had been away. The crowd at the rock, mostly all Buddhists, seemed indifferent to greed and competition, and the mood of righteousness and superiority taking over the Buddhists in the country. None of the people passing Anjali seemed angry or disillusioned, they were much too busy cuddling babies and nestling little children against them, as they climbed up the thick stone steps. Teenagers helped up old grannies in saris who were clutching huge handbags and wearing inappropriate slippers. In baskets, Anjali glimpsed plastic bags of wet jasmine flowers washed ready for temple, packets of joss sticks and Tupperware with picnic lunches, thermos flasks full of tea perhaps, or Nescafé made thick and sweet with condensed milk. Young couples giggled and teased and flirted, falling behind the others. Bodies brushed against her, but gently, no one jostled to get ahead.

They reached the first rock plateau and went into a cave where a giant Buddha was seated meditating, smiling benignly down. People pushed forward to lay flowers and fruit on a white marble shrine table. They lit incense and paused to pray, heads bowed, eyes closed, hands pressed together. Anjali felt the crowd behind her, shifting and alive against her as she murmured a prayer and laid her lily next to Dan's on the white marble before being carried in a hushed, warm-bodied surge back to the entrance. Outside, monkeys sat in a line on a wall eating stolen shrine flowers. Mango stones from fruit similarly acquired, lay sucked clean on the ground. Anjali and Dan went with the crowd to the next flight of steps, which gave way to worn rocky ledges leading up to the second plateau.

The shrine here was in a long low cave. The Buddha statue reclined, its large fine head propped on a red plaster bolster cushion,
the gentle painted eyes quiet and reflective. The walls were covered
in murals of lush forests and quiet lakes, peacocks, storks, ele-
phants, deer grazing on green grassy plains. The fires of Hell
burned in a panel beneath, with tortured figures being punished
forever. Anjali knew the stories from Sunday school. She showed
Dan the evil Angulimala wearing the necklaces of fingers cut from
his victims. In the next panel there was a repentant Angulimala,
fallen to his knees, being offered forgiveness by a haloed Lord
Buddha. In the panel that followed, Angulimala himself stood in
saffron robes, redeemed and with a yellow-orange haze of goodness above him to prove it.

"This place is amazing," Dan said.

When they went outside, the families had settled around a
stepped pond cut into the rock, full of still green water. The scents
of rice and curry filled the air as the Tupperware was opened and
plantain leaf wrappings of lunch packets were unfolded, but the
young couples went on and Anjali and Dan followed.

The third plateau was shaded by forest. The couples dispersed,
easing away through the trees. Anjali and Dan went alone to the
shrine, small and blue-painted, formed of a rocky crevice. Two clay
lamps burned in an iron stand beside a Buddha lying flat on his
back, dead. The glossy yellow-painted feet touched the end of the
cave, the rock chiselled out to fit them – such huge rounded toes,
white nails outlined in a thin line of red. The figure was so large
it felt potent, alive, and Anjali felt suddenly afraid. She felt herself
stirring awake, a sudden quiet joyfulness in her, and her secret wild,
golden self coming to life again. In that small blue room smiling
avatars flew in painted clouds across the ceiling. Orange-robed
disciples made of plaster with sweet solemn faces, bowed chipped
shaven heads, averting their gaze as if aware of her aliveness. She

went outside into the light, and stood at the edge of the forest's dark shade. A breeze passed through the trees teasing, caressing.

"So where do you suppose the priest's house is?" Dan said, coming out to join her.

"Maybe it's at the bottom."

"Or higher up," he said, and went on.

But the path came to an end, and there were no more steps to climb.

"Oh well, that's it." Gladly Anjali turned back to go.

"No, look!" Dan touched grooves cut into the rock and clawed his way up, fitting his feet into the hollows. He reached down for her and she grasped his hand, scrambling up behind him until they reached the dense rustling quiet of the fourth plateau.

"It's just jungle up here," Anjali said.

The voices of the couples faded, lost below.

"There could be snakes," she added. "Or weird people."

Dan didn't listen, he went deeper into the trees and Anjali edged behind him. Monkeys shrieked high in the branches. Birds cackled. A woodpecker tapped hollowly.

A clay-tiled roof showed through the green up ahead.

"There it is!" Dan was triumphant. "Jesus! Imagine living up here all alone – no wonder he's gone mad."

"I didn't say he'd gone mad."

"Better stay back a little, just in case," Dan said as they approached the house.

"Hello!" he called, from the edge of the veranda.

Silence gripped the house and the garden.

"Maybe you should say something in Sinhalese?" Dan suggested.

"He speaks perfect English, you idiot! He's extremely well-educated."

A superior mind, Grampa had said of the priest, predicting

that he would one day be among the country's top clergy. How wrong he had been; how misplaced his admiration. Dan went up the two low steps and onto the veranda.

"Is anyone there?" he shouted.

His voice echoed around the clearing. There was a feint shuffling sound inside the house. Then came the slap of bare feet on a cement floor and, from deep in the shadows of the house, a figure in a monk's ochre robes came towards them.

&

It was time to go. Ria left her bungalow for the last time, all her possessions with her, the nest she had made for herself dismantled, abandoned. The room waited, emptied out for whoever came next to make it theirs. At the main house, Soma had made lunch as usual, but instead of rice there were stringhoppers – surely not because of her? He brought out creamy yellow kiri hodi gravy to moisten the soft matted noodle-mass of the stringhoppers stacked on her plate. And there was more: a dark peppery-hot king-fish curry and seeni sambol, with the onions fried dark and crisp, the way she liked it best. He had remembered everything she had said in a conversation they had had about her favourite Sri Lankan foods. He beamed, watching her eat, taking a spoonful of each, tasting turmeric, fenugreek, coconut, black pepper and tamarind – that magical complex mixture of savoury and mild, sweetness and pepper-heat that felt of belonging and being cared for.

There were others too, eating on the veranda: Padma sat with Gerhardt at the table where Anjali and Dan usually sat; Rohan ate alone. He and Padma stole glances at each other when they thought no one was looking. Gerhardt kept looking up, too late to see them. He seemed anxious, but it wasn't enough to undo the calm of the villa, and the solid base of pleasure and contentment on which that whole world seemed built. Soon Ria would be outside their enchanted circle and back in a world that knew nothing of the wonders of openness and kindness and welcome that she had found. Outside, only striving was possible, and fleeting stalled connections, strangers turning away unnerved when you smiled at them. There was no shelter outside, no gathering places, no place to dream and feel dreams come alive. Ria's throat tightened. Her eyes filled with tears, remembering. Long ago, she had left another perfect world, but that first time she left Sri Lanka she hadn't known to cry. She had grinned and waved goodbye to her grandparents left behind at the barriers in the airport hall. She had not known then what she was losing; not known that she was being taken away from the only people she had ever belonged with, away from the place she loved, where she had been loved completely. At the villa she had found her way to an echo of that earlier life, but once more she was leaving.

The taxi arrived to take her to Colombo. They all came down to the gate with her, Padma, Gerhardt, Rohan, with Soma carrying her bags.

"Stay in touch, okay?" Padma pleaded.

"Of course!"

"Don't forget us."

"I won't."

"Yes you will! You'll go back to London and never think about us ever again!"

"I promise, I won't ever forget."

And then it was all over. Ria sat in the taxi being driven away while they stood in the lane waving goodbye. Soon they would go back inside and be together. They were waving still, tiny faceless figures, then the taxi drove around the bend in the road and they were gone. Villagers stared in at her. In the entrance to an alleyway stood the bald man and his unpleasant young friend who had sent

Louis and her to the turtle watch beach. They glowered into the
taxi, at her. The taxi reached the stalls at the top of the lane and
she was alone again, the girl leaving once more, letting herself be
taken away from a place where she belonged. That first time, at
the airport, Gramma and Grampa had waved goodbye, beaming
with gladness for all that she would gain in the new great country,
all that they had wanted her to see and learn and have – they had
wanted so much for her. They had waved, sending her and her
parents into the great wide world beyond their little island, she and
her parents dressed in their new clothes made by Grampa's tailor
especially for the journey. Further and further away they walked
through the pale bare marble departure hall. Ria hadn't known
then that she was leaving forever, or that everything left behind
could be lost, and so completely. Why hadn't she protested? Why
hadn't she looked back?

In the taxi now, she took off her sunglasses and wiped her eyes.
The taxi driver glanced at her in the rear-view mirror and politely
looked away. The sea was so blue, so bright without her glasses.
It stayed by her side as the taxi hurtled along the road, and the
emptiness that lived in her, a quiet smothering presence returned
to take its place. But she pushed it away now, and remembered
that she had looked back in the airport hall, turning at the last
doorway to see small plump Gramma hunched sobbing against
the tall figure of Grampa who was bending over her, holding her
as he too cried, those beloved faces crumpled with sadness and the
arms that had hugged and held her each day were now wrapped
around each other, consoling themselves as she went away, and all
that they had had together was lost. What might she have become
if she had stayed? If she had run back, crying and pleading not
to be sent away? In their bungalow at the edge of the city, in a
garden full of fruit trees and flowers and an orchid house and
frail roses wilting in Colombo heat, how might she have grown?

Wrapped in their love and concern, cushioned in the soft bed of their acceptance, who might she have been? She had felt their world so close sometimes at the villa: in the smell of the sea in the mornings, the noise of traffic and crows. She had loved to hear the muezzin's calls at the mosque over the road in Colombo and the priests' chanting in the temple next door, to feel the silky saris of Gramma's friends seated close at bajaans, singing to the drone of a harmonium. She thought of fresh flower garlands hanging in the flower stall outside the kovil, bright paper lanterns in the gardens at Vesak, the green parrots in the mango trees and lurid pink candy floss at the Vel festival. How lulled she had been hearing the voices of women in gardens behind the villa, talking in what seemed a foreign tongue, until she realised that she had understood every word, for those words lived in her still – all this she loved; it was what beautiful meant to her, what it would always mean.

To know what one wanted was a gift, and a burden for she couldn't deny anymore what she wanted. Gerhardt had raised a whole world from a shack on a dubious road with questionable neighbours – a valiant attempt, a triumph, even, for it was the effort that counted, after all, to have dared to try. Padma had often talked of a yoga institute in Colombo, and there were a great many chambers in Colombo – so many places where she could ask for work. She didn't need permission from the family, or an invitation; she didn't even need them to want her back. What could be more natural than to work in the city of her birth, to have a home of her own and a lover, perhaps, and make the family she wanted for herself, one day – just as Gerhardt had. Nothing was ever truly lost; old worlds could be remade. Even the people that would never come back could be found in new others. At the villa an old lost life had flickered alive and now she felt its small bright flame inside her. The taxi paused as they reached the main road and with an excited jolt joined the cars and trucks and buses full of people going on to somewhere else.

&

"Lovely girl, that one," Soma observed as they went back into the garden.

"I hope I see her again," Padma said.

"Of course you'll see her again," Gerhardt scoffed.

"Not here, I won't, she's never coming back."

"For goodness sake, you don't know that!"

"Yes I do, she told me."

"She told me too, but that doesn't mean she won't change her mind."

"Ria's going to Goa next year instead of here, she was quite sure. And she'll carry on living in London for the rest of the time."

"What an extraordinary young woman." Gerhardt looked impressed.

"It's easy to be extraordinary when you don't have a guest house to run," Padma snapped and the others stared at her.

"You can go to Goa if you want," Gerhardt said, looking shocked.

Soma hurried away to the house. Rohan walked silently at her side.

"And who would run this guest house?" she asked Gerhardt.

She was suddenly angry, and unfairly, for the guest house had been her idea, not his. He had only helped her to set it up.

"Soma and I could look after things here if you wanted a break," Gerhardt said. "Or we could close for a few months."

"We just opened! How can we close so soon?"

She had no right to be angry, he had done so much to help her. She was the most ungrateful person alive.

"Just ignore me," she muttered and walked faster up the path.

"Are you okay?" Rohan asked, coming with her.

"I have to check Ria's room in case she's forgotten something," Padma said and ran away.

He didn't follow her and she was glad. She wanted to be free of everyone, even him; alone with her ingratitude and dismay. Gerhardt had given her so much, but they were heavy gifts and too big; they filled up the smallness of her world. She stood in Ria's room, soothed by its emptiness. From the window she saw Hema Amme coming past the villa's gate. The shrivelled old head peeped around the gatepost then retreated as she saw Gerhardt on the porch. If Hema Amme had news, Padma would only receive it if Gerhardt was helped to go away.

Padma went over to Gerhardt sitting typing on his phone.

"Aren't you going to your site visit?" Padma asked.

"No, I'm just letting the client know I'll be going tomorrow instead—"

"There's no need, Gerhardt, go and see him now!"

"But are you okay?"

"Of course I am. I'm sorry I was so rude earlier."

They hugged and the ugliness faded. There was always space with Gerhardt to move aside from the bad things you did, and begin again.

"I'm sure Ria will come back to see you," he said.

"Yes, maybe. Anyway, you'd better go Gerhardt, you're going to be really late."

He left finally and moments later, Hema Amme was back at the gate. Padma stayed hidden behind bushes and watched the stooped old woman with her hooked nose and crumpled toothless jaw, scowling up at the house, a white envelope dangling from her hand. How long she had hovered near the villa to give Padma that envelope. So much patience was needed to spy; so much time

316

used up. There was so much to do with one's life, yet those who watched others didn't seem to resent all the hours they lost, all the effort wasted; they only seemed to resent other people, people like her. Padma went down to the gate. Gustav came running behind her and gave the old woman a warning bark, but Padma hushed him.

"Here – it's urgent!" Hema Amme thrust the white envelope at Padma and stepped back from the gate, eyeing Gustav with loathing.

"It's from your mother – she needs your help at once!"

"Why? What's happened?"

"She's really sick, she needs more medicine. It's all in that letter."

"How ill? Is it very bad?"

Hema Amme strained to see past Padma into the villa garden.

"You're seeing guests now, I hear?" Hema Amme said.

"I see them every day, this is a guest house."

"But you're seeing one of them, aren't you? Everyone knows. Is he paying you extra?"

Hema Amme was the only villager to use 'umba' for 'you' with Padma. Umba was used by poor villagers to address animals and each other. Even Sunny used the more respectful 'oya' with her, as did the other villagers, forced by the fact of her adoption to acknowledge her elevation to a world above theirs.

"That's right, I'm sleeping with guests all over the place, I'm shagging everyone. Would you like a shag as well?"

"What a way to talk to your elders!" Hema cried. "Gallivanting on the beach with strange men, canoodling in full view of everyone. Aren't you ashamed?"

"Isn't it worse to be a pervert hiding behind rocks watching the canoodling?"

"Even those girls up the road go inside for that kind of thing. And they get paid! You're doing it for nothing."

Padma thought of Rohan guiding her away from the spy and

his friend, who was possibly Mukul, and she remembered the weight of Rohan's arm around her, shielding her from them, taking her to safety.

"At least I get to marry a rich, handsome man and leave this cess pit of a village to go to England," she said.

"He's never going to marry you!"

"Oh, really?"

"He's not going to take you to England!"

"That's what you think!" Padma laughed seeing the disbelief waver in the old woman's mean watery eyes, blue-grey with cataracts.

"You think you know so much about me, don't you?" Padma jeered, seeing the old woman's envy expand and fill her. She looked pained, as if Padma had physically hurt her. There was such power and freedom in knowing the source of another's envy, a way to cause pain; sensing exactly where the secret hurt would fester.

"So make sure you tell that nice son of yours to enjoy the show while it lasts, because I won't be around much longer."

"Disgusting, you are! Good riddance to you, that's what I say. The sooner you go, the better. Your poor mother, what a thing to have a daughter like you."

Hema Amme shuffled up the lane, still cursing. Padma heard 'whore' and 'hussy' and 'worthless' while she tore open the envelope and found a letter to Leela from the hospital. Blood tests had shown a streptococcal infection and she needed antibiotics straight away: two tablets to be taken daily at the same time each day, for one week; the course to be completed. Leela had written a short note, asking for money for the prescription. Padma ran to the office and paid it at once into Leela's account. There were new emails to read – one from the yoga institute in Colombo. She didn't dare open it. At last she clicked on it, and it was from Mrs Gunesekara, the director herself. She had written that she was delighted to hear from Padma again, and of course Padma could take the exams whenever she was ready. Mrs Gunesekara was looking forward very much to seeing Padma again, as were her two daughters, who were themselves teachers at the institute, one of whom had taught Padma.

Padma closed her eyes, returning to their world, back at once in the cool high-ceilinged rooms with a walk-in cupboard where rolls of pale-green yoga mats were stacked and wooden blocks, baskets of jute belts, rough-spun cotton blankets for shoulder stands. In each of the rooms there was an alcove or a shrine with a dancing Lord Shiva and incense burning – the same incense she used still, its scent drifting through the rooms of the villa. One day she would show Leela this world and she too could share in its goodness; no more would she be thwarted and denied and enfeebled. One day soon it would be time for Padma to return to the institute and keep on learning.

## 24

FROM THE SHADOWS of the priests' house, the robed figure approached. Anjali stood by the steps, Dan suddenly stepping in front as if to protect her. A monk stepped out from the darkness. It was the head priest from the old temple. He started to smile at Dan, but he stopped, seeing Anjali. He stared at her.

"Is it really you, Duwa?" he murmured.

He looked exactly the same: the same pale-gold skin, the round shaven head, three fat wrinkles at the back of his neck.

"I didn't know if I would ever see you again, Duwa."

She had forgotten that he had called her daughter in Sinhalese - that small sure word, so old-fashioned and gentle, proudly, quietly claiming her as someone important to him.

"You haven't changed," she said.

"It's the altitude. Very good for the skin, I hear."

She smiled and knelt on the ground and worshipped him.

"Suvakka veva," he recited over her, the silky words of blessing wrapping her up, protecting her against the unknown, the unseen.

Dan bowed, handing over the bag of Marmite and Horlicks.

"Very kind of you both," the priest said and blessed Dan as well.

"This is Dan," Anjali said. "A friend."

"Dan. Welcome."

The priest pulled over a wooden bench for them to sit on and settled in a chair draped in a sheet, the way chairs were meant to be before a priest could sit on them. Even at the airport, there were seats for clergy, covered in white linen.

"You know Dan, I have known this Duwa since she was a baby, three days old," he reflected. "I was only a young novice then, but I remember her parents and grandparents bringing her to see the head priest. How happy we all were that day."

The priest beamed fondly at her, the way everyone had once when they thought her clever and good and the perfect daughter. Astonishingly, the priest still seemed to feel the same way about her.

"I thought you were in America still, Duwa," he said. "I didn't get a chance to see your parents before I left." His voice trailed off. "Are they well?" he asked. "Your father - he is - happy with the new post?"

"Yes. Very."

And he was shocked by that, she could see, just as she had been. No one had forced her father to change job, as some of the relatives still believed. Each day he was content to go with the new driver and the van following, full of security men - to his world of official secrets and bad deeds to defend.

"Are you qualified yet, Duwa?" the priest asked.

Dan glanced nervously at her, sympathetic at last.

"The thing is," she said carefully, "I've decided to become a teacher, not a lawyer."

"Ah, very good." The priest nodded approving.

"You think so?" She searched his face.

"Oh yes, I always thought you would make a very fine teacher."

"A *kindergarten* teacher? With your academic qualifications?" her father had exclaimed, so shocked he had seemed to be amused.

"Why do you want to throw your life away?" her mother had cried.

"You were so patient and kind with the Sunday School children," the priest observed. "Your pupils will be very lucky to have you."

"I do like teaching," Anjali confessed and for once it didn't matter that he had known her before as a superiorly clever girl destined for far greater things than most people.

"The kids at the orphanage really did love her," Dan told the priest. "They grew so confident just from being around her."

The priest and Dan looked proudly on at her. She shifted on the bench, suddenly so happy, she thought she would burst.

"The kids were so sweet. They'd come up and tell me all kinds of silly things." She smiled, remembering the solemn taps on her arm and the earnest little stories they'd told her. She saw again their upturned faces, the small warm hands, slightly sticky, uncurling in hers. She couldn't quite explain the feeling in words.

"And how are you finding Nilwatte Beach?" the priest asked her.

"The locals are awful," she blurted. "Always staring and asking questions; they hate me - I can see it in their eyes—"

"No, they don't hate you, Duwa. They see your happiness and they envy what you have, that is all. They probably think you're very wealthy."

"But I'm not rich!" Anjali exclaimed.

"You and I know very well why you're happy." The priest smiled and glanced at Dan. Shame rushed up in her like heartburn.

"By the coast the people are a little excitable," the priest added. "They see the tourists with all their dollars and it makes them feel angry – and who can blame them? There are advertisements everywhere for luxury goods and hotels and holidays abroad, all the time the rich are getting richer – that's all they see—"

He talked a lot about money, Anjali observed warily. Had he got into debt? Gambled? Had he stolen from temple funds? Or tricked a wealthy donor? She'd recently read of a priest going to prison for just those reasons.

"Of course, in another way, you *are* very rich," the priest added.

He had always known that her family had money and especially now, after her father's promotion. But would he believe that she could no longer ask her parents for funds? She readied herself for the priest's demands, or even worse, some revelation about his shameful secret.

"Love is a very precious commodity," the priest said.

"Love?"

Her mother had talked a lot about love recently, but only in terms of the duties and obligations of a daughter who truly loved her parents – a love for reining in desire, and giving up what you really wanted. This love would silence the protest in you, as you did as they asked. Love was the biggest hindrance of all.

"Maybe sometimes it's nice to love," she muttered.

"And to *be* loved," the priest added. "True love, that is, offered for free, without any conditions."

Was there really such love? Love that was just given and didn't ask for something in return? Was it love, then, that simple good feeling she had about Dan – always, even when they argued? How she wished that the priest hadn't been weak and fraudulent so she could believe him, and feel the simple gladness she had once felt knowing him.

"For so long in this country, people have felt deprived," the priest went on. "They've had nothing to hope for, and not just the poor. In all these troubled times, so many educated people have been unable to achieve their best work – they couldn't get any recognition, or reward – for some that matters. It matters very much. It can make them do things they would never have dreamed of."

He meant her father, Anjali knew. The priest was trying to ease her disillusion; trying to help her understand. She heard his forgiveness. She listened to the sadness in his voice.

"If only we could all have what we needed," he said wistfully. "Then we would all be happy on our beautiful island. But it is hard to find contentment without having what one truly desires—"

"It's not possible to have everything one wants!" Anjali said fiercely. "You can't just take what isn't yours."

"If something is important to you, Duwa, you must do everything you can to try and get it – as long as it doesn't hurt anyone else, of course."

Anjali studied him, confused. He didn't seem to be advocating stealing.

"It's funny," Dan mused. "Everyone thinks Buddhism is all about denial."

"Yes, that's the trouble. But the Buddha never said to deprive yourself. When he tried giving up everything, all that happened was that he wasted away and nearly died. In fact, it took a kind gentle woman bringing him milk rice every day to stop him starving to death, and this is what helped him to renew his search. She showed him a way through hardness and self-denial with her love and generosity. She helped him to grow strong so he could resume his ascent to enlightenment – everyone needs such reminders sometimes, everyone needs to find their joy."

The priest shifted in his chair, making himself comfortable. She remembered this, his eagerness to discuss and explain; it was always about learning, for him, and trying to understand. There was the same brightness about him still.

"You know Ryokan? The Japanese priest?" he asked, but neither she nor Dan did.

"I learned of him during my time in Japan. He knew all about this need for joy. He wrote beautiful poems about looking at flowers, trees, even drinking and being drunk and playing with children. When he was very old, he fell in love with a young nun. She stayed with him for the rest of his life. He was so happy in his life, and he had so much love for everyone – his poems are very loving, so full of inner freedom."

Anjali smiled. The priest was exactly the same as before, he hadn't changed one bit.

"Now let me get you some pirith thread," he said and went inside the house.

"Your priest's really cool," Dan whispered when the priest had gone. "I swear your mother's insane."

He had leant in close. Anjali could smell his aftershave. His hair brushed her cheek, it was soft like fur. She rested against him. He took her hand, turning a little ring that he had given her. They sat silently returning to each other, the jungle before them.

They heard the priest's footsteps inside the house and Anjali slid away from Dan and they sat apart once more. The priest sat down, unwinding a ball of orange thread.

"Come, Duwa," he said, and she went to him.

He looped the thread around her wrist and chanted a blessing over her, his voice so familiar, so kind, at peace with himself, and she knew that he hadn't stolen anything or hurt anyone. The jungle breathed out with a sigh. 'At last!' it seemed to say. A breeze touched her face, toying with her, as if teasing her for being suspicious. The birds and the monkeys jeered at her, rejoicing. The priest tied a double knot and tested the thread for strength. He broke her free of the spool.

"I'm very glad I came to see you," she said.

"Me also. And now that I've met Dan, I am very happy – I can't think of two nicer people to have found each other."

It was the first time an elder from Anjali's old life had offered her and Dan the blessing of approval. She was filled with new gratitude for him.

"Dan? You also want a pirith thread?" the priest asked.

"I didn't know if I was allowed. I was born Catholic, but I think I might be an atheist."

"Everyone can have a pirith thread," the priest said, and Dan jumped up, his arm already outstretched.

The priest wrapped orange thread around Dan's wrist and started the chanting. again.

Anjali sat gazing up at the trees towering over the clearing. A kingfisher darted across, landing with a metallic blue flash on a branch by the track they had followed to find the priests' house. Something moved there now – a figure all in white – a woman wearing a white skirt and white blouse. She was slim and rather plain, her long hair tied back in a ponytail, a quietness in her face and in the movement of her body – so still seeming, even as she walked. She stopped, seeing Anjali and Dan on the veranda. The priest was still chanting behind Anjali. But when she turned to tell him about the woman, he was looking up already. And Anjali saw then what he didn't have time to hide – the joyful defiant gladness in him, and tenderness – and Anjali knew then what he had done to be sent away from the old temple. The trees shook in a gust of wind and the sun burst through, blazing in gold patches over the lawn and the woman's face and her slender neck and arms. The black rock gleamed, a gilded shield around the priest and the woman, the whole of the dark inscrutable jungle closing around that terrible couple, protecting them from the world outside.

The priest tied a double knot and broke off Dan's pirith thread as the woman slowly approached.

"Some people came and left rice for tomorrow's lunch," the priest told her. "And someone brought jak curry, I think. This is Anjali," he added. "I knew her as a small baby."

The woman gave Anjali a gentle, easy smile; not seeming at all ashamed of what she had done. "I'll make some tea," she told the priest and walked away, passing behind a line of trees, her skirt a white flicker between them – like the white butterflies that flitted through gardens, barely seen above all the colours and flamboyance, a firm pure whiteness when you looked closely.

"Duwa, would you like some tea?" the priest asked.

"No, we have to go."

Dan looked surprised as Anjali stood up, but he didn't argue for once.

"Yes, of course, thank you for coming," the priest said meekly.

Anjali knew she should walk away without another word and never return. She had every reason to be angry. His betrayal was not just of her but of everyone who had believed in him and willed him to reach the great heights he had seemed destined to achieve, yet he had been weak and ill-disciplined and broken one of the most profound rules of Theravadan Buddhism. He would definitely have been made to disrobe if he hadn't had friends in high places, but they had covered up for him.

The priest came with them to the edge of the veranda. And despite everything Anjali now knew about him, she could sense the promise of something important in him still, and she knew he was just as determined as before to find his way to a place of dignity and truer feeling than most people. She longed to stay close, and to learn from him, the way to her own true feelings and the secret undeniable depths of her heart, that already she had glimpsed in his presence. This he had given her. She knelt and worshipped him, his pale rough feet before her, the nails clipped short and clean – the same feet she had watched her father wash when the priest came to their house for meal offerings.

"Go and come," the priest said, with the same smile of pride and approval he had always had for her.

He stood on the steps and watched them leave. He was still there when she reached the end of the garden and turned back to wave as she had at the gates of the old temple. She saw his surprise and saw him laugh, waving back wildly as he had used to.

"Well, he was very nice, your priest," Dan said. "What could he possibly have done to offend the good Buddhists of Colombo? People are so dumb, sometimes, don't you think?"

"They do worry about the wrong things."

They searched for the way up to the last level and found only a rusted ladder nailed to the rock. Dan tugged the ladder which rattled and shook and came away from the rock in places.

"Let's go, this looks too dangerous," he said.

"Give up now? After coming all this way?" Anjali reached for the rail and started to climb.

"*Now* you have to go and get daring," Dan said, but he followed her. "Watch out! That next step is loose – talk about public safety!"

"No one cares about that in this country!" Anjali laughed and hauled herself up.

The ladder creaked and swung a little as she climbed. When it ran out, she crawled over the next boulder and on to the top, the dusty plateau shaded by thin stunted frangipani trees, their bald spindly limbs enmeshed in each other. Dead flowers rotted on the ground, filling the air with a sweet heady scent. Nearby was a small dagoba, its white greyed with mildew. On the old cracked tiles of the shrine, fresh new frangipani flowers had been placed in a neat half-circle before a marble Buddha standing with one hand raised, aware and knowing, radiating calm. She saw the kingfisher again, perched on a branch at the edge of the rock. It didn't fly away as they went close, to stand watching the sky turn gold and rosy. The sun started its descent over the green paddy fields and the lake they had passed earlier, a glassy deep blue from above. And there was the road that the tuk-tuk had taken, a journey belonging already to the past. Anjali gazed at the beauty of the world spread full and lush before her.

"I've always loved late afternoon," she said. "No school, no homework until evening, everyone busy with their own things, letting you be."

She looked on, loving her world, loving the life she had.

"Let's find work around here, and settle here for a little while," she said to Dan.

"Sure, why not."

A new gladness surged through her and she kissed Dan full on the lips.

"What are you doing? We're still in a temple you know!" But he kissed her back. "You should go to temple more often," he told her as they climbed down together to the driver waiting for them.

⁂

Padma had tea with Rohan on the veranda with the house fallen silent and the bungalows both empty with Anjali and Dan still away at the rock temple.

"It seems strange to think of Ria gone," Padma said.

"It'll be me next," Rohan added, a jolt to hear him say it, yet she had always known that he would be leaving; she had noted the date on the calendar herself.

"How shall we see each other once I've left?" he asked.

"What do you mean?"

"Would you ever consider coming back with me?"

"To London?" If only Hema Amme could have been there to hear him!

"It isn't safe here," he said.

"Is London so safe?"

"Your uncle could come back at any time."

"He hasn't though."

"He said he would."

"But I have a business to run!"

"Couldn't Gerhardt hire a manager?"

"Yes, but then we'd never make any profit. Anyway, London wouldn't suit me."

"Even for a holiday? Just to see what you thought?"

Why was it that she never longed to go abroad like other people? She never felt as if she were missing out when she heard of fine monuments and palaces and museums, or the best restaurants and shops. It was only India that she longed to return to - in India she had felt something new, a new eagerness and desire; a new strength. Once at the cave temples of Ellora she had gazed in astonishment at the dancing statue of Lord Shiva in a cave full of bats, and been moved in a way that she had not known before - such beauty, so quiet and humble and exquisite in the contours of that chiselled stone, such pleasure and abandon captured in those elegant angled limbs.

"But how can we lose what we have?" Rohan insisted. "I've never felt this way with anyone else - have you?"

"No. But—"

He didn't sound like someone having a mere holiday romance - but how many amorous men must decide to rescue a poor local on holiday, and return home relieved to have failed? It would be better for them both to part cleanly, and let the good feelings fade.

"One day I'd like to live in Goa and teach yoga - just for a while," Padma said.

"How nice to live in Goa," Rohan mused.

"Okay, let's go!"

"And what job would I do?"

"You could rent out your flat in London and live on the profits! You'd have enough, wouldn't you?"

"If I slept in a shack and ate coconuts."

"Sounds good! Anyway, I'd help you out."

"Ah, you'd be the main breadwinner hippy, would you? I like it!"

He thought she was joking - which she had been, but now she wanted it for real.

"You might think up a brilliant business idea while you're sitting on the beach," she said.

"I have ideas all the time, it's choosing one that's difficult - believing in something enough to work all the time at it. The friend I told you about - Tom - he never doubted himself, even when other people turned him down."

"You need to be courageous to live creatively, Jarryd says."

"Or crazy!"

"He says you must let yourself step into the unknown and trust that the universe will hold you."

"Intriguing."

If only Rohan could have believed in that life; if only she could. The silence ran on. Padma forgot how it had begun.

That night, the veranda felt incomplete without Ria. Padma still lit the lamp on Ria's table and placed a vase of flowers on it, just as if Ria might appear at any moment. Anjali and Dan leaned close, murmuring excitedly to each other, their feet entwined under the table.

"Doing nooky all the way home," Wilson had reported. "I was worried they'd start doing sexy stuff all over my new seat covers."

Anjali was glowing and lovely in the lamplight. Dan held her hand, studying it like a precious jewel. They were both wearing pirith threads – possibly they'd had a religious conversion at the rock temple; Anjali looking adoringly at Dan as if seeing him after a long absence.

## 25

L ATE THE NEXT morning Rohan walked to the stalls. A
man selling lottery tickets followed him, begging him to try
his luck. Rohan stopped before the women selling fruit and vegetables, women who sat on the ground all day, blackened by sun,
shrivelled and sharp-tongued. They held up mangoes, paw paws,
bunches of small yellow kolikuttu plantains that Padma loved
which Rohan always bought for her. The women wrapped some
for him now and a large pineapple that he planned to take back for
dessert, the only contribution they would let him make to lunch.
The lottery-ticket seller had paused nearby, waiting to resume
when the fruit had been bought, but now without any protest
from Rohan, the man went away.

"Excuse me, sir," someone said behind him.

He turned and there was Padma's uncle, Sunny, standing right
behind him, a little too close. Rohan stepped back.

"I was just passing by and saw you there, sir!" Sunny smiled. "How
are you, sir? You remember me? We met at Gerhardt Hundsler's
villa?"

The memory of that night would never leave Rohan. He
glanced around at the stalls, but no one was watching for once;
everyone was looking the other way. The old women before him

busied themselves rearranging the fruit, covering their heads with their saris.

"Of course you remember me," Sunny said. "So how are you doing? I hear you're having fun at the villa! Enjoying yourself very much, from what I hear!" He smiled nastily. "The thing is, sir, you must be careful with that Padma - maybe no one has told you, but she isn't quite right in the head."

"Really? She seems fine."

"Can you imagine a young girl giving her body to an old foreigner - all for money! Just think, disgusting, no? That is why I was angry with her when you saw me last time."

"Okay, I have to be going." Rohan walked away from the loathsome little man, but the man came with him.

"Sir - you don't know anything about her. She is treating her own people very badly, very disrespectful, that one. She's trouble - don't get involved with her, sir."

"Maybe her people deserve it, because she seems alright to me."

"Ha! You don't know anything about her! Did you know she has more than one old foreigner - one of them dances nude on the beach - can you imagine? If you don't believe me, I can show you - you want me to show you?"

"No, thank you." Rohan walked faster, but the man stayed with him, easily keeping up. He was fitter than he looked.

"Old men with wrinkles and bald heads and hanging bits - that's what she likes, I'm telling you, sir. You should keep away from her. There are much nicer girls around here. You want me to find one for you, sir?"

"No."

"Any type you like, I can find. Much better looking than her."

Rohan stopped in the lane.

"Leave me alone - do you hear me?"

"Then stop seeing Padma."

"Or what?"

"Or you'll find out."

Sunny grinned and Rohan saw the madness in him, the simmering fury waiting for a reason to be unleashed.

Rohan started walking and this time Sunny didn't come with him. Rohan looked back as he reached the lane and Sunny had gone. Rohan walked slower, stepping to one side as a motorbike roared behind him, coming alongside, suddenly close, two men in black helmets turning to look at him. Then an arm swung out holding a metal pipe crashing into Rohan's chest, throwing him down into the drain as the scooter roared off. And then someone behind him clamped a hand over his mouth and pulled him back.

Rohan struggled and kicked as he was dragged into an alley between deserted back gardens of houses. The man threw him into a barbed wire fence, the spikes piercing his chest. A hand searched the pockets of his trousers, taking his wallet and phone and something that rustled – a receipt briefly inspected and thrown to the ground. Rohan didn't fight back, he didn't resist; soon the mugger would see there was nothing else to take.

"Go back to Colombo," the man said, pushing his face close to Rohan's.

The man smelled of alcohol, sweat and dope, and deodorant working too hard. Rohan glimpsed a dark face, chipped yellowed teeth; tangled black hair, and he was sure that he had seen the man before, hiding on the beach with the spy, watching Padma and him.

"You stay away from our people, arsehole!" The man punched Rohan in the ribs. "And don't come back. Or we'll get rid of you ourselves – then you can see how you like it here – swanning around like you own everyone. Who the hell are you, to swan around here?"

The man rammed Rohan into the edge of a wall. The guy was just a jittery hoodlum with sweaty hands, nothing like the muscled mob reeking of aftershave and whisky and eerie professionalism that had dragged Rohan out of his parents' house on the night before the court case. The mugger gave Rohan one last shove and ran away. Rohan listened until he couldn't hear him anymore. In the silence he turned. The alleyway was empty. In one of the gardens, a dog lay sleeping in the shade of a tree. A buffalo trampled out through a fence and nosed in the bag Rohan had dropped, inspecting the bananas and pineapple. Rohan went stumbling out into the lane, back to where people were passing – but no one seemed able to see him anymore. He straightened his shirt and saw that he was bleeding. No one came over to help. As on the night before the court case, he was alone in something unknowable. He walked, then ran towards the villa.

Padma was on the veranda laying the table for lunch.

"What happened?" she cried and rushed to him. "You're bleeding!"

He flinched at the pain as she touched him.

"I got mugged. I need to ring my bank and insurance company."

"Was it Sunny?" she whispered.

"No, someone else."

"Soma! Come quickly!" she shouted, leading him into her room.

He sat on her bed as she and Soma cleaned his wounds with Dettol and iodine and covered them with a dressing from a bright-red First Aid box. Soma telephoned Gerhardt while Rohan used Padma's phone to call the necessary emergency numbers, calm efficient voices in England, assuring him that his bank accounts were unaffected, and now safely locked; his phone disabled.

"Have you ever seen the mugger around here?" Soma wanted to know.

"Maybe once, on the beach."

"What's he look like?"

"Young, skinny, longish hair – a bit crazy looking."

"Could it have been that spy fellow?" Soma pondered.

"No, it wasn't him. It was someone else."

"Mukul? He's also been seen around these parts," Soma said.

"Who's Mukul?" Rohan asked.

Padma smeared ointment onto the bruise on his ribs with small cold fingers.

"He's just some guy – but he wouldn't come this way without Sunny. You're sure you didn't see Sunny?"

"No, he wasn't there."

Why frighten her? He had left Sunny far behind at the stalls before the men on the bike appeared. It was probably coincidence that Sunny had been there as well. The mugger and his accomplices were most probably locals envious of Padma's business, wanting to scare off her guests.

Then Gerhardt arrived, anxiously checking on Rohan while Soma laid the table for lunch. They ate together, Rohan feeling quite restored after sipping the vintage brandy that Gerhardt had brought from his house.

"It was just bad luck," Rohan said. "The bank said nothing's happened on the cards, so everything's fine."

"Obviously I'll lend you any money you need," Gerhardt said.

"There's no need, the insurance company is sending someone over with cash in the next few hours."

"Who the hell was it?" Soma was still puzzled.

Padma stared out at the lane.

"It couldn't have been anyone from here, everyone knows Boss looks after us," Soma said.

"Maybe whoever it was didn't realise Rohan was with us," Gerhardt considered.

337

"Everyone knows he's staying here," Soma insisted.

"It must have been someone new in the area – I keep seeing loads of new people going past these days," Padma said.

"Those are tourists. If there was anyone new taking control around here, we'd have heard about it," Soma said impatiently.

"The minister's brother's wretched business is attracting a new sort of person down here," Gerhardt reflected.

Soma sighed. "Boss won't get involved with the minister's brother's people," he admitted.

"Exactly, it must have been some of them," Gerhardt said. "There's nothing we can do for the moment."

"Or ever," Soma added glumly.

Rohan remembered Padma saying that the minister looked out for Gerhardt and the villa – so why had the minister's men let Padma's horrible uncle hang around? Surely Sunny could have been made to leave the area by the minister's men?

The telephone started to ring in the hall and Gerhardt went to answer it. He came out a moment later, looking to Rohan.

"It's your mother," he said.

Her timing was extraordinary. Rohan paused to drink down the brandy, then he gulped down the water in his glass, instinctively, as if she might smell the brandy on his breath. He rose slowly and went to her.

"Hello?" he greeted her, as if nothing had happened.

"Rohan? Darling! Are you alright?" She was breathless and agitated. "Your insurance company called just now about sending a courier – what's all this about a mugging?"

He had forgotten that until just weeks before, he'd had no address in Sri Lanka, other than his parents'.

"Everything's fine, Ma. There's nothing to worry about," he said.

"Fine? Were you, or were you not mugged earlier?"

"Yes, but it was nothing serious."

"Darling – you must come home at once! It's clearly a very dangerous place you're staying in."

"It isn't. I'm not hurt, no money was taken, all the cards are cancelled."

"It's the staff at these places who're usually involved. You mustn't stay there a moment longer. Shall I send the driver for you or will you arrange a taxi?"

"It's got nothing to do with the villa, Ma," he had lowered his voice to the barest whisper, terrified of the others hearing.

"Darling, if you don't come home this instant, we're coming to find you. I mean it, Rohan – the car is waiting, Thaththa has told the driver. We'll be driving down this afternoon, if we have to."

He ground his forehead against the wall. His parents above all had to be kept away from the villa, and never allowed to come trampling into that trusting gentle world. He couldn't bear to think of his mother's suspicious gaze on Padma, and the awkward embarrassing questions she would ask Gerhardt, without ever believing his responses.

"Alright, tomorrow I'll leave," he said.

"Tomorrow morning?"

"No, afternoon."

"Alright, but any later we're coming for you."

"Fine."

"Ah, very good, darling!" His mother accepted his sacrifice. "Now make sure you keep your door locked at all times, and leave as soon as you can. Shall we send the driver?"

"No, I can arrange a taxi."

"Don't let those guest house fellows force one of their crooked drivers on you."

"They wouldn't do that."

"You don't know that."

"I do, actually."

"Who can tell what these people are up to? They could be tipping off thieves and robbers, getting a cut for themselves, that's how it is these days."

"My mugging had nothing to do with anyone here," he snapped. He glanced shamefully behind him, in case anyone had heard.

"Is he coming or not?" he heard his father say in the background.

His mother covered the receiver to tell him, her palm loudly scuffling. Rohan cut her off and returned to the veranda.

"I have to go back to Colombo – the insurance money has been sent to my parents' house," he told them.

"I could send a courier to get it for you," Gerhardt offered

"It's okay. I have to leave tomorrow."

"Will you come back in the evening?" Padma asked.

"No, they want me to stay."

Padma looked as if she didn't understand. But it had arrived, the moment that had been waiting for them, always there up ahead. Their time had run out. How they had worked to forget that it would, fearlessly defying it each hopeful, glittering morning as they lay in each other's arms with the whole of the new day just beginning. And he saw now, that in only a few days, he would be back at his desk with the view over London – a view of shining glass and steel, a cold impassive hardness that hung over everyone, even when the sun shone and the sky was blue and cloudless. He had no interest anymore in his view or in the hard-won office hung with expensive art and a soft leather sofa to rest on. He didn't know why he had stayed so long, or how he could ever return there.

"Of course you must go, your parents must want to see you before you head back to London," Gerhardt said as Padma turned away to face the garden, and it seemed to Rohan that the whole of the villa was turning away from him, filling with a sullen silence.

He went to his room to pack. Padma didn't come with him. He folded some shirts then went to knock on her door, but she didn't answer. At dinner she barely spoke to him when she brought him his food, going to sit with Gerhardt on the porch then passing through, not speaking to him as she went into the house. Rohan ate alone, Anjali and Dan talked on and on together.

Padma stayed in the kitchen watching Soma cut up a newly-baked wattalappan, serving the warm wobbling milky-brown squares into clay bowls, spooning the hot syrup over them. Padma sprinkled on dried rose petals, a deep red-pink against the blue of the bowls. Gerhardt came to join them in the kitchen and stood drinking his beer.

"Maybe you should go and talk a little to Rohan," he told Padma.

"Now you want me to talk with him! But what if we go and have a holiday romance, all of a sudden?"

"I just thought he looked a little lonely. The other two are not being very sociable."

"Oh God, those two lovebirds!" Soma complained. "After all that trouble moving single beds, now they've gone and joined them together, Varuna says. The two of them are joined by their tongues these days!"

"Soma, that's very crude," Gerhardt admonished.

"Not to mention joined by other things."

"Oh, good grief!" Gerhardt exclaimed. He was laughing though, more relaxed than he had been in days.

"You're happy he's going – aren't you?" Padma said.

"What?"

"You wanted him to leave – admit it!"

"Considering what's happened, maybe it is for the best!"

"How can a paying guest leaving early be good?"

Soma spooned the last of the hot syrup from the baking dish over the wattalappan, acting as if he couldn't hear them. He put the bowls on a tray and gave it to her.

"Don't forget to bring back the other dishes; I can wash-up while they eat," he said.

She went slowly towards the veranda, longing to linger in the hall. It would only be worse when dinner was over and Anjali and Dan had gone, and she and Rohan were left in their last hours together. What else could they say to each other? And then the day would end and the next the morning she would watch him go. Her eyes smarted with tears. Every day from now on, she would walk from kitchen to the veranda taking food to strangers, returning with dirty plates, and she would do it again and again, day after day with no end. She felt lightheaded, her head swam, the hall floor tilted and the tray in her hands slipped to the floor in a crash of smashing crockery. Shards of blue pottery and wattalappan like brown scrambled eggs, spread in a lake of syrup. Soma and Gerhardt came running.

"What happened?" Soma cried.

"Are you alright?" Gerhardt lead her back from the spillage.

Rohan too had come to the door.

"I'm fine, I'll get the broom," she said.

"I'll do it, you go and see to your guests," Soma said and pushed her towards Rohan.

"Come and sit down," Rohan said, taking her arm and they went to the veranda.

"Dessert will be slightly delayed," she told Anjali and Dan.

"No problem," Dan said. "Are you okay?"

"A slight accident."

"By the way, Padma, about those yoga lessons – if you're still interested so are we," Anjali said. "I'm sorry I wasn't more enthusiastic when you asked."

"No problem, I'd love to," Padma said.

Wonders would never cease. That rock temple really must have had magical powers.

"Just tell us how much you charge," Anjali said.

"I was offering for free."

"No, no, we'd like to pay," Anjali insisted.

"I'd better warn you, I have no coordination whatsoever," Dan said.

"And I've only done an introductory course a long time ago at university," Anjali added.

"You did yoga at Harvard?" Dan asked Anjali disbelievingly.

"It was the nicest thing I did there. Of course, my father decided that it was taking me away from my studies so I had to give it up. And my mother had already decided that yoga was making me anorexic, because I'd become a vegetarian, so it was easier to stop."

"Your mother!" Dan groaned.

Anjali giggled, and they smiled at each other, lost in each other again.

"We can start the yoga tomorrow," Padma interrupted. "How about the morning?"

She tried not to think how it would feel the next morning with Rohan about to leave.

"Yes! Great!" Anjali and Dan said and Padma moved away as they held hands again and kissed, leaning over the table, all lips and tongues.

Padma stood by Rohan's table, refusing to sit down.

"I'd better go and help Soma," she said and went back to the kitchen.

She stayed there for the rest of the evening, refusing to leave. Soma served the last squares of wattalappan into new bowls, scraping the baking dish and filling up the bowls with sliced mangos.

He took it to the guests himself while Padma slumped at the kitchen table pretending to read a recipe book.

"What are you doing?" Gerhardt asked, frowning over her shoulder at the book.

"I'm reading," she snapped. "Why don't you go home now? It's getting late?"

"Are you going to be okay?"

"Of course I am."

Finally he left and she waited while Soma cleared the tables on the veranda and the guests had gone to bed. When she heard Rohan closing his door, she ran to her room.

That night, like on all the other nights, he came to her door and she let him in and they eased into their secret private world. Afterwards he held her, but more tightly.

"I don't want to leave you here, come with me, please?" he said.

"I happen to live here."

"It's not safe - can't you see that? I need to tell you something - I did see Sunny earlier—"

"What? Sunny attacked you?"

"No, I saw him by the stalls before I was mugged. The mugger was younger, he might have been connected to Sunny or it could just have been a coincidence . . ."

"Yes, a coincidence . . ."

The younger man could have been Mukul, with Sunny in the background directing, that she could believe. But to go to so much trouble for a phone and some credit cards?

"It was probably some of our dear neighbours trying to scare away our guests," she concluded. "I'm so sorry . . ."

He put his arms around her. She stroked his back. He winced and she withdrew her fingers from the edge of his wounds.

"So what happens to us now?" he asked.

344

"Maybe there is no us, outside of here."

"Of course there is."

But he was a guest, and guests came and went; that's what guests did. She would never let herself get so close to one again.

"You don't mind if we never see each other again? You don't care?" he demanded.

He would care if he ever found out the truth about her. What would he feel if he ever discovered that she came with Sunny attached, and probably Mukul - what an entourage! Already he had been burned; when he understood why, he would run like the wind.

"We can keep in touch," she said.

"Oh sure, let's write letters! And we can give each other likes on Facebook!"

"Don't be angry."

"Please come to London - you don't have to stay if you don't want to."

"But then what?"

How could she ever be happy in that place full of strangers? From a trip with Gerhardt years ago, she remembered shy polite people and wandering the streets bundled up in a raincoat.

"Things will settle here. Gerhardt will give Sunny some money to bugger off - and he will. That's all he wants."

"He seemed really pissed off at me."

"You? No, Sunny's just greedy, that's all."

"So you want to stay?"

"I've got no other choice!"

He turned from her, pulling away, the sheet shifting. But he didn't storm out, he stayed lying beside her. She had been sure he would leave - they usually couldn't get away fast enough when she turned them down, but he stayed, lying on his back, his arm shielding his face, silent next to her. She could see his chest rising, falling. She blew out the candles and in the darkness he took down his arm. They lay side-by-side, awake. Her mind filled with the whir of the fan.

26

GERHARDT CANCELLED ALL his meetings the next morning and stayed at the villa after breakfast. It was a day of some importance, he sensed, a day to tread carefully through, alert to signs and signals. Before breakfast Padma had gone away to Anjali and Dan's bungalow to give them a yoga lesson. Rohan had booked a taxi for later. When the breakfast things were cleared away, Padma joined Varuna and needlessly supervised the daily cleaning of the bungalows, staying away from the house. Only Anjali and Dan seemed oblivious to the strange mood hanging over the villa, like a storm brewing. He had a headache, just as on such days. He sat on the porch re-scheduling his cancelled meetings. Anjali and Dan went past.

"Bye! See you later" Anjali called up to Gerhardt.

"Bye! Are you off to the beach?"

"No, to the rock temple," Dan said.

"Again? You liked it that much?"

"Actually, we're visiting an orphanage close to the temple – we're going to see if they need any volunteer teachers," Dan said.

"We're thinking of staying on in the area," Anjali added eagerly.

She really was a very beautiful young woman, and thoroughly transformed, suddenly brimming with life and purpose.

"I'm sure they would love to have you," Gerhardt said and Anjali smiled gratefully back at him.

Gerhardt was about to suggest that she take Padma with her to offer yoga classes to the children, but Rohan appeared.

"Gerhardt, can I have a word?" he asked

He looked so stern and serious, Anjali and Dan quickly left.

"Take a seat," Gerhardt told Rohan and gestured to Padma's chair.

"I think we should talk in private," Rohan said, not sitting.

"But there's nobody else here!"

"I'd prefer to go inside."

"Fine, let's go into the office."

Gerhardt led the way. What on earth could Rohan want? His taxi was booked for eleven o'clock. Gerhardt glanced at the office clock – just ten-fifteen. He had never known a morning to pass so slowly. He sat down behind the desk, ready for battle. Battle! What a ridiculous idea.

"Take a seat," he told Rohan.

"I need to talk to you about Padma," he said and stayed standing.

So the fellow wouldn't sit down. Gerhardt stood and faced him.

"I've asked Padma to come to London with me," Rohan said.

"Oh yes?" Gerhardt knew to stay detached while this new strand unravelled; he had to show no panic, no concern. "And what did she say?"

"She refused."

"I see." Gerhardt held back a smile. He couldn't blame Rohan for having feelings for Padma – she was very lovely. But Rohan barely knew her! They must have talked a little, now and again but how could he possibly know if Padma felt the same way about him? Had he been this impulsive with his first wife? No wonder things had ended badly.

"I'm afraid, there's not much I can do if she's said no," Gerhardt said, and he gave a rueful smile just to be clear that he wasn't gloating. "I'm sure Padma was very touched by your request."

So much for Ruth's dire predictions! Padma clearly had no desire to leave the villa just yet.

"You need to do more to protect her," Rohan said.

"Oh yes?"

"She's not safe here. She needs to go away, but she'll never leave unless you help her."

"Not safe here? She is extremely safe here. What on earth do you mean?"

"People watch her outside - in the lane, on the beach—"

"Ah! You mean our spy! It's very nice of you to be concerned, but he's just the village idiot. She's in no danger from him."

"But there are others. They've been hanging around us for a while."

What bothered Gerhardt was the way Rohan used 'us' for Padma and himself, as if they were an actual unit, already defined and decided.

"You have to help her, Gerhardt."

"You do realise this is her home?"

"And it's her business too, I know, and she feels responsible because you've spent loads of money building bungalows—"

"She loves those bungalows!" Gerhardt objected.

"But she can't go out without weird men watching her. And that ghastly uncle of hers is always hanging around."

"What uncle?"

"Sunny."

"*Sunny?*" Now this was new. Until now Rohan had merely sounded overwrought.

"What do you know about Sunny?" Gerhardt demanded.

"I know he's exploited her for money since her parents' died.

349

There's no use pretending, Gerhardt, she's told me everything."

"Yes, I can see that. And you say you've seen Sunny?"

"*Seen* him? I've had to stop him attacking her!"

Gerhardt had nothing to say. He could only stare at Rohan who seemed serious enough, but how could what he was saying be anything other than a complete fabrication? The fellow was a fantasist, or a downright liar. Possibly the shock of the mugging had made him unstable.

"He came into the garden late at night a few weeks ago," Rohan said.

"Sunny came in here? Into our garden? Where was the dog?"

"He was inside at first, that's probably how Sunny got into the garden. By the time Gustav went out, Sunny was there and Padma thought he had a gun, so she held Gustav back. I was on the veranda and I could hear him barking At first I thought Padma was just talking to a neighbour or someone asking about the guest house, but then I went out to check and Sunny had his hands around her neck and she was gasping for air—"

"Alright, that's enough! There's no need to invent silly scenarios – do you think I'm stupid?" The boy was impossible! Gerhardt was fast losing patience with him.

"Ask her about it!" Rohan challenged. "But I'd better warn you, she didn't want you to know, in fact she specifically asked me not to tell you, so she may well deny it."

"I'm sure."

The fellow was not only mad, but manipulative and divisive, trying to cause a rift between Gerhardt and Padma. As if Padma would keep such a thing a secret! So why then did Gerhardt think of his last encounter with the minister – for hadn't he too warned that Sunny was in the area, and talked of Padma being hurt? A baseless threat, Gerhardt had taken it for. His head hurt even more now. And his eyes ached. Sunny was the enemy, not Rohan. Rohan may have made up his far-fetched tale simply to make Gerhardt pay attention; he meant well. He wasn't to know that Gerhardt had already made a plan and set it in motion. If only the lawyer would telephone. Every time Gerhardt called him, he was out at a meeting or in court. He didn't return phone calls these days, it seemed; or reply to emails. If only Rohan would go soon. The moment he left, Gerhardt would telephone the lawyer and this time he wouldn't stop until he got the man. He would go and wait outside the courtroom if he had to.

"I am going to deal with Sunny, don't you worry," he assured Rohan.

"All you do is give him money, but it's the last thing she wants! She's sick of being paid for!"

"She said that?"

Rohan's silence confirmed it. How much could Padma possibly have talked? She who was usually so private about the past, and about Sunny in particular.

"I assure you, I know exactly how to deal with that tedious little man," Gerhardt said. "Possibly I know him better than her."

Rohan looked unimpressed.

"I've been managing Sunny for a great many years," Gerhardt insisted.

"I don't want Padma getting hurt. There's something strange going on – more than you think, Gerhardt. I saw Sunny just minutes before the guys on the scooter—"

"That's not what you said yesterday."

"I know, I didn't want to worry Padma – but I told her later."

"Later?"

"Yeah, I sort of bumped into her . . . but something strange is going on. Sunny came up to me when I was at the stalls just to tell me not to see Padma anymore—"

"But you're not," Gerhardt reminded him.

Rohan was silent. Gerhardt looked hard into his eyes: the pupils didn't seem too dilated. Rohan hadn't seemed interested in drugs, but he could have been doing anything; English public-school boys were known for it. All the more reason for Padma to avoid him – someone with a drug habit was the last thing she needed.

"Sunny said some disgusting things. He's vile," Rohan said.

"Yes, he is."

Gerhardt sat down in the desk chair, suddenly needing to. He had to stay calm. Rohan was stirring up trouble, that's what he wanted – for everyone to get over-excited and panic and for Padma to run away with him to London. A schemer, just as Gerhardt suspected. Soon he'd be gone, though. When Gerhardt rang the lawyer, he would authorise him to increase his offer to whatever Sunny wanted. It could all be arranged before the day was over.

"Sunny's never going to let Padma be," Rohan went on.

Oh, what a maddening fellow!

"We both care a great deal for each other," he added.

"Is that so?"

"That's why I asked her to come to London."

"But didn't she say no?"

"She did. And I know I can't force her. Just look after her, okay?"

Gerhard watched helpless, wrong-footed as Rohan went to his room – Gerhardt's old room. How simple it had all been then. He rang the lawyer again and found him away once more at a meeting.

"Can you tell him to call me? Please tell him it's urgent," he told the secretary, who promised that she would.

While he waited for the call, Gerhardt moved money around his accounts, ready to make payments to Sunny; he would take on more work if needed. He sent emails to those who had approached him with work in recent months and let them know that he might now be available. All the while, he kept seeing Sunny sneaking into the garden at night, those vile murderous hands reaching for Padma. It hurt to think of Sunny hurting her. How frightened she would have been – surely it could never have happened? There was no change in her; no sense of anything new having occurred. But he thought now of how she had started to leave Gustav outside at night. Even after the commotion with Anjali, she had insisted. Had he been too complacent all this time and missed the signs?

Across the hall, Rohan packed to leave, hangers rattling in the wardrobe, drawers being opened and closed. When Rohan emerged they settled the bill, carefully conversational as they waited on the porch for the taxi. Padma stayed away. Gerhardt kept seeing her going between the bungalows pretending to be busy. Even when the taxi arrived and the driver had taken Rohan's suitcases away, she didn't come over.

"Padma!" Gerhardt shouted. "Rohan's leaving!"

At last she came out of the large bungalow.

"Come on now! Hurry up! The taxi's here!" Gerhardt cried impatiently.

She walked the longest way over, even stopping to play with Gustav.

"Is it time already? Are you all packed?" she said breezily to Rohan.

Gerhardt walked with Soma, following Padma and Rohan down the path. Neither Padma nor Rohan spoke, walking side by side, staying apart. Padma looked straight ahead, Rohan glanced at her a few times. At the gate Rohan shook hands with Gerhardt and gave Soma a hefty tip. Only Padma went with him to the car.

"Have a safe trip," she said.

Rohan touched her arm and they looked at each other in secret private communion.

"Will you come to Colombo? I'll be there for another week," Rohan said.

Gerhardt started. An ambush at the last moment! He hadn't been expecting that. To his relief Padma just shrugged and looked uninterested, and even Rohan had to give up.

"Well, bye, then," he said, and they hugged.

Rohan kissed Padma on the cheek. She kissed him back, a simple gesture of farewell, nothing more. Then Rohan got into the taxi and it drove away.

Soma and Padma waved and Gerhardt joined in. He bore Rohan no hard feelings; in fact, he would miss having him around. But what an almighty relief to see him go! Now Padma could concentrate on running her business; Sunny would accept the money and leave them in peace, and life would go on as it should. A movement caught Gerhardt's eye and he looked down to see Padma's feet in her rubber slippers the toes flexing and un-flexing under the straps – the same frantic pulsing of the night long ago when he had known, body and soul, that he must help her. He watched her, so strong and poised beside him, yet so unknowable.

She stood looking at the lane, even after the taxi had turned the corner. Soma counted his tip, nodding approving.

"He turned out to be a nice guest, didn't he?" Soma said, putting the money into his shirt pocket.

Padma ran past them, up the path. Gerhardt called to her, but she didn't stop.

"What's the matter with her?" Gerhardt exclaimed. "Well? Do you know what the matter is with her?" He turned on Soma.

But Soma would never tell him. Soma always stayed clear of emotional entanglements, which was what made him so easy to live with.

"They like each other," Soma blurted.

"She told you that?" Gerhardt stared.

"Rohan Mahaththaya will be good to her."

Padma had gone into the house. On the veranda Gerhardt saw her wipe her eyes with the back of her hand. He tried to go to her, but she was in her room by the time he reached the house. Her door was closed.

"Padma, can I come in? Can we talk?" he called, but she didn't answer.

There was silence behind the door, not even the sound of the fan. He went to Soma in the garden.

"Have they been seeing much of each other?" Gerhardt asked.

"I think so."

"Just talking?"

"Maybe. And maybe more."

Gerhardt knew he had been blind; of course there had been more. How could he not have known?

"Did Sunny ever come into the garden and hurt Padma Baba?" he asked.

"No! That could never happen."

"Exactly. Rohan made that up. I thought so."

"Rohan Mahaththaya told you?" Soma looked worried. "If Rohan Mahaththaya said, then maybe something . . ." He looked fearfully up at Gerhardt.

"Has Boss said anything about seeing Sunny around here?"

"Not near us, but someone did see him by the stalls the other day."

"Yesterday? When Rohan was mugged?"

Soma nodded. Gerhardt checked his phone – the lawyer still hadn't called or even sent an email to say when he would – but there was no time to be polite anymore. He drove at top speed through the village, heading to the lawyer's office. He wouldn't leave until a new contract with Sunny had been drawn up and Sunny brought in to sign it. He wished they had never begun a guest house at the villa. Ruth had been right to worry. But what was Gerhardt supposed to do – Padma had begged to return to the villa! He couldn't ban her from her own home! And yes, he had suggested building bungalows in the garden, but only in response to Padma wanting to run a bed and breakfast in the front room. She had agreed of her own free will, he hadn't forced her. He defended himself now to an invisible audience.

The roads through Tangalle Town were full of traffic, irritably honking and cutting across each other. A cyclist shouted at a taxi. A bus honked at a scooter. Everywhere shone white with heat, the sun was remorseless, unforgiving.

Padma lay on her bed, trying to visualise a pink cloud of comfort spreading through her, but it kept thinning to nothing and she was left with the emptiness of the day ringing in her ears, racing through her body. Whenever she had ended a relationship before the sadness had lasted only for a while, but all she kept seeing now was Rohan leaving – Rohan not forcing her to choose, letting her be. She could still feel his kiss on her cheek, but his presence around her was already fading, and she knew that he had gone. A sob broke free; she buried her face in her pillow and cried for what she had done, what she had so determinedly given up – it was more than she had wanted to lose, more than she could bear. She had nothing now. For the first time, the villa wasn't enough. She sat up. All she had was the email from the institute in Colombo and the director's hand extended to her, calling from another world. She would go to it. She needed to be on new soil; to have something more.

She left the bed and stepped into the hall. She had heard Gerhardt go earlier. Soma was in the kitchen. She slipped into the office and brought up the email from the institute and signed up for the teacher-training exam. There was a week of preparation before the exam, which she had to attend. It began in three days. She emailed Ruth, asking to stay with her. Anjali and Dan were due to leave in a couple of days and there were no other guests booked; the timing was perfect.

⋈

Gerhardt had never before arrived unannounced at his lawyer's office. He'd known the security guard for years, so he was able to go straight past the gate of Mr Aluvihare's grand town house and to the office in the annexe. In the reception, Mr Aluvihara was greeting a client, his secretary holding a file behind him. All three stopped to look at Gerhardt standing in the doorway. The lawyer smiled at once and came over to shake Gerhardt's hand.

"Ah, how nice to see you, Mr Hundsler. Thank you for coming. I have been waiting for a moment to call you, I have been so busy."

"I need to speak with you urgently. It has to be today."

"Yes, of course. But I have a client with me, as you can see—"

"I will wait right here until you're finished."

The client, a man with a briefcase, looked away, embarrassed. The secretary sat down at her desk and rummaged intently in a drawer.

"Wonderful, I will see you in half an hour," the lawyer said smoothly. "Please, Mrs Krishna, offer Mr Hundsler something to drink, anything he likes."

The lawyer gave his other client a reassuring smile and ushered him into the office.

"Would you like some tea? Or a soft drink?" the receptionist asked Gerhardt.

"A glass of water please."

To himself he sounded like someone ill and needing help, desperate to be told that frightening eventualities could be avoided. He perched on a teak armchair amongst the potted palms. A matching coffee table bore the day's newspapers, arranged in a fan. The secretary brought him the water and retreated to her desk. Gerhardt opened a newspaper but could barely stop to read it, his mind full of what Rohan had said. How could it be true, what he had told him about Sunny? What troubled him most was that Padma might have been keeping secrets from him. When had she stopped talking to him? Why? If she had hated him paying Sunny, how would she feel if she knew what Gerhardt was about to do? He was making things worse. But what else could he do?

The lawyer finished with his client and Gerhardt was ushered into the office, once a sanctum where calm was restored, where so many of his troubles had been dissected and solutions found, apportioned into manageable steps taken one by one, until the problem was resolved. Over the years, Gerhardt had grown to trust Mr Aluvihara implicitly. The latter's recent slackness in returning phone calls was no doubt a sign of how busy he had become.

"Please, take a seat," Mr Aluvihara said. "I'm afraid I have another client coming soon, so we will have to be quick."

"Did you get my messages?"

"Yes, yes I did." The lawyer looked uncomfortable.

"And have you spoken with Sunny? I'm afraid the matter is somewhat urgent."

"In what way urgent?"

"I have reason to think that Sunny may have threatened my daughter – possibly violently. I need him to agree to keep away from her. Can you speak with him today? Tomorrow at the latest?"

The lawyer sighed. "I have already spoken with him," he said.

"You have? Why didn't you tell me? What did he say?"

"I've been very busy, I'm sorry—" The lawyer looked down at his blank notepad. He picked up his pen and put it down.

"Doesn't matter, what did Sunny say?"

The lawyer looked up wearily. "He has turned down the offer, I'm afraid."

"Fine, fine, offer him more. I suspected he would try to haggle – it's fine. I don't mind paying even double—"

"I'm sorry, Gerhardt, but he has refused any payments of any kind."

"Sunny turn down money?" Gerhardt laughed. "He's just playing hard to get – don't believe a word that rascal says. Please, Mr Aluvihare, I know this man well, make him a revised offer."

"Gerahrdt, he made it very clear that I wasn't to bother him again on this matter." The lawyer paused, considering his words. "My impression is that Sunny now has a new source of income."

"Where from?"

"I have no idea."

"It must be a lot for him to turn my money away."

"Possibly."

"Do you know who it is?"

"I can only speculate—"

"Not the minister?" It was a ludicrous idea, a scallywag like Sunny being elevated to the minister's secret employ. "What on earth can the minister want Sunny for?"

The lawyer shifted in his chair and glanced at the clock on his desk.

"I'm afraid, Mr Hundsler, I can't help you anymore in this particular matter. And now I have a client due."

Gerhardt rose, still trying to understand.

"Is this how the minister and his brother intend to get us out of the villa? That is a poor show – getting Sunny to pester Padma.

There has to be something we can do – this is my daughter's safety we're talking about,"

The lawyer stayed seated. "Mr Hundsler – Gerhardt – as a father myself, I understand your fears. I too would be concerned in your position. I wonder – why not move your daughter to your other home and rent out the villa? Or even sell it?"

"I see. To a certain high-profile tenant and his brother?"

"Well, yes, but then you and your daughter could move on from certain associations – surely that would be beneficial – for her, most of all? Selling would be preferable, I imagine, so you would not have any further dealings—"

"And meanwhile the minister's brother gets his hands on the home we love?"

"Could you not see it simply as a sale – does it matter whom the property goes to next?"

"Of course it matters!"

"I see."

Mr Aluvihara got up and opened the door and stood waiting for Gerhardt to leave.

In the reception, there was no client waiting. The secretary was playing Patience on her computer; hurriedly she closed it down. The newspapers on the coffee table had been arranged back into a fan.

"Thank you for coming, I'm sorry not to have been more help," the lawyer said to Gerhardt. "Have a think about what I suggested."

Gerhardt strode out without saying goodbye. He returned to the villa and sat with a beer on the veranda – his veranda, his house. He would not be bullied into giving it up. What a precedent to set Padma! All he needed was to find another way to manage Sunny. Sunny, enabled by the minister, would be harder to control and until then Padma had to be sent away, out of harm's reach. He would talk to Ruth – she and Padma could travel abroad after all. He could join them some of the time. Padma came out of the office.

"Feel better?" he asked.

"I think so."

"That's good."

She joined him at the table, sitting, stretching her legs, pointing her toes, flexing them back. She had been good at ballet, and excelled at Baharatanatyam dance, but she had given them up in Colombo. It was only yoga she had continued with. He wished sometimes that he had resisted pushing her along the routes of all clever, educated children and let her choose her own way. She had not known at sixteen the career she wanted – they should have waited until she did. He should have shown her that it was courageous to hold a void and to not rush to fill it. Instead he had urged her to follow the herd, she who was so much her own person.

"Did Sunny ever come into the garden and hurt you?" Gerhardt asked her.

"What?" Her face looked hot; he had made her uncomfortable.

"Did Sunny ever come in here and try to strangle you?"

"What are you talking about?"

There! It wasn't true. How could it have been? It was an outrageous fabrication! But he noted that she didn't ask why he was asking, or who had given him such an idea – she didn't say another word.

"You must get away from here, just for a little while," he told her. "How about if you go and stay with Ruth?"

"Yes, I've already emailed her."

"You have? You were planning to go to Colombo? Are you going to meet Rohan?" he blurted.

"Only if I have time. I'm booked onto the next yoga Teacher Training exam and it's next week."

"Next week? So soon?"

"I have to do a week of preparation with them, so I'll be leaving in three days."

"Of course." He was baffled and delighted.

"I've worked out what my problem is," she said.

"Oh yes?"

"I don't have something I love, that I can make money from. I've always wanted to create my own yoga retreat."

"Here?"

"Maybe. I could charge guests more, and you wouldn't have to keep giving me money then, and I can start to pay back your loan."

"But I like helping! I want to help! That's what parents do!"

"You've done so much for me already, Gerhardt."

She hugged him then, all of a sudden, oh such a loving precious child! He held her tightly, if only he need never let her go.

"It's up to me now," she said, sitting back alone, stirred by a new force.

There was something so determined about her as they sat watching the sun setting over their perfect glorious view. The sea turned red and silver, the crimson sun bleeding into dark steel ripples. Padma was unsmiling and distant, blind to him.

## 27

I T TOOK MANY hours for Rohan to reach his parents' house, the first time he had been glad of rush-hour traffic. The taxi turned into their road, the big pale houses imbued with the solidity of generations indifferent as ever to the mayhem of the main road. Long ago he had gone to parties in those houses, and spend-the-days; known the names of servants. Some of the children he had played with still lived behind those iron gates, with families of their own – people uncertain of him now, smiling politely if they passed in the road. He made the driver stop outside his parents' house, seeing as if new its pristine whiteness, the dark slatted shutters; a peach-coloured bougainvillea growing over the garden wall and on an arch above the gate. He had lived away from that house for most of his life, but it was where he was linked to – the address on school records and where his university magazines still went; his flat in London was merely an outpost. For so long the house in Colombo had rooted his rootless life; it could claim him as now, and haul him back. Only the villa existed apart from it, secure in its otherness. So far away it felt now, another country, a magical island where he had been made new. Where was that self he had been there? Who was he now, returning?

He paid while still seated inside the taxi, a refuge, a last link to the villa. Then he stepped outside into the lane and went to ring the doorbell. The young sulky maid opened the door and stepped back, eyes lowered, to let him in. She refused to meet his gaze or greet him – she had heard all the rumours about him and was terrified. His mother came rushing out of the sitting room and gave an excited gasp as if surprised to see him.

"Daddy! Daddy! Rohan is here!" she cried.

The study door opened and his father came out.

"Ah, here you are. How was the drive? Did you get caught in traffic?" his father asked.

"You look thin. Have you been eating properly?" his mother said.

"I've eaten very well actually."

"I had the girls make you the Japanese teriyaki chicken you like. Or would you prefer to go out for dinner?" his mother said.

"Chicken teriyaki is fine."

At the villa it had grown harder each day to imagine this life he had left behind. Now its reality took over, trying to defeat everything he had inside.

"Did the insurance company send a new phone?" he asked

His father brought over a package.

"Check the money, make sure they've sent the right amount," his mother instructed.

"I need a shower first."

"I've left new towels on your bed."

He climbed the stairs, hearing the silence behind him and feeling their watchful concern yet refusing to turn around to re-assure them. Through the bannisters he could see into the pantry, the cook and the maid standing alert at the kitchen island, listening – the drama of family gatherings during his court case had heightened their expectation of gossip when he was around. They bustled back to work, seeing him on the stairs.

In his room he took out the new phone and put in the battery and the SIM card, then dialled the number from the villa's business card. It was the first time he had needed to call Padma for she had always been somewhere nearby. The call went to voicemail. Her voice, playful and light, asked him to leave a message. He told her he was missing her and asked her to call him back. He waited, sitting on the new bed, a double, bought to replace his teenage single bed, for visits back as a married man, but which he had mostly slept on alone during the weeks of the court case. When he and Shalini had come back on holiday together, they had always stayed at her parents', where Shalini and he had been given a wing of the house. His phone didn't ring.

He showered, back in his old bathroom again and changed into clothes washed by the villa's dobi. He paused on the landing, in the upstairs family sitting room with its pale cotton-covered sofas and silvery blue Persian rug, slightly faded at the edges. The drapes were half-drawn across the windows to protect the bookshelves full of Readers Digest condensed novels and textbooks – both his father's and his own from the school a short way across the city, where he had been prepared for his launch into the great and famous boarding school in England. It didn't fill him with dread anymore to think of the trajectory from those years of promise to the shame of a courtroom some weeks ago, for now his life led out from the pit he had descended into and climbed towards the villa, to Padma. He had never known a world so truly beautiful as hers with Gerhardt, so full of love and fun, welcoming even strangers, as he had been once. Even with Sunny prowling outside, and envious neighbours full of scowling resentment, no one within ever seemed deprived. How earnestly they cared for each other at the villa, a glorious nest, a magical palace in the mountains; a glowing hut in the woods, rich with contentment.

"Rohan! Dinner is ready!" his mother called and he went downstairs.

"By the way, you had a phone call earlier," she told him as they sat at the table.

"Who was it?"

"Tom."

"*Tom?*"

"Your friend from school, you remember?"

"I know who Tom is! I haven't spoken to him in ages. Was he in London?"

"Yes, but he's going to be in India for business."

"What else did he say?"

Tom had to be ringing because of Rohan's letter. Post travelled faster than Rohan had hoped. He'd written instead of sending an email for that reason.

"I told him you would be in Colombo for a few days," Rohan's mother added. "He said he'd call you."

"Did he say anything else?"

"Like what?

"I don't know . . . anything?"

His mother looked puzzled. Possibly she would have been too embarrassed to talk about the court case. He cringed from the thought of Tom hearing about it from her.

"It sounds like Tom's finally started to do well," his mother said. "He always seemed such a dreamer to me. Good for him, pulling his socks up. His parents must be mightily relieved! He says he isn't married, though."

So they were equal now, except Tom had a life that he had worked for steadily, getting closer little by little to what he had always wanted.

"You should call him," Rohan's mother said.

"Yeah, maybe."

"He was hoping to come and see you after his meetings."

"Here?"

"He said he'd try."

Rohan hadn't imagined meeting Tom so soon. Tom wouldn't have been surprised by Rohan's news; relieved, perhaps, maybe even glad. Tom may well have felt vindicated, for he had disliked Shalini from their first meeting. Shalini had despised Tom with surprising vehemence, vocal in her disapproval of his restless search for the right work, travelling abroad to volunteer on charitable projects and ethically-run businesses. Shalini admired only the commercial success of her father and uncles and the parents of her friends. Socially beneficial enterprises were of no interest to her, and she had feared perhaps that Rohan might one day succumb to the lure of Tom's modest and itinerant existence. Tom had been unusually silent when they had met for dinner after Rohan and Shalini were married. The next week Tom had invited Rohan for drinks after work, just the two of them, like in the old days, and they had gone on meeting for a few more times, but it had never felt like the old days again. Rohan had sensed Tom's contempt for Rohan's City career and new life with Shalini, and her cousins and old school friends, living in an exclusive, elegant London, gathering at weekends in splendid homes and at many-starred restaurants, their talk of investments, shopping and spectacular shows; weekends away in Europe - a constant search for pleasure and distraction, a sly current of rivalry and comparison coursing under the conversation.

Rohan had been welcomed into this world, admired for his education and career accomplishments. In those days he had been proud, himself, of his achievements: his apartment in a prestigious conversion, his frequent travel abroad from work to the great cities of the world, flying First Class and staying in exquisite hotels, and meeting others with credentials as impressive as his own. But all this meant so little when he was with Tom. Afterwards Rohan was unsettled and resentful. Tom's mere presence was a reminder of their student years when they had vowed to each other never to succumb to the temptations of a life of gilded mediocrity, like all the people around them. Tom had stayed true to his vision and talked when they met of quests for funding and research trips to far-flung lands, travelling in Economy and on local transport. He had forged new friendships with people as driven as himself, collaborating on projects that strived to put right what was wrong in the world. Every time, Rohan returned home doubting his own achievements and the life he had built, fearful of having made an error too big to correct.

It had become easier to postpone meeting Tom. He would wait for a more suitable date, which never came. Tom went to China for six months, and they lost touch. Only a year and a half had passed since then, but it was enough time for a marriage to unravel all the way to divorce and an almighty mess. It was hardly what Rohan had hoped to show for himself when they next met.

"Give him a call, I have his number here," Rohan's mother said, tearing a page from a notepad. "Maybe you two could go back to London together."

"I don't know when I'm going back."

"I thought you were leaving next week?" his father said.

But he couldn't leave without seeing Padma. They had barely said goodbye, or had a chance to talk about the future. There had to be a future for them.

"Aren't you due back at work?" his mother enquired.

Both she and his father were watching him, alert to even this minor variation of a plan made long before his time at the villa, a plan that didn't seem relevant anymore.

"There's no fixed date for going back," he lied.

"But I thought you said—" his father began.

"No, it was left up to me."

"But the days are flying past!" his father exclaimed.

"They won't wait for you forever!" his mother added. "There'll be plenty of others wanting your job."

"But not so many who can do it."

"I'm sure there'll be some."

Always the last word. She had to be the one to win. He let her. She wanted him back in his life in England. She had always been so sad when he left Sri Lanka, he'd imagined that she hadn't wanted him to leave, but the divorce had challenged her belief that she knew him – in the court room, in tense family gatherings, she had seen him as he was now. No more could she think of him as the eleven-year-old boy she had sent away to England with his cases of suits and shirts and books and bow ties. She, so much a product of her family of conservative right-wing intellectuals, was acutely attuned to difference and distrusted it in anyone – even him. She wanted him back in his life a safe distance away, back living the way they had determined for him, so many years ago. But that eleven-year-old boy had had his own inkling of the life he should lead; it didn't feel so long ago anymore. He was the same boy still, full of the same dreams.

"I might not go back to England," he said.

"Where will you go instead?" she demanded.

"India." It came out unchecked.

He saw the sea and a beach in Goa, a palm-thatched hut under coconut trees; he couldn't quite see what he would be doing in such a place, yet it felt real.

"Doesn't your bank have a base near Delhi – in that newish place?" his father asked.

"You mean Gurugram? Yes."

"That's the one! I was reading about it – a whole city built for commerce! Businesses are coming from all over the world." His father beamed approving. "You must ask your bank for a transfer – Asia is the new great economy."

"It would be much easier to find a nice girl, if you lived nearby," his mother reflected.

"I don't want you to find me anyone, Ma. I think I mentioned that already."

"Next time we'll look into the family much more. I've heard about people using private investigators – who knew such things! No one needed them in my day, but don't worry, we also will get one next time. No stone will be left unturned."

"So you do accept that she was lying?"

"I don't know what happened with you and Shalini, but you are only twenty-eight years old and you will learn from your mistakes."

"The mistake I made was to marry a total liar!"

His parents looked shocked. No one in the family had spoken openly of Shalini's accusations, always referring to them obliquely, and always in the context of the legal defences required to refute them. But now he had spoken as he had grown used to at the villa, saying what he felt, not edging around the facts.

"Do you really think I was violent with her?" he challenged his mother.

Her eyes widened. She seemed annoyed at being forced to respond.

"I don't know what to think," she retorted.

"Well, I wasn't. I was never violent with her."

"Of course, we knew that," his father said.

Was it only now that they believed him? Did they even believe him? It mattered surprisingly little now that he felt able to speak as he liked.

"You will marry again, darling, don't worry," his mother said.

"I'm not worried."

"That girl would have driven anyone mad! The more I hear about her past, the more, I, myself want to wring her neck."

"I didn't hurt her."

"It doesn't matter now. We will find you the right person next time. And don't you worry, we will go through their past with a fine-tooth comb."

"No, Ma. I will find myself the right person."

"Oh yes? And how will you do that?"

"Maybe I already have."

They both looked at him in horror.

"You're not thinking of trying again with Shalini, are you?" his mother pleaded.

"Huh?"

"That is all over now! You have to forget her! Just put her out of your mind!" his father urged.

"I certainly will."

"So you're not planning on going back to her?" his mother confirmed.

"That, I can promise you." Sometimes he couldn't believe how little they knew him.

"We will help you and the girl to get settled next time," his mother said. "Daddy and I will rent a place nearby and come each day to look after you both – that's what Mrs. Seneviratne did for her daughter, she also was in London. Somewhere near Kensington Gardens, I believe – the poor girl found it very hard at first. It's England I blame, there's far too much rushing around. And all that rain and bad weather, it's bad for the health."

London would certainly be a difficult place to be in after living at the villa. He thought of his apartment abandoned for weeks, with only the cleaner coming in to those stark silent rooms waiting for him, the parquet floors and high ceilings; an ornate fireplace where sometimes pigeons dropped cherry stones from the trees in the garden below. It was a garden kept locked for residents' use only, with soft weak grass and flowers in tasteful muted colours; plane trees and the cherry trees and a giant pink magnolia under which Philippino nannies sat scrolling through Facebook while their small toddling charges played alone. London was lonely for everyone. Padma had been right to refuse to go there. He remembered waking at the villa with her warm body languorously stretching beside him as she turned to the window to watch the morning arrive. She would lead him out to the sunrise and they would walk in the garden gilded with dew. In England there were often moments of beauty: a sunset over the Thames; summer sun over sheep-flecked fields in East Sussex – but that world didn't beckon to him anymore; his life there had ended as another began at the villa.

☙

Padma walked outside in the early morning, still in pyjamas, her dressing gown left open, for there were no more guests at the villa. Anjali and Dan had left the day before and there were no new guests expected with the rainy season fast approaching. Padma herself was leaving for Colombo the next day to begin her week at the yoga institute.

Rohan too was in Colombo. He would be waking there on his first morning back. Would he try calling her again? Or would he already have begun to forget her? If he called, she wouldn't answer. His absence would soon cease to gnaw at her, and left alone, his presence in her thoughts would fade. She had to forget, to undo the damage of letting herself open to him, to let herself heal again.

Down by the gate, a misshapen figure was waiting: Hema Amme, weighed down by a giant cloth bundle on her back. She took in washing these days, Padma had heard. How the old woman would have loved rooting in other people's pockets for things she wasn't meant to see – secrets for gossip and blackmail. Hema Amme peered up at Padma and waved a white envelope, gesturing to Padma to go down to her. Another letter from Leela, no doubt. The letters were coming more frequently; the treatments seemed more serious and the medicines seemed stronger each time. Leela didn't seem to be getting any better. Padma ran down to the gate.

"Is Leela alright?"

"It's all in here." Hema Amme passed the letter over the gate. "She needs more medicine and some new treatment," Hema Amme added.

"Didn't the last treatment help?"

"Not really."

Hema Amme looked up at the house, her eyes roving over the garden.

"Everyone's leaving your place, no? Where's your future husband? He's gone, no? I heard he was attacked. Can't imagine him coming back here again!"

"Oh, so you think he was scared off, do you?"

"Looks like it!" Hema Amme laughed showing the stumps of her teeth, yellow-brown and randomly planted in pale purple gums. "Now who's going to hump you?" she cackled.

Poor Leela, having such a woman as her only friend.

"Actually, he's gone to buy the ring," Padma said. "Of course, I will be choosing the necklace – his family always use the same jeweller in Colombo – quite a famous one, I'm told. Such beautiful pieces they make! I can't wait! I'm joining him tomorrow – he says I can have anything I like, but I'm thinking of designing something myself. I love emeralds and rubies, don't you? I'll have lots of those. Only problem is I'll have to keep it in a safe in a big bank in Colombo, it'll be too valuable to keep in the house."

The old woman listened with horrified fascination to the fairy tale.

"You wait till his parents meet you, then you'll be out on your ear," she said.

"He's a big grown man, he's doing all the choosing himself!" Padma tossed back her hair and walked away.

"He'll change his mind when he sees what you're really like!" the old woman shouted. "You wait till he finds out about you!"

Padma knew not to listen and not to care about what Hema Amme had to say, but it was hard to ignore such determined ill-will. They lived in the midst of so many who followed their every move, and hated every beautiful thing they tried to make. In that hostile savage glare it was hard to feel proud; to feel glad to have created a beautiful place. Padma felt Hema Amme's malevolent watchfulness follow her into the house. Padma shooed Gustav outside to scare off the woman at the gate.

In the kitchen Padma turned on the kettle for tea and hacked at a twisted stump of ginger.

"What's the matter?" Soma asked, as he made pancakes for breakfast.

"Nothing." Padma dropped the shards of ginger into a cup and poured on boiling water. "I hate that old hag," she muttered.

"Who?"

"Hema Amme."

"When did you see her?"

"She just came past when I was outside."

"What did she want?"

"Nothing."

"Tell the truth! What did she say to you?"

"Oh . . . she was just happy that we don't have any guests anymore."

"That woman is a devil! So full of spite!" Soma glowered. "Her sister's the same. Don't worry, the gods punish people like them – already the sister is sick, really sick; something's gone wrong with her kidneys—"

"Kidneys?" Padma sipped the ginger tea, but it was too hot. Her lips smarted.

"Yes, and the kidneys are important – if they stop working, you die."

"Which hospital is the sister in?" Padma asked.

"How should I know? Planning on visiting, are you? Going to take her some fruit and flowers?" Soma laughed.

The letter in Padma's pocket grew heavy and so big it filled the room. A malignant darkness swirled around her, shrieking with mirth, doubled up laughing at her so alone in her folly, a dank cavern of regret and smallness.

"Where are you going?" Soma said as Padma hurried out of the kitchen.

"I have to get dressed."

"What about your tea? And now your breakfast is ready!"

But she ran to the office and ripped open the white envelope. Under the desk lamp she examined the letter: yes, it could have been a photocopy; yes, they would only have needed to change the name and address. And yes, 'Leela Sugathapala' and the address of Sunny's house had been typed in a different font, and there was a faint line that could have been the edge of a pasted-on piece of paper, a simple small stuck-on addition to turn a blameless hospital letter into a smug little scam. The latest letter was for an appointment for dialysis – there was a charge for that of course, and a prescription for several new drugs. A further note was attached with a paperclip, on which the charges were handwritten and totted up for Padma's convenience so she could transfer the right sum into the account Leela had set up. Below the paperclip

375

Leela had written: 'My Dearest Duwa, thank you for helping me,' in wistful misshapen letters.

How innocent it still looked, and so plausible. Padma turned on the computer, determined to ignore her suspicions. It may not have been a trick at all. A name could have been typed in a different font by someone, and the almost-invisible line around the address could have been an accidental smudge of the printer. So many people suffered from diseases of the kidney, it was a fairly common complaint. What if she was denying Leela vital treatment? But Padma couldn't bring herself to give away her money; the protest in her was too loud. She swivelled the chair, turning from the computer to the window. She sat looking outside, the garden so empty and bright and distant from the shadowy office. She tore up Leela's note and the hospital letter into the tiniest fragments. Only the paperclip was left. She didn't add it to the pottery dish of paperclips and staples on her desk; like something contagious, she threw it into the bin.

She remembered how life at the villa had felt incomplete when she first came to live there; every interaction so puzzlingly simple; no need to be alert for tricks or to track back through what people had said to discover the start of a betrayal. And there had been no sudden anger to fear, no beatings, no sadness, no shame. Much later, at the yoga institute, she had felt a similar disbelief at the rightness of how it had felt, so easy just to be there and to be herself, that it had seemed something was missing. But now she knew there was no need to search beyond that ease, that rightness. She pushed away the morning. She would be leaving the villa the next day, and the jeering new knowledge of her failure; leaving for the institute in Colombo, that clean simple world waiting for her.

# PART III

## 28

EARLY EVERY MORNING, the taxi Padma had arranged to take her to the yoga institute came for her at Ruth's house. Ruth had offered her driver and car, but Padma had refused, and this time, unlike when Padma was going to university, Ruth hadn't argued. There were no recriminations, just a quiet retreating; a new separation, easy and painless. Each morning Padma drove away with a wave to Ruth and her security guard Joseph closing the gates behind the taxi, and entered a Colombo of her own.

The roads were almost empty at that time, the shops still locked up and shuttered, the only cafés open the ones where the workers went for breakfast. Early-worshippers went in through the gates of the kovil with small plastic bags of flowers. Without the dread of university dragging her down, the city felt hers. Somewhere nearby was Rohan. He could have appeared anywhere, yet he seemed too far away; she couldn't imagine seeing him. The taxi drove past the turning to his parents' road. A car paused at the top, about to ease out onto the main road. It was a stranger driving – an elderly man with neat combed hair and a moustache. He could have been a neighbour or Rohan's father, or just someone driving through from another road. Padma's taxi drove on. Now the shops were starting to open. She thought only of the institute and the morning ahead.

She was the first of her group to arrive. The caretaker was unlocking the doors to the practice rooms. She stretched alone. She heard teachers coming into the building, and other students, then her own group arrived, nine others preparing to take the teacher-training exam. They were continuing from that year's course, only Padma had transferred from a different year. She hadn't stayed in touch with any of her former classmates; she had barely known them at the time, always having to run off after class to attend tutorials and lectures. She had been so determined to keep that other life apart from what she loved she had told no one why she kept leaving early. The students on her previous course may have grown as close as these latest students had become. They welcomed her in without hesitation; she had never belonged so easily in a group before. The thrill of it was almost like pain; she was forever ready for a sudden awkward question and the discomfort of having to lie, but it never came. She sat in their midst in the leafy courtyard, talking freely, the only past that mattered the one that had brought them to the institute. A shared gladness at being there was their connection, the truest Padma had felt among strangers. With people at university and at the parties at Ruth's, it was only one's family of birth that mattered, what they needed to know before they could know you. Adoption by Gerhardt did not redeem her to people in such circles. What they didn't seem to know was that it was the people you loved and those who loved you, who formed you – they were the ones to know about. Work formed you in the same way, she was starting to see – the work you loved made you grow; the right work took you to the right people.

In the shade of the courtyard she talked of plans with her new friends, they telling her of businesses they hoped to start or had just begun. They talked of teaching contracts they were applying for, and retreats to try abroad. Padma listened, but she didn't mention the retreat in Goa. Guiltily she withheld it from those others who spoke so trustingly sharing what they knew with her. All through their conversations Padma guarded her secret. She hadn't known until then how afraid she was of it being taken away.

That afternoon when she was back at Ruth's, she emailed the retreat in Goa and asked if they had work for a new yoga teacher. She would be free over the next months, she told them, for the guest house was likely to stay quiet for the rainy season. There had been one booking the day before, for a couple staying a few days, but there had been no other enquiries. She added in the email to Goa that she was a friend of Ria's. Once she would have hesitated to mention names to try and gain an advantage, but it seemed important now to try anyway she could to impress the retreat's owners. A new part of herself had stepped forward and taken control, making her guard secrets and name-drop – anything to get her what she wanted. She wanted to teach yoga in Goa, she knew now, as if somebody had just told her.

Gerhardt woke from an afternoon nap to a room rosy and glowing, a flare of sun caught in a rose-pink and orange band of the curtains. There was a smell of jasmine oil, sweet and joyful and sickly. For a moment he didn't know where he was, then he remembered: he was in Padma's room, at the villa. He had offered to run the guest house while Padma was in Colombo for her yoga teaching exams. The blades of the fan were a pale blur circling above him. In his first years in Sri Lanka he'd imagined fans coming loose and falling down onto him on the bed, slicing him up – even though he had never heard of a fan coming away from a ceiling. He'd worried about a great many far-fetched happenings in those days.

Misplaced guilt, Ruth had called it, for leaving his mother behind in the chateau in the fir forests and reaching for a life beyond her grasp. But his mother had always known that he would leave her; even as a child he had searched for different ways of living, more curious than the rest of his family about the workers on the estate. He had gone with them to their houses and workshops and seen inside their buildings and learned their crafts. He had longed as a young man to be stirred by the places he stayed in, and to make places that would stir the hearts of others. It was important, he had sensed even then, to live and work in beauty, to live life gladly, owning every hour, every day, year after year.

He followed the lines of the ceiling beams, past the fan. He'd been right to raise the ceiling to almost double its original height. He loved the spaciousness of that emptiness above him, and the innocent simplicity of white-painted boards in the style of old Dutch houses and churches. There were many aspects of the villa, clear, considered design decisions that had the vague and diffuse effect of making one feel happy and serene, just to be there. So little it took, yet so much effort was needed to exert the necessary restraint. He had been happy at the villa, and Padma too. Everyone who visited had marvelled at his lush precious nest with the beautiful child at its centre, he holding away the threatening force of Sunny to let her thrive. He no longer had that power, he could no longer provide her with the freedom and safety she deserved. Perhaps, after all, it was time to rent the house. Could he ever bring himself to sell it? For now, he would try to find a good tenant, putting out feelers discretely. Perhaps the lawyer would agree to undertake the task.

He sat on the edge of the bed and stretched, feeling the ache in his limbs, a new tension cramping his muscles. Work at least was going well. Two of the holiday cottages had been rented out already and the third was nearly completed. As for clients, he had more than he knew what to do with, for all those whom he had written to had been delighted to know that he might soon be able to take on more projects – but of course now he didn't need the money anymore as Sunny had declined to be paid. Sunny declining money! This was one change he would never have predicted!

A gust of wind came in at the window and left, sucking the curtains ribbed against the window bars. Surely the jauntiest, kitschiest colour scheme ever conceived, those curtains, with their red, orange, lemon-yellow, candyfloss-pink and even a lime-green stripe, but somehow it worked – that was the beauty of the design and Padma had seen it. He thought back to the shopping trip at the famous Barefoot boutique in Colombo, seeing a younger Padma march straight past the more predictably coloured bolts of cloth and straight for this. Caught in its cheery cosy glow now, he was aware of how much the room felt of her; the happy eagerness that shone through her that she would take everywhere she went. He felt her absence. Even in the years of her being at university there had always been a sense of her still there, about to return. But the villa felt empty now with a heavy new emptiness. The curtains blew in, released from the iron bars, lifting to reveal the ripening sun low over the garden. The afternoon, always a time for rest and reflection, had tipped over into the earliest edge of evening, the sunset still a promise in the deepening colours. Soon it would be time to watch the display, the day's brilliant achievement. This was the appeal of the Tropics: the distinct phases of day, each broken into clear components, the parts defined by light and heat and the strength of breezes. In Europe the day was a nebulous continuum, too short in winter, and in summer stretched to extraordinary lengths, yet one was led guilelessly to believe in those long light evenings, only to be disappointed as the days shrank through autumn and the bleakness of winter gravely took its place. Time passed so confusingly in Europe; no one quite knew where it went. A life could be over before you knew it.

He glanced at his watch: three thirty. Time to begin the evening. Slowly, carefully, he stood up. One needed to ease oneself out of the lostness of sleep. Out of reach of the fan, his body, so stiff, so old seeming, was damp with sweat. He didn't mind. It felt healthy to wake hot and needing to wash, as if some necessary physical exertion had taken place. He took a shower and emerged renewed to dress in clothes he had brought in a suitcase, like a guest. In the hall, he listened for a moment outside the guest room where a couple were staying – rather an unlikely pair: Nimmy and Prakash, middle-aged, well-to-do Sri Lankans from Colombo, who had booked and arrived on the same day. They hadn't liked the bungalows or the guest room and just when he had expected them to leave, they had asked to stay, and opted for the room in the house. The room was cheaper than the bungalows, but he felt sure it wasn't a question of money; there was an anxiety about the two that made him suspect they felt more secure inside the house. There was something a little strange about them turning up out of season, during the monsoon – but it wasn't as if it rained all day, or even every day. Still they did not seem like people who were taking a restful off-season break – they went out early every day, for some hidden purpose, and returned late, never talking about where they had been. There was no sound from their room now. Possibly they had gone out, or not returned after lunch. He couldn't imagine them ever sleeping during the day.

On the veranda, the winds from the sea had turned frisky as the sun's strength waned. The late sun fell on the dresser and a package that had arrived earlier for Padma, sent by Rohan from Colombo, according to the postal stamps and return address. The package had been delivered by postal van, the postman tottering up the path burdened by its weight, and hanging around curiously in case Gerhardt opened it. But of course Padma had to open it. Gerhardt had put away Jarryd's books with a guilty spurt of relief and put the package in their place, awaiting Padma's return. Soma came out after his own afternoon nap and settled under the mango trees to smoke. His eyes were bleary with sleep; he was quiet, disgruntled looking. A little marijuana would have helped but he never smoked dope while Gerhardt was staying. He still observed the rules of long ago: ganja only after dinner had been cleared away and to be smoked well out of sight of Padma and absolutely never to be shared with her. He thought about telling Soma to go ahead and smoke if he wanted to, but the new guests could return at any time and one could never tell with strait-laced people how they might respond. It always surprised him when conservative people took offence at another person's liberties, even when unaffected by it themselves.

The couple returned as the sun was starting to set. He noted their sandy slippers with surprise: why go to the beach and not stay for sunset? The sky already looked exquisite: pink, blending through shades of orange, to red. Even on the veranda the new guests sat unheeding of it, turned away from the view.

"Would you like some tea? A beer? A soft drink?" he offered.

"Nothing for me," Nimmy said wearily.

"Oh, by the way, Gerhardt, do you happen to keep a guestbook here?" Prakash asked.

"A guestbook?"

"Yes, you know, where people write comments and leave contact details," Nimmy added.

"Already you have comments?" he joked, dreading a complaint.

"It's just – oh it's really nothing! – but our daughter stayed here some months back." Nimmy forced a little laugh. "She was with a – a friend of hers. And we were wondering if—"

"No, *you* were wondering," Prakash corrected her.

"Alright, so it's me that's wondering. Does it matter?" she snapped.

She turned again to Gerhardt. "You see, they've forgotten to tell us where they're going to next, can you imagine? These young people, how funny they are! We're just trying to find out where they've got to, that's all."

"Ah, now I see! You're spying on your daughter and her boyfriend!" Gerhardt teased.

"No, we absolutely are not!" Prakash retorted. "What a ridiculous thing to say. Parents don't spy on their children."

"Of course not, I'm sorry. I'll go and look for the guestbook. What are their names?"

"Anjali Panditharatne," Prakash announced.

Gerhardt started.

"And Daniel Gomes," Nimmy added.

"Yes, Gomes," Prakash said, with explicit distaste.

"He also might have written in the book," Nimmy protested.

"I'll go and see if we have such a book, we may not, of course—" Gerhardt was suddenly nervous of showing them the leather-bound guestbook that Padma kept in the office.

"You spoke as if you had one," Prakash said sharply.

"No, no, I merely assumed. You see, it's my daughter who runs this place. I have no idea if she even has such a thing. I'll have a look." And he hurried to the office.

Inside, with the door closed, he read carefully over the recent pages. Luckily, Anjali and Dan had written nothing. Padma probably hadn't offered it to them, and why would she? They hadn't really left. But why didn't the parents know? Why had Anjali kept her whereabouts from them? Outside he heard the spatter of the hose as Soma watered the plants, and Gerhardt longed to be outside with him, with the house just there for them, like in the old days. He took a deep breath and went out to the couple. They were waiting, watching the door, expectant like baby birds in a nest. They pored over every page of the guidebook, all the way to the last entry, Ria's sweet melancholy farewell to them. Prakash handed back the guidebook, a new desperation showing through his superior veneer. Gerhardt understood that terrible need to know. Had Padma been aware that Anjali and Dan were running away? Was it yet another secret she'd kept from him?

"Maybe this isn't where they stayed," Prakash said.

"But it's the name of the guest house in her letter," Nimmy protested.

"She wrote to you?" Gerhardt sounded more exasperated than he had meant to.

The father gave him a startled glance, but really, what was the matter with these people? Anjali could hardly be accused of deserting them if she'd written and told them where she was.

"We're just concerned parents." Nimmy's voice wavered. "She's our only child and we're worried about her. She's forgotten how dangerous it can be in this country – you're sure you don't re-member her, Gerhardt?"

"They must see so many people here, how do you expect him to remember just one?" Prakash scolded.

"Two," she corrected him miserably. "Anjali's quite small, about my height," she told Gerhardt. "Light brown eyes, black curly hair."

Gerhardt swallowed, thinking of Anjali with her newly bleached hair: white-blonde and bizarre-looking, and beautiful. She'd always wanted to do it, she'd said afterwards, but she'd never been allowed to, or had the nerve, even while she was living abroad. He thought of her so alive, so altered in the little cottage among the paddy fields that she and Dan were renting from Gerhardt. When he and Padma had visited, they'd found the two of them reading together in a big green hammock, entwined like a pair of contented silk worms. And so oddly alike with their golden-brown skin, cut-off jeans and loose t-shirts, so relaxed and glamorous, Anjali preparing vegetarian salads for lunch while Dan made cocktails for the four of them. They were good sweet kids, that much he knew, whatever their story. And resourceful – in just the short time they'd been in the area they'd managed to find teaching jobs at an orphanage, and a village school run by the priest of the rock temple. There had to be a good reason for their secrecy. It would be wrong of him to intrude on the life they had so quietly and determinedly arranged for themselves.

The parents sat slumped in silence. Gerhardt noted their expensive watches, the pristine clothes and expertly-dyed hair, the effortless polish of them. What if Prakash were someone influential, with enemies that Anjali needed to be protected from? Was she being left vulnerable by Gerhardt's reluctance to get involved?

"You know, maybe I do remember them," he said.

Nimmy and Prakash sat bolt upright. But there was no joy, no relief in their expression – only something incongruous – it felt like . . . triumph. The thrill of the chase. They wore the look of hunters in the forests around his mother's house, alive and brimming with purpose and almost crazed, before the hunt. Even as a boy he had shrunk from them and their slavering dogs; he had never longed to join in, like his cousins and his friends. He regretted revealing what he had; he had done wrong, the youngsters were far more to be trusted than the parents.

"Actually, I'm not sure they were the couple I'm thinking of," he said. "I think the young man was Indian. And the woman was from Hong Kong – or maybe it was the Philippines—"

"And where is this couple now?" Prakash demanded.

"I have no idea."

"You don't remember any places they mentioned? Somewhere that they might be headed?" Nimmy asked.

"No, sorry, nothing comes to mind."

"In actual fact, this is all academic. We could find her in a matter of hours if we really had to," Prakash declared.

"Yes, my husband could put a trace on her," Nimmy explained importantly. "We could find her just like that." She clicked her fingers. "In minutes, not even hours. You see, when you work for the Governm—"

"Yes, okay, no need to broadcast the fact," Prakash interrupted.

"But he won't do it," Nimmy complained. "It's a matter of *principle*, apparently."

"Yes, I believe it to be in very poor taste to expose one's family concerns to colleagues."

"We still need to know where she is, Prakash! What kind of parents don't know where their daughter is living?"

"What sort of daughter disappears without telling her parents?" Prakash's fine features were distorted by anger. "She wants to be left alone, so let's leave her alone; in fact, wasn't that the gist of her letter?" Prakash took a step away, composing himself.

How hard it must have been for Anjali to write that letter, to ask for independence from such a man; to request her release, to be allowed her own existence. She would have hoped for her freedom to be given without rancour, without the loss of affection, but clearly no blessing was forthcoming from the people before Gerhardt now. Why were such clever accomplished people threatened by a child's will? Her most natural desire for freedom?

"How can a daughter ask a mother to leave her alone?" Nimmy wailed. "So secretive she's become, all of a sudden."

"It's the age," Gerhardt said. "My daughter too can be quite unreadable. These last few weeks, for instance—"

"She never used to be. She would tell me everything. We used to be so close."

Accusation hung in the air, aimed at the amorphous corrupting force that had invaded the world that Nimmy had made for herself and her daughter. In the silence the sounds of Soma in the kitchen drifted in. Gerhardt thought longingly of the clean tidy kitchen, and Soma purposefully preparing dinner, a last simple act of creation in the day.

"I must go and check on dinner," Gerhardt said leaving.

He arranged with Soma to have his dinner brought to the office. He didn't dare eat with the couple until he had discussed with Padma what they were to do about Anjali.

He called Padma late that night, after the couple had retired to their room. Padma and Ruth were watching a film, Padma informed him - a thriller. He wanted to be with them in Ruth's cool pale sitting room with its white sofas and white linen drapes rippling with the fan and the huge new flat-screen television. He imagined Ruth patiently waiting for the call to end, the image on the screen paused shuddering.

"How was today? The course still okay?" he asked Padma.

"Yes, it's great, we're covering a lot."

"And the people?"

"Everyone's really nice, really friendly."

She was happy, he could hear it - the satisfied stillness in her voice. She was right to have returned, to have gone back into the one world that had always called to her.

"By the way, something came in the post for you," he told her.

"A letter? Who from?" she sounded worried.

"Not a letter, a great big heavy lump of a package."

"What is it?" She sounded terrified.

"I don't know, I didn't open it! It's from Rohan."

"Oh, Rohan!" She sounded relieved! "You're sure it's from him?" she asked.

Who did she think would be sending her things? "His name's on it, and an address in Colombo."

"It probably is from him then. Open it! See what it is."

"It might take a minute or two, it's very well wrapped." He took the package to the office and cut string and tape and unfurled layers of cardboard and wrappings to reveal a bronze statue of a Dancing Shiva. It was exquisite.

"What is it? Tell me!" she demanded.

"It's a Shiva Natraj. It's rather wonderful, in fact."

"Ah! It's because I told him about the cave in Ellora!" she said.

Gerhardt looked closer at the statue and saw that indeed Rohan had sought a replica of that ancient stone statue in the famous cave complex that he, Ruth and Padma had visited one year. Rohan must have searched hard for such a close match. It would have been expensive; the workmanship was impeccable. Gerhardt couldn't stop looking at the statue; it defied him. He had been wrong about Rohan; he had missed something vitally important about the man.

"Gerhardt?"

"Yes?"

"You're very quiet."

"Have you had a chance to see Rohan?"

"What for?"

"Maybe I was too hasty to judge him—"

"Why? Because he sent me a present?"

"I don't think I got to know him properly, I was too quick to—"

"It doesn't matter now. He's going back to England soon, and anyway, I'm too busy."

"Maybe send him an email and say you're in Colombo?"

"What for?"

"You have to thank him for your gift. It really is a very fine sculpture, you're going to like it very much, I think."

She was silent. He thought he heard her sigh.

"How are the new guests?" she asked brightly.

"Ah, about that—" He ran to the office door and carefully opened it to check that the guests weren't outside in the hall.

"I think they might be Anjali's parents," he whispered into the phone.

"What?" she shrieked. "Oh my God!"

"What is it?" he heard Ruth in the background.

"Why are they there?" Padma cried.

"They're looking for her," Gerhardt said softly.

"Don't tell them anything! Whatever you do, don't say one word! You haven't, have you?"

"Of course not!"

"Gerhardt? Have you said something?"

"No! But they are very concerned about her."

"It doesn't matter, you absolutely mustn't tell them. They mustn't find out where she is, they'll ruin her life!"

"I really don't think we're in a position to judge—"

"Her mother was so mean to her! She called her a whore!"

"Really, Padma!"

"Who is this person?" Ruth demanded.

"No-one you know," Padma assured her.

"I know everyone!" Ruth protested.

"She'll definitely know the father," Gerhardt said.

"That doesn't change anything - you can't tell them where she is! They don't want her to be with Dan, her mother's furious. But what sort of mother talks to her daughter like that?"

"People say things when they're angry, it doesn't mean—"

"Fine. You go and tell them - ruin their happiness."

"Maybe I'll call Anjali first and discuss it with her."

"And then she'll get worried and they'll have to run away again."

"Or maybe she and her parents will talk and start over?"

"Oh sure!"

Padma was right, and he knew it. And he didn't really feel sorry for Nimmy and Prakash. He couldn't help feeling that they had brought this rejection, so harsh and unthinkable, on themselves.

"Maybe I won't say anything for now," he conceded.

They were guests, not friends; he didn't owe them anymore than guest-house hospitality. He didn't need to suffer their private pain; they certainly wouldn't thank him for it.

"Please hurry up! I'm forgetting the plot here!" Ruth shouted.

"Lost the plot, has she?" Gerhardt said and Padma giggled and told Ruth.

"She's making faces at you," Padma reported.

"Tell her I'm making faces back."

"He's making faces back at you," Padma told Ruth.

"The winds may change!" Ruth yelled.

"Enjoy your film. Don't forget to thank Rohan for the gift."

"I won't forget. Goodnight, Gerhardt."

"Sweet dreams."

"I love you," she said.

"I love you too."

Why did he stand in the dark with tears running down his face, missing her as if she had gone away forever? Missing the girl he had surrounded with love, and people who loved her. She drew such people to herself now, all by herself. The Dancing Shiva gleamed, rising out of its wrappings. He had always wanted to see Padma fly out into the world and shine as her true self. She had begun her ascent. Already she had taken her first true steps away from him. He had to set her free; he couldn't let her be caught any longer at the villa. In that house he had intended once for his solitary pleasure, its rooms silent and patiently waiting around him, he stood in his shadowy office, crying without knowing why.

## 29

THE NEXT MORNING Nimmy and Prakash set off with the grim righteousness of secret agents out to find traitors and bring them to justice. They were gone for several hours, returning in the evening from who knew where, and asking for tea and cucumber sandwiches. They took these on the veranda, Gerhardt warily joining them. They sat in surprisingly easy silence together, as the sea winds grew strong, stirring the garden, and the colours of sea and sky deepened along the horizon. Nimmy reached for another sandwich. Prakash sat working on an iPad, pausing absent-mindedly to sip his tea.

"She was at Harvard, you know, our daughter," Nimmy said to Gerhardt. Pride crept into her voice, as if from habit. "She read Law. She got a First."

"A First from Harvard! My goodness! I didn't realise!" Gerhardt blurted.

"Realise? Realise what?" She was onto him like a shot.

Prakash too, glanced up and watched him closely.

"That – that we were talking about someone so academic," Gerhardt stammered. "Now I'm certain we're discussing two totally different young women."

Prakash returned to his work.

"Was she intelligent, this other woman?" Nimmy enquired.

"Oh yes, very clever, but she didn't come across as an intellectual, she seemed much more—"

"You thought she was one of those traveller types, I suppose. That's how she likes to act these days, ever since she met that awful boy. She doesn't realise how much better she can do for herself. How can *she* become a kindergarten teacher?"

Nimmy stopped, a thought just occurring to her. "She doesn't actually *look* like one of those hippy-types, does she, Gerhardt? With matted hair and one of those awful nose studs, like some dirty charwoman? Did she dye her hair some awful colour? She used to talk about wanting to, long ago. Or a tattoo! Oh, my God, don't tell me . . ."

"It wasn't your daughter staying here, I'm quite sure."

"So she did have a tattoo? Did she, Gerhardt? Did you notice one?"

"No, no tattoos. None at all."

"I'm sure she's gone and done something . . ."

"For God's sake! Enough of this nonsense!" Prakash went to stand by the parapet. "What makes me so angry is the waste of it. How hard my generation worked to get where we are now - we created the very advantages she takes for granted. It makes my blood boil! I got her into one of the best Chambers in Asia - others would kill for such an opportunity - and she simply threw it away without a moment's thought."

"You don't know that, she may have thought very hard about it," Gerhardt said.

"I doubt that very much."

"There are so many pressures on young people these days. We think we're protecting them, but in fact we burden them with our expectations. I'm not judging you, I merely speak from my own experience." Gerhard gave the stern countenance before him a rueful smile of consolation. "It's only recently occurred to me that it must feel oppressive to them, to be so constantly aided and guided by us, to have our long shadows fall across their bright new horizons."

It was a confession, a revelation, but it was easier spoken out loud.

"A lack of gratitude – that's Anjali's only problem," Prakash said.

"What was the point of all the sacrifices, that's what I'd like to know," Nimmy added.

But all there could ever be was the pleasure of having nurtured and loved one's children. Love was attachment and lead to sorrow, the Buddha had warned, but looking back at the worry and sleeplessness, there was always the delight of seeing her thrive from his care and the gladness of simply having her be his- she had been his greatest luck, his greatest joy. He had been blessed with more than he could ever have hoped for.

"We can look on with pride at what we have done," he told the couple. "That's what we have. All those years when they were so small and needing us . . ." His voice wavered and he stopped, stemming the flood rising in him, threatening to spill over.

"Of course it's different when they're young!" Nimmy scoffed. "There's no problem keeping control of them then! It's now that they don't listen."

"But how can we tell them how to live, when we know nothing of their secret hopes, or their dreams for themselves?" he pleaded with her.

"Speak for yourself, Gerhardt. I know everything there is to know about my daughter," Nimmy retorted.

"If we did anything wrong, it was being too lax," Prakash declared. "One day Anjali will regret not taking our advice, and I for one will not be bailing her out from whatever mess she finds herself in."

His phone beeped and he studied a message with sudden concentration.

"I need to make a phone call – do you think I might get better reception in the garden?" he asked.

"Best place is by the gate" Gerhardt knew to give up; defeat was inevitable.

"Why don't you use the phone in the office. No charge, it's on the house." It was all he could think of to help the man.

"No need, I'm calling Beijing - far better done on expenses, I'm sure you'll agree!" Prakash smiled, returned to his world of work. He strode past Gerhardt into the garden.

Gerhardt and Nimmy sat on in the fading light.

"I hope I didn't offend your husband," Gerhardt said.

"It doesn't matter."

"All I meant was that we didn't really know what it is to be our children; they probably know better than us what's right for them. Our time of being central to their lives is over."

"So you think we're irrelevant?"

"Well, yes." He smiled. It was the way it should be – young people should never be made afraid of stepping towards the life they wanted. It was all they would have one day to look back on, and accept as what they had done with the time they were allotted.

Nimmy gazed through the frangipani trees at Prakash pacing up and down in the lane, talking on his phone.

"I certainly *feel* irrelevant," she murmured. "I try to meditate and free myself of this . . . this . . . tightness. Just here." She put a thin hand to her chest. "Sometimes I think I'm about to have a heart attack, or a stroke, or something. My heart starts beating so hard."

"A panic attack?"

"Of course not! No one in our family has any kind of mental illness. It's all this worry about Anjali. If anything happens to me, it'll all be her fault."

The red glow on the sea darkened to a shimmering gun-powder grey. Padma had possibly always known what she wanted to do, only he had kept pressing her to get a degree - to have a safety net, he'd explained - but he had assumed so much that wasn't true; he had imagined she could be happy anywhere, among all people; that one could own what one did without belonging to it, without it calling to you. How could he not have known, he who had always listened to his own call and gone only towards what he truly wanted. He had never thought to look down to see if a net were in place.

But he had once longed to belong where he had made no impression. All he had hoped for, at one time, was acceptance by Ruth's family, her brothers and cousins, mostly all lawyers- witty, urbane, effortlessly successful men, bolstered by an arrogance that charmed with its warmth. To be allowed by those languid, erudite men into their circle was what he had hoped for when working on his first projects in Sri Lanka, but he had never managed to impress them. Yet those minor projects with their uncertain goals had made him the architect he was now. He would never know if a more conventional career would have made him less happy - all he had was what he had chosen and the respect of certain people whom he himself admired. This was the path he had chosen; one had to accept the decisions one took. To choose honestly, bravely, without compromise, holding on for what one really wanted, was the one protection against regret.

The night winds swept onto the veranda. And the darkness came slinking in, a veil, a net coming over, concealing the garden.

"Anjali could be anywhere, she could be mixing with unsuitable people," Nimmy said. "One of these days, she's going to be attacked."

"No!"

"Oh yes, she definitely will if she goes out wearing the awful clothes she's started wearing recently. Looking provocative for the sake of it! Just asking for trouble! She used to be so well-dressed before, she always took my advice on everything." Nimmy paused. "By the way, that couple you mentioned, I suppose they shared a room?"

"I'm sure it wasn't you daughter and her boyfriend staying here," Gerhardt assured her.

"Even so, was it a double room or a twin they had?"

"I think it was a twin."

"What's the use! They would have just pushed the beds togeth-er." She took a slow shuddering breath. "She has no values anymore, none whatsoever! I saw her once, you know, at home, in my garden. With that man. I just happened to be in the room upstairs looking out of the window – something told me to look out of the window, some instinct – I just knew they were creeping about downstairs the moment my back was turned. And sure enough, there they were. Disgusting. I was so shocked. I felt *sickened*."

"They were doing it in the garden?"

"Just like in the films, all open mouths and pawing at each other—"

"Just kissing?"

"Yes, kissing! What else would I mean?"

"Oh."

"Obviously you don't understand our culture one jot, Gerhardt. Here in Asia people are expected to behave respectfully in public."

"But didn't you say they were in your garden?"

"Yes, and any one of the neighbours could have seen them. She has picked up all the worst morals of the West. Other people's children go abroad and come back perfectly unchanged – but not her! If I'd known she was so weak, I would *never* have agreed to send her. She's become shameless, like some cheap American woman. White trash, they call them, even over there."

Her eyes went to Prakash still talking in the lane.

"He wouldn't listen. How many times I told him we should get her married before something happened, but he was all caught up with her career. So many judges we know have sons, any one of them might have considered her, but it's too late now, everybody knows about her. Who would want their son marrying someone like her?"

"There really is no shame in young love," Gerhardt said. "I'm sure even Sri Lankans fall in love now and again, don't they?"

"Oh yes, and it always ends in disaster."

"At least she'll be safe travelling with a boyfriend."

"*Him!* He's the one who's going to attract attention. With that horrible hair of his. Whoever heard of an Asian boy from a good family bleaching his hair? Ridiculous he looks." Nimmy sniffed, taking off her spectacles, wiping them with a handkerchief. She re-balanced the glasses on her small straight nose – the same nose as Anjali, Gerhardt noted, startled by the likeness. But how different the tight little face of the mother, to the laughing and alive daughter. How terrible to thwart that spark in her. But he understood; he had known it himself, the fear of that youthful aliveness, like defiance, a dismissal; it felt dangerous, stirring up one's own missed chances, bringing them to the surface.

"You also have a daughter?" Nimmy enquired.

"Yes, Padma."

"Ah. You chose a Sinhala name?"

"Actually, she is Sinhalese. I'm her legal guardian."

"Legal guardian?"

"She's adopted."

"You're not married?"

"No."

"Must have been hard looking after a child on your own. You didn't want to meet a nice woman and start a family with her?"

"I did meet a nice woman."

"And what happened?"

"She married my best friend."

"And you didn't find someone else? Surely there must have been others you could choose from?"

"Not like her, no."

He found it strange to be talking of Ruth to this stranger who may well have known her and possibly disapproved of her – for Ruth's flagrant independence had never endeared her to more conservative Colombo society, despite her wealth and connections.

"I hadn't planned on bringing up a child on my own, it just happened that way," he said. "And then my whole life changed."

"Tell me about it," Nimmy muttered.

"Obviously the life I'd imagined was never meant to happen."

"You mean Fate, I suppose? You sound more like a Buddhist than a Christian. Are you a Buddhist, Gerhardt? Often Westerners find it a far more intelligent choice than their own religions."

"I have no particular religion."

"I see, an atheist."

"No, I like them all. Mostly they say the same things."

Her lips tightened. Religion was where the fault lines were drawn for most Sri Lankans, separating them from each other, trapping them in a logic of division. And after religion came class, an obstacle even harder to surmount – and to confront. But it was there under the surface of so many polite conversations, an edge to be caught on, a barrier that tripped, a threshold never to cross.

In the darkening light, Prakash came up from the lane.

"Any progress?" he asked, glancing at Nimmy.

She shook her head.

"A child becomes a separate person, they stop being a part of us," Gerhardt reflected. "Yet we still feel their hurts, and suffer with them – such a visceral connection, yet they are entirely in-dependent of us."

"Maybe in your case," Nimmy said. "Your daughter isn't *actually* yours, is she? For us it's different."

"I meant for everyone. 'Life's longing for itself', someone called it. Our children are not ours—"

"I've never heard that saying." Nimmy looked impatient.

"I must concur, it sounds a little too mystical for my tastes," Prakash added.

"In our culture, children are very *much* a part of the family," Nimmy said.

Gerhardt stayed silent. He didn't regret keeping back the truth, not anymore. He might even have telephoned Anjali to warn her to keep out of sight, but he didn't want to disrupt her peace – clearly it was hard-won.

"I have to do the accounts," he said and went to the office.

Padma must never have to hide her life from him; or be held back. She had to be free to go wherever she desired, to follow her dreams. The villa must never entrap her. The guest house had been an experiment, but it was too heavy a burden. It was time. He telephoned the lawyer and instructed him to search discreetly for tenants, starting immediately. Then he telephoned Jarryd to arrange his escape for the night.

Jarryd was waiting for him with a bottle of chilled dry Spanish Fino, which they took out onto the veranda. Through the trees, over the lake, lights glowed in the luxury huts of Jarryd's retreat. There was a distant beating of drums and cheers and clapping.

"The guests are having a jam tonight," Jarryd said. "So what's happening with your guests?"

"Soma's taking care of them."

"Oh dear."

"I'll be glad when they go. After that I'm going to be renting out the villa."

"What will Padma do then?" Jarryd asked.

"Whatever she wants. Travel, teach yoga – it's what she would like, I think. The guest house is what's keeping her here. And me, I'm holding her back."

"Or maybe she stays for reasons of her own . . ."

"Like what?"

"I don't know!" Jarryd grew vague. "But isn't her old family nearby?"

"She isn't staying here for Sunny!"

"What about her mother?"

"Leela?"

"A girl does need a mother at key transitional times in her life . . ."

"What on earth would she want with Leela? The woman's as bad as Sunny!"

"You don't know that, Gerhardt."

"She let her daughter be sold to a stranger – what sort of mother does that?"

"Maybe she didn't have a choice. She has been at the mercy of a violent man for many years, who knows what control he exerts over her? She may have a very different story to tell if asked. And what if one day she manages to escape Sunny? Then she and Padma could be reunited."

"Leela is no downtrodden housewife, believe me. Ruth is quite convinced that Leela's the brains behind Sunny."

"Poor Leela is a sad ailing woman."

"How do you know?"

"That's just what I heard. But Gerhardt, you mustn't feel threatened if Padma has feelings for her old family."

"What are you talking about?"

"Oh nothing, really – I am merely hopeful that one day some elements of Padma's past life will be redeemed."

"Like Sunny?"

"Oh good heavens, that man is beyond redemption! No, I meant her mother—"

"Good God, Jarryd! You are one hell of an idealist!"

Jarryd smiled. It was never an insult with him.

"Shall we eat?" he said.

Dinner was a salad of beansprouts and tofu, raw grated beetroot, gottukola mallung and red rice with a sauce made of ground cashew nuts. It tasted better than it looked. Afterwards they drank coffee in the sitting room, Gerhardt still troubled by what Jarryd had said. Surely after the debacle of her recent trip to the family's home, even Jarryd could see that Padma should stay away? Had Padma hinted at wanting to see more of Leela? Why had she confided in Jarryd instead of Gerhardt? Jarryd had never dealt with people like Sunny and Leela; Jarryd was as misguided as the locals in his unquestioning respect for familial bonds. Family could be damaged, family could destroy their own. Family sometimes had to be left behind.

"I'm sorry, I didn't mean to intrude. You know Padma best of all," Jarryd said gently.

Gerhardt smiled at his friend. It was hard to stay angry around Jarryd because he always meant well, there was kindness in his every act, however misguided.

"You'll find someone to rent your villa," Jarryd added. "I expect they'd pay quite a lot. You'd get even more if you had a pool."

"I could put one in."

"Or you could rent the place to our dear minister's brother?"

"Of course!"

Jarryd chuckled. "Just imagine those nubile young women draped around your veranda, tempting the passers-by . . ."

"A lovely thought."

"The man is ambitious, no harm in that! In fact, one must admire his entrepreneurship!"

Jarryd was right, the minister would be first in line to rent the villa if he knew; Gerhardt would ask the lawyer to act exceptionally discretely. Jarryd went around the room, turning on more lamps – which was when Gerhardt saw the broken glass in the French doors.

"What happened to your window?" he asked.

Jarryd pulled the curtain closed, hiding the jagged exposure.

"Just some jokers from the village." Jarryd settled back on the sofa, repositioning a stool to prop up his bad leg.

"Which jokers?"

"Some friends of our honourable minister and his brother. They want me to remove my book from all shops in the whole of Sri Lanka, no less. Can you believe that?"

"And you said no?"

"Of course I said no!" Jarryd laughed.

"But now they are throwing rocks through your window!"

"One little stone, let's keep this in perspective. There was very little damage done. The worst of it was that they gave poor Geetha a fright. She heard the noise and came running from the kitchen and saw the thugs outside. Luckily no one did anything to her, she's fine."

"Jarryd, this can't go on, these are not people to fool around with—"

"No one got hurt."

"This time."

"It was just some silliness, hardly worth mentioning. That fool of a minister is trying to intimidate me. According to him, I've made him a problem for the great powers in Colombo. He says I am living in his constituency and spreading dissent. As if my little book is going to influence anyone!"

"You really don't want to annoy him, Jarryd, he's a strange fellow—"

"Dissent is an essential part of good governance – don't you think?"

"Yes, but those idiots in government don't understand!"

"It's about time they did."

"Just take care, will you. Call me if anything else happens? Anything at all."

"What an old fuss pot!" Jarryd laughed.

"I'm serious, Jarryd. You must come and stay with me if anything else happens."

"Alright, I'll call you and maybe I will stay with you if it gets really bad here."

The minister would soon tire of smashing glass. When would Jarryd realise how dangerous these people could be if provoked? The new breed of nationalistic Sinhalese were brazen and bullish, full of a jeering lawlessness emboldened after the war that was won so cruelly and without remorse. Now they surged behind a government that no longer cared for the West's approval, turned to China, Russia, Iran, a different heartless power propelling them.

Gerhardt stayed at Jarryd's after dinner, waking nervously through the night to look out from the window, checking the garden for intruders. In the morning they took coffee in the courtyard at the back of the house. A gardener arrived for work, followed by the staff of the yoga retreat, one of whom Jarryd reminded to call the glazier to replace the broken glass. In the easy splendour of the morning the shattered glass seemed innocuous, the break a fractured star, edges glinting in the sun.

"You should withdraw your book for a short period, just until the elections are over," Gerhardt advised.

"All because some silly fellows got carried away after some beers!"

"You need to be seen to be obeying the minister, that's all he wants. Then he will look like he's asserted himself and call his hooligans off."

"So you think I must bow to bullying and thuggery?"

"If it means you stay safe, yes. You can still sell the book abroad."

"But what message does that send to all these young men? Is this how a society should be? We need voices in this country. All voices must be heard, not just this one angry majority. The young in this country have been told such warped stories about themselves, about their nation, they must be enabled to hear the views of others – even such small contributions as my personal effort. How can I let them see me cowed? Silenced by one petty act of aggression?"

Jarryd always had been stubborn, and idealistic – but they were all guilty of that, they who had set out to define a life in a place of wonder, on the magical isle that reached deep into their longing hearts. But there would always be people, people who did not see, who did not understand. One day Jarryd would accept the precariousness of his rooting, and accept like Gerhardt that the dream must fade before the reality of their borrowed belonging.

"Would you like to join me in morning puja?" Jarryd asked.

"No, I should be heading back."

"Make sure you talk to Padma and find out what's going on," Jarryd said.

"Is something going on?"

"I don't know, but you must talk to her."

Gerhardt was aware of the presence of secrets, an invisible buried threat, as yet unthreatening. He was helpless to unearth it; all he could do was help Padma to leave, to go with his blessing to wherever she needed.

"I should get back to my guesthouse duties," Gerhardt said standing up to go.

"Good luck with your guests!" Jarryd chuckled.

"Hopefully they'll be out hunting their daughter when I get back."

Jarryd stood between the pillars of his veranda, a tall lone column of his own, as Gerhardt turned to wave before driving away.

# 30

U P AT THE house, Nimmy and Prakash were still seated at breakfast when Gerhardt returned from Jarryd's. They looked strangely unhurried, although it was late-morning. Prakash calmly read Gerhardt's morning papers and Nimmy sat scraping out the last of her paw paw. As Soma brought Gerhardt a glass of king coconut water, Nimmy started on scrambled eggs, thumping out Heinz tomato ketchup and eating gazing placidly over the garden.

"Anjali said there were mynahs," she murmured. "There are three over there – look, Prakash."

"Ah, yes," Prakash agreed, not looking up from the newspaper.

"This *has* to be where she stayed," Nimmy said. "I'm sure if we search hard enough we'll find someone who remembers her. We could go for a walk and ask in all the cafés – what do you think?"

She looked hopefully across the table, but Prakash carried on reading.

"I take it you don't want to try and find her? Prakash?"

"Huh?"

"Aren't we looking for her anymore?"

"Today? No. I have work to do."

He put down the paper and began making notes on a document

beside his plate with a silver Mont Blanc pen. He worked with an intensity of focus, the kind Gerhardt knew.

How many times a young Ruth had playfully yet wilfully disturbed him as he tried to work; Nimmy's tight-lipped resignation reminded him. And he glimpsed now the rejection that Ruth might sometimes have felt. Ronny had only ever worked enough to achieve success; never more; he had never let himself be driven by the work. Nimmy sullenly watched Prakash writing, his big pale hand moving over the pages, making smooth blue inky strokes. Gerhardt edged indoors.

"Gerhardt?" Nimmy called and he turned back slowly. "Anjali mentioned a nice chicken curry you do here – with potatoes, she said, and quite spicy. A red curry, I think, not black. I also would like to try it, if I may."

"Okay, I'll tell the cook."

"Thank you." She smiled, restored by that most modest of attentions.

She spread her toast with red watermelon jam, swinging her feet under the table.

"Before you go, Gerhardt, could I possibly use your scanner?" Prakash asked.

"We don't have one here," Gerhardt said.

This was a lie, but Gerhardt knew that he must not let Prakash cross the threshold of the office. It would lead almost certainly to further intrusion. One would never be let off serving such a man.

"You don't have a *scanner?*" Prakash exclaimed.

"No, it's all rather basic here, I'm afraid."

"Printer then?"

"Sorry, the printer's not working at the moment. You could try the café up the road."

"Is it secure? I have highly confidential papers to send."

"Confidential? Then I definitely wouldn't. Why not go into town, to the hotel?"

"A hotel? Now that's an idea." Prakash looked pointedly in Nimmy's direction.

"Yes, send the scan from there," she agreed vaguely.

"Well then, Gerhardt, could I trouble you to arrange some transport? I'd rather leave the car here," Prakash requested.

"Of course."

"I need it immediately. Perhaps you could send your help to fetch a taxi from the top of the lane? It might be quicker than phoning."

Soma was not impressed by this new task, but he didn't protest, just as he had agreed to make lunch for the guests. He seemed already to know, without Gerhardt having to tell him, of Prakash's leading role as a senior Government official – a fact that Gerhardt had discovered through searching the internet. Had Soma deduced it from Prakash's cold-eyed aloofness, his air of unquestioning superiority and dismissive arrogant gaze as one spoke with him? Gerhardt had noted with some discomfort Soma's subservience towards the new guests as he waited on them at mealtimes. It was undignified, not only for Soma, but for Prakash too, to profit so easily from the threat of his power. Power in Sri Lanka had corroded its people. Surely it was through learned respected figures such as Prakash that change could be effected for everyone, yet they did nothing for the country, merely prospered alone. They were no better principled than the ambitious and uneducated rising through bribes and favours and mutual pacts of corruption. What use was an education if it failed to inculcate the moral?

Prakash left for their room and returned wearing a more formal shirt and carrying an elegant leather briefcase. He sat with Nimmy and waited for the taxi as Gerhardt hovered nearby, feeling he should be of assistance.

"I'm sorry about all this," Prakash told Nimmy. "But this is an extremely urgent case."

"You always have an urgent case," Nimmy said. "It's impossible to have a holiday with you."

"*Holiday?* I didn't realise we were on holiday! *Here* of all pla—" Prakash stopped, remembering Gerhardt. "I thought we were here on a mission!" He added an awkward laugh.

"Why should only Anjali get to travel and have holidays? Maybe I also want to be taken to places now and again," Nimmy said, just as the taxi stopped at the gate.

"I'll be back as soon as I can," Prakash said, hurrying to the door. "Don't wait for me if you want lunch, I might have to stay for a response from these people."

"Alright. Take care."

Nimmy sat watching as Prakash climbed into the taxi and it drove away.

"This is what it's like," she told Gerhardt. "People think it's all official functions and glamorous parties, but *this* is what it's like for the rest of the time. It's impossible. At least before, my daughter and I could have gone shopping or sightseeing or something."

"I can see you miss her. It's so hard when they leave."

"But yours is coming back next week!"

"Not for long. Once she has her yoga teaching certificate, she'll be off travelling, I hope."

She would have gone sooner if he and Ruth hadn't intervened. Ruth had dragged her to parties and thrown sophisticated soirées in her grand house - all in the hope of Padma encountering eligible young men, and women to grow networks with, but Padma had run away from the crowd to hide. Ruth would complain about her sitting chatting with the chaperones, the mothers and old aunts drinking tea in the back rooms. On one occasion Gerhardt had found her alone on a balcony overlooking the beach and the old railway line, and they had stood together in the dark, watching the trains rattle by with their last lone passengers. Poor Padma. Neither Gerhardt nor Ruth had been much help to her in the past years. If only he hadn't made things worse by building her a guest house. Sometimes the best one could do for one's child was to step away, to know when to give up.

"Yoga teacher training?" Nimmy was unimpressed. "Another one wanting to teach. What is the matter with them all? You don't mind her not having a career?"

"Teaching yoga is a career."

"But how will she make a living when she's older? These days a girl can't just rely on a husband to look after her."

"Yoga doesn't have an age limit, as far as I know."

"Everything has an age limit. Nobody wants you for anything when you're old, especially we women."

"But you're not old!"

She didn't reply. She scratched at a jam stain on the tablecloth.

"The one thing nobody can take away is an education," she said. "It was always the boys in my family who got to go to Oxbridge. We girls had to fight simply to be allowed to go to any university at all."

She wiped her finger clean in a corner of her napkin.

"My sister and I were the first women in the family to get degrees – from Colombo, not Oxford. And what was the point, you might ask, we only had careers for the brief window before marriage, and after that came the pressure to produce children and of course look after them. The great myth of the fulfil-ment of women – the endless giving of ourselves. And after-wards, it's too late for us to do anything – that's the joke of it." Her eyes shone with terror and rage. "You talk of joy and pride, but having children is the end. For a woman it is a kind of death."

Gerhardt longed to show her in some small way that all was not lost.

"If that young woman who was here was your daughter, then I can assure you, you have done something very wonderful, you can be very proud of her."

Nimmy listened intently.

"To have brought such a loving, passionate young person into the world, someone so determined to help others—"

"Do you know where my daughter is, Gerhardt? Because I get the distinct impression you know her better than you're letting on," Nimmy said.

"Oh no, no, I know nothing of your daughter!"

All he knew was that with Dan Anjali was adored and enabled, basking in the love that only a lover could give.

"Anjali thinks she's in love," Nimmy said. "She's all flushed with this so-called romance of hers – she thinks that kind of thing lasts forever."

"For some it does."

"What nonsense!"

"Call me an old fool, but I still believe in love. Your daughter and her boyfriend might make each other very happy for a long time, if not forever."

"We have different views of love in the East. For us, marriage is a commitment, a clear-headed decision – none of this whirlwind romance nonsense. Everybody knows that kind of thing never lasts. Look at all the divorces in the West. You have to choose a partner carefully. How can you just rely on feelings?"

Feelings were the one true guide: delicate, ephemeral, faltering, but still the only light to follow. He thought of Rohan listening as Padma talked of her visit to the Ellora caves with Gerhardt and Ruth. They had followed the guide to the cave with the giant Dancing Shiva and stopped before it, speechless. He had felt such an overwhelming sense of elation then gratitude, moved to tears before that greatness and the humbling devotion of unknown ancient masters making their art. Padma, Ruth and he had been joined in that perfect moment, full of gladness for what they had seen and being there together. Padma had chosen to share it with Rohan, she had guessed that he would understand. And he had – the statue was proof. How rare it was, such accord; it had to be nurtured. He had done wrong to interfere; Padma and Rohan had to find their way back to each other.

"Of course, it's easy to be fanciful at the start," Nimmy reflected. "The men do make an effort then – oh yes, even Prakash. We used to go out every evening for months before our engagement. He used to come for me at my parents' house on his little scooter, and after dinner we'd go to see a film, then ice cream later." Nimmy gave a harsh little laugh. "It was all very innocent in those days. Straight home afterwards. Not even any hand-holding in case anyone saw you."

It was fear that stopped one letting a child go – fear of hurts and betrayals that might befall them. But there were other quieter, more secret fears; the fears one had to own: fears of losing and being left behind, such were the terrors of aging.

"I can't sit here all day waiting for Prakash!" Nimmy exclaimed, rousing herself. "Anjali mentioned a nice view from the top of a rock – I might take a look, myself."

"Ah, the rock temple."

"Rock temple? Not *Sudhugala Temple?*"

"Yes, that's the one!"

"But it's where that awful priest went! I told her categorically not to go anywhere near him, but she's totally disregarded my instructions!" Nimmy was incredulous.

"Which awful priest is this?"

"The new head priest, of course! The *only* priest there, thank goodness – at least he can't corrupt anybody. He was thrown out of Colombo for misconduct – an *affair*, would you believe, with a woman much younger than himself – an ex-nun. Can you imagine such a thing? And he was one of the most learned men you could meet. I tell you, this country is going to the dogs. I can't believe Anjali's been to see him – I can't imagine what that awful individual would have said to her—"

"Young people these days know more about these things than we care to imagine," Gerhardt tried to console Nimmy, but she looked affronted.

"Call me a taxi will you please, Gerhardt. I am also going to see that view from the rock – why should it only be Anjali doing what she wants. Even the clergy are doing whatever they like these days – why not me? I don't have to visit the priest – if I see him, I'll just look the other way."

"That really is quite a climb, you know. Shall I organise a guide for you? He may not be available immediately, but give him an hour—"

"No, no, I have no need of a guide, I'm not an invalid! I'll be fine as long as I stay clear of the temple. Just call me a taxi."

She marched inside, a woman possessed by a new fire, emerging several minutes later in a sun hat, pressed linen trousers, a blouse buttoned up to the chin and impossibly white trainers.

"Right, where's that taxi?" she demanded, her eyes crazed with adventure.

She returned in time for lunch, grim-faced and gleaming with sweat. Her hair frizzed furiously, escaped from her bun; the white trainers covered in the red soil of inland.

"I don't suppose Prakash is back?" she demanded as Gerhardt came out to greet her.

"Not yet. How was your trip?"

"Totally bloody useless - you're right, we're far too old to be climbing rocks. I almost fell and broke my neck trying to get up that stupid ladder. I had to give up." She fanned herself with her hat. "Did you manage to convince your boy to make us some lunch?"

"Yes, it's all ready - shall I ask him to serve it?"

"Not yet, I'll wait until Prakash gets here. Could you ask the boy to bring me a bottle of water? Nice and chilled, please. Tell him to leave it outside my room, on the table, no need to knock. I'll take it when I'm ready."

She walked stiffly into the house.

She was showered and changed and seemingly fully restored by the time Prakash returned. They sat down to a late lunch of vegetable curries, fish curry and rice.

"This is good fish," Prakash declared. "You know, you're right, Nimmy, in a way, this does feel like a holiday, now that I've settled the case. It was a very satisfactory outcome, if I say so myself. At last I can relax. Let's make it a holiday, we might as well—"

"How can we relax?" Nimmy snapped.

"But this morning you said—"

"This morning was this morning. Now it's this afternoon and soon it will be evening and your daughter is still running around the countryside going wild. It's no use sitting about, we have to go into the village and talk to more people. Someone must know something."

They didn't stay for dessert. Gerhardt ate his mango in the office, watching from the window the two rush out into the scorching whiteness of the afternoon. He refused to imagine where they might go, whom they might talk to, how close they would come to finding Anjali. Padma must never long to run from him, the way Anjali had; to have to hide to free herself. She had to go out into the world and find the love and generosity of others, and never have to fear the price of a gift. He set up his drawing board on the veranda like in the old days, a new white page stretched over it. As always the thrilling blankness met him, challenging him and pulling him in.

## 31

O N THE DAY before the final yoga teaching assessment, classes finished early at the institute. Padma took a tuk-tuk back to Ruth's, but as they came close to a certain turning off the main road, she gave the driver a new address. He darted obligingly across oncoming traffic into the lane of large stately houses where Rohan's parents lived. She made him stop before they reached the house and asked him to wait while she approached the house alone. There was no one to be seen, no cars parked in the driveway. Pale curtains were drawn behind elegant dark-framed windows sealed against the midday heat, and the dust and noise. She paused at the gate. There was no barking, no sign warning of dogs. She went to the front door, hesitating before ringing the bell.

"Yes?" Someone had come around the side of the house, a woman, hostile, wary. "Everyone's gone out," the woman told Padma.

Padma had no role at that house; she had no claim there. The maid could tell. Padma always felt that something of the village remained in her on such occasions – a giveaway sign of her first life that marked her and revealed her to those who looked for such signs: the arrogant affluent elite and those who served them.

"Who do you want to see?" the woman asked Padma.

"Is Rohan here?"

"They'll all be back after lunch."

The woman was a maid, Padma decided, from the woman's unremarkable clothes and un-styled hair tied impatiently back from her face, which itself was unadorned and uncared for. Very little else distinguished the woman from Padma; they were probably the same age and probably the maid came from a village just like the one Padma had come from. Would Rohan see this about her if he saw her now? The family would not welcome her in, Padma sensed; the flawless white house frowned down on her, the heavily-curtained windows repelled her intrusion.

"Who shall I say came?" the maid asked, as Padma retreated.

"It's okay, I'll try again later."

The maid eyed her suspiciously. The white-painted stones at the edge of the path were bleached to nothingness in the sun. The iron gate was hot, clanging shut behind her. The maid bolted it at once. The tuk-tuk driver was waiting, lying back in his seat, his legs up on the dashboard. He scrambled to sit up as she got back in, and they returned to the main road. The hot diesel-tinged air buffeted her as she went towards the peace of the afternoon at Ruth's. And here, an email arrived later for Padma, from a Mrs Isobel de Souza, the owner of the yoga retreat in Goa, who, following a glowing reference from Ria, wanted to offer Padma a beginner's yoga class to teach the next month. It was Padma's first job offer, her first true success. She had got what she wanted now.

Gerhardt worked on the veranda, deep into the afternoon. He was designing a retreat by a lake near Galle for an American musician. Gerhardt had envisioned a raised wooden building with windows looking out over jungle to blue skies, and a veranda to sit with the lake below. He had been thinking of huts high in the mountains of his childhood and he saw again the clear blue skies of autumn, the giant rocks rising to a bright white summit, almost impossible to reach. After all the years of tropical green and rooms opened onto courtyards and gardens, as he prepared to relinquish his villa to strangers, he was drawn back to the interiors of his past, to the safety of those intimate spaces.

A car pulled up outside the gates. It was Nimmy and Prakash. They came up the path, talking in low urgent voices. Something was different about them. Something had happened Gerhardt started to pack away, suddenly longing for the office.

"Ah, Gerhardt, just the man," Prakash said, with icy displeasure. They came to stand before the drawing board, side by side the two united against him.

"We understand that you arrange property rentals?" Prakash said.

"Yes, that's right." His heart jolted and skipped, beating too hard.

Just think if he had a heart attack because of these people. It would serve him right for getting himself involved in their problems.

"We thought maybe you'd arranged a property for our daughter to rent?" Nimmy took over the questioning. "A man in the village seemed to think you had."

"I've arranged quite a lot of rentals, recently."

"I'm sure you would remember my daughter."

"I'm an old man, my memory is not what it used to be. As it is, I seem to have confused several young women with your daughter."

They didn't believe him. Their animosity pinned him down. He struggled against them, trying to get free. How astonishing, the power of such resentment, this desire to control. What fury they felt for the young vibrant life that had broken loose from them. He wanted them gone, but they would never leave. They would stay until they had what they wanted.

"You know, now that I think of it, I may well know where your daughter is," he said.

"Ah, so you *do*, remember her. I thought you might," Nimmy said.

"I'm not sure if it's her - after all, many people pass through here, which is why I didn't mention it earlier—"

"Yes, yes, just hand us the address," Prakash interrupted.

"Let me see now, it was a rental I arranged a few weeks ago, for a young couple - a Sri Lankan woman, I believe, and a young man from—"

"We don't need a biography! If you could just give us the address, we can be on our way at once," Prakash said.

"Of course. I'll have a look through my paperwork."

"We'll help you," Nimmy said.

"There's nothing I would like more, but clients' details are confidential, I'm afraid," Gerhardt said as he slipped out from behind the drawing board.

"My goodness, what a lot of progress we have made in a single afternoon," Nimmy observed as he went to the office.

"Come Prakash, let's pack!" She led the way to their room.

From the office Gerhardt could hear her sandals thwacking on the floor as she marched around the guest room, extracting their possessions. He went out to meet them once more on the veranda and Prakash checked the bill, paying in cash.

"Keep the change," he said loftily, taking the notepaper Gerhardt offered him with the address of his first rental cottage.

"I don't know what exactly happened here with my daughter,

Gerhardt, but at least you finally helped us find her," Nimmy said nobly.

"Nothing happened. She was merely a guest."

"Nonetheless, you felt the need to conceal the fact, don't deny it. It took a considerable amount of probing on our part to find out. Don't worry, I want you to know there are no hard feelings."

"Thank you."

He waited in the house, not seeing them to their car. He heard the engine start up then the sound of them driving away. At last they were gone. He was left with the weight of their emptiness, the loneliness of their hunger. It hung in the rooms of the villa; there was nothing there anymore to console him. The villa seemed to sense its abandonment by him. He felt it recede from him and let him go.

⚜

They stopped the car in a village lane. Nimmy got out first and looked over the fence at the cottage.

"Come, Prakash," she called impatiently.

He was dilly-dallying in the car, looking for an excuse to stay inside while she did all their dirty work. She waited until he joined her. In front of the house was a small garden, its lawn only roughly mown, the edges left unclipped. A tangle of pale purple bougainvillea grew wild over the porch. A Nepalese paper lantern hung around the porch light, long red tassels blowing in the wind.

"What a place to be living," Nimmy muttered.

She felt suddenly hesitant, even afraid – of what? Of Anjali? Whoever heard of a mother being afraid of her daughter?

"You go in, Prakash. She'll only get angry if she sees me," Nimmy stepped back from the gate.

"I'm not sure we should have come like this," Prakash said,

backing away from the gate as well. "Let's just go. We've seen where she's staying, it looks fine to me."

"And leave with our tails between our legs?"

"What do you plan on doing anyway? She won't simply get into the car and come back with us."

"Oh yes she will! And I'm going to give her a good piece of my mind while we're at it. As if we didn't have better things to do than to be driving around the countryside looking for her."

Prakash stood looking at the house. He seemed nervous and unsure, rather undistinguished, in fact, standing there hesitating, shuffling his feet like an old man. What a way to behave. This is what Anjali had reduced them to. Nimmy pushed past Prakash and swung open the gate. She went into the garden.

"What are you doing? We should wait a little before barging in like a bull in a china shop," Prakash grumbled.

"No one's barging anywhere, we're just visiting!"

He followed her into the garden and they stood behind a giant camellia bush that had turned unruly, left to grow in all directions and covered in fleshy, pink flowers. A young man came out of the house.

"Who's that?" Prakash whispered.

"How should I know? Must be some friend of theirs."

Whoever it was hadn't seen them. He disappeared behind the house.

"Look at the types she's mixing with now - his hair is all matted. Dreadlocks, they call it - they do it on purpose, never washing or combing their hair. Fine thing, for a girl from a good family to be hanging around people like that."

Just then a young Asian woman came out of the house and went where the man had gone.

"Who on earth are these people?" Prakash muttered.

The couple came back with plates, glasses, beer bottles and a saucepan – the remnants of an outdoor meal. They stopped, seeing Nimmy and Prakash.

"Very sorry to disturb you, dears, but can we have a quick word with you?" Nimmy said, approaching the couple.

"You talk to them, Prakash," she instructed.

"Me? What am I to say?" he hissed. "Oh. Er . . . yes, hello." He almost bowed to the couple. He looked ridiculous – what was the matter with him? Surely he wasn't afraid of a pair of kids?

"Have you just been to visit Anjali and Dan?" Prakash asked.

"Anjali and Dan?" The man looked puzzled.

"I don't think they're here, Nimmy," Prakash said, smiling nervously at the couple.

So foolish, he looked. And it was all Anjali's fault. What a mockery she was making of them.

"There's no one here called Anjali or Dan," the woman said.

She was Sri Lankan, but she had an accent from England. She had an unfriendly look about her. She seemed thoroughly immodest, wearing the shortest pair of shorts Nimmy had ever seen, with no bra under her vest – and she certainly needed a bra with a figure like hers. What people Anjali associated with these days. No polish whatsoever! Drinking beer in the daytime, and no doubt smoking and doing drugs as well. Had Anjali gone the same way? The couple looked tense.

"What is this about?" the young man said.

"Who lives here?" Prakash asked.

"We do," the woman said, so rudely.

She had no manners, no class, no breeding. Was she covering up for Anjali? Was Anjali hiding in the house? Maybe Gerhard had telephoned to warn them. Or . . . Nimmy gasped, understanding at last.

"He's tricked us," she said.

"Who?" the couple demanded.

"Gerhardt's sent us on a wild goose chase," Nimmy told Prakash.

"Nonsense! Why would he do that?"

"Why indeed!"

"Excuse me, what exactly is going on here?" The man was English, not American and the woman was nowhere near as pretty as Anjali. There was no way Gerhardt had mistaken these two for Anjali and Dan.

"Someone told us our daughter was living here," Prakash explained. "There's been a misunderstanding."

"It *could* have been a mistake," Nimmy reflected. "After all, one mixed-race couple might look like another to him."

The couple looked startled. The woman was frowning. There was no need to get so high and mighty; Nimmy had merely stated a fact. If the proverbial cap fitted, one had to put it on.

"We're very sorry to have troubled you," Prakash said, and once more he was acting all sheepish in front of those unpromising young people.

"Come, Nimmy. Enough. We're going home." Prakash gripped her arm, steering her back to the car. She pulled out of his clasp – who did he think he was, dragging her off like a naughty child? As if he was so much calmer than her. It was strange though, to feel him hold her; to be held by him. In public they never touched, and at home there was never time, and a certain habit of shrinking back just enough to avoid clashing, that had crept into their movements when they were together, which was not often. She blamed his constant busyness – there was always something he had to do, all the emails and phone calls and top-secret messages that couldn't wait.

She sat in the car that had already become hot and stifling.

"Right, turn around, back to the villa!" Nimmy commanded. "I'm going to give that man a piece of my mind!"

But Prakash kept driving straight on. He didn't look at her.

The grimness of his expression silenced her. She let him drive out of the village and onto the main road and start the long drive back to Colombo. He looked straight ahead at the road with its shimmering cloud of heat up ahead. It was impossible to know what he was thinking.

"Not once in all my years have I been so humiliated. By my own daughter – a salutary lesson."

The air-conditioning took over, cooling the car to a comfortable chill. Outside, villages paused in the afternoon were left behind; dogs dozing in gardens, children playing in the shade of verandas. In the paddy fields, the women worked stooped over in the long green lushness. Silent, distant, the world safely removed, Nimmy felt her mind grow still, her head stopped throbbing, even the ache in her legs from the terrible climb up the rock, eased away.

"I felt so ashamed just then," Prakash said.

The anger had left his voice. He seemed tired, as if resigned to a defeat. But he was never defeated – one of his most admired qualities was that he never gave up.

"The two of us acting like a pair of criminals, creeping around that garden was the lowest I'm going to sink on Anjali's behalf. I don't even know what I would have said to her if she'd been there. I'm done, I'm not battling her anymore – she's keeping in touch, she says she's fine, so let her be. That old fool Gerhardt has done us a favour, as far as I'm concerned."

"You're not going to try finding out where she is?"

"I don't *want* to know. If this is what she wants, then fine. We've done everything we can for her. She can regret her decision all by herself one day."

"You're still angry. See – this is what she's done to us. I also am angry. After all the sacrifices we've made for her. So little gratitude! Is this how a daughter should behave?"

"Actually, it's that idiot Gerhardt I'm angry at. Acting like some great pundit on child-rearing, sitting in his ramshackle house—"

"Oh I know! People like him have no standards."

"The whole place gave me a bad feeling," Prakash said.

Nimmy gazed towards him, relieved. So it hadn't just been her feeling unsettled by the guesthouse.

"What a way to end up, scraping any old work together." Prakash shook his head. "As if *he* ever had any important commercial projects! I don't think I'll even bother checking out that story. Did you see the so-called designs he was working on? It was some kind of shack. Maybe it's for a fisherman."

This made Nimmy laugh.

"Why not strive to make something impressive, even at this late stage in life?" Prakash went on. "He's only ten – maybe fifteen years older than me – that's all the time I have left to leave my mark. It's terrifying, frankly."

"*You'll* never be like him, Prakash, what a thing to suggest!"

How could Prakash possibly harbour such doubts? Yet it was strangely soothing to know that he too had those fears, those dizzying, terrifying moments of uncertainty and irresolution, the long puzzling trail back to whom you had been once and to this self now that you had become, that you had wanted to be. But how could Prakash, of all people, doubt what he had achieved? He turned to her, giving her a sudden smile of gratitude that brought back an older, more united time. A time when he had needed her and desired her opinion and approval for the decisions he had to make. Her encouragement had certainly steadied his first steps up the craggy slopes of his brilliant career. She had played a part in that climb past so many, to a success unimaginable – even fantastical – to the rest of the family.

She watched the road run on in the heat, the far-away wavering line beckoning them home to their house, so big and fine and quite splendid, in fact, – a great leap on from their first home on a too-shaded plot and smaller than her sister's, in a rather down-trodden neighbourhood of the city.

"Do you want to go out this evening when we get back?" Prakash asked. "How about somewhere really nice? I feel like it, after that bloody guest house. How about Pierre-Gerrards?"

"*Pierre-Gerrards?*"

"Why not? I can get us a table. A few strings pulled now and again can't do any harm!"

"But won't you be too tired?"

"Not in the slightest. In fact, I need to do something to shake off that awful place."

"The cobwebs?" she joked.

"Indeed." He smiled. They had often laughed together in the old days. He had liked her sense of humour, even though he called it cruel.

"Not to mention the clouds of dust on that mosquito net," he said.

"What a useless net that was – holes big enough for an elephant to come through, let alone the mosquitoes."

"We shouldn't poke fun," Prakash said. "The old guy has obviously made a total failure of his little business venture – not to mention his paltry cottages. Imagine ending up designing shacks for fishermen!"

They sniggered together, like naughty children. She was glad to put that strange Gerhardt well behind them. Nothing he said had made any sense – but then people stuck out in the wilds were bound to be backward. She wasn't missing anything. Anjali was welcome to people like that.

## 32

AFTER THE FINAL Yoga Teaching assessment, Padma and the other trainees went for a farewell tea to a South Indian café across the road from the institute. They shared a large platter of potato bhondas and two types of vada: the crisp-skinned doughnut ulundu vadas, and Padma's favourite crunchy lentil vadas, and drank chai tea or pink rose-scented faludas or thick sweet mango lassis. Everybody exchanged email addresses, promising to connect on Facebook and Instagram and to like each other's business pages. Padma still didn't speak of the retreat in Goa. Someone mentioned it in passing, and she listened wide-eyed and anxious as they discussed the facilities for staff, and wages, and even as she longed to reveal her news and see them turn admiringly to her, she was too afraid to speak. Betrayal lurked close behind success; there was always someone wanting what you had, wanting to take it from you. Some people seemed only to ever want what others had, and didn't stop until they had taken it from you. Afterwards they all said goodbye, hugging outside on the pavement, promising to meet again. Maybe some would. For now there was only the villa for Padma. If only she dared to accept the job and boldly go to Goa. If only she could have known that it would be a success and turn out well, but there was so much she couldn't know.

Everyone left. After the waving and shouting she found herself alone in a taxi heading back to Ruth's. She had hoped to buy a gift for her so she stopped at Barefoot, her favourite shop in Colombo. She lingered among the rolls of bright cloth with their scent of new cotton. Jazz played softly on the stereo. In another room she roamed around rails of skirts, blouses, dresses, kaftans made of the bold strong handloom fabric that the shop was famous for. She chose a red and blue silk shawl for Ruth and bought a necklace for herself. For the first time, Padma didn't want to go back to the villa. Leela had drawn her into a new silence of unease and slyness, moving money around accounts and lying to everyone. The new secrets swarmed over her, an infestation. She tried naming her feelings as Jarryd had taught her to in meditation: Anger. Anger. Betrayal. Sadness. Was it possible that Leela had been telling the truth about her illness? Could she and Hema Amme's sister have grown sick at the same time with the same condition? And even if Leela had lied, wasn't it only because she was desperate to escape Sunny? After years of living with him she would only have known his way of getting what she needed. Padma decided to talk once more with Leela They would start again with the truth, and Padma would make Leela understand that Padma would never betray her.

Padma looked over a grey cotton sari with a delicate maroon and gold embroidered border. She remembered Leela mending clothes in the afternoons, sitting outside in the shade: re-hemming frayed edges, re-attaching hooks, stitching tears closed. The straggling thatch of Leela's darning had spread over her blouses and skirts until the cloth thinned to almost nothing, then Leela ripped the clothes into strips and rolled them into wicks to take to temple for the oil lamps. Padma would hide behind the trees in the temple garden and watch Leela place the wicks in the burned-out lamps, pouring in coconut oil she had brought in an old medicine bottle wrapped in a hanky to catch the drips. The lamp's flame would come to life, in the line of lamps on an iron stand thick with grease. What had Leela wished for before that wavering brightness? Padma would follow her to the shrine rooms of the Hindu gods, where Leela would kneel earnestly praying before a picture of Goddess Laxmi surrounded by lotuses and pots of gold coins, a plastic flower garland draped over the greasy gilt frame. Padma bought the grey sari for Leela and added a piece of matching grey blouse material. For some time now, she had wanted to give Leela a gift – something beautiful but not overwhelming, carefully chosen. She would have to find the right way to offer it, for they had no history of giving gifts.

Ruth had returned early from an afternoon wedding, and was waiting for Padma at the house, the table laid for tea.

"A celebratory dinner will follow later," Ruth announced, pouring out milk and tea into fine China cups and cutting up a Green Cabin chocolate cake.

Padma took a small slice. It had been her favourite tea time treat as a child, a chocolate sponge cake covered and filled with chocolate buttercream. Ruth and Ronny had brought a Green Cabin chocolate cake with them when they first came to meet her, rushing down to see the child that Gerhardt had suddenly acquired. She had eaten half the cake in one sitting, much to their amazement, and from then on they had couriered a chocolate cake in a cool box to the villa every week, along with a package of clothes and toys and Clarke's shoes and Enid Blyton books.

"I see you went to Barefoot, did you buy anything nice?" Ruth asked, seeing Padma's bags.

"A present for you!"

Ruth beamed, admiring the shawl and wore it at once.

"And for you? What did you get?"

"This necklace."

"Lovely. And a sari? Is that a sari in the bag?"

"Oh yeah, it's just something I quite liked." Padma held the bag closed.

"Let me see!" Ruth tugged at it and Padma was forced to relinquish it.

Ruth examined the sari with a frown.

"It's a little dull, don't you think? When you're young you can wear bright colours—"

"There's red in the border, and gold—"

"But it's grey! It's very muted for Barefoot - they usually have such beautiful colours. Why go for a fuddy duddy old-lady sari?"

"Actually, I was thinking of giving it as a gift." It was a relief to drop the pretence.

"To whom?"

Padma hesitated. This was new territory.

"Who's the sari for?" Ruth pressed, sensing a secret.

"I thought I might give it to Leela."

"Leela? You're not taking it to her yourself, I hope?"

"No, of course not, I'll post it."

Sending a letter through Hema Amme, asking to meet, was almost like post. Hema Amme couldn't be trusted to deliver an expensive sari, but she would deliver a note to Leela, and when Leela came Padma would question her until she had confessed.

"It's nice of you to think of Leela, but don't get dragged into anything," Ruth said.

"I won't."

"Don't let yourself be distracted, especially now that you've got started on your yoga. Just imagine, our girl a fully-fledged yoga teacher!"

"If I've passed."

"Of course you've passed. I've seen you, you're wonderful!"

Padma smiled. She had always thought Ruth would be

disappointed if Padma didn't progress to a high-flying career, like the children of her friends, but Ruth had seemed genuinely proud when Padma chose to complete her training.

"Just like Gerhardt," Ruth had said wonderingly. "You're so alike! You both know exactly what you want to be doing, following your own path!"

"Were you sending Leela a present for a reason?" Ruth asked now.

"Not really." Padma started up the stairs.

Ruth came with her and sat on the bed while Padma packed the grey sari into her suitcase.

"I never knew what to make of Leela," Ruth said.

"I didn't know you'd met her."

"Just once. A long time ago, at the attorney's office when Sunny came for his cash. Ronny and I wanted to see for ourselves what was going on. Of course Gerhardt never went, he always tried to forget about the unsavoury side of the arrangement."

Padma herself used to flinch from the mention of those irregular dealings, but she saw now that they had been necessary, like certain painful injections.

"Gerhardt was always afraid that Sunny would change his mind," Ruth said. "So he avoided any contact with him, but Ronny wanted to see Sunny for himself. Ronny was convinced that Gerhardt was storing up trouble for later. I went just to see what kind of person gave up a lovely girl like you."

"But how did you meet Leela? I thought only Sunny came to collect the money?"

"The time I went, they were both there. Leela hung around in the road while Sunny came into the lawyer's office. Quite brazen he was, not at all ashamed. He didn't seem bothered that Ronny and I were there. While he was with the lawyer and Ronny, I went outside to talk to Leela."

"You spoke with Leela?"

"Oh yes. She's a strange one, that's for sure. Do you know, I even offered her a job here so she could leave Sunny and get to see you regularly, but she wasn't interested."

"Maybe you took her by surprise. She wouldn't have known what to think."

"I was very clear that I would look after her."

But Sunny would never have let Leela go, and Leela would never have defied him. "She was probably afraid," Padma said.

"No, no she didn't seem frightened at all. I remember she gave me a rather contemptuous smile. It was very odd. It was as if she was thinking how stupid I was, like I had got everything wrong. I did sometimes wonder if she wasn't the real boss out of the two of them."

"No way! Sunny's the one in charge! Leela must have been afraid he'd see her talking to you. Sunny can get really angry."

His anger was silent, invisible; it had a way of seeming to have slipped away before it struck hardest. She remembered the smoothness of his hands tightening around her throat, and in his eyes the bright dancing madness seeing her fear and knowing he was hurting her. She had seen the desire in him to hurt her more – a longing almost too strong for him to resist. How could she ever tell Ruth about that night? Or Gerhardt? She felt ashamed of her powerlessness, her naivety in thinking she was safe, and turning her back. Her silence joined her to him, she was alone in the darkness of that night.

"Leela never seemed like an abused wife to me," Ruth said.

"Like you know any abused wives."

"One thing I know is that like attracts like, not opposites. Leela is no innocent, not by a long shot."

"You don't know that."

But Padma knew that Ruth listened when people spoke, and she heard the unspoken. She saw through to what pooled and festered underneath.

"I'm sorry if that upsets you, darling," Ruth said.

"No, you're probably right."

Leela had forgotten how to be kind, she had forgotten about love and softness. Who wouldn't, living with a man like Sunny. Padma could guide her to another world, if only she could make Leela trust her.

⁂

Padma returned to the villa, a qualified yoga teacher. To Gerhardt she seemed older, her body taller, stronger, her arms more muscled, as she sat in a wicker basket chair that had been brought back to the veranda from the storage shed. The old dining table was also back, and the new tables and chairs for guests put away. Padma had not commented on the changes, she seemed barely to take them in. She sat gazing at the new Shiva statue, a faraway look in her eyes.

"So, have you made any plans?" Gerhardt asked.

"For what?"

"For teaching yoga. Ruth says many people do yoga in Colombo these days."

"There's no rush"

"Actually, there is. I have something to tell you – I've decided to rent out the villa."

"Our villa?"

"Yes."

"To whom?"

"Anyone who'd like it, as long as it's not the minister or his brother."

"But the guest house! We've only just opened." She looked anxious. "Have I done something wrong?"

"Not at all. None of this is your fault; I should never have pushed you into this."

She looked surprised but she didn't contradict him.

"Did you get to see Rohan in Colombo?" he asked.

"No, I didn't have time. I did email and thank him for the statue."

"It's a shame you didn't get to see each other again."

Padma gave him a strange look. "Didn't you say he wasn't serious? Just a holiday fling, right?"

"I was wrong. He clearly cares a lot for you."

"Well, he's going back soon anyhow." She turned to assess the statue.

"Why don't you ask the institute in Colombo if you could run a few classes?" he suggested.

"Maybe." She sat in her chair, unmoving. "I contacted that retreat place in Goa where Ria teaches," she said.

"Yes? And?"

"They've offered me a job in a few weeks."

"My goodness! Really? That is fantastic!"

"Is it? What am I going to do in Goa all by myself?"

She slumped in her chair looking indifferent. Yet she had arrived. It was the moment of flight. She had reached the edge of the nest, about to step off into nothingness. He had to help her. She had to learn to trust in flight; he would carry the safety of his net alongside her for a while, just while she needed him.

"I could come with you, " he offered.

"To Goa?"

"I'd like some time away from here, and I could bring my work. It would be good to have a change of scenery." He would stay until she was settled, then quietly leave.

"Do you really mean it?" she asked.

"Yes! Give them a call and say you'll come. And ask them for somewhere to stay – say it's for two people."

She was already reaching for her phone, her eyes wide with excitement.

꩜

The next morning Padma sat on the porch and wrote a letter to Leela, asking to meet. There was so much she wanted to say, but she couldn't write it in case Hema Amme saw or anyone else who might have got hold of the letter. A different silence filled the villa that morning, thick and restless. In the past it had always been a relief to return to Nilwatte Beach from the clamour of Colombo, the snarling horns of traffic, and voices of strangers shouting, begging. Her ears rang with their absence. Over the road, the sea was grey, with the waves grown lifeless, idle-looking. The garden cowered under chill gusts of wind running hard at the coconut trees, making them bend and sweep their branches in helpless bowing submission. Padma used to feel safe and contained on these cold, wild, monsoon mornings, with their glowering light and otherness, but that day they seemed a portent of change.

"What are you doing?" Soma asked, coming up behind her.

She hadn't heard him approach. She folded the note, casually, as if it were a simple shopping list. She stood up.

"Where are you off to?" he asked.

"To the stalls."

"Fine, let's go."

"You don't need to come. I won't be long."

"Gerhardt Mahaththaya told you not to go out alone."

"I'm only going to buy some kadala."

"I can get it for you."

"Soma! I can't stay locked up in here all day - it's like a prison!"

"Oh, fine, go then! Go on!"

"Thank you."

The path to the gate seemed shadier, more overgrown. It seemed as if Gerhardt had given up on the garden when he decided to rent the villa. She walked along the lane and she felt the same freedom as in Colombo, a sense of going away. She didn't care whom she met, she wasn't afraid. She reached Hema Amme's garden and rattled the gate. The dog snarled and danced and yacked in a frenzy until the old woman hobbled out of her house.

"What is it?" she croaked.

"I've got a note for Leela."

Hema Amme took it.

"How's Leela? Is she any better?" Padma asked.

"A little. If she keeps having the treatment I'm sure she'll be cured."

"Oh, and how's your sister? I hear she isn't very well?"

The old woman bent over the dog and inspected a black rounded growth at the back of its ear, squeezing its rubbery darkness.

"I heard your sister also has kidney trouble?" Padma persisted.

"Hmm?"

"Kidneys. Your sister. Is she better?"

"Oh, yes, much better. Just an infection they think. She'll be fine."

The shifting eyes in the shrunken old face were unreadable. But what exactly had Padma hoped for? A confession? A plea for forgiveness? The dog wandered away. The grey sky hung heavy over the dark little house.

"I have to go," Hema Amme said.

She was looking past Padma at someone in the lane, but when Padma turned around there was no one there. Hema Amme scuttled back to her house. Padma walked towards the top of the lane, turning to check behind her, but there was no Sunny, no Mukul, no spy. She longed to talk with Jarryd. There was so much to tell: Leela's lies and the good fortune of Goa. But it was the gift of the sari that bothered her most. Was it wrong to give it? Would Jarryd still insist that Padma forgive Leela when he knew about the lies that Leela had told? Padma needed him to tell her; she needed to know what she was: a good kind daughter, or just gullible.

"Is it true Gerhardt is selling the villa?" the kadala man asked her, up at the stalls.

Nothing was secret in Nilwatte Beach. It was only the thoughts in one's head they didn't reach. She rang Jarryd, but there was no answer. She left a message to say that she was coming round and went to the tuk-tuk rank and chose the least annoying driver – Pratik, a friend of Wilson's.

"Baba, it's going to rain, go visit Jarryd Sir another time," he said.

"Let's go now." She climbed in and sat waiting. Reluctantly Pratik started the engine and they drove through the village.

"Jarryd Sir is saying bad things in a book, no?" Pratik said as they started inland.

"It's hardly a book – he's just written a little pamphlet for tourists."

"Is that so? People are saying he's written lies about our country – that's not nice, no? After all, this isn't even his own country, we welcomed him in and now because of him people from abroad will think badly about all of us."

"He doesn't mean anyone any harm, he loves Sri Lanka," Padma protested.

"All I know is what people are saying. You should tell him to stop spreading rumours. Nobody likes people saying bad things about them, no? And after everything that our people have suffered, he shouldn't be making it worse."

"He's trying to help. He wants everyone to love Sri Lanka, just like him."

They reached Jarryd's gates. Pratik said he was too busy to drive up to the house and let Padma out on the road. He whirled around and sped away. As if Pratik had anything urgent to do – having a nap, more like. Well she was glad not to have him hanging around waiting. She needed to talk to Jarryd in peace to decide what to say to Leela.

"Jarryd!" she called into the house. "Geetha?"

She waited on the veranda. No one came. They were often busy; sometimes they were both over at the retreat. She waited, but still no one came. The doors were never locked. Padma went inside.

"Jarryd? Geetha?"

The house was silent. It felt empty. In the sitting room, there was a book of poetry on the floor by the sofa. On the coffee table was Jarryd's silver Moroccan teapot from which he drank mint tea at night. The pot had fallen over. A greenish dark stain was on the floor. The tea in the glass was cold.

"Jarryd?" she called.

The bedroom door was open. He would have closed it if he was with someone. Surely if he'd been asleep, he'd have heard her by now? She peered around the door. The bed was still made, a yellow and white striped handloom bedspread smoothed over, his blue baboushka slippers on the mat on the floor.

"Geetha?" Padma called in the hall, but she knew even before going round to the kitchen that the house was empty.

A house, even with its possessions intact, could feel unowned and abandoned. A vacuous quiet patiently waited in the rooms and the hall, so empty feeling. Padma could have claimed Jarryd's house right there, making it all hers, that yellow sitting room with its high shelves of books and carvings, and the corner where he had made himself a den to write his book, a desk and stool tucked into a recess lined with maps and notes and pages from magazines, a thick red curtain put up across to hide it from view if someone unsuitable came round. She looked into the dining room with its teak table and chairs, the red and black batiks hung against pure white walls. She could have taken over that house so lavished with care and attention; she could have settled in right then and no one would have resisted.

She stretched out on the sofa in the yellow sitting room and picked up a book from the floor. Was it occupancy alone that gave a house its life? Would their presence linger at the villa once they had gone: ghostly shadows of Gerhardt, Soma and her; an essence of their being lingering in rooms? Her phone rang. It was Soma. She didn't answer. She left the house, closing the doors of the veranda behind her. No one would ever know that she had been there. Only a book picked up, left on a chair could reveal her.

⊰❦⊱

Gerhardt returned early for lunch, but Padma was not at the villa.

"Where's Padma Baba? Is she sleeping?" he asked Soma.

"She went somewhere."

"On her own? But I told her not to—"

"She wouldn't listen, she just ran off."

Soma came closer.

"Sir, maybe Padma Baba is getting herself into trouble—"

"What sort of trouble?"

"When she went, I went behind her—"

"You followed her?"

"How else to find where she's going? She went to Hema Amme's house and gave her an envelope."

"What on earth for?"

"I don't know, sir."

Gerhardt's mind raced. Was it money in the envelope? Was Sunny using the old woman to extract money from Padma? But Gerhardt had offered him far more than Padma would ever have. He couldn't see how anything fitted.

"Where is she now?"

"I don't know, sir, she took a tuk-tuk somewhere."

"To where?"

"I don't know, maybe she went to see Jarryd Sir? I can go and find out from the drivers?"

"No need, I'll talk to her."

Why hadn't she talked already with him? They had always been so open with each other. Gerhardt sat trying to understand.

"Sir, shall I bring the lunch?" Soma asked.

"No, just some water. I'll wait for Padma."

He tried ringing her phone, but she didn't answer. He walked in the garden, trying to be calm. Ruth had telephoned the night before to warn him to watch out for Leela. Ruth was convinced that Padma might be involved with Leela somehow. Gerhardt hadn't seen Leela in a great many years, not even the morning after the party at her house when Gerhardt went to fetch Padma. He walked over now to Hema Amme's house. She came when he called, stopping halfway before she reached the gate.

"Where's Padma?" he asked.

"How would I know?"

"What did she bring you earlier?"

"Nothing." The old woman gave him a slow crooked smile.

He turned from her, his heart beating hard. Nothing had happened to Padma. He called her again and sent a text telling her to come home at once. A large black Mercedes appeared at the other end of the lane – just like the minister's car, but the minister and his brother were never seen in Nilwatte Beach, not during the day. The car came closer. People stumbled into the ditch, out of its way. It stopped outside the villa gates and waited for Gerhard. Two security guards got out on either side and stood to attention, eyeing the lane in both directions. As Gerhardt reached the car, the window went down and the minister was inside, calling his name. Gerhardt went to him.

"Hello sir, I'm afraid I am in a bit of a rush."

"I won't be a minute. I hear you are renting your place?"

"Really? You heard this?"

So much for his lawyer's discrete enquiries! Had one such enquiry been passed by others to the minister, or had the news taken a more direct route? Gerhardt recalled the lawyer's discomfort at their last meeting, the quiet hostility of conflict, perhaps, as a professional man prepared to betray his client.

"As I have told you many times, I am very keen to purchase your little place," the minister told Gerhardt.

"It's not for sale, sir, as I keep saying."

"What will make you sell? What price?"

"You don't need my little house, sir; you own so many fine properties."

"Yes, but yours is in the way. And I know you are already planning to rent it, so why not just sell?"

The lawyer was fired. Gerhardt had a good mind to report him to the Law Society for breaching client confidentiality.

"And I understand congratulations are in order," the minister said. His big smooth head creased as he beamed.

"For what, sir?"

"Your daughter's engagement!

Gerhardt burst out laughing. "Padma's not engaged!"

"That's not what I heard."

"I'm afraid you've been misled, sir. She's not engaged to anyone."

"But it's just a matter of time, isn't it? A beautiful young woman like her. You might as well sell and use the money to buy her a place somewhere more suitable."

"Thank you, sir, I'll consider it." Gerhardt turned to go.

"What will make you sell your house to me, Gerhardt?" the minister asked.

"With all due respect, sir, no one can *make* me sell my house."

"Oh I can." The minister withdrew into the car. The window rose with a hum and the car drove away.

Gerhardt felt his phone buzz. At last a message from Padma: she was on her way from Jarryd's. Gerhardt waited with Soma on the veranda.

"Have you heard anything more about Jarryd Mahaththaya's book?" Gerhardt asked Soma.

"People are talking about it. I don't know how many have read it, but they're all getting angry because the minister's saying he's written bad things about the country. Sir, why don't you tell Jarryd Mahaththaya to stop selling the book until the elections are over? Everyone is angry before elections, no?"

"Oh I've tried telling him alright, but he won't listen."

Soma stood at the parapet, looking out at the lane.

"The minister and his brother are a bad pair. Lots of people have disappeared after falling out with them." Even Soma, who wasn't afraid of much, lowered his voice to speak of the minister and his brother.

"I'll give Jarryd a call and see if he's okay," Gerhardt said.

"Sir, sometimes they bug the phones, I hear. Just be careful what you say."

Why did he suddenly feel afraid? Nothing had happened, and

probably nothing would. All Jarryd had done was write an opinionated essay and print it with some good photographs. Surely one needed to do far worse before the clandestine forces of power bothered to strike?

"Let's go over to his place later and take a look," Gerhardt suggested.

"I can get Boss to come with us," Soma said.

Padma came sauntering up the path.

"Where have you been?" Gerhardt demanded.

"Out for a walk."

"We need to talk."

"Okay." She was impassive. He felt her resistance.

"I want you to be open with me—"

"I'll bring your lunch," Soma said, and quickly left.

"I have to wash my hands," Padma said, stalling.

"Fine. I'll wait."

Padma sat down at last to red rice, dahl, gottukola mallung, beetroot curry and jak curry, a reassuringly usual meal while something unnatural seemed to be brewing beneath them all.

"I want you to tell me the truth about what's going on," Gerhardt told Padma.

"Nothing's going on."

"Did you give Hema Amme an envelope today?"

"How did you—? Oh I get it, Soma was spying on me, was he? So that's why Hema Amme was so jumpy."

"Were you giving her money?"

"No."

"Was it money for Sunny?"

"No it was not!"

"Padma! Tell me! Enough of all these secrets!"

"It was a letter." Padma sat on the edge of her chair.

"I'm not angry, I just want to understand," he said.

Still she said nothing. They sat divided. This was what Sunny did best, creating suspicion between people living their lives in peace, loving and trusting each other. Sunny couldn't stand Padma living happily at the villa – it wasn't what he had planned for her, although he had made just as much money, if not more. What Sunny couldn't bear was that Padma had become a part of Gerhardt's world; for Sunny this was the affront, a betrayal almost. He had been waiting to pull Padma back for all these years.

"The money was for Leela," Padma said. "I've been giving her money for hospital treatment."

This was new. Sunny had never tried asking for money for anyone else before. A novel approach, and he had succeeded. Sunny knew exactly where Padma's defences were weakest: kindness and compassion were weaknesses to a bastard like him.

"I see Sunny has been up to his old tricks," Gerhardt said.

"Sunny's got nothing to do with this."

"All roads lead to Sunny, I'm afraid. I was worried the minister was involved in some way, but I don't see what he would gain from Sunny getting some cash."

"Gerhardt, I'm telling you, the money went to Leela, not Sunny!"

"It doesn't matter anymore. We'll be out of here soon, even if we don't find tenants we'll be in Goa – won't we? Just don't give Sunny – or anyone – anymore money, please."

"Don't worry, I won't."

"If he approaches you or sends Hema Amme – send them to me, okay?"

"Fine."

They ate in silence.

"Did you go to see Jarryd?" Gerhardt asked.

She looked up startled.

"When you went for your 'walk' earlier?"

"Okay, it wasn't exactly a walk, and yes, I did."

Why had she gone all that way to talk with Jarryd? Surely it wasn't only to talk about yoga? What was it she wanted to tell Jarryd that she hadn't felt able to tell Gerhardt?

"How was he?" Gerhardt asked.

"He wasn't in."

"Where the hell is he?" Gerhardt reached for his phone, the unease growing stronger in him, all other worries toppling.

He listened to Jarryd's phone ring. He left another message for him to call. Soma came out to join them, reading a text on his phone.

"Boss says there's a big rally being organised in town later this week and the minister's people are rounding up anyone who's said anything bad about him."

They all three stared at each other.

"That guidebook hardly counts," Gerhardt said.

He didn't feel hungry anymore. He pushed his plate aside and phoned Jarryd again, and left another more urgent message for Jarryd to call back.

"Let's go to his place," Gerhardt said.

"I'll come too," Padma said.

"I'll call Boss." Soma was already on his phone.

They went in Gerhardt's car, with Boss and his men following in their van, their dark windows inscrutable. Jarryd's house was still empty. Geetha usually left after sunset, but there was no sign of her at only three o'clock. Beyond the lake, they could see figures moving about the yoga retreat. Three of Boss's men crept through the coconut plantation to check on them, and Boss and two men checked the rooms of the house and the garden. They found nothing out of the ordinary. The glass was still broken in the French doors. Padma showed them the teapot fallen on its side. Where the hell was Jarryd? Gerhardt refused to think the worst. They stood on the veranda looking out. Jarryd had to be somewhere nearby.

The men returned from the retreat, reporting that all the tourists were attending an evening yoga class as usual. No one had seen Jarryd, but then he didn't always go over there.

"Maybe he's gone on a retreat of his own," Gerhardt said, for Jarryd sometimes went to practise meditation with the priests at a remote temple.

"Did Jarryd mention going anywhere?" he asked Padma.

She shook her head. She looked terrified.

"Has something happened to him?" she whispered.

"No, I'm sure he's fine."

But he didn't believe it anymore. Something wasn't right. The minister, so smug, so sure of himself, haunted Gerhardt.

"There was a book fallen on the floor," Padma said. "I didn't think much of it at the time. Or the teapot. Maybe it was a cat? "

"Yes, a cat. It was probably a cat," Gerhardt agreed.

"Let's call Ruth," Padma said.

"Not yet, there's no need. He'll be around here somewhere."

He had to stay calm for all their sakes. They drove back through the village, passing people going on with their day, the new bunting fluttering in the trees for the rally.

"I'll call the forest temple, that's bound to be where he's gone," Gerhardt said.

"Boss is going to Geetha's village to find her," Soma said.

They returned to the villa and Gerhardt called the forest temple, but Jarryd wasn't there. Gerhardt called the doctor, the dentist, expat friends in the area. Jarryd could have gone on a hike, someone said; another mentioned a new woman Jarryd had met, a German tourist, but no one knew her name or where she was staying. The mention of the German woman was a balm, a reminder of the innocent playful possibilities of Jarryd's life.

They were subdued that evening. Gerhardt helped Padma to write a CV and a choose a photograph of herself for the Goan retreat's website. It was reminiscent of their time filling in forms for university, but this time there was a real sense of order forming, a clear new path begun. Then late at night, Boss came with news that Geetha had been tracked down. She had received an anonymous note two days previously telling her to stay away from Jarryd's house and not to talk to anyone, so she had hidden away at a relative's house in a different village. She knew, as everyone did, that no good came to people who didn't do as they were told.

## 33

IT WAS HARDLY the day to be thinking of saris, but Padma unfurled her gift to Leela, casting her eye over its soft elephant grey and restrained elegant border. Was it something that Leela would wear? That she would enjoy owning? Padma folded the sari and wrapped it in tissue paper. Gerhardt was in the hall, talking on the phone with the police, reporting Jarryd missing. Gerhardt and Soma had already been to Jarryd's again early that morning and come back silent with concern. Boss, his brother, Gerhardt and Soma had gone into the office to talk for almost an hour. Padma had heard them calling people they knew, speaking fast, in low voices. Now Boss had gone and Soma was making breakfast while Gerhardt asked to speak with the Chief Inspector.

Padma's job that morning was to stay by the phones - she had her phone and the office phone with her, fully charged and ready, waiting for Jarryd to call. She thought of Jarryd happy and safe on an adventure somewhere, unaware of all the fuss. He had merely switched off his phone to enjoy himself, or it had run out of charge. The things that sometimes happened to other people wouldn't happen to them. Geetha was a drama queen. The note she had received may have been a joke by some village kids - everyone knew how silly and jumpy Geetha had become.

Jarryd was most probably contorting under a mosquito net in a house somewhere, in the company of a beautiful agile yogi with hennaed hair and a nose ring. Let it be that, Padma silently begged; nothing else seemed possible – for how could the worst have happened?

Late morning Gerhardt went to meet the Police Inspector. Soma went with Boss and his men, spreading around all the villages near Nilwatte Beach to talk to villagers. Ruth rang to say that none of her contacts in Colombo knew anything.

"How many times did I tell that man to withdraw his book!" she fumed, her fear making her breathless.

"Maybe nothing at all has happened," Padma said.

"People disappear all the time these days for far lesser things. They asked him and asked him to stop. How we all begged him—" Ruth's voice broke.

"Don't panic, Ruth. He's probably just gone on holiday. And everyone's looking for him. Boss and his guys are going to all the villages around here."

"As if Boss and his little bandits are a match for your minister! His men are invisible. They come and grab and disappear, nobody sees them or finds them again. They're hidden from high up. Everyone here is too frightened to help – I've rung lawyers, judges, opposition ministers and everyone is terribly sorry but they won't get involved."

"He could call up at any minute, laughing at us for getting all worked up."

"I want to believe you, darling, I really do. I'll get off the phone. Call me if you find out anything."

"Of course."

"And you stay inside, my girl, please don't put yourself in any danger. Is Soma with you?"

"No, he's gone with Boss."

"Gerhardt's left you all alone in the house?"

"Ruth, I'm fine."

"Lock the doors, darling. Please lock everything."

"Okay, I will."

For once Ruth's fears didn't seem far-fetched. Padma locked the doors and windows and diverted all calls to her mobile. But she had agreed to meet Leela that day, and soon it was twelve o'clock. She left the house. She had to go, now more than ever she needed to know the truth about Leela. There was no more time for lies; their lives had to be simple and innocent, that was all Padma wanted now.

Leela was already there, waiting by the dustbins behind the café, looking anxiously around.

"I thought you'd never come," she said to Padma, a little pointedly.

"Why? I said I would."

Leela glanced over her shoulder at a police car driving past. The policemen inside seemed to glance more alertly at everyone, then they drove slowly around the stalls and into the lane.

"How are you feeling?" Padma asked.

"I'm alright."

"The medicines are helping?"

"Oh yes, very much, yes."

"But now about your illness—" Padma began.

"You went away?" Leela asked.

"Yes, and before I left, I learned that Hema Amme's sister—"

"You went to Colombo?"

"Yes, but as I was saying—"

"Ah, you went to see your friend?"

"No, I was taking a course, so I can teach yoga."

"Yoga, is it? Ah, very good."

Leela was determinedly slippery, flashing eel-like between Padma's words. She would never let Padma pin her down; the truth would slip away, that was her power.

"So anyway, I have to be going," Leela said. "But I want to give you—"

"Ah, I nearly forgot! I got you something." Padma took out the sari in its tissue paper wrappings.

"What is it?" Leela eyed the package.

"It's just a small present. It's nothing much. Open it and see if you like it."

Leela looked horrified.

"Take it." Padma pushed the parcel into Leela's hands.

Leela prised apart the wrapping and pulled out the grey blouse material.

"That's for the blouse," Padma said.

Leela tore away more tissue paper and inspected the sari. She handed it back.

"You keep it," she said.

"But it's for you."

"If I take it home, Sunny will ask questions."

Padma took the sari back. Released from its wrapping it sank loose and formless, to the bottom of the bag.

"Anyway, I wanted to tell you, I can't make the payments anymore," Padma said.

Leela didn't flinch. "Doesn't matter, I'm much better these days. The doctors think I won't need the operation now after all - all thanks to you."

"Really? You're fully recovered? Isn't that amazing."

Leela fumbled in her own bag, moving aside an umbrella and a scuffed old plastic water bottle.

"You know you don't have to make things up, to ask me for help," Padma said.

"Here, I have something for you." Leela brought out a large red cardboard jewellery box in the shape of a heart.

"What's this?" But Padma already knew.

Leela undid the brass clasp and lifted the lid, holding up the box like a vendor. And Padma saw, laid out on purple furry velveteen, an ornate necklace of rich yellow-gold, studded with rubies and emeralds and diamonds. It was Leela's most prized possession, the last remnant of her dowry that she had not let Sunny sell.

"You like it?" Leela asked.

Leela had kept the necklace hidden in their house, but Padma had searched for it tirelessly, and discovered Leela's hiding place in an alcove of the room where Leela slept with Sunny. The box had been wedged into a crack in the wall of the alcove, and covered over with old newspapers and a battered cardboard suitcase, which Padma had stealthily moved when she was alone in the house to unearth the red heart. And she would wear the necklace, a cold heavy collar and stare in the mirror at the jewels, glistening like wet, licked lollipops, and at herself adorned; a princess, a queen.

"I know you used to like it - you used to wear it when you thought I wasn't looking," Leela said.

"You saw me?"

"Of course I saw you." Leela's silence of those years felt unnerving now.

"It's yours. I can't possibly take it," Padma said.

"Please, you must have it. It's all I have to give you. I wanted to thank you for everything you've done for me."

"Don't worry about it—"

"This is my gift for when you get married. It's soon, no?"

"I'm not getting married."

Leela laughed and pressed the box into Padma's hands.

"What a fine wedding you'll have! How happy I am for you. All I want is for you to be happy . . ." Leela's eyed filled with tears.

"Really – I'm not getting married. I just made that up to annoy Hema Amme."

How was Padma to know that the stupid old woman would go running to Leela, or that anyone would believe such a ludicrous story.

"Don't worry, I won't tell anyone. Nothing will come between you and your lover," Leela said slyly and Padma flinched.

'Lover' sounded strange coming from a mother, but then Leela had never quite been Mother to her. Real mothers and daughters were joined by wordless understanding; a mysterious binding. Between Leela and her there was only confusion; glimpses, and shadowy forms; unexpected edges to trip over. Leela was separate, her motives hidden from Padma. Leela pushed the jewellery box at Padma with surprising force and Padma gave in.

"Keep it locked somewhere," Leela ordered. "Gerhardt Mahaththaya must have a safe, no?"

A safe was the first place a burglar would look for – surely Leela knew that? Padma put the box inside her bag, tucked under the sari.

"I'd better go," Leela said. "By the way, what has happened to Gerhardt Mahaththaya's friend Jarryd?"

"What do you mean?"

"I heard Sunny talking with someone this morning." Leela dropped her voice. "I thought I should mention it to you – you're friends with this man, no? Tell Gerhardt Mahaththaya to talk to the minister. He's the only one who can help."

"The minister?"

"It's something to do with the minister."

"Are you sure you heard right?" Padma couldn't breathe. A hard, terrible truth was untangling and growing undeniably real.

"Tell Mr. Gerhardt to hurry up if he wants to see his friend again." Leela stopped but she was holding back the rest of what she knew.

"Please, where is Jarryd?" Padma cried, but Leela was already leaving.

It was no use begging for more, she knew that from long ago. Leela would never give more than she wanted to. She could seal herself up and face your crying and never give out another crumb. Padma watched Leela haul herself onto a waiting bus, scrambling up the steps with a new sprightly vigour. Grabbing a leather strap, she swayed wide and free as the bus turned. Padma ran home, ringing Gerhardt and Ruth on the way. Nobody understood her at first, there was so much she had to explain.

⁂

For the first time, Gerhardt was made to wait for the minister in the lobby of his office. Usually Gerhardt was ushered straight into the minister's private sitting room within the office suite, a new wing separated from the rest of the house by a light-filled hallway, both designed by Gerhardt in happier times. A Special Security Force guard stood blocking the way now to that pleasant, tasteful room. The minister had let his wife run amok with the decoration of the main house, but for the new wing he had given specific instructions to the interior designer: cream sofas, mahogany tables and chairs, burnt-copper lampshades, dark-stained wooden shutters. He had been keen not to flaunt his flat-screen television, delighted when an antique armoire had been specially adapted to conceal it. Gerhardt recalled the minister's insatiable desire to learn from anyone possessing the knowledge and training that he himself had been denied during the early humble years of his life. The minister had often revealed himself to be remarkably well-informed about history and architecture, asking insightful questions at all stages of the design process, retaining everything, even years later. It took a certain expansive intelligence to maintain such an effort in all of one's dealings; Gerhardt sometimes found himself almost liking the man. But there were always the moments of unexpected candour or an attempt at humour, sometimes an aside that would reveal the darker depths of the minister's mind. His cruelty was an unshakeable fact about him, his strength. Gerhardt felt it now as the minister arrived and greeted him unsmilingly in the hall. Unusually for their meetings, at least in more recent years, he was formally dressed in the white collarless Nehru shirt and white trousers of Sri Lankan politicians' traditional attire. He stood aside as two security guards stepped forward and, for the first time in their acquaintance, searched Gerhardt, instructing him tonelessly to spread his legs, to lift his arms, patting him down while the minister watched. Then the minister led the way to his study and, placing himself behind the gleaming expanse of the mahogany desk, he gestured to Gerhardt to be seated. There was no offer of whisky, like in the old days, not even tea or soft drinks. Gerhardt heard the guards' footsteps slowly pacing outside in the hall.

"You wanted to see me?" the minister said.

"I'm worried about my friend, Jarryd. No one seems to know where he is."

"Jarryd? Now who is this Jarryd?" The minister wrinkled his face in apparent concentration. "Is he the one who wrote that book recently?"

And so the game began.

"Ah, not really a book, more of a pamphlet – a bit of fun, I think. The thing is he seems to have disappeared."

"My goodness! But how can I help?"

"I think there might have been a misunderstanding about that pamphlet—"

"Misunderstanding? What is there to misunderstand? According to what I have heard he has slandered our beautiful island – a paradise isle, many call it – a country that has welcomed him in, given him a home . . . Now is that a way to behave towards the people who have treated one well?"

It was not the time to argue, or to keep trying to explain. Gerhardt decided to avoid mentioning the book. That bloody book. How many times had he warned Jarryd about flaunting it in Colombo.

"I can arrange for those pamphlets to be removed from every shop – I will need only a couple of hours, I will see to it personally," Gerhardt said.

"Yes, that would be helpful to your friend, but many copies have already been withdrawn."

"In that case, he can be released? I can assure you he won't be putting out any more of his publications."

The minister pondered. He sighed deeply, dramatically.

"For you this is a simple matter, but there has been much pressure on me to stop this defamatory item spreading its lies. Your friend should have thought of the consequences. You see, his actions have been noted much higher up than my lowly powers could ever reach."

They both knew this to be untrue – the minister could reach very far into the cabinet, comprised as it was by several members of his family. One word to any of those illustrious relatives and Jarryd would be out of wherever he was being held, possibly unharmed.

"Please, sir, Jarryd, for all his youthful ways, is an old man, like me," Gerhardt appealed. "He is injured from a terrible robbery at his home only two years ago, he still walks with a limp. He wishes no one ill. He has done so much for the villagers, helping families with jobs, paying medical bills when their children get sick, sending young people to university—"

"Yes, yes, from what I hear, he is quite a character. He dances in the sea, does he not, wearing an amude?"

The minister chuckled with contempt. For him, a foreigner like Jarryd, formed outside the colonial mould, undesiring of its power and prestige, would be incomprehensible. Had the minister merely looked away as orders were given from higher up, or had he given them himself? One thing was certain – he knew what had happened to Jarryd. He held the knowledge within him; it was all his to withhold or reveal; to be used as he determined. This was power. Gerhardt sat before the starched white of the minister's shirt, the dyed, blue-black thatch of his hair shining with hairspray; the minister was an impenetrable edifice. He smiled.

"Is he dead?" Gerhardt asked.

The bright bulging eyes stayed clear and impassive, revealing nothing.

"You know, I am glad you visited," the minister said. "I have been waiting to find out if you had changed your mind about selling your villa?"

"Renting it, you mean?"

"Ah, you are not thinking of selling? What a shame. If you were selling, it might have helped your friend."

"You mean, if I should sell the villa to you?" Gerhardt followed the trail laid before him. Blindly, meekly he went where it led. All the years of knowing of corruption didn't prepare you for when it crawled out of the bog and pulled on you.

"If I sell the villa – to you – we will find Jarryd, is that it?" he checked.

"Oh no, no, not in such a simplistic sense." The minister grimaced with distaste.

"Alright, I will sell it, but only after Jarryd is returned."

"I see. So there will be no more talk of renting?"

"No. I will sell it, but only after Jarryd is back."

"So you would sell your place to help your friend . . . hmm. I had a feeling you would." The minister stood up.

So this was how it ended, their wary dance of many years, the careful tread of avoidance weaving in and darting out, playing on one's luck. Gerhardt had always known that the luck would run out, but he hadn't seen how or when. When the minister would lose patience waiting to own the last house on the best part of the coastal stretch, and when Jarryd would taunt the wrong people and make himself bait for a trap. How could anyone have foreseen such separate strands of folly and hubris gathering to this knot, which nonetheless seemed inevitable?

"It won't be easy for me to find your friend. He has angered a great many people," the minister said. "And everything between us must be settled before he is found. How much do you want for the place? Cash can be arranged."

"I need to see Jarryd before I accept any money," Gerhardt said. "You know you can trust my word."

The minister was silent. Outside, a black Mercedes van drove slowly and parked in a bay under a row of red frangipani trees. Two Special Security Force guards climbed out and walked across the garden, their blank eerie gaze perpetually alert. The two security guards on the porch swapped positions. There was the sound of splashing and children's squeals; a woman's voice calling out in Sinhalese that it was dangerous to run near a swimming pool, that they could slip and fall and break their necks.

"I'll see what I can do," the minister said. "You're on your usual number?"

"Yes."

The meeting was over. The minister opened the door and Gerhardt left the room. Past the guards in the corridor, he walked towards the carved teak door that he had overseen being installed. Outside he moved as in a dream through the garden with its shrill perfection ablaze in the hurtful glare. Even the trees offered no shade, no shelter.

The call came that afternoon. He was seated on the porch at the villa talking to Ruth on Padma's phone, keeping his own free, when it rang with an unknown number. A male voice said: "The old school. In two hours."

"Is Jarryd alright? I want to speak to him. Jarryd? Jarryd!"

They ended the call. He tried calling back, but the line was dead. Padma stood frozen. She was holding her phone with Ruth still there, a tinny shrieking far away.

"What's happened? What's happening? Padma? Padma - are you there?" Ruth cried.

Padma was gazing up at him, Soma stepped closer.

"The old school, in two hours," Gerhardt said. He shook his head at the question in their faces. He took Padma's phone and spoke to Ruth.

"They said to be at the old school in two hours. I suppose they mean the one inland."

"Oh my God." Ruth moaned. "I don't know what to do. I'm coming over now. I'll bring Doctor Wijeysuriya—"

"Ruth, I don't know if we'll need a surgeon."

"He said he wanted to help, so I'm going to ask him. He can at least pull some strings if we need it . . . Oh my God, Gerhardt!"

"It'll be fine. Jarryd will be alright. We're all going to be alright. I need to go now and make sure we are ready."

It wasn't fear that he felt, more the desire to protect himself - from what he might see, what he might be forced to know. He longed to hide like a frightened child waking in the dark, still feeling the presence of malevolence from dreams. In those days one could huddle under the sheets and wait for the monsters to be gone, waking once more to a safe dull reality. He longed for the call to have been a hoax, for Jarryd to not really be missing. He was aware that the minister had guaranteed nothing; he had offered no assurance of what was being returned. Gerhart thought of the weeping women and children with banners at a recent protest march – families of the disappeared, haunted for ever by what they might never know, tormented by the unending hope of a miraculous return. Not knowing might seem easier now, but there was no end to what the mind could construct, the horrors it could invent. To face the worst was an end in itself. He put his arm around Padma. She was shaking.

"Ruth's coming with Dr Wijeysuriya. We'd better get a doctor of our own, just in case," he said.

"I'll call Dr Perera." She was calm as she rang the doctor, even as she stood trembling holding the phone.

Gerhardt listened to her explaining simply, clearly what they knew. How much she had grown. When had she become this new person, this woman in the hall knowing what to do, even as the worst happened? Gerhardt sank into a chair, the garden, his attempt at paradise, finally riven open, for here was the serpent that had lurked in the undergrowth, reclaiming its hold over the land. Sunny, who had loomed so large over their life at the villa for so many years, had been merely a distraction, a spectre arisen from a rottenness spread vast underground. The violence of oppression was a part of the island so desired, so used, so mutilated. A black bile glistened beneath the roots of its ancient trees, under the foundations of houses, the glorious views and sunset skies that could make one cry with their innocent purity. Even a tsunami had not been able to wash away injustice or sweep in togetherness or compassion; the black poison still lay at the bottom of the hearts of those with power, and it was they who controlled what people thought and felt and what they did. The man Gerhardt had spoken with had sounded like a local, young – a young man like any other one might pass in the lane, at any time – perfectly ordinary-looking perhaps, unmarked by any particular branding of evil.

## 34

I T WASN'T THE way it was in films. Padma sat at the back
of the car with Soma while Gerhardt sat in front, with Karu
driving; they could have been going on an ordinary trip. For one
thing, it was daytime, not night, and the meeting place wasn't
in a lonely far-away place but the road behind their lane, a few
minutes drive away past the brothel and the beach bars. Dr Perera
rode behind them in an ambulance that he had borrowed from the
hospital, with a driver and a paramedic. Boss was there, of course,
with his brother and five other men seated in their van, out of sight
behind the dark windows.

It wasn't at all the way it was in films, it was eerie and unnatural to be driving in convoy with Boss, his men and an ambulance
to the marshy end of the lane where they never went, where a river
pooled in a dark pond covered with pale creamy scum, humming
with mosquitoes. Karu turned past the pond into the road that led
past paddy fields to the abandoned school. The road was empty.
They stopped in front of the deserted schoolyard. Padma looked at
her phone – they were ten minutes early. Gerhardt and Dr Perera
had already driven over to the school soon after the phone call, but
they'd found no one there. The doctor had advised Gerhardt not
to stay, in case it put the kidnappers off. The kidnappers wouldn't

care who saw them, Padma suspected. They were untouchable. The minister would see to that. One of his nephews had raped a tourist in a café, in broad daylight with a crowd of people watching, and the guy was still cruising around town with a grin on his face – no chance of ever seeing him in prison. Gerhardt was staring straight ahead at the point in the road where a car would first appear if it was headed for the school. Gerhardt's stillness, his steady quiet strength, held them all inside the car. Padma had seen bodies in newspapers and on television: shot, bombed, stabbed, torn open by grenades. Blood was a red liquid, flesh was wet and pink; bone, hard white. Already she knew that Jarryd was dead. They all knew it; even the villagers who had come to gawp at the ambulance as it waited outside the villa. Gerhardt looked at his watch.

"It's two now, they should be here," he said.

They all watched the road, but nothing came.

"Let's go closer," Gerhardt said and Karu drove slowly up to the entrance of the school yard.

Nothing moved inside the empty classrooms. The open, unglazed windows gaped hollowly where once sea breezes would have stirred over children seated in rows reciting times-tables, copying lines from a board as a teacher stood scribbling with chalk or striking a ruler across an outstretched palm. A motorbike appeared in the road. It drove towards them. A man was at the front, a woman behind. They peered into the car as they passed, slowing by the ambulance, trying to look in. The ambulance driver gestured impatiently to them to go. Boss's driver wound down his window and shouted to the couple and they moved on, but stopped and watched from a distance.

At two-twenty, Dr. Perera came from the ambulance to the car to confer with Gerhardt. "I don't think anyone's coming," he said.

"Do you think it was a hoax? Shall I ring the minister?" Gerhardt asked.

"Let's check the school."

The doctor was middle-aged, short and rounded, but he was suddenly younger and toughened, the young man he had been once perhaps when he was training with the army.

"Soma, you stay here with Padma Baba," Gerhardt ordered and went out to join the doctor.

The two walked together into the yard, headed for the school building. Boss and his men piled out of the van and followed them.

Gerhardt and the doctor walked outside around the ground-floor classrooms looking in at windows. Gerhardt climbed over a window sill and the doctor followed, then Boss's men jumped into the classroom as well. Padma watched them disappear. Minutes later, Gerhardt, the doctor and Boss and his men trooped out into the yard again. They moved so slowly. Why didn't they split up and search all over? There were so many buildings, so many rooms, so many places where Jarryd could have been waiting gagged and tied up or lying hurt. What if the kidnappers had been there long before? Jarryd could have been waiting alone and in pain for hours. Padma opened her door and ran to the school.

"Padma Baba! Come back here!" Soma cried, but she didn't stop.

Padma ran through a shadowy hall, her footsteps echoing, and out through a door at the end of a corridor into a playground. A rusted netball hoop was fixed to a wall, white lines were painted on the ground, marking out an old netball court. The doctor and Gerhardt came after her. Boss and his men ran past, going on into the building in front.

"Padma! Get back in the car!" Gerhardt yelled.

They heard someone shouting - it was Boss from inside the building up ahead. Gerhardt started to run, the doctor went with him. Padma followed them in, going past crumbling empty rooms, a door half-fallen from its hinges, a table covered in bird droppings. One of Boss's men came running out, going back to the yard.

"Bring the ambulance! Bring the medics!" he shouted. "Ambulance! We need help here!"

Through the doorway where the man had come from, was a hall where the whole school might have gathered once to sing songs and chant prayers and have prizes awarded. At the far end, where the men had gathered, was a long misshapen bundle on the dusty floor.

"Is he alive?" Padma heard Gerhardt say.

Boss's men crowded over the bundle.

"Stand back, don't touch him," Doctor Perera ordered.

Dr Perera and Gerhardt crouched on the floor by Jarryd. They had left him out of the sun at least, but without a mat, without a covering, just naked, a discarded animal form, the same body that had danced proud before the dying sun, now broken and bound and lifeless. Padma stood at the door, unable to move. The ambulance driver and the paramedic came rushing past her with a stretcher.

"Here come the medics! Quick! Get them in here!" Boss's men shouted, leaping around.

"Jarryd, Jarryd, it's me, Gerhardt. We're here now, you're safe," Gerhardt said.

The paramedic placed an oxygen mask over Jarryd's face. Padma glimpsed a blindfold, a dark-stained cloth, a large welt on Jarryd's cheek, blood dried in his hair, brown smears along one leg. As Jarryd was rolled onto the stretcher, more bruises, welts, cuts were revealed before they were all covered by a thick cotton blanket.

"Jarryd? Can you hear me?" Gerhardt reached for the blindfold.

"Careful! Don't touch that," the doctor warned, moving Gerhardt aside

The doctor pointed a torch at the blindfold, a yellow dot of light roaming slowly over the ragged bandage. He took a knife from one of Boss's men and sawed at the plastic cord binding Jarryd's wrists. Jarryd moaned, a thin child cry of helplessness and pain.

"He's alive, he's alive!" shouted Boss's men.

Doctor Perera lifted an edge of the blindfold. A trickle of blood ran out from under it onto the stretcher. The paramedic wedged in fresh cotton wool under the bandage. The doctor filled a syringe and sank the needle into Jarryd's arm. The ambulance men lifted up the stretcher.

"Please, Lord Buddha, Lord Shiva, Lord Ganesha, please let him be alright," Padma prayed, stepping back into the dark hall as Jarryd was carried away. The new cotton wool under the blindfold was already staining, the colour of strawberries and buses and pillar boxes in imported children's books, the cheery happy red of birthday balloons.

"I'll go in the ambulance," Gerhardt told Padma. "You go back with Karu and Soma and wait for Ruth. Call her and tell her we've found him. She'll already be on her way - tell her to go straight to the hospital."

Padma rang Ruth as Karu drove back to the villa, Ruth speechless, then murmuring: "Yes, yes, we'll go straight there."

There was no such thing as a truly evil person, Jarryd used to say, no such thing as intrinsic evil; people were products of their experience. They were triggered to act badly by their pain. But what made someone do what they had to Jarryd? What anger, what pain? What sort of country gave birth to such people?

"Devils, that's what they are. The bloody fuckers must be sent straight to hell!" Soma ranted beside her.

Jarryd had claimed there was something to gain, something to learn in everything that befell one. She had struggled to believe him sometimes, to see a longing for love and joy in Sunny or people like the minister and his rapist nephew, but she had tried, for Jarryd's sake. How wrong he had been.

"We have to find all of them who hurt him and burn them alive. We have to make sure they suffer slowly . . ." Soma gabbled on.

Padma could see Karu's wild-eyed gaze in the rear-view mirror holding down his horror and sadness. He kept blinking away tears, swiping them away with the back of his hand as she asked him to drive first to Jarryd's house to pack clothes for the hospital. And she would find any belongings that he could have near him – talismans to remind him of the beautiful life he had made and so gloriously lived, which he must have again – he had to; she, Gerhardt and Ruth and everyone else who loved him would make his world beautiful for him again. She trembled with the memory of his damaged crumpled body – could that hurt ever be undone? And what will have happened to the sweet soul within?

Rohan stayed in bed, listening to the household awake downstairs, the morning progressing without him. Even after so many days of sleeping alone, he was surprised not to find Padma curled under the sheets beside him, to turn under the sheets and not encounter her smooth slender limbs, to feel her arm wrap around him. Nine-thirty a.m. It was the longest he had ever stayed in bed without the excuse of illness or a hangover. He reached for his phone. There was no message from Padma. He read again the email she had sent to thank him for the statue: 'Dear Rohan, Thank you for the Dancing Lord Shiva, it was very kind of you.

Love Padma.' He held on to the 'Love' of 'Love Padma', but it was weakened by the 'Dear' of 'Dear Rohan'. He searched between the distinct little words she had typed, for meaning, searching in the words themselves for something revealed, offering hope. There were voices outside: the calls of vendors and conversations of passers-by; the maids in the garden next-door were calling to the children. From the main road came the impatient rumble of traffic as the city surged on to schools, offices, factories, banks; or to the courts where lives could be mangled or set free.

He lurched out of bed and went to shower. It was mid-morning when he went downstairs. A place was still set for him at the dining table, but the jam lids had been put back on, the butter covered up and the bread returned to its sealed container.

"Ah, darling, how would you like your eggs?" His mother appeared from the kitchen wearing an apron.

"I don't want any eggs."

"Then what will you eat?"

"I'll have something later."

"Are you sure? I can make you an omelette? Or how about waffles? Or pancakes?"

She often spent her mornings in the kitchen making little concoctions of rich dainty additions to lunch - sometimes an elaborate salad or an ornate vegetable dish prepared with utmost concentration and effort, taking over all the work surfaces in the kitchen so that the maid and the cook had hardly any space in which to prepare the rest of the lunch.

"Some tea, then?" his mother asked.

"A coffee, please. No milk, no sugar."

"Decaf?"

"No, very much caf."

The disapproving look she gave him was because she had read somewhere that normal black coffee corroded the gut. She had banned him from drinking it, but this time it appeared there was to be no lecture. She brought out a tiny cup of weak Nescafé and placed a hopeful jug of milk beside it on the table.

"Now don't forget, this afternoon I won't be here, I have my ladies' lunch," she said.

Once a week, when his father and ex-work colleagues met in a members' room at the Chamber of Commerce, their wives met for lunch in a private dining room at the Colombo Hilton: each week those well-dressed refined middle-aged women with their air of entitlement and casual comfort met in the same room, bound by their years of loneliness and privilege running homes and staff and children for absent husbands.

"Daddy's already gone," his mother said.

It was inexplicable to Rohan how his father could look forward to these meetings of trustees' talk and pretend work, but his father had always liked the atmosphere of business, and even the buildings and the people that had surrounded him. Rohan could not imagine ever wanting to meet colleagues from his bank when he retired. It was hard to think of returning to be with them even now. Some of them who had so helpfully agreed to cover for him while he was gone, had already surreptitiously begun to charm his clients. Rohan had received messages from several concerned clients whom his colleagues had attempted to poach. He should have been back at his desk by now, shooing those vultures away, showing them all that he was just as ruthless and determined as before – yet the merest thought of resuming that old life brought up a violent new resistance in him; a super-human force pushing him back. Already that week he had asked his manager for more time, blaming bureaucratic delays and archaic legal practices. As they spoke on a video call, he had seen the bright wintery sun falling in through his boss's glass office, and glimpses of others roaming around behind the partitions. It had been almost midday there, and he had thought of them all about to ride down the great towers, spilling out through an opening at the bottom to search for lunch, like ants. They would all crawl back in with their crumbs, returning willingly to that world, but it had become impossible for him to do the same now. A fierce new apathy gripped him.

His mother was reading the Society section of the morning papers. Rohan reached for the main pages He glanced thought the news: new improvements in the North, a series of vitriolic claims against a potential opposition leader, a missing journalist, a school prize-giving. On page five he saw: 'German ex-dancer found wounded near Nilwatte Beach.' Two words jumped up at him: Jarryd Gunnerson. The article reported that Russian drug lords had attacked Jarryd after a deal had gone wrong. Jarryd had been found severely injured four days earlier, possibly fatally.

"What is it?" his mother asked.

"Someone I know is hurt." He reached for his phone.

"And it's in the papers?" She pulled the pages to her, scanning them blankly. "Where? Which one? Who, Rohan?"

But Rohan was ringing Padma. She answered this time.

"Hi, it's me – what's going on? I just read the news."

"Who are you calling?" His mother watched him suspiciously. He went outside into the garden, away from her.

"Are you okay? What's happened to Jarryd?" he asked Padma.

It didn't seem possible, the things she described in her sad steady voice, acts of such cruelty and senselessness. How could they have happened without the rest of the country knowing? All the people going about their day, no one hearing, no one seeing; no one rushing to intervene. And even now there would be no search for the wrong-doers; no judgment passed, no punishment. Only the sly little lies in the paper, a trail obscured, people getting away with what they had ordered and what they had done, even able to profit.

"Which hospital is he in? Is there any way I can help?"

"Who is in hospital?" His mother came up behind him.

"Is Soma with you? You're not alone in the house?" Rohan asked Padma.

"Is it someone you know from England?" his mother whispered.

"No, Nilwatte Beach," he mouthed to her.

"Who do you know there? Who is this on the phone?"

He moved away from her again.

"I'll call you later," Rohan told Padma.

"Who are these people you've been mixing with?" his mother demanded as he ended the call.

He didn't stop to answer; he rang for a taxi, ordering a car to Nilwatte Beach, to leave immediately.

"What on earth do you think you're doing?" his mother said.

"I have to go."

"You can't just go haring off to the wilds at the drop of a hat!"

"I have to, Ma."

He was already on his way upstairs. His mother ran up behind him panting.

"Have you gone mad? I must say this is some guest house! Why are you so mixed up with these people? You barely know them."

Yet they felt like the only true people anywhere; the only people he needed to be with.

"A friend has been hurt and another friend is all alone, I have to go to her."

"Her? Who is this woman you're running to? Is she young or old?"

He had never fully unpacked, it was simply a matter of adding his toothbrush and comb to the small suitcase, with some t-shirts and trousers and underwear.

"Rohan, please answer me – who exactly is this woman you're going to see?"

"She's the manager of the guest house."

"And who's the owner?"

"Gerhardt Hundsler. He's an Austrian architect who lives here in Sri Lanka."

"And he's in hospital?"

"No, his friend is."

"What's his friend got to do with you?"

Rohan closed his bag and headed downstairs to wait for the car. His mother came too, bringing the newspaper from the dining table.

"Is it this one – this story about the Russian drug lords?" she demanded.

"Yes, it's certainly a story. None of it's true, apart from Jarryd being seriously wounded."

"You know him? This drug dealer?"

Jarryd's injuries had been too severe to move him to Colombo, or even to Galle. He was being treated at the hospital in Tangalle. Broken ribs, concussion, a swelling on the brain, and there were genuine fears that he had lost his sight. A specialist had been rushed over from Colombo Private Medical, but there was nothing to do but wait, to see how much damage had been done.

"How did you get muddled up with these people? Were you buying things from that drug dealer? You don't owe anyone any money, do you?"

He had nothing more to offer her; she would believe what she chose to; he knew that from before.

"Rohan, once and for all, are you taking drugs or not?"

"No, I'm bloody not!"

"Then why are you getting so angry?"

The maid came to say that a taxi had arrived for him and he ran out to the car, his mother close behind him.

"So now you're going to stay with this Austrian woman?" she cried.

He turned at the gate and kissed her on the cheek.

"She's not Austrian, Ma, she's Sri Lankan. And right now she's probably the loneliest person in the world."

His mother watched him go. She didn't wave. Her reproach followed him up the lane, but then the car turned onto the main road and he was free. Free to feel the full truth of all that he had just learned, and to fill with sadness. Yet there was hope, there had to be hope – he had learnt at the villa that there was always a reason to hope.

The taxi passed through the city to its edges where blocks of government flats rose up above the road; lives boxed and stacked, their balconies filled with bright-coloured washing blowing in the hot harsh air; AC fans with dusty blades slowly turned. The loneliest person in the world was not Padma – surely it was Jarryd in his coma, induced in the hope that the fluid in his brain drained out. Jarryd alone with his memories. What visions, what horrors flickered inside his battered skull? Poor Jarryd. Poor wonderful trusting hope-filled Jarryd. Why him? The one man to still believe in the intrinsic good in men, in their power to question and search for truth and be transformed by beauty? Padma hadn't known how his eyes had been hurt. She said no one did. Possibly the facts were deemed too distressing for those who loved him. If only their love could run in him now, to flow over the damaged tissues, to pulse in his blood and resurrect him. For the first time since he was a boy Rohan prayed, thinking of wet clean frangipani flowers around the veranda and rose incense in Padma's pink room, red hibiscus dancing over the lawn in the mornings and Padma smiling. He prayed for love and all that was pure and true and good in the world to undo what had been done.

35

PADMA WAS ON the veranda of the villa, her phone on the table before her, closely watched. They kept their phones with them at all times these days, ready to receive or pass on news of Jarryd. It had been four days since Jarryd had been found – four days for an idiot journalist to write a so-called report in the paper – they hadn't had the nerve to reveal their name, calling themselves merely 'staff writer'. How could they live with themselves? Surely it was its own hell to have to work each day in a job like that? Jarryd would have loved that ludicrous article, he would have framed it and put it on the wall. She had kept him a copy for when he was better. She could only think of him getting better, of them all returning to a new life soon, a new chapter.

The morning before, Jarryd's heart rate had stabilised. Padma was there when the doctors announced it, she and Gerhardt seated at Jarryd's bedside, Ruth just waking from a nap in the spare bed. But there was still no knowing how Jarryd really was, the doctors said. There was a high chance of significant brain damage, and the trauma could have affected him in many different ways. Jarryd might not return to them the way they had known him, the doctors warned. Ruth and Gerhardt were already talking about how they would care for him – whether it would be in one or other of their homes, or in his; and who would move where – but it was not possible to make plans anymore. Jarryd's life was suspended in the hushed solemnity of the hospital, his life was diaphanous, ethereal; detached from the substance of his presence, his consciousness. They waited, suspended themselves, for his return to them.

Padma walked around the veranda. In the past days, the lane had grown quiet – too quiet. The women in the brothel had been told to go home and lie low for a while, Soma had learned from Boss. The whole of Nilwatte Beach felt deserted. Usually it took a murder to make everyone stay at home. Even the few tourists about seemed subdued. Locals scurried past the villa keeping their heads down. No one was bothered about the villa anymore – everyone knew that it had been sold to the minister and his brother. Were they all rejoicing that the minister had forced Gerhardt's hand? Let them find out what it was like to have the minister and his brother in charge of the lane, because they would soon enough. Even a whole stretch of coastal land with the best views would cease to be enough for those two – already there were rumours that the brother planned to bring in Eastern European women to replace his local set at the brothel. Russian prostitutes were all the rage, according to Boss; in Colombo a visit to one cost a small fortune, he said, and he had heard that the minister's brother hoped to draw foreigners to the South for a cheaper alternative. Foreign clients, however miserly, would bring in more money than the local riff-raff.

A car door slammed in the lane. Gustav scrambled up and ran out barking.

"Hello, boy! Where is everyone?" Rohan's voice came over the garden to her.

She ran to the porch and he was coming up the path, returning. Their days apart shrank to nothing as she went to him and they held each other. It was instant, the relief, being with him again, something returned to her, an essential component. Soma came out because of Gustav's barking and gladly took Rohan's bag to the guest room. He made tea for them and rushed to the shops to buy more food for dinner.

"Gerhardt might take Jarryd to Austria for treatment," Padma told Rohan. "He's found a brilliant eye specialist who might be able to help. But Jarryd needs to be stronger before he can travel."

They sat together at the big pine dining table, and she was aware of the villa having changed in his absence, returned to a former arrangement, a new composition, become again the house she had grown up in. How strange to be seated beside him with the old table between them, with its familiar dents and scratches and faint splashes of colour where candles had dripped

"What will you do after here?" Rohan asked. "Do you remember how you wanted to teach yoga at a place in Goa?"

"They've just offered me a job."

"So you applied? That's great! Now all you need is your teaching certificate."

"I've got that."

"Have you? But I thought—"

"I took the exam."

"You did? When?"

"Last week."

"In Colombo? Wasn't the yoga school in Colombo? Were you in Colombo last week?"

She felt her face grow hot. She could have said anything and he may even have believed her, but she was tired of secrets; so many stories she had told to so many people; there were too many versions of the truth to remember.

"I didn't want to feel sad again, we both know you'll be leaving soon," she admitted.

"I'm not sure if I will be going back."

"Aren't you expected at work at the end of the week?"

"I've told them I've been delayed, but I don't want to go back."

"What will you do instead?"

"I don't know." He sighed. "Being here is the only thing that makes sense."

He turned to look at the beach and the waves curling and rolling over; it was her view too, what she looked to when her mind churned, but she never learned anything new. These days the right decisions seemed to appear from inside her, as if she had always possessed them.

"It's so beautiful here," Rohan said. "When will you go to Goa?"

"I don't know now; I need to be here for Jarryd."

"But he's going to Austria with Gerhardt."

"Only when he's better."

Padma's phone lit up and buzzed and jigged, throbbing against the table. It was Gerhardt calling.

"Jarryd's blood pressure's stabilised and the internal bleeding has stopped," Gerhardt said.

"Thank God!"

Every day they clung to these miniscule signs of progress, which kept coming, one by one. She would not think of a time when they might end. She silently thanked every god that she had prayed to. Like most Asians she believed easily in both science and the divine and she had prayed fervently to the Buddha and significant Hindu gods for Jarryd's recovery. Soma had gone to the kovil and made a bargain with Goddess Kali, promising a sacrifice – he'd told Padma he had offered money, but she suspected that he had bargained much harder, offering a live chicken or maybe a goat.

"The doctors here are very pleased," Gerhardt said. "And now the eye surgeon from Vienna has offered us a consultation. That's a little way off, of course. His contact in India will fly over for an initial examination to assess the situation."

No doubt this required Jarryd to regain consciousness, but neither she nor Gerhardt spoke of that. She had allowed herself to blur the details of Jarryd's prognosis and not settle on any outcome. Having already once steeled herself to find Jarryd dead, she should have known to guide her expectations to stay low, but instead they soared to new heights. Hope knew no restraint for those one loved.

"Rohan's here," Padma told Gerhardt.

"Rohan? He's at the villa? Now?"

"He'll be staying in the guest room," she said quickly.

"You've told him about Jarryd?"

"He already knew. He saw it in the papers—"

"Ah, the great failed drug deal."

Gerhardt had read the item in silence. He had looked so defeated by it, so angry and helpless.

"So Rohan came back when he saw it?" Gerhardt said. "What a good fellow he is. I'll be very glad to see him."

So much was changing; the whole world had shifted and broken, but it was forming new, tiny shoots of enquiry breaking through.

"What a thing, him racing back to be with you . . ." Gerhardt mused.

Padma walked with Rohan in the garden. She showed him places of the past, where she had hidden once in certain nooks; the trees she had climbed; clearings where she had built huts and the mango tree where her rope swing had hung. She took him into the potting shed and showed him the inside of the door where long ago she had drawn oil-pastel sunsets and flowers and comical big-headed figures of Gerhardt, Soma, Gustav and herself. Gerhardt and

Soma had preserved these relics of her youthful art under strong varnish, and carefully painted around them whenever they painted the shed. Rohan took photographs, but Gerhardt had already told Soma to remove the door from the shed to take away with them. No memories were to be lost when they left. Memories could be replanted, Gerhardt claimed; they would go on living and breathing anywhere you put them.

"Gerhardt's glad you're back," Padma told Rohan.

"Really? You're sure?"

"Yes! He's been telling me to contact you for days."

"But you didn't."

"No. But I did come to your house—"

"You did?"

"—you weren't in, though."

"It's strange, I had a dream that you were in my garden."

"I was, and I had a lovely chat with your grumpy maid."

"The young one? She's a cow! Was she rude to you? Next time, call me first."

"Okay."

He took her hand. "I don't want us to end. Do you? How do you feel about us? Please, Padma, tell me the truth."

But she didn't know how she felt, or how to say it; all she could hold onto as they walked together was how right it felt to be with him.

"Can I go with you to Goa?" Rohan said.

"But I'm not going, I just told you."

"Jarryd's going to be in hospital for a long time. And you can always come back if he's sent home—"

"If?"

"Yes, if. He's in bad shape."

"He will get better. Don't you think he will?"

"I really want him to." Rohan stopped walking. "Jarryd would be the first to tell you to take that teaching job," Rohan said.

"And you'd come with me?"

"Yes."

"What would you do there?"

"Research."

"Oh yes? What research?"

"For a retreat of our own – didn't you say you wanted to run one? Well why not you and I together? I'll be able to observe how it's done while I'm there and then we can buy some land and build our own! We could make it just like the villa – Gerhardt could design it. I have some savings left, I always meant to invest it in a business – so why not our business, you and me together, living by the sea, somewhere beautiful?"

It was strange how simple a dream could sound, broken into its essential components.

"Do you still like India?" Rohan asked.

"I love India."

"And I love you. So we should do it!"

She smiled. It was the life she had imagined sometimes for herself; a life that Jarryd had guided her to in the years he had taught her. A natural, he had called her; a born yogi and teacher. His home had been her haven, her ship to explore the world in – and to this same house a van had come sneaking up, faceless figures spilling out and running inside, bursting into that glowing gentle light – such ugly demonic men, and so cruel that they could only have been demented, or – how else could they have returned after what they had done to lives with wives and children and friends and passed among them like ordinary people? She kept seeing Jarryd in his yellow room in the honey-gold lamp-light, sitting dreaming among his paintings and books, perhaps humming along to the Ravi Shankar CD they had discovered in the CD player left on and overheating. Jarryd sipping mint tea brewed in the silver teapot he had bought in Marrakech, in a market full of magicians and storytellers and acrobats. The minister's men had trampled through Jarryd's sweet nest, his life of music and beauty and love. Jarryd had loved everyone, but could that love survive what he had endured?

She had always wanted to live like him, with playfulness and a desire to serve; a life of purpose and fun, doing what he loved. Jarryd's love was in her, and she could pass it on. Rohan was right; Jarryd would have rejoiced to see Padma become a teacher.

"Let's do it," she said.

"Really?"

"Yes!"

That afternoon they made plans, lying in her bed entwined in each other, weaving a new life.

"I'll rent out my flat in London, that'll bring us some cash for now," Rohan said.

There were no further calls from Gerhardt; no further improvements in Jarryd's condition. When Rohan fell asleep, Padma sent a message to the owner of the retreat in Goa to say that her father couldn't come anymore, but that she would be bringing a friend, adding that they would no longer need two bedrooms, or the loan of a drawing board.

In the evening Soma packed dinner in plastic boxes for Gerhardt and Ruth and Karu drove it to the hospital. Soma laid the table for Padma and Rohan and they sat down to chicken curry, roti and chick pea dal with spinach. In most Sri Lankan homes there were many more dishes at mealtimes, especially when there were guests, but how soothing was the restraint of those two clay bowls of curries and basket of rotis on a pale-blue tablecloth with the quiet spaces in-between. For the first time in days she was hungry. They ate peacefully together.

After dinner, while Rohan unpacked in the guest room, she

walked around the garden with Gustav. The bungalows were locked-up, silent and dark inside. Waiting. Who knew what depravities those sweet false homes would witness when the minister's brother took over the running of the villa? Gerhardt planned to take out all of the furniture, the rugs and pictures and books and put them in the new cottages. The life of the villa would go on in the new places. They would leave only bricks and tiles and beams behind; walls, windows, doors – that was all the minister and his brother would have of the villa.

Padma looked into the outdoor kitchen, then she walked past the sheds. Gustav started to growl as they came near the shed where her scooter was kept.

"Is someone there?" Padma called in Sinhalese.

Her voice sounded small in the darkness; Soma and Rohan would not be able to hear her from the house; she would have to have screamed to be heard. She turned, imagining Sunny behind her, about to clamp a hand over her mouth – but there was no one. Gustav pulled on his lead and barked and dragged her closer to the shed.

"Who's in here?" she shouted and threw open the door with a crash.

Her scooter gleamed untouched. Gerhardt's tools hung as always above the workbench. She took the machete with her as she followed Gustav out of the shed. Leaves rustled nearby and Gustav started to bark.

"Hello!" said a voice from above.

Sunny was looking over the garden wall, which Gerhardt had planned to extend higher, but Sunny still had to be standing on a ladder to be able to look over. He steadied himself holding onto the iron spikes, put in to deter burglars. Until only a few months earlier there had been a family living next door: father, mother, three grown sons – reticent, fearful villagers who had run a garage tending mostly to the minister's vehicles. The family had hardly ever spoken with anyone at the villa and they had left without saying goodbye. Everyone knew that they had sold their house and the coconut grove behind it to the minister's brother.

Gustav hurled himself at the wall, snarling up at Sunny.

"What do you want?" Padma asked Sunny.

"Just to see how you are. How are you these days?"

"You should watch out, the minister's brother owns that house now," she told him.

"That's true, you don't want to annoy the minister or his brother. Look what happened to your friend."

"It could happen to you as well."

"Actually, I'm good friends with the minister and his brother."

"I'm sure."

"I hear your friend is back," Sunny said.

Rohan must have been seen arriving, so Sunny had come to see for himself. It seemed vaguely like proof that Sunny had been involved in Rohan's mugging, but as always it wasn't clear. Most of the exhaustion of dealing with Sunny was never knowing what he wanted and what he was trying to make you do. It was always too late when she linked up the clues.

"You're going to Colombo?" Sunny asked.

"Maybe. Or maybe we'll go to London. Want to come?"

How crazed Sunny was, to come so far from home to balance on ladders and trespass on the property of a psychopath minister – just to find out about Padma's private life. Would Sunny ever grow old like other people? Would he ever start to tire easily and need to sleep in the afternoons for hours and sit slumped on a veranda, mumbling with the neighbours?

"How lucky for you, going to London. Must be nice having a rich man to pay for everything – and this one is young. He must be having all his teeth and far fewer wrinkles than your other boyfriends, no?"

She dragged Gustav away and left Sunny up there, laughing like a maniac. She walked, glancing over her shoulder all the way back to the house; he would never be taking her by surprise again. Inside, she locked all the windows and bolted the back door.

## 36

ROHAN WOKE UP at dawn, alone in darkness, rising up from the depths of dreams. At the villa he slept so deeply, he woke not knowing where he was; without present or past, no signs to guide him. He reached for Padma, but she wasn't there. The fan throbbed above. He heard her speaking outside in the hall.

"I'm on my way. I'll be there soon," she told someone.

She came into the room, pulling off her nightdress.

"Jarryd's awake," she said, starting to dress.

"I'll go and get ready," Rohan said.

He was crossing the hall when Soma appeared.

"Who was that on the phone?" he asked, squinting at Rohan.

He didn't seem concerned that Rohan had come out of Padma's room in only his boxer shorts.

"Jarryd's woken up," Rohan said.

"Has he spoken?"

"I don't know."

Padma appeared, tucking in a t-shirt.

"What's happened?" Soma asked her.

"He's woken up. Gerhardt said he's very weak."

"Can he see?"

"His eyes are still bandaged. The specialists have said to keep them covered up for now."

"He's going to be blind," Soma said.

"No, he isn't! Not necessarily!" Padma cried.

"And his brain must be damaged."

"No, it's not! What's wrong with you, Soma - you're so negative! Jarryd knew who Gerhardt and Ruth were, and he understood why he was at the hospital and why they were with him - so his brain's working perfectly."

"Can he use his legs?"

"He hasn't even sat up yet, give him a chance!"

Soma stood anxiously watching as Padma rang the driver and arranged for him to come for them at the villa. In the guest room Rohan dressed, buttoning a shirt, carefully prising in one button after the other. He was suddenly unsure if Gerhardt and Ruth would want him to be at the hospital, intruding in their tight, small circle at such a time. A part of him wanted to stay away, to never have to see what that circle contained now at its centre. But Padma needed him. Soma clattered in the kitchen, preparing a hurried breakfast for them of Nescafé and cheese toast. They sat on the porch toying with the food, waiting for the driver.

"I'll stay here," Soma said. "Somebody needs to keep an eye on the house."

"Good idea. Keep the doors and windows locked. And make sure you leave Gustav outside," Padma said, looking carefully over the garden.

The car appeared in the lane and hooted for them. Soma gave Padma a sandalwood Lord Ganesha to place next to Jarryd's bed. "Say hello to Jarryd Mahatthaya from me," he said, his voice sounding strained.

Padma walked determinedly down to the car. Rohan walked

beside her. He would not let himself think of what they would see.

Jarryd had a room at the hospital with a large glass panel, over which a curtain had been drawn, thus delaying the moment when they would witness the reality of what had happened to him. Rohan had never known such dread, such acute uncertainty in his own ability to take in something so irreversible; for there was a terror in him and repulsion, resisting seeing damage so wilfully inflicted. Padma went first into the room. She had been shaking in the hall, her teeth chattering, her hand ice-cold in his, but her fear seemed suddenly to leave her as she entered the room, a new calm sweeping into her face, an accepting generous kindness; she was ready to receive, to give. He had not seen her so steely, so strong before, or this hidden toughness under her soft surface, risen up now when it was needed.

Jarryd lay sleeping, his head and eyes bandaged, a drip in one arm. A sheet covered him up to the neck. Gerhardt and Ruth, seated at the side of the bed, turned to them, Gerhardt opening his arms to Padma. She went to him and held him, and Ruth held Padma's hand. Rohan stood behind them and together in silence they watched the figure on the bed.

"He's gone back to sleep," Ruth whispered

Jarryd was so still, he could have been dead, only the beeping of a monitor confirmed activity within him: a heart pulsing, blood surging. Or maybe the blood trailed weakly to the torn broken tissues, swollen and seeping. Was there a steady secret repair taking place within that still form? How much lay outside its capabilities? Ruth reached for Rohan's hand, drawing him into their silent togetherness. To anyone going past, glancing in through the door, they would have looked like people gathered at the bedside of a relative. In a sense they were a family, bound by an unspoken affinity, impossible to define. In that white room with the shades pulled down, alive with the hum of machines and air conditioning, there was a peacefulness that had settled, pushing away the wildness and injustice and horror of the world outside.

"Did he speak?" Padma asked Ruth.

"He muttered something."

"It sounded like 'where am I'?" Gerhardt said. "He was speaking in Sinhalese."

"He must have thought he was still with those devils," Ruth murmured.

She turned away, hiding her crying.

"Can I get you some tea? Some water?" Rohan asked her.

She shook her head.

"Gerhardt? Padma? Can I get you anything?"

He longed to serve them, to be of use to them and make them strong, to stand with their beautiful dignity against despair and hopelessness. They, of all people, could not be allowed to succumb and be defeated. People like him needed people like them to live their sweet charmed lives – they had to be enabled to stay trusting in goodness and beauty and kindness. People like them had to be allowed to build the worlds they wanted, so that all the others could see.

Jarryd lifted an arm, then it fell back onto the bed. A leg twitched under the sheets. His head turned on the pillow. Padma rushed to his side and leaned close.

"Jarryd? Jarryd, it's Padma. You're safe with us now. Gerhardt is here. And Ruth, and Rohan, we're all here. We're right here with you."

"Gerhardt?" The voice was faint, but it was Jarryd's voice.

"Jarryd, yes, yes it's me, Gerhardt."

Gerhardt went at once to Jarryd's side, gently touching Jarryd's bare shoulder.

"I can't see—"

"I know, I know, we're going to find out what we can do. You just need to get stronger."

Gerhardt bowed his head onto the bed. Padma kissed Jarryd's hand, her tears streaming onto the sheets.

"Padma is right here," Gerhardt said.

"Padma? My little Padma?"

His hand probed the air. She held that pale shaking hand in both of hers. He gave a small moan.

"Jarryd, we're going to look after you. You're going to be okay," she said, her voice so calm and strong and certain.

"My eyes, they hurt so much. I can't see. What has happened?"

There was a pause, the silence of gathering the right words, the right way to speak – did Jarryd read it and understand? He turned his head away. He didn't ask again.

"We're going to take you to Colombo to see a specialist," Ruth said. "Then we will know about your eyes and what needs to be done."

"Ruth," Jarryd murmured. "You are so good. My friends . . . so good to me."

A sigh, a choking sobbing came from the thin old man stretched on the bed. Rohan stifled his helplessness, willing love and goodness to flare in those beloved others, for it was they more than anyone who could soothe a damaged soul and return it to wholeness; heal wounds that seemed impossible to mend.

For the next two days Jarryd grew steadily stronger and it was decided that he could be moved to a hospital in Colombo where the eye doctor from India could examine him. As yet there was only pain in his eyes; he had regained no sight. Even in a darkened room, when the bandages were lifted, Jarryd saw nothing, not even shadows. A private ambulance was arranged and Ruth and Gerhardt prepared to travel with him.

"Will you stay on for a few more days?" Gerhardt asked Rohan.

"Yes, of course."

"Thank you. It's a comfort to me knowing that Padma and Soma aren't alone in the house. Do you know how long you can stay?"

"As long as you need me."

"Haven't you got work to get back to?" Ruth asked.

"They'll wait."

"Did they say that?"

"Yes." It didn't matter that this wasn't strictly true. His work could do what it liked, he wasn't going back; he knew that now.

"Your company won't wait for ever, you know. Don't trust everything they say," Ruth warned.

"Don't worry, I don't trust them at all."

Padma glanced up with a smile. Neither she nor he had told Ruth or Gerhardt about going to India. It didn't seem the right time, but soon they would announce it, and then perhaps the plans would feel more real. For now, they floated, fantastical wistful clouds before him.

## 37

IT WAS TIME to start packing up the house. Padma began with the office. Rohan kept asking to help so she had him fill boxes with books while she shredded papers, letters, emails from guests and cast away the traces of her short-lived business. Still, she didn't regret it, one never knew how a life would feel until one wore it; but it was important to know when to shed it, when it was time to start again, to be able to go on growing.

"Would you like a beer at Boss's?" Rohan asked.

"I can't, I have to finish packing this room today."

"There's no rush."

"The house is going to be sold at the end of the week!"

"It'll be weeks before everything is finalised."

But on that final Friday, they would leave for Gerhardt's house and the villa would belong to the minister's brother. He and the minister would be free to walk around the garden under cover of night when they wouldn't be seen. They could sit on the porch and drink beer and make plans while Special Security Force guards patrolled the garden or stood silent in the shadows, poised to hurt anyone who came too near.

And soon the foreigners would come to stay, to loll around on the veranda or in the bungalows with women bought by the hour and maybe even a child or two from the village plied with gifts. This was what Sunny had once wanted for her. After all these years of defending the villa against him, Sunny's dream was coming true. But it was too late for him; he would not profit from this latest change; she consoled herself with that.

"What shall I do with Jarryd's books?" Rohan asked, bringing over a box of the unsold copies. There were so many still to be sold, but for now they had to stay hidden. She flicked through the thick cream pages, the copy in her hand falling open to a strange unsettling section:

## THE ALLURE OF SRI LANKA

Sri Lanka to outsiders is a secret small whole, a glimpse of perfection. One is drawn deep into its hushed murmuring watchful greenness, its close moist heat. There is a wild raw beauty about Sri Lanka, yet this is a trap, a poison, it ensnares you and then you will never escape. The island's beauty is most clearly seen by those who are free to leave, and those who have left – people free of the angry warring spirit that maintains divisions between the people left living together, pulling apart and resisting each other, each defending their divided depleted terrain. For those who long to claim a place of their own in a paradise world, somewhere to hide from the dullness of life and the rigours of their world, Sri Lanka has offered itself, the perfect magical isle where one can lose oneself.

Paul Bowles, Pablo Neruda, DH Lawrence each felt this pull and for a time enjoyed the island's splendour, but they all succumbed to dark currents and forces, encountering difficulties with people. The island lures and embraces and longs to be embraced, to be admired by those who are unaware of the secret discontent of its inhabitants, and the ugliness that lurks behind their smiles of greeting.

These days Sri Lanka is an excellent luxury holiday destination. Tourists are a breed apart and treated well, unless they interfere or intervene in any ugliness they witness. There is a darkness behind the bowing beaming welcome of garlands and mango cordial offered in hotel receptions; or the famed generosity of the poor, sharing their meagre meals with outsiders. Stay away from altercations even those between locals, do not take sides, do not try to help. And do not speak openly of what you have glimpsed, then the country will show you its sweetness and offer only kindness.

For the locals there is a reward to be had in these acts of generosity, for in caring for visitors, they gain a chance to transcend their lives of fear and struggle and bask in the gratitude of strangers. Tourists in Sri Lanka can remain unaware throughout their stay, and even afterwards, of the people's true feelings and their seething resentments. Visitors pay and are granted a gilded way through the fury and sadness at the heart of this fierce, deflowered island. For the tourists, the island spreads its peacock tails in the sun and dances, determined to impress, and to rise above the sadness of its weary soul, its tortured beauty.

Jarryd had cared so much for the country. He had wanted so much to help. He had thought that by exposing the ugliness to the light, it would lose its potency, but the ugliness had turned on him. She packed Jarryd's books in her bags for Goa. Jarryd would never be silenced, she would give out the books for the world to see.

Now the dresser shelves were empty, only the stereo was left and the Dancing Shiva. She stood, leaning against a pillar, the silky white plaster warm with sun. Here, the men coming to stay would cavort with women paid to perform friendship and attraction, hollow imitations of love and togetherness. She almost felt sorry for those deluded stupid men travelling all the way to Nilwatte Beach to be conned, but possibly they were fully aware of the artifice of what they were receiving, reassured by a transaction; for paying gave one the power to have, and even an artifice could be felt as real.

She went into the garden, trailing her hand around its skin of bark and leaves and petals, its needles and spikes and eruptions of flowers. Gustav started to bark.

"Hello? Hi? Is anyone there?" a man shouted up from the lane.

He was young, white, British sounding; a tourist with a backpack. Gustav ran to the gate.

"Is this The Villa Araliya?" the man asked.

"Yes, but we're closed." She stopped, refusing to say 'closed down', with its suggestion of failure.

"Is Rohan staying here?"

"Rohan?"

"Rohan Fernando. I'm a friend of his."

The man was tall, slim, about the same age as Rohan. He was tanned, with brown hair lightened by sun. He could have been anyone – maybe Rohan's manager, sent to talk him into returning to London.

"Please, could you let him know that Tom is here to see him?" The man extended a hand over the gate to Gustav. Gustav let himself be patted, wagging his tail, not barking anymore. She trusted that. Gustav knew about people.

"Okay, wait here," she said and went back to the house.

"There's someone called Tom to see you," she told Rohan.

He was sealing up boxes and stared blankly up at her.

"He says he's a friend of yours."

"Who?"

"Someone called Tom."

"*Tom?* Where?"

"He's waiting at the gate."

He raced past her into the garden.

"Tommy! What are you doing here?" he shouted to the man.

Rohan opened the gate and he and the man hugged on the path, Gustav bounding around them.

They came up to the house together.

"This place is beautiful," Padma heard Tom say. He sounded surprised. "From what your mother said, I thought—" He stopped as Padma went out to join them.

She felt his gaze on her, the sudden keen interest assessing her as she stood next to Rohan.

"This is Padma," Rohan said. "Padma, this is Tom, my oldest friend from England."

"Padma's the manager here," he told Tom, and she and Tom shook hands.

"Rohan's mother seems to think you're Austrian," Tom said.

"My mother sounds very confused," Rohan replied.

"I'm sorry I left you standing outside, I thought you were his boss," Padma said to Tom.

"Like my boss would ever come looking for me." Rohan laughed.

"You need to talk to your mother; she told me you'd gone running to a den of iniquity," Tom said.

"And you came to rescue me?"

"Of course."

"She said you'd been mugged."

"That was ages ago. I'm fine now."

"He was hurt quite badly by some barbed wire," Padma said.

She would have diminished such an incident to a stranger usually - a local habit, even a national trait, not to dwell on the small everyday dangers when talking to outsiders - but she felt an inexplicable urge to unsettle the newcomer. She felt his pull on Rohan, they were bonded by a deep closeness that she could already feel, a new current pushing her away.

"Wow, what a view - this is a very lovely house!" Tom said, looking approvingly out from the veranda.

"It's been sold, that's why we're closed," Padma told him.

Just then Soma came out to the veranda and stared at Tom.

"He's a friend of Rohan's," Padma explained.

"If you're closed I'd better find somewhere to stay," Tom said.

"Can't he stay here, Baba?" Soma urged.

"We're not really set up for guests at the moment." Padma frowned at Soma to make him stop.

"No problem, I saw loads of guest-house signs when I was coming here," Tom said.

"But how can he stay in those places, Baba?" Soma protested. "Shall I call Gerhardt Mahaththaya and ask him? I'm sure he won't mind a friend of Rohan Mahaththayya's staying here for a few days."

"Gerhardt's got more important things to think about right now, don't you think?" Padma said sharply to Soma.

"Gerhardt Mahaththaya won't mind - you just stay here," Soma told Tom.

Soma sounded desperate. What a time to start being a good host.

"I can go now and make up the bed in the small bungalow," Soma said, and Padma gave in.

Soma went inside and opened up the linen cupboard. So he was afraid; possibly he imagined they would all be safer with a tourist in the house. Boss and his men were no match for the minister, but the minister might hesitate to tangle with a foreigner. Everyone knew about the politician in the next town who had raped a student from England and killed her boyfriend and avoided prison because his uncle was a cabinet minister, but only until the British High Commission intervened. The little shit was locked up in prison now and still waiting for a pardon, but that would only come when all the fuss died down.

"Please, how much do I owe you?" Tom asked Padma and she told him the usual room rate. Charging him felt safer, a barrier between him and them.

Padma sat with Rohan and Tom at the dining table. Soma returned to say that the bungalow was ready.

"Can I bring sir a drink?" Soma asked Tom.

"Tea would be great, thank you," Tom said.

"I'll make tea for everyone."

"When do you go back to London?" Tom asked Rohan.

"He's not going back," Padma said.

"For a while or ever?"

"Who knows?" Rohan said.

"You're quitting the bank?" Tom looked delighted.

"We're going to Goa to stay at a yoga retreat. We're planning to set up one of our own," Padma said.

Not only Tom, but Rohan too looked startled. She'd exposed him to his friend. It seemed necessary, a test.

"Wow! That's great! Whose idea was that?" Tom said.

"Both of ours," Padma said and felt Tom look at her with admiration.

He was impressed – by the idea itself or perhaps merely its otherness, but he was excited for them. His neat even features that had seemed so unexceptional earlier were suddenly alive and attractive. She felt his approval and his kindness and knew that he meant no harm to them. No damage he caused would be wilful.

"Padma's a yoga teacher," Rohan explained.

"And what will you be doing?" Tom asked Rohan.

"He'll help me run the place," Padma said.

Soma brought out the tea and they settled at the table.

"What work did you have in India?" Rohan asked Tom.

"I've just signed up a client. It's early days, but it looks promising."

Padma felt Tom's unsettling energy, even as he sat quietly beside her. He seemed familiar. She knew his drive, an eagerness rather than a hunger; she knew that confidence and quiet intelligence; he made her feel nervous of her own ideas, so much smaller seeming near him. It was how she sometimes felt around Gerhardt. Gerhardt would like Tom very much. She sat back in her chair, in their strange new circle of three.

"So your company's actually growing," Rohan mused. "I'll be honest, I never thought you'd pull it off."

"I know!" Tom grinned.

"He came to me with this crazy idea—" Rohan told Padma.

"Not that crazy!" Tom added.

"Clearly," Rohan agreed. "I'm impressed. In fact, I'm amazed."

"There's still time to join. A dynamic socially-engaged enterprise - how about it? Both of you? We can all be partners. I'm looking for partners."

Padma laughed.

"I'm serious," Tom said.

"He really is," Rohan said wryly to Padma.

"Not for me, thanks." Padma wanted their talk to be over and for Tom to be resting in the small bungalow. Three was an unstable number, its pairs constantly changing, its bonds always under strain.

"We could all go to London together," Tom said.

Tom's London would be a different city to Rohan's, a place of vibrant neighbourhoods of artistic, ambitious, flamboyant people, people with ideas and knowledge and belief; finding each other in intriguing places: sleepy daytime pubs, galleries and great libraries; museums and private clubs.

"I'm not going back to London," Rohan said.

"We could share a flat," Tom said. "We could work from home, and Padma, you could still teach yoga classes - there are hundreds of yoga studios in London. And we could all hang out in the evenings—"

Rohan shook his head.

"You know you want to . . . you know you miss London . . ." Tom coaxed.

"I don't miss it at all," Rohan said with certainty.

"Of course, you'd have to move out of that deathly boring neighbourhood of yours," Tom said. "And just think - no more going into the bank - no more suits, no more wankers—"

Rohan smiled and looked away. He watched the waves, big and restless and far away, their roar filling the silence.

⚹

After lunch, Tom went to his bungalow and Rohan lay beside Padma on her bed. He was thinking of Tom, and feeling a familiar needling anxiety; the way Tom used to make him feel when they met after work for drinks. If only he could have hidden his new life a little longer, he and Padma had only just started to piece it together, such frail strands still forming. In the bold clear light of Tom's vision, his work so strident, Rohan's plans wavered unrooted. It was precisely what his mother would have intended, sending Tom to stir up old ambitions.

"Are you sure you want to go to Goa?" Padma asked.

Could she have sensed his sudden uncertainty?

"Of course I want to go! I suggested it."

"You won't change your mind once we're there?"

"Not at all."

"But if you do, I'll be stranded."

"I wouldn't leave you."

"I don't want you to feel trapped," Padma said.

"I won't!"

They were too tired, too stirred up to make love, although the afternoons were her favourite time. She fell asleep against him. Padma slept better in the afternoons than at night. He had often found her wandering the house in the early hours of the morning, or seated on the porch steps with Gustav, watching over the garden, waiting for the dawn. He heard a door close outside. He eased away from the bed. From the window he saw Tom leaving, crossing the lawn. He wore a handloom cloth bag over his shoulder – it looked like a handbag, but it wouldn't have bothered Tom. He had never appeared to care what others thought of him, but he cared alright that he stayed different to all the usual public schoolboys. He wanted intensely to be seen for himself; to never be mistaken for a type. He marched over the garden, the cloth bag a bright holster at his side. Of course, another possibility was utility – the little handbag was exactly the right size for carrying an iPad, a notebook and pen; Tom had always known what he needed. It was a talent, or perhaps just a skill made better with practise, to know the exact nature of one's desires, and to be clear about what one truly hoped to achieve. How freeing to work only in the service of one true goal, to never worry that another truer calling was being ignored. Rohan put on his clothes and went outside.

Tom hadn't gone far. He was standing in the lane discussing cafés with a local man who wore the eager helpful demeanour the locals reserved for tourists; a best-self kept for show. Rohan looked the man over; could he have been involved in Jarryd's abduction? Since the attack, everyone in the neighbourhood was a possible torturer.

"Sir, if you want a café, go to the Kingfisher Café," the man told Tom.

It was one of the row of beach bars owned by the minister and his brother.

"There's a better bar this way," Rohan said, steering Tom in the opposite direction while the man glowered at him.

They went in to Boss's bar. In the kitchen, off the entrance, Boss's wife was washing up. She greeted Rohan as he took Tom through the empty bar and out onto the cliff-top garden. Boss scrambled up from a deck chair.

"You want beer? I'll bring it to you in one minute, okay?" Boss sat tousled and tired-looking and lit a cigarette.

Rohan and Tom sat at the table at the edge of the garden, looking down the cliff to the beach and the black laterite reef. The sun was growing gentle, its yellow deepening, spreading. Soon Jarryd would have come by with his limping swinging gait, undressing at the next table and descending to the waves. His music would have followed him wading towards the sunset glow with its burning red centre.

"Everything alright?" Tom said.

"There used to be an old guy who came here and danced in the sea at sunset."

"Cool!"

"He came every evening to celebrate his day. He lived each day so fully, so completely. They'd play his music for him on the bar stereo."

"I can't wait!"

"He's not coming, he's in hospital. He was attacked. He's probably been blinded."

"Jesus. Poor guy."

"It was a robbery last time, but this time they wanted to punish him. He dared to say how he really felt – and that's what did it. Nobody's allowed to speak their truth in this country."

"Who's they?"

"The local minister, most probably. And maybe it wasn't even his order initially, it may have come from above, but he's certainly made use of it - he's managed to extract some valuable land on the back of it. He's the new owner of the villa."

"What a shame! It's a beautiful house."

"Padma always thought she'd come back to it - but maybe one shouldn't ever go back."

"Depends where to."

"I'm done with my old life."

"But was it your life really? Working for an investment bank?"

Rohan had thought he had chosen, but maybe he had merely been led. Like so many others, he had been seduced while still at college by the fine talk and attentions of the elite young executives sent by the bank to charm them: witty, polished, beautiful gym-toned, young women and men, only a few years older than him yet already full of a sophisticated worldly confidence, inviting the selected students to dinner and drinks. It was only after succumbing to join them that one saw them as they were beneath the veneer: addled by doubts and nerves and secret afflictions and astonishing insecurities.

"It's what happens to most people," Rohan said.

"But not me! And it shouldn't have been you either - you got well and truly sucked into the sausage factory, my friend."

Rohan smiled, glad to return to talking in their old way.

"Come back with me! We'd work so well together," Tom said. "We might even do something amazing! At least we'd make a difference. We always said we'd only take on work we cared about - remember?"

"Of course I remember."

"Padma would come too if you asked her."

"I can't do that to her - she's finally going to do what she loves, I'm not taking that from her."

Boss came to take their order.

"How's Jarryd?" he asked Rohan.

"He's out of his coma. He was talking a little, he remembered everyone."

"Did he talk about what happened?"

"No."

"He was so stubborn! We all told him to take that book out of the shops."

"But everything he said in it was true."

"Who cares? Only a fool goes upsetting a politician like the minister. He's the only one who can do what he likes."

Tom listened wide-eyed.

"Where's Padma?" Boss asked.

"She's at the villa."

"You tell her to be careful with that father of hers, it looks like he's big buddies with the minister now."

"Gerhardt's not buddies with the minister!" Rohan exclaimed.

"Not Gerhardt - Sunny!" Boss gave Rohan a puzzled glance.

"Sunny . . ." Rohan repeated and then he understood. He understood everything. Padma's father hadn't drowned in the flood she had once told him had swept away her parents.

"Is Padma's mother still alive?" he asked Boss.

"She was wandering around the market just the other day!"

Did Padma have brothers? Sisters? Poor Padma; what a way to be orphaned.

"Who's Sunny?" Tom asked when Boss left to get their order.

"The local bad guy pain in the arse. He's been hassling Padma for ages."

"So if you two ever get hitched, he'd be your father-in-law?"

"Don't be stupid."

A frightened little voice in his head that sounded like his mother told him to back away, to say sorry and feel cowardly and deeply ashamed, but run. Run for his life.

## 38

GERHARDT DROVE HIMSELF and Ruth to the villa for dinner, leaving Karu watching over Jarryd who was sleeping, sedated for the night. Karu was under strict instructions not to leave Jarryd's side and to call the nurses if he saw anyone suspicious lurking nearby. It was all they could do to make up for not being with him the one time he should not have been alone and defenceless. Could anyone have saved Jarryd that night? They would have come for him sometime. Once the order was given, the forces of malevolence unleashed, nothing could have stopped them entering his world, so wide open and unguarded.

Each day they guarded him now, watching over his quiet steady breathing, like the sound of morning waves in the room. He would sleep for many hours, the time of danger receding. The beeping, whirring machinery had been wheeled away, unpinned one morning from the body lying gathering itself, its bruises healing, bones mending, its gaze under the bandages turned inward. Jarryd barely spoke when he was awake. They played his music for him and recounted happy times as they sat with him, dwelling in gentle memories. Or they talked of good news, of small new happenings – he liked hearing about the planning of Padma's impending trip, and how Rohan's return had surprised her – although they didn't say what had prompted it. Jarryd assumed at once that it was romance that had drawn Rohan back to the villa, and Gerhardt knew then that the old Jarryd was still alive inside the broken body; a hopeful loving nature was built into a person's mind perhaps; maybe even its cells. He stayed by Jarryd's side, willing those cells to grow and proliferate and spread their magical goodness all through his friend.

One thing they never mentioned near Jarryd was the sale of the villa. And they never asked him any questions that might lead him back to a too-dark place. When he spoke he didn't offer them any glimpses of what he had endured, only murmured concern for his eyes that still hurt him. The doctors had ascertained that a sharp instrument had been used to pierce Jarryd's eyes; membranes and tissues had been ruptured in several places, on separate occasions. Pain flared in Gerhardt as he tried to assimilate the facts, questions in him that he could not find answers to: how anyone could possess the necessary anger and hatred for such measured steady violence. For Jarryd, the memories came to him at night. Gerhardt held him as he screamed, dreaming himself back into an unknown hell, remembering.

Ruth had arranged for a trauma specialist to attend to him – a highly recommended young Harvard-educated son of one of her friends. The young man spent several hours each day alone with Jarryd, talking in the strictest confidence. He had worked with many similar cases of abduction and torture, he had told them, words he uttered as fact. The young psychologist was baffled by Jarryd.

"He knows, he remembers, but he already seems to be working through the trauma by himself." The psychologist was impressed. "He's working so hard, all on his own. All day long he must be lying there quietly processing what happened to him."

"He used to meditate a lot," Ruth said.

"It's incredible; he's remarkably strong mentally."

Gerhardt held on to the psychologist's admiration, it was consoling to know that even the experts were alert to the impressive attributes of his friend. Already the medical staff showed a heightened interest and concern for Jarryd, possibly they would do more than was usual to help. Gerhardt clung to this hope; the kindness of staff was all they had, those solemn stern nurses, starched white angels, watching over his friend.

He drove with Ruth silent beside him to the villa. The lane was empty. No one seemed to be going to the brothel anymore. The bars were still open, but their gardens were empty. Could he ever have known that he would one day have few regrets about leaving the area? But parking by the gate, strolling up the path to the white-pillared form of his villa and its warm yellow glow, he felt the same pride. There were voices coming from the veranda. An extra young man was seated at the table with Padma and Rohan. Padma was talking, the two young men turned to her, admiring and attentive. They all turned to look as Gerhardt and Ruth went in.

"How's Jarryd?" Padma asked.

"He's sleeping," Ruth said.

"We've left Karu with him. I'll go back after dinner," Gerhardt added.

Rohan and the new young man had stood up for Ruth, and now the new young man came over to shake hands.

"This is Tom, an old friend of Rohan's," Padma explained. "He'll stay the night in the small bungalow. Soma's made up the bed."

"I hope that's alright," Tom said.

An Englishman, very English, with an air of immense confidence. There was still a select segment of that nation who could travel the world cushioned by privilege. Class, wealth, a liberal education; cultured, intelligent – an unassailable combination.

"You were at university together?" Ruth asked him.

"Different colleges," Rohan said.

Ruth smiled, approving. She was predictably impressed, like all those of her particular niche of Sri Lankan society who were easily seduced and reassured by an elite British education.

"We were at school together," Tom said. "We both boarded. Rohan used to stay at my house during the holidays when he didn't come back to Colombo."

There was an authenticity and openness to this Tom, a steadiness at his core. Well-loved by a mother, Ruth would say, her explanation for strength of character and the likeability of a person.

"What about Padma?" Gerhardt had challenged her.

"Mother or mother-figure," Ruth maintained.

*He* was that mother-figure, according to Ruth. She even included Soma in that category.

"Fussing over her like a pair of old women. I'm the one who's more like a father to her."

Gerhardt and Ruth joined the three at the table. There was something familiar about that trio of young people, an excitement about them, kindred spirits finding each other in a particular place, in a particular moment in the wilderness of the world. He knew well the headiness of that recognition, the embracing warmth of that connection. What tangles would they weave, those three? How much heartache would they cause each other?

Soma came out and Ruth discussed the dinner arrangements, checking on the quantities of oil and coconut milk in the curries, and instructing him to skin the chicken pieces. It seemed to Gerhardt she had always been there, analysing the dinner; he couldn't imagine a life without her. Somehow they had always been together, despite Ronny, despite everything. Now more than ever he knew that he needed her; and that he needed to be near her – the past days had proven it.

Padma went with Ruth to the hospital the next morning to relieve Gerhardt from his watch. He rose stiffly from the fold-up bed and went outside with Ruth to drink coffee and discuss the night – the new dreams and utterances that had defied the sedatives while Jarryd slept. Jarryd looked bigger in the bed that morning, more present, more alive.

"Hi Jarryd." She kissed his cheek. His cheekbones were hard and pointed under the stubble, his skin pale.

He smiled and reached for her hand.

"Hello, my Padma. How are you?"

"Good. And you? Are you comfortable?"

"Getting there."

"Do you need anything?"

"No. Thank you for coming to see me. Aren't you very busy packing?"

She had to remind herself that he meant Goa, not the villa's sale.

"It's a few weeks away," she said.

"Gerhardt says you'll be teaching a yoga class."

"I don't have to go, I can wait until you're home."

"But this is what you have worked for! You're my best pupil – blaze a trail, please! Show them all what good teachers we both are!"

"I will." She kissed him again.

"And Rohan is still planning to go with you?"

"Yes."

"Big changes for him." Jarryd grew thoughtful. "Whatever he does, you must stay true to your path," he said.

"You think he'll change his mind?"

"I don't know. He also is searching – he too must find his way. But you are each very good for the other, I can tell."

Jarryd fell silent. He seemed to have fallen asleep. His broken ribs and fractured limbs were fusing whole again, the most recent X-rays had revealed. His body was steadying, recovering, readying itself to go on before the next wave hit – this was how he had always lived. Perhaps it was how all lives progressed, despite all the effort one made to avoid falls and collisions.

"Is Ruth here?" Jarryd murmured.

"No, she's outside with Gerhardt. Shall I get her?"

"No. I wanted to ask you – how is your mother?"

"She's much better. In fact, the treatments have been so successful there's no need for me to send her money anymore."

"Ah, that is good to hear! Aren't you glad you were able to help? The poor woman must have felt so desperate – thank God she had you."

"Yes, thank God. And now I'm so glad because you're getting better."

"Yes, I am better."

Jarryd's fingers suddenly tightened around hers.

"I've been damaged before, but I danced with my damaged leg. I will see again with my damaged eyes."

"You will, Jarryd, of course you will." She was trying not to cry; she wiped away her tears so that he didn't feel them as she kissed him.

"I will see," he said again. "Even blind, one sees."

Maybe she too would find a strength like his, if she had to. Like him, maybe she too would one day close her eyes and see everything. Ruth came in and sat at the foot of the bed. She massaged Jarryd's feet and he smiled in that new way of his, looking in the wrong direction, thanking her. Ruth joked about the size of his long big toes; he said something lewd and she tutted at him. Padma held Jarryd's hand until he fell asleep.

Tom left that afternoon. Padma and Rohan walked with him to the gate to see him to the taxi.

"Call me whenever you're in London!" Tom shouted to Rohan as he left.

Over the road, a hooded figure appeared behind the coconut trees. Padma saw with a start that it was Leela, her face half-covered by a brown shawl. Padma had never seen Leela so close to the villa before. Padma glanced back as she and Rohan went into the garden. Leela raised a small dark claw of hand and beckoned to Padma.

"You go in, I'll be back in a minute," Padma told Rohan.

"Where are you going?"

"To Boss's"

"I'll come with you."

"No, no! You go inside, I won't be long."

"But why can't I come with you?"

"Please don't worry, I'll be back in a minute."

There was a heaviness in her head as when a storm was brewing.

"I just want to sit by myself for a little while," she said, actually wishing that she could.

Rohan looked worried, but he went on alone. Padma went back to the lane, but now Leela had disappeared. Padma walked up the lane, checking as she went that neither Rohan nor Soma had followed her. Leela was waiting for her at the entrance to the alley where Rohan had been mugged.

"This way," Leela called.

Was it a trap? Why this same alleyway? But Padma went in. She was stronger than Leela. She stepped carefully around the potholes, going past the wire fences of the dishevelled little village houses. A woman came out of one of the houses and scraped out a plate of rice for a mob of scrawny cats. She looked up and saw Leela and Padma and drew back into the house. The cats snarled and scrabbled and scratched each other for the scraps.

"Come here!" Leela called to Padma.

She waited in the middle of the alley, a dark, hooded totem, an omen.

Padma took a step forward then stopped. Everything in her told her to back away, yet she was suddenly afraid of not doing as Leela wanted. This was new. She had only ever felt afraid around Sunny – he was the one who would hurt you if you disobeyed.

Padma stood still. It took Leela a moment to understand that Padma wasn't going in any further. Padma wanted to back away to the lane, but she didn't move as Leela came towards her, stopping a few paces away.

"I've been waiting around all day to try and see you," Leela said cheerfully. "How is your friend Jarryd?"

"He's doing well."

"Lucky I overheard Sunny, no? So I could tell you what I heard."

Padma felt her body tighten, the muscles clenching so sharply they hurt. 'The body never lies,' Jarryd used to say. 'Our bodies are the most truthful part of ourselves, the best guide we have.'

"He's blind now, no?" Leela said.

"We don't know that yet."

"That's what I heard. Everybody's saying he's blind."

There was a strange excitement in Leela; so new and alive that it was barely suppressed, and an air of importance, almost triumph. Even if Sunny had been involved in Jarryd's abduction, why should Leela feel anything other than horror or disgust? The only reason perhaps was that Mukul had taken part. Could Mukul really have been involved in such horrors? Mukul, the precious son that Leela had asked the gods to give her, and made bargains at the kovil for – Mukul, Leela's pride and joy – had he joined the ranks of the minister's men and proved his worth with Jarryd? The possibility persisted in Padma like stomach ache. Mukul was strong, he boxed well. One of Boss's men had encountered him in a match in a nearby village and Mukul had won. Mukul was known to be vicious, and to fight dirty. Had this qualified him to torture old men?

"I suppose you'll be leaving for England soon?" Leela said.

"I told you, I made that up."

"Before you go, can you give me my necklace back?"

"But you gave it to me."

"Only to borrow."

"No, you said you wanted me to have it because I was getting married."

"I want it back now."

"But I was going to wear it to my wedding," Padma taunted.

"You give it back, or I'll come and take it myself,"

"You'd better hurry then, did you hear the villa's been sold?"

Leela studied her with narrowed eyes.

"So this is how you treat your mother, is it?"

"I give you money for fake medicine, don't I?"

"What money? When did you ever give me money?"

Padma knew she should return to the villa. She should never have been out alone. Leela had nothing to give her, no secret pure love of a mother for her daughter waiting for a chance to show itself.

"What did you do with my money?" Padma demanded.

"I had to pay the doctors."

"But there were no doctors, were there?"

"Give me my necklace," Leela said.

"Did you think I wouldn't care about your lies if you distracted me with jewellery? Is that what you think I'm like? How were you planning on getting it back? No use sending Mukul to mug me – don't forget he ended up in prison last time he tried stealing jewellery. He's useless at everything he does."

"Mukul's not useless." Leela's eyes were black burning coals.

"Never mind him, I'm keeping my necklace. Maybe I'll sell it and get back the money you stole from me."

"I didn't steal any money, I was sick! Ask anybody. I was so sick last month."

"Then I'm glad you're feeling better."

Padma backed out of the alley, and started for the villa.

"That necklace is mine, you can't keep it!" Leela shrieked behind her.

Padma didn't look back. Her greatest power was the freedom to walk away. She need never return; or ever regret it.

"I will curse you! I will curse you!" Leela shouted.

In the lane, people stared but Padma didn't care, soon she would be leaving them all, and going where they couldn't follow. Something hard hit her back, then her hip. She stumbled forward. A stone shot past the side of her face. Padma turned and there was Leela, her arm raised, about to throw the next stone. Padma ducked as she hurled it. It was a small rock. It just missed her and rolled into the drain. Padma walked faster. A stone caught her arm, breaking the skin; blood spurted onto her dress.

"Bitch!" Leela shouted. "Thief! You won't get away with stealing my things!"

More stones came, but Padma refused to run. Running away was what frightened children did, and animals who had no shame: stray dogs, abandoned, damaged and forever afraid, ran away yelping from the people who hurt them, who relished causing pain. She was hit on the calf, the back of her leg, her neck; the stones were thrown with surprising precision. Hate was strength, hate perfected aim. Leela didn't have to stop to find new stones, she must have had a pile ready, gathered before they met – like the village boys preparing to hurt sparrows, choosing the stones with sharp edges. Padma started to run. She ran all the way back to the villa.

## 39

"WHAT ACTUALLY HAPPENED?" Soma asked as Padma sat resting on the veranda, her wounds cleaned up and covered with plasters.

"I told you, some kids were throwing stones." Padma rubbed her head where a bulge throbbed hidden in her hair.

Rohan stood silent by the parapet.

"Which kids?" Soma demanded.

"I don't know! I've never seen them before."

"This is all very strange." Soma closed the bottle of Dettol and packed away the plasters and cotton wool. "How old were they?"

"Please could I have a cup of tea?"

"Girls or boys? I'm going to have a look for the little shits."

"What about my tea?"

"I'll make it for you, Soma, you go," Rohan said and Soma marched off.

"They won't be there anymore, they ran away!" Padma shouted after him, but he went anyway.

"Was it Sunny?" Rohan asked.

"No, I told you, it was just some kids."

"So you didn't go to Boss's bar?"

"No. It happened before I got there."

518

"Boss seems to think Sunny's friends with the minister now," Rohan said.

"The minister can have him."

"But Sunny would be far more dangerous with the minister's backing, don't you think?" He was looking to her with a strange new force, a new directness, almost accusing. She looked away. Why should she feel guilty?

It had already occurred to her that Sunny may have offered to help the minister buy the villa. One thing Sunny could claim was a connection to Gerhardt. He had already tried using it to arrange a marriage for her. He could have gone to the minister offering information, to advise when and how to apply pressure to force a sale. But could a man really have been made blind because of some sea-front real-estate? She felt dizzy. Might Jarryd have escaped with a broken leg if it hadn't been for his links to the villa? And the villa was always linked to Sunny because of her. She rubbed her eyes,

"What is it?" Rohan asked.

"I'll be glad to leave here," she said.

What she would miss were the old days, when Sunny took Gerhardt's money and stayed away and the minister and Gerhardt had pretended to be friends. An artificial bought peace was as good as any.

She had a nightmare that night, of being chased down an alley, of being wounded and left for dead in an empty school yard. This time she was her own age in the dream, no longer a child; she woke sitting up, gripping the edge of the bed. She went to the veranda. Gustav lay on the porch, sleeping so soundly he didn't hear her, even when she went right up to him. Something glistened on the floor by his mouth spreading mottled and pale. She knelt to look: it was vomit. She touched him and he moaned and was sick again.

"What is it boy?"

He lay panting. She brought him his water bowl and he lapped weakly at it then slumped on the floor. She ran down the hall and banged on Soma's door; he came at once and crouched by Gustav, studying him, while Padma mopped the floor.

"I'd better ring Gerhardt Mahaththaya," Soma said.

"We shouldn't wake him, he's going with Jarryd to Colombo later today."

"I don't think we should wait," Soma said and called Gerhardt at once.

She heard his voice, low and urgent in the hall, then he went to dress and was ready in minutes. Soon Gerhardt was at the villa, bending anxiously over Gustav, prising his mouth open, peering into his drooping eyes. Meanwhile Soma carried a pile of old sheets to the car and spread them over the back seats and the floor.

"He's probably just eaten something," Padma said.

"We need to have him checked," Gerhardt said.

Soma ran back from the car. Padma had never seen him so energetic.

"Let's go," Gerhardt said.

"You're going now? It's five o'clock in the morning!" Padma exclaimed.

"It's okay, I've called the vet, he's expecting us. Come, Soma."

Between them they carried Gustav into the car and Soma sat at the back holding him as Gerhardt drove them away.

Padma poured the soiled water down the drain outside and washed out the bucket and mop with the hose. The garden was restless, a wind stirring in the trees, a sign that the day would be stormy. The sea was moody and grey. Padma went inside and dressed in the dark of her room, silently, so as not to wake Rohan. Then she waited alone on the veranda, more lonely than she had ever been there, with no Gustav beside her guarding the house.

Gerhardt returned with Soma, but they didn't have Gustav with them anymore.

"Gustav's been poisoned," Gerhardt said.

"Poisoned? How? He's been in the garden all night." Padma tried to understand.

"Somebody must have thrown in some poisoned meat, that's how they do it," Soma said.

Padma thought of Sunny looking over from the empty garden next door just a few nights earlier. She started to shake. Gerhardt drew her to him.

"Gustav's going to be fine, he's strong. They pumped out his stomach and he had already thrown up a lot of it."

"Why would anyone want to hurt Gustav?"

"I've no idea."

"Was someone trying to burgle the house?" Rohan asked.

"Then it's no one from around here. Everybody knows I don't keep any valuables in my houses. I've made that clear right from the start."

"It could be Sunny," Rohan said.

"He knows better than anyone that I keep all my money in the bank."

Gerhardt kissed the top of Padma's head, stroking her hair. He kept her close, hugging her so tightly she almost couldn't breathe.

"Maybe it was the minister's people showing off," Soma said.

"I'm sure it wasn't them, but I think we should all stay at my place tonight, just to be on the safe side."

"But it's our last week at the villa," Padma protested.

"We'll eat dinner here, then sleep at mine. You too, of course, Rohan."

"Jarryd has to travel to Colombo later," Padma recalled.

"Ruth can go with him and settle him in. I'll go tomorrow, that's when the specialist arrives."

When it was fully light, Soma searched the garden and found a red raw hunk of meat dropped into the bushes at the back by the wall. He wrapped the meat in plastic and Gerhardt drove with it to the vet for tests. By the end of the day the vet had phoned to say that Gustav was going to recover. In a few days he would be able to come home. That night, Soma produced a dinner of hoppers: both plain and egg hoppers, seeni sambol and mutton curry - a defiantly celebratory meal.

Padma barely tasted what she was eating, thinking of Gustav lying weak and alone in his pen at the vet's, and Jarryd in his new bed at the Colombo hospital, not knowing what lay ahead.

Rohan was quiet, sitting tense and thoughtful, drinking a beer. Padma dragged her fork through the centre of her egg hopper, trailing the yellow yolk through dark meaty mutton curry and seeni sambol.

"Aren't you hungry?" Gerhardt asked Padma, glancing at her plate.

She shook her head. Gerhardt laid down his fork and spoon, the meat bones left neatly on the side of the plate, then he finished his beer. He called Soma to clear the table and they sat listening to the clatter in the kitchen as he washed up, the coffee spluttering in the coffee machine. The winds trailed through the garden, making the leaves shudder whispering. The gate latch clicked, but when Padma stood to look there was no one there. The sea sounded nearer that night, the air was more chill, more empty.

"What's the matter?" Gerhardt asked.

"I thought I heard the gate," she said, returning to her seat.

There was no Gustav to run down to see who it was. Someone stepped in from the porch - a man with a black stocking over his face, pointing a pistol at them.

"What the hell?" Gerhardt jumped up.

"Sit down," the man said – it was Sunny, of course.

He was wearing a tight turtleneck top that clung to his body, small and thin except for a flabby little pot-belly.

"I said, sit down!"

Sunny's voice sounded distant. He had muffled it with a sponge or a cloth – he must have thought that would make him unrecognisable. He sounded as if he were choking. Padma wished someone would choke him.

"There's nothing here to take," Gerhardt said, sitting down.

Sunny advanced, pointing the gun. He wouldn't shoot, he wouldn't dare. So this was what Gerhardt had paid to keep away. But in those years they'd had the minister's shield over them. That shield was gone now, they had no one.

"If anyone tries anything, I'm using this," Sunny warned, brandishing the gun.

"I don't know what you're expecting to find here, but please could you hurry up?" Gerhardt said.

Padma studied the round masked head, the veiled reptilian eyes. To wear too-tight trousers and a sock over your head to go and rob your daughter. She wanted to laugh. Let him take what he wanted, anything he took could be replaced.

From the kitchen there came the sound of glass breaking.

"What the fuck is this?" Soma shouted and the sound of a scuffle ensued.

There was more glass breaking, pans crashing to the floor, then silence spread through the house. A second masked man came from inside and stood framed in the doorway: taller and stronger and young. *Mukul?*

"Hands back! Down! Back! Behind the chair," he shouted.

It was Mukul alright. He was all excited, like an idiot. And high as a kite. He could have been on anything. She could smell weed on him as he came close and wound a nylon rope around her. She thought of Jarryd's bloodied wrists and hands and the seeping stained bandages wrapped around his eyes and suddenly she was afraid. Was this what Mukul was capable of now? He pulled the rope so tightly it bit into her arms and breasts; she couldn't move. He crouched, tying her ankles to the chair legs, his round black cotton head studiously bowed, like an obedient dog, stupid and dangerous. Through the sock, she saw his eyes, the same shape as hers and Leela's, and she was repelled by the similarity. He was slower than she had expected, breathing hard, with sharp whistling breaths, his gloved hands clumsily unbuckling her watchstrap as he slid her watch off. He had always had a thing for watches, even as a boy. There was no hesitation as he took hers, only a sense of entitlement. He tied the last knot, tugging it to check, ignoring her cries of pain.

Mukul tied Gerhardt to his chair and checked through his pockets, finding nothing to take. He took off Gerhardt's watch and slipped it into his trouser pocket

"Right, now him." Sunny waved the gun impatiently in Rohan's direction.

"Leave the boy," Gerhardt said. "Is it money you want? Let me write you a cheque. Or we can go to the bank in the morning."

"You! Shut up!" Mukul shouted at Gerhardt as he tied Rohan up.

Sunny strutted over to the dresser, opening drawers and helping himself to handfuls of Ikea knives and spoons and forks, dropping them noisily into an old rice sack.

"What's the number for the safe?" Mukul asked Gerhardt.

"There's nothing in there," Gerhardt said.

Sunny took a step towards Gerhardt. "Give me the number," he ordered.

Gerhardt recited it.

"It had better be right," Sunny said and went inside the house.

Mukul went with him. They seemed to know where the office was. The light came on inside. Gerhardt and Rohan struggled against their ropes. Rohan strained trying to get one of the dinner knives.

"Can you reach your phone?" Gerhardt whispered, but no one could.

From inside the office came the click-click-click of the safe code, then the squeal of its door opening. They would find mainly documents there, her adoption papers and EU passport. Her more expensive jewellery, gifts from Gerhardt, Ronny and Ruth, were kept in a bank vault in Colombo as Ruth had insisted. Padma longed for Ruth to turn up and rescue them all; she was the one person the robbers might have listened to. But Ruth was far away in Colombo, with the new nurses and doctors, and no doubt worrying about meals and massages and checking on Jarryd, unaware that at the villa the very events she had been warning of for years were occurring.

The black egg of Sunny's stockinged head looked around the hall doors, checking on them.

Inside the house there was the sound of doors being flung open, drawers thrown down. They would be searching the cupboards. Mukul had always taken what he wanted of her things and destroyed what he hadn't. As a child he had broken her one doll and torn up her schoolbooks. He had thrown any pictures she drew into Leela's cooking fire. Sunny came out of the office carrying the computer. Mukul ran out with her iPad and phone from her bedroom and made a pile on the porch, adding the stereo from the dresser.

"You don't have much," Sunny observed. "I thought you'd have a lot more things."

He came to a stop before Rohan.

"You're not going to get much of a dowry here. Good thing you're rich," he told Rohan.

"I'm not getting married," Rohan said.

The masked features moved. Was he smiling? Pulling faces? Sunny swung back his arm and hit Rohan across the face with the gun. Blood spurted from Rohan's cheek.

"No!" Padma said.

"You arrogant jumped-up shit!" Mukul shouted at Rohan. "People like you think you can do what you like – but not anymore!"

Sunny punched Rohan in the stomach. Rohan doubled over, gasping, blood dripping from the cut in his cheek onto the floor.

"Leave him! We're not getting married!" Padma screamed.

"Nobody's getting married, I can confirm it!" Gerhardt shouted.

Sunny glanced over at Padma as he paced before Rohan, a bounce in his step, coiled and ready to spring. There was so much energy in the wiry old-man's body, an unquenchable anger like a madness fuelling him. He seemed unable to stop moving. His face, distorted under the mask, seemed to be smiling. He was enjoying himself. He wanted her to be watching. The fear in the room was all made by him, by the pain he could inflict – this was what he lived for. He would never tire, no matter how old he got, he would always have this hatred in him, driving him on until he was dead. Sunny spread his legs, steadying, readying himself, the way he had raised his umbrella once to beat a neighbour's dog that had dared to bark at him as he went past. The poor dog had been tied to a tree and unable to run away as the blows came, the umbrella whizzing through the air in a frenzy. Padma, unable to look away, had stood by the kitchen door and watched, seeing

Sunny panting and spent, staggering with the effort of the beating, spitting as he left onto the crumpled animal, spread on the ground in a bloodshot puddle of piss.

Rohan straightened, sitting up defiant and strong, looking back clear-eyed and unafraid at Sunny. He didn't flinch as Sunny swayed, preparing to strike again, his fist clenched ready, the arm rising with such slow determined viciousness, even Mukul stood frozen, watching.

"We all know it's you, Sunny! If anything happens to him, we know who you are!" Padma yelled.

Sunny paused and turned to her. She saw the gleam of his attention behind the black nylon of the mask. He giggled. She should have known not to taunt him, and to be more afraid. She had dragged Rohan into the trap with her, now Sunny wouldn't stop until all that was innocent and good in her life was destroyed. Sunny wanted her hurt, he wanted her damaged and in pain if he couldn't use her for his own gain. Sunny was never going to let her be unless she left.

"I'm not going to England, I only told you that for a joke," she said.

"That's true enough. Nobody's going to England."

Sunny slammed his fist into Rohan's chest, sending him crashing back, his chair hitting the table. Rohan gasped and cried out in pain.

"No!" Padma shouted.

She had to set Rohan free, he had to survive and go back to London and the life he deserved. The life he had been ready to give up for her.

Sunny swayed, and readied himself again, fists raised. And Padma knew that he could not be stopped. He would keep going until there was nothing more to break. The neighbour's dog had stayed afraid of Sunny until its dying day. It would cower and whimper and hide whenever Sunny walked by, sometimes it wet itself, remembering.

"Please, don't," she begged Sunny. "Hurt me instead."

There was the sound of someone gasping for air, someone choking.

"Urgh. Arghh!" A gurgling wet animal sound, desperate, helpless.

It came from Gerhardt.

"My heart! Oh God, it's my heart! Padma! Come quickly!"

"Gerhardt?" Padma held back a sob. It was finally here, the night of all of her nightmares. Sunny had made them real.

"What's wrong with him?" Mukul muttered.

"He's having a heart attack! Let me go to him!" Padma cried.

Sunny strode over to Gerhardt.

"I didn't know you had a heart problem." Sunny nudged Gerhardt in the chest with his shoe.

Gerhardt gave another weaker, more anguished groan.

"Looks like the old bastard is dying or something," Mukul said worriedly.

Padma struggled against her ropes.

"Untie me, will you?" she screamed at Mukul. "If he dies, Mukul, you'll be done for murder!"

"Shut up!" he snapped at her.

"You'll be *hanged!*" she cried. "The minister won't help you then! Not for murder, he won't - he'll deny ever knowing you. You'll be all on your own going to the gallows—"

"Fucking shut the fuck up!" Mukul rushed at her, his fists clenched.

"Aagh! Aagh! Oh God, oh my heart," Gerhardt yelled. "Padma get me my heart pills, will you? The ones in the fridge, in the brown bottle - you know the ones. On the middle shelf?"

The heart pills? The *heart pills!*

"Let her get me my pills, that's all I ask," Gerhardt pleaded.

"He's a doctor," Padma said, looking to Rohan. "Let him get them. He knows about medicines."

"Yes, send the boy," Gerhardt panted. "He'll know what to do. Go, Rohan, they're in the fridge. Second shelf, at the back. A brown bottle. Orange pills."

Sunny considered for a moment, Padma held her breath.

"Let him get the pills," Sunny told Mukul. "But you go with our doctor here."

Sunny pointed the gun at Rohan. "You try anything stupid, and you're dead, right here, in front of her."

Mukul sliced through Rohan's ropes and dragged him inside, the knife pressed against Rohan's neck.

## 40

WHAT THE HELL was Padma doing? She really was an
idiot sometimes - calling him a doctor, sending him to get
medicines - Gerhardt needed an ambulance, not heart pills. All
the years of denying the dangers around them, thinking themselves
immune to Sunny, well here it was, the bad guys always won in
the end. First Jarryd, now the villa; the ugliness should never be
confronted, it was too big to fight.

"Slow down!" the burglar warned. Mukul, Padma had called
him. So she knew him too.

The man's voice was familiar. The cold blade of the knife
pressed harder into Rohan's neck. There was no use struggling or trying to run. The burglar smelled of sweat and dope
and aftershave. He'd taken something stronger than marijuana; his hand shook, the blade juddered, scraping Rohan's
skin.

"Don't mess with me, I mean it," he said.

Rohan had definitely heard that voice before. Why couldn't
he put a face to it? He shuffled through the dark hallway, the
man gripping him. The kitchen was bright up ahead, eerily silent.
When they entered, there was Soma lying gagged and tied-up on
the floor. He looked up wild-eyed at Rohan.

"Don't try anything," the burglar said as Rohan went to the fridge.

The mugger! That's who it was! He had told Rohan to leave the villa and to stop taking their things – what things? Rohan opened the fridge.

"Get the medicine out slowly," the mugger warned.

Inside in the brightness, past a butter dish, a packet of cheese and a stack of Tupperware full of leftovers, was a brown glass bottle. As Rohan grabbed it he saw the label: multivitamins with added zinc and magnesium. For a moment he was puzzled, then he almost laughed out loud. They *were* crazy, Gerhardt and Padma, and all the bold clever people of their small precious world, so brave and silly and reckless; so gloriously defiant. They had style. God, how he loved them! He wanted to be deserving of them. He wasn't afraid anymore.

"Hurry up, arsehole!" the mugger said and shoved Rohan away from the fridge.

"He'll need water to take the pills." Rohan started filling a glass from the fridge dispenser.

When the glass was half full he let it drop. It smashed across the floor.

"Oh damn!" Rohan leaped away to the other side of the room. "I need another glass – where are the glasses here?"

He opened cupboards and drawers until he found the knives and dropped a paring knife on the floor while rummaging in a cupboard, rattling saucepans.

"What the fuck are you doing?" the mugger shouted leaping after him.

Rohan kicked the knife in Soma's direction and grabbed a bottle of water from under the sink.

"Never mind, let's take this." He ran back into the house, the mugger chasing him.

"Here! Here! Take these!" Rohan ran to Gerhardt and placed two vitamin pills in his mouth, holding the water bottle to his lips.

Gerhardt swallowed dramatically.

"This man needs to lie down, untie him," Rohan ordered. "And bring her over here so she can hold his head."

He must have been convincing because the burglars obeyed. Both Gerhardt and Padma were released.

"Take the stuff to the van," Sunny told the mugger who put the iPad and phone into the rice sack and carried it outside with the stereo.

Sunny leaned against the parapet and watched as Rohan pretended to take Gerhardt's pulse while Padma sat holding Gerhardt in her arms. Rohan felt Sunny's gaze on him. It felt like a lull before something was concluded. Rohan tried to think of a way to run out and fetch help.

The mugger returned. "Let's take him now," he said. He and Sunny suddenly swooped on Rohan and dragged him up by the arms. Padma was shouting. Rohan struggled and kicked. This was not the robbery anymore. They had come for him.

'Please, no,' Rohan begged.

Sunny pointed the gun.

"You're coming with us," the mugger said.

How could this be the end? The end of him, while everyone else went on living in the world. It was too soon, he hadn't done anything yet, nothing that mattered.

"Please, is it money you want?" Rohan pleaded.

Sunny laughed delightedly inside his mask.

"I need to take the old man to the hospital," Rohan said.

"No you don't, you're coming with us. You need to be taught a lesson."

Rohan struggled but the mugger and Sunny dragged him

towards the door. His mind was empty. He heard himself screaming.

All Padma knew was that she must save Rohan. She left Gerhardt and ran over and dug her nails into Mukul's stocking, pulling it across his eyes. "You're not taking him anywhere!" she shouted.

"Padma, get back!" Rohan cried. He shoved Mukul off and kicked out at Sunny. Mukul pushed her and she felt herself falling.

"Leave her!" Gerhardt shouted, running at Mukul.

"Heart got better, did it?" Sunny chuckled.

Sunny tried to punch Gerhardt, but Rohan jumped in the way and Sunny hit him across the head. Rohan fell to his knees and Mukul turned on him.

"You think you can do what you like? You think you can fuck with our people?" Mukul shouted.

"I'm not your people!" she shouted and hit Mukul with a chair.

"You fucking arsehole!" he shouted and grabbed her wrists, squeezing so hard she thought the bones were crumbling

"Leave her! Leave her!" Gerhardt screamed and hit Mukul with the Tiffany lamp, glass smashing on the floor.

"You're going to die!" Mukul swung round to Gerhardt.

Sunny, the gun dangling from his hand, was tussling with Rohan, pulling him nearer to the porch. She clawed at Sunny's arm.

"Come and take him!" Sunny growled at Mukul and Mukul left Gerhardt and came running. She and Gerhardt clung to Sunny and Mukul, both trying to overpower Rohan and were dragged along with them.

"Get him in the van!" Sunny panted.

"Like hell you will!" she shouted.

Outside in the lane, a car horn sounded.

"Someone's coming," Sunny said, and he stopped to look.

533

"We need that bloody necklace or she'll never shut up," Mukul muttered. Padma gasped.

"Is that fucking necklace what this is all about?" she shouted. The horn signalled its warning again.

"Is that her?" Padma demanded.

How hard Leela had thrown the stones, how nimbly she had jumped onto the moving bus. Now she was in a car, or a van parked in the dark, the look-out for Sunny and Mukul. Leela was no victim. This time Padma had been well and truly conned.

Sunny was running in and out of the garden.

"You bring that necklace out this second, or I'm going to shoot him," he said, pointing the gun at Rohan. "I swear I will."

The car horn blared on and on. Mukul let go of Rohan and started to run.

"Where do you think you're going?" Sunny yanked Mukul back by the shirt.

"I can't get caught! I'm not going back in that prison!" Mukul yelped.

"Where's the necklace?" Sunny shouted at Padma.

The gun catch clicked off and Sunny placed the gun on Rohan's forehead. Sunny was crazy. All her life, as long as she could re-member, she had known that he had killed many people.

"It's outside," Padma said and ran out to the porch.

"Padma! Come back!" Gerhardt shouted.

"Get her! She's running away!" Mukul cried.

She could hear Sunny coming after her as she ran down the porch steps. His feet thudded behind her. She dropped to her knees at the pond and reached into the water.

"Shoot her! Kill her! She's getting a gun!" Mukul yelled.

"The necklace is in the pond," Padma told Sunny who was skipping madly around her. Her arm sank deep into the cold water.

"Don't mess around," Sunny warned. He was breathing hard,

animal and hoarse, he was right up close to her. Mukul was running up and down the path, as the car horn went on calling. Gerhardt and Rohan hovered close while Sunny's gun waved over her. But she wasn't afraid. She felt underwater for the package she had hidden, never wanting it in the house, and brought it up from under the stones and sand and slime at the bottom of the pond.

Sunny ripped the plastic wrapping apart and prised open the red cardboard heart, then he ran over the lawn, Mukul right behind him. They disappeared into the bushes, then scrambled up the wall like crabs. Then they were gone, crashing onto the tin roof of the garage next door. There were shouts, a shot, and dark figures ran into the garden from all sides.

"Padma! Come!" Rohan pulled her inside and she ran with him and Gerhardt into the guest room and hid behind the bed. They listened to shouts in the garden, the screech of brakes in the lane. The door of the room flew open. She almost screamed, They curled up together, holding each other tightly.

"Padma Baba! Gerhardt Sir?" Soma shouted, and there he was in the doorway, waving the axe from the outdoor kitchen.

"I went and got Boss," he panted. "I didn't know how many were here."

Boss and his men crowded in to report that the robbers had escaped.

"The woman was hiding in the van," Boss said. "She was the one pushing the horn. Somehow those bastards got in and she took off."

"She can drive?" Padma muttered.

"Which woman is this?" Gerhardt demanded.

"Leela," Padma said.

Gerhardt stared.

"Ruth was right about her," Padma admitted.

"Ruth is always right," Gerhardt said. "None of this is your fault. We're all okay, that's all that matters." He hugged Padma and Rohan to him. Rohan stumbled and held onto the desk. He had closed his eyes.

"He's going to faint," Gerhardt said and one of Boss's men grabbed Rohan and pushed him onto the bed.

"Hold his head down! Put his head between his legs!" Boss instructed.

Padma heard Mukul's voice again and again in her head: "Take him, take him now". That was why they had come; for him and the necklace, although for Sunny and Mukul, Rohan was the main event, she suspected. Where had they planned to take him? The abandoned school swam before her, and Jarryd laid out on the floor of the ruined assembly hall. If Leela hadn't sounded the horn, if Boss hadn't come with his men, if Soma hadn't been able to escape from the kitchen ... "When your time comes, it comes," Sri Lankans liked to say – it was an actual saying. She had never believed in such fatalism, but now it seemed a sign. Rohan had to live the life he deserved, she couldn't let him give it up.

Gerhardt came with a bottle of iodine and cleaned Rohan's cheek. The cotton wool came away soaked in blood.

"You might need stitches," Gerhardt told him. "I'll call Doctor Perera. Poor man, he'll be glad when we're gone."

Padma took Rohan a glass of water. She couldn't tell if he was angry with her; she would have to tell him everything. He would consider it a lie, what she had told him about Sunny. Rohan had suffered so much already from a lying ex-wife; she didn't dare meet his eyes. Rohan reached for her hand.

"I'll make that call," Gerhardt said. "And I suppose I'd better tell the police, for what it's worth. They can write a report about it, at any rate."

Rohan watched the door until Gerhardt had gone and Boss and his men had followed him out.

"I know about Sunny," Rohan said.

"What do you know?"

"I know who he is."

He wasn't angry, he wasn't disappointed; she couldn't understand what he was feeling as he held her close. "I'm sorry," she murmured. "I didn't mean to lie. I've told so many lies, I'm so sorry . . ."

"It's alright." He stroked her hair. "We'll leave here and you won't ever have to see them again. They'll never come anywhere near us in Goa."

"No, you have to go back to London. You and Tom will do amazing things."

"No!"

"You'll regret not joining Tom while you can."

"Maybe I could work for Tom from Goa," he conceded.

"But you need to start in London, that's where the investors are, that's where he needs you."

"We could still live in Goa one day, or anywhere you want. I'll come and find you. It wouldn't be too long, maybe a year."

"Of course." Maybe he would come back, or maybe he would meet someone else; or what they had felt could fade; so much could change.

"I want to be with you for the rest of my life," he said. "But you're right, I don't want to feel thwarted, I don't want to feel what I felt when I looked into Sunny's gun. Regret is so bleak and hollow."

"I'm so sorry," she whispered.

"I felt so empty, so angry."

"You will do wonderful things. We both will," Padma said.

He took her hand. "Will you wait for me?" he asked.

"Yes."

"Really? You promise? I don't want to lose you."

"Of course I'll wait. I can live like a nun if I have to."

"Oh yeah? Like Maria from *The Sound of Music*?"

"Exactly. I'll be singing at the top of my voice on the mountains."

"It shouldn't be hard to spot you then."

She smiled.

"I really am coming back," he said.

"I know."

In the hall, Gerhardt was talking on the phone with Ruth. Boss left with his men.

⁂

Doctor Perera arrived and Padma went outside as he stitched the cut on Rohan's cheek. She sat on the porch steps with the pond still and calm below her. Inside it, life would be going on as always. A girl at school had once told her that fish only remembered the last ten minutes of their lives – in which case they would have been swimming around in their cool, wet, green darkness with the disturbance of earlier quite forgotten. They would have no recollection whatsoever of the plastic-wrapped package with its hard red heart that she had placed in their midst a few days earlier, nor its abrupt removal. Its presence in their lives would have been erased; for them it no longer existed.

She could hear Gerhardt talking with the doctor, telling him about the night. The doctor had said earlier that Rohan's wound wouldn't mark him significantly, a little discolouring might be all that remained, perhaps a faint trace of a scar.

"You'll still be handsome, but with added intrigue," Gerhardt had joked.

Wherever Rohan went he would wear that scar, a reminder of

his return to Padma. She and he were forever joined by the mark that Sunny had anointed him with.

"Padma?" It was Gerhardt.

He came to sit beside her on the step. He put his arm around her and they sat as they used to. Then they had looked up at the stars, naming constellations and sipping hot chocolate that he had made – proper hot chocolate, like in Europe, he used to say, melting real chocolate into the milk. She remembered the sound of the spoon stirring, rata-rata-rata-rata against the side of the pan. That was how the nightmares had gone away. Now there was no need to talk, no need to explain. They sat listening to the sea, so muted and hushed and distant that night, so far removed from the lives of people. It was just another night in the endless life of the sea.

## 41

GERHARDT LOOKED OUT at the shimmering tarmac of the runway, the coconut trees a dull haze at its edges, the sky paled to whiteness. Beside him Jarryd lay on the stretcher he had travelled on in the ambulance, which had been wheeled into the special bay in Business Class and strapped in, curtained off from regular fliers. A nurse was with them, seated in Economy, available for emergencies and to change dressings and make the elaborate trips to the toilet with them. It was a strange way to be returning to Europe. The holidays of the past with Padma, when he had taken her to see Paris and Berlin, the Rembrandts in Amsterdam, even his home city of Vienna, had seemed like excursions to new lands, but this time, needing help for his friend, needing to be restored himself, he was truly returning. Europe this time was for making a safe, quiet nest for Jarryd and himself, and Ruth too, when she arrived in a few days, after seeing Padma off to Goa.

While Jarryd was at the eye hospital in Vienna, he and Ruth would have time to wander in the great city of his youth, to eat lunch together in ancient squares, being just the two of them alone again in Europe. As before, he had no guide, no knowledge of how to proceed, only time would tell what they might have been, what they still had to give to the other.

"Gerhardt?" Jarryd said.

"Yes?" He touched Jarryd's arm, the way they all did now, responding instinctively in touch to the solitary figure who lay with them, so alone seeming in his silence.

"I once went to Vienna with a girlfriend."

"Did you now? And who was this lucky woman?"

"She was called Gerda."

"I see."

"Yes really! She was! She was a singer, the most beautiful singer you've ever heard. She played the guitar and sang old songs from her country. Hungary, she was from."

"We'll go and listen to music when the doctors let you out," Gerhardt said.

"That'd be good, wouldn't it?" Jarryd smiled.

Life could be started again, no matter how badly it was paused. Life could begin, over and over.

⚜

Padma woke in the dark. She walked through the house, Gerhardt's house that felt only of him although there was a room always kept ready for her. Gustav heaved himself up sleepily and padded along with her to the veranda and they sat as they used to at the villa, and waited for the dawn. Here the view was of paddy fields and a gleam of pale sky above a black faraway plateau of rock. She strained to hear the sound of the sea, but there was only the hiss of trees stirring, in a breeze that had travelled inland. In a couple of days she would leave for Goa and she would be by the sea again, the same sea as at the villa.

Rohan was in London. A year wasn't so long. Sometimes one had to return before moving on. Padma listened outside Soma's new room. He was snoring peacefully. She left the note she had written on the kitchen table in case he woke up before she came back. He would be furious when he knew that she had disobeyed orders and gone alone to the one place she had been told never to go back to. She walked to the corner shop and roused the solitary tuk-tuk driver parked at the side of the road. He didn't seem to know who she was, not even when she asked to go to Nilwatte Beach. He started up the engine without protest. Once or twice she saw him looking at her in the rear-view mirror, but she pretended not to notice; he was curious, that was all. There could only be a strange reason for a respectable-seeming young woman to be going to that dubious stretch of coast at such an early hour.

They drove over the fields, past the town, and entered the old village. The shops were still closed, the stalls at the top of the road just poles and tarpaulin, no one there as yet to set up. Around the bus stop it was only just starting to get busy with a few workers boarding a bus – no one she knew. They entered the old lane. How could so little have changed after all that had happened? Padma pressed back against the seat, keeping out of sight as they drove past Hema Amme's house. Hema Amme was on her front step, throwing food to the dog. She squinted at the tuk-tuk going past but it was travelling too fast; she wouldn't have been able to see Padma hiding inside.

"Which house?" the driver asked.

Padma made him stop four houses away.

"I'll be back in a minute, wait here please."

She walked towards the villa gate, still cheery white and sturdy. The guest-house sign had been taken down and thrown into the ditch outside, the wood already starting to warp, and the hibiscus flowers that Gerhardt had sketched for the sign-painter blistering into thin red strands of paint, curling and broken. The 'Beware of the Dog' sign was still up, but there was no barking as she went near. Soma had told her that rich Russians were renting the place.

"Terrible people, selling drugs and guns. We must never go anywhere near them," he had said.

He had lost all interest in the villa now that they had left. Like his home in Colombo after the mob burned it down, it had become just a place for him. He talked only of what happened in places, the good and bad and the people who'd been in them; the buildings didn't matter, he said, not once you'd left. Gerhardt disagreed: buildings mattered hugely, he said; buildings had to be preserved and fought for, he insisted, but on the subject of the villa he seemed uncertain.

Padma unlatched the gate and stepped into the garden. Why would the minister let rich Russians - business rivals - occupy a house that he and his brother had bought to extend their own business? She saw something move in the doorway of the hall - a curtain? It looked like a curtain, yellow with brown flowers. It was hard to imagine the drug lords moving in and putting up curtains. Someone came out to the veranda, moving behind the frangipani trees. Padma stepped back into the lane. The figure on the veranda stood at the parapet, just as Padma once had, and looked out at the lane. Padma knew where to stand so she couldn't be seen. It was a woman, on the veranda, holding a broom - someone cleaning for the Russians, perhaps. Padma scrambled up the wall where the hibiscus bushes grew tall and peered through. She could see the veranda more clearly now: the woman gazed out from behind the white-studded frangipani branches; the woman was Leela.

Leela turned her head and called into the house and another figure appeared: Sunny. Side by side they stood, watching the lane. They stood close together, bound to each other. They had always been bound to each other. Sunny smoked a cigarette and strutted around the empty veranda. Of course there were no rich Russians living at the villa. Sunny and Leela had found a way in at last. This was what they had always wanted. And thanks to the minister and his brother they had what Padma had been given; they had it all. Soon the perverts would come to stay and Sunny and Leela would proudly welcome them in.

"Missy, is it the wrong address?" The driver was below, looking anxiously up at her.

"Yes, all wrong."

She jumped down from the wall and went back to the tuk-tuk and left Nilwatte Beach forever.

Back at Gerhardt's house, it was still early morning, as if no time had passed. Soma was still asleep. It was as if she had never left. She tore up her note and made coffee. She sat in the courtyard by a blue-tiled pool that Gerhardt had designed. The goldfish darted under the lily pads, believing perhaps that they had always lived there, the dark square pond by the villa's porch, all gone, not even a memory.

"How about kiribath for breakfast?" Soma asked, appearing in the doorway.

"Kiribath?"

It was not the first of the month or a Poya day, and it was not New Year or Sinhala New Year, Pongal or Christmas. But the day was auspicious; a day of endings and a new beginning.

"Yes, kiribath," she said, and he went inside to start.

Soon there was the hiss of oil and mustard seeds popping, the smell of onions frying as he made seeni sambol to eat with the kiribath. She went into the house. In the dining room, her suitcases waited, half-packed for Goa. She lit a candle before the Dancing Lord Shiva. The flame gleamed, moving in the dark bronze limbs. Trust Sunny and Mukul to overlook the one thing of value at the villa. Lord Shiva smiled, blissfully, dancing inside his flaming circle. Agile and sure he thrilled in his dance of destruction, removing all obstacles, giving life to the future. She opened to that sunlit brightness, and all that it might hold.

# Acknowledgements

I AM DEEPLY grateful to Chris and Jen Hamilton-Emery for opening the doors of the wonderful Salt to my novel and me.

I am indebted to Andrew McDonnell for his generosity and kindness in supporting my work long after my novella Lantern Evening won the Gatehouse Press new Fictions Prize 2016. It is entirely thanks to Andy that my novel *Beautiful Place* found its way out of the wilderness.

A huge thank you to Philippa Sitters, the most enthusiastic, positive agent a writer could wish for.

I would also like to thank Kathy Gale who read an early draft and offered invaluable feedback and encouragement, and Martie de Villiers for all our years of reading and editing in cafés together.

To my daughter Kezia, a thank you for just being her and to my husband Jason, the biggest thank you of all, and all my love.

This book has been typeset by
SALT PUBLISHING LIMITED
using Neacademia, a font designed by Sergei Egorov
for the Rosetta Type Foundry in the Czech Republic.
It is manufactured using Holmen Book Cream 65gsm, a
Forest Stewardship Council™ certified paper from the
Hallsta Paper Mill in Sweden. It was printed and bound
by Clays Limited in Bungay, Suffolk, Great Britain.

CROMER
GREAT BRITAIN
MMXIX